【トランスルーセント】
translucent
彼女は半透明

3

STORY AND ART BY
KAZUHIRO OKAMOTO
岡本一広

TRANSLATION BY
HEIDI PLECHL

LETTERING BY
JIM KEPLINGER

CONTENTS

FOR NEW READERS

At times partially transparent and frequently completely invisible, eighth grader **Shizuka Shiroyama** suffers from **Translucent Syndrome**. She's easily overlooked, and her disappearing body makes her painfully aware of this fact.

On the other hand, because of her condition she has become close friends with her classmate, **Mamoru Tadami**. Spending time with the bright and cheerful Mamoru has helped to give her the drive she's needed to continue pursuing her love of acting.

Two other good friends of hers are the student body class president, **Okouchi-san** (who is, by the way, very stubborn), and **Keiko-san** (who is completely translu-cent—and also engaged!). **Takazawa-sensei** is Shizuka's romantic-yet-pushy doctor. They all adore Shizuka!

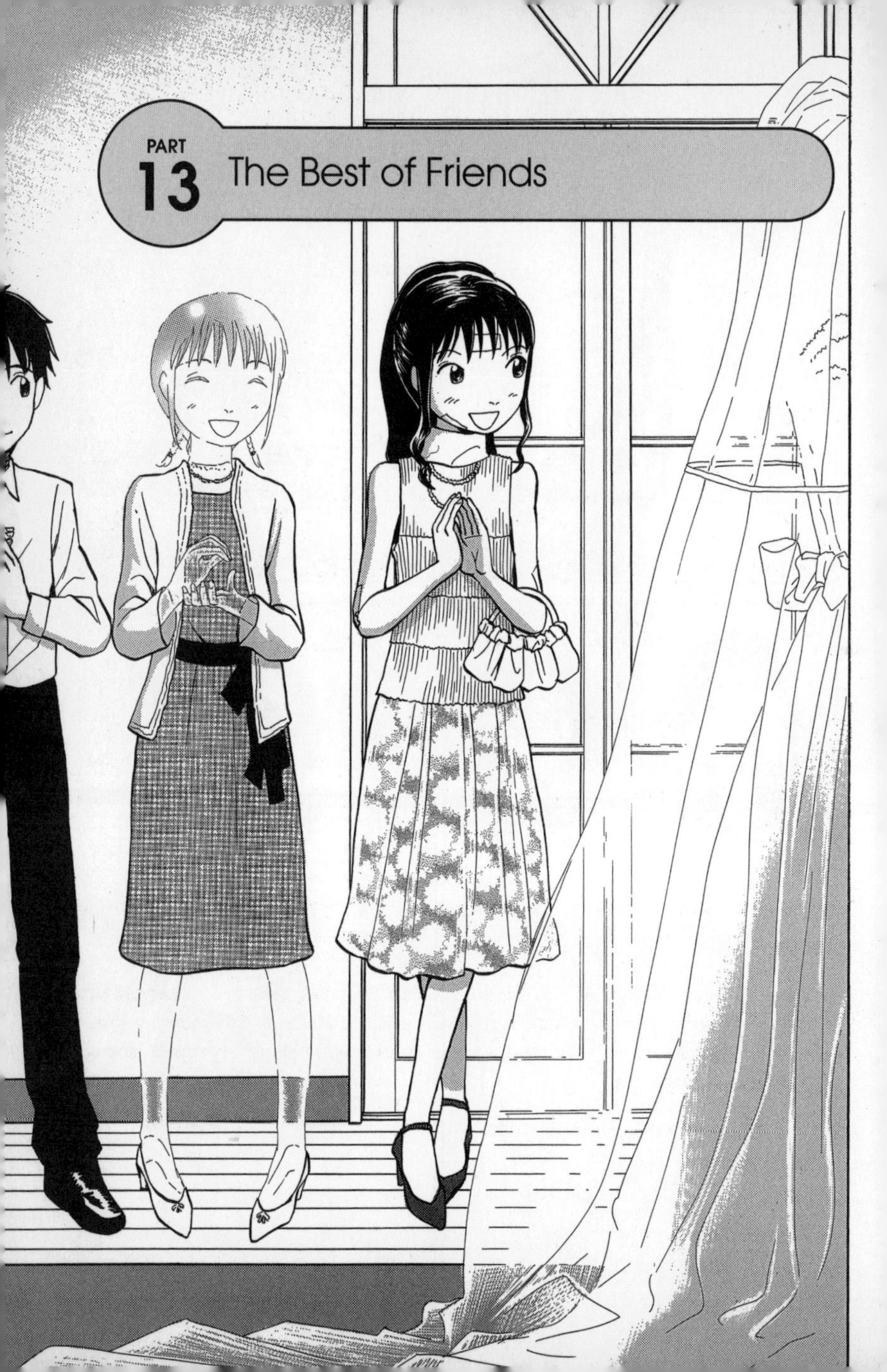
PART 13 The Best of Friends

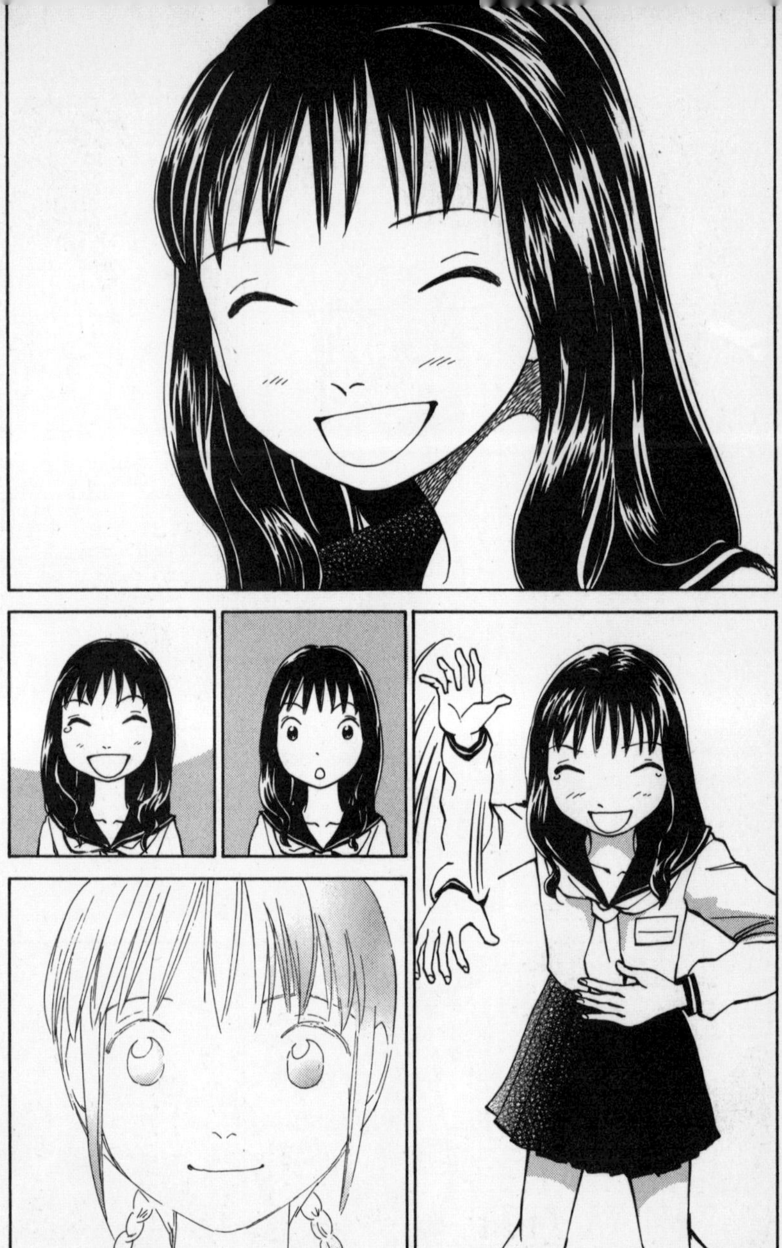

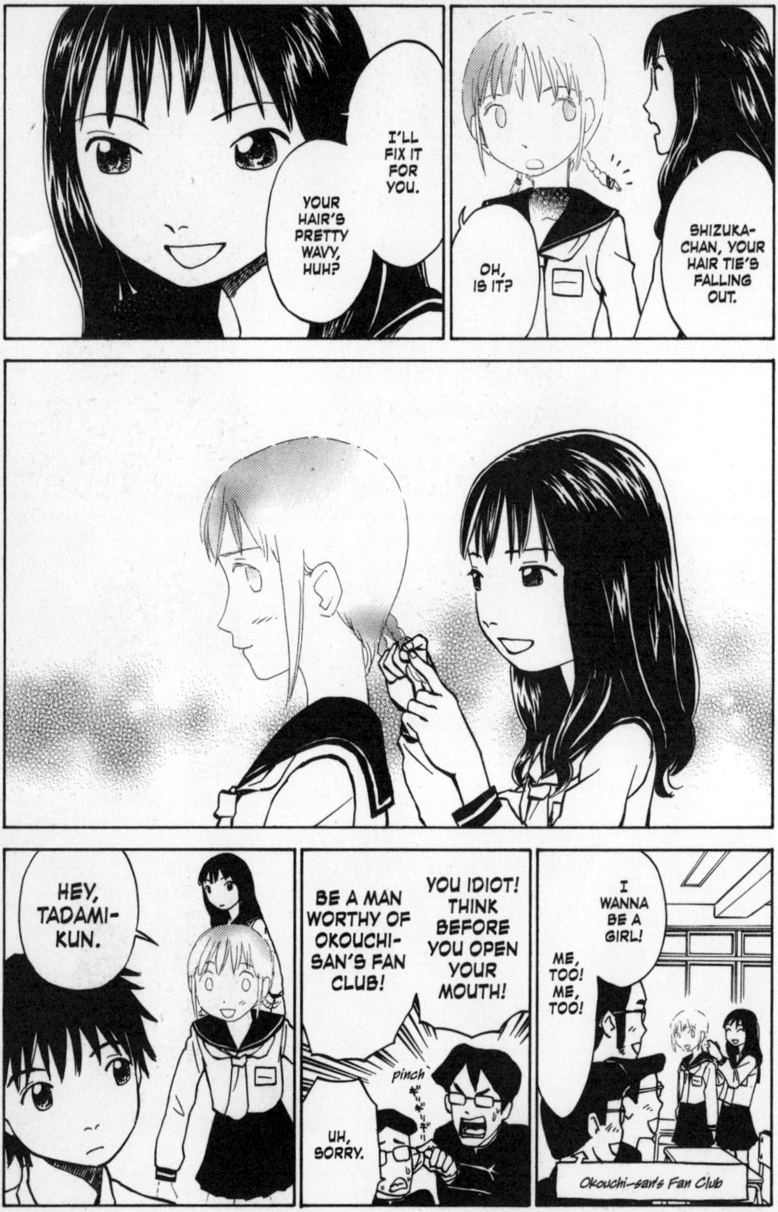
SHIZUKA-CHAN, YOUR HAIR TIE'S FALLING OUT.
OH, IS IT?
I'LL FIX IT FOR YOU.
YOUR HAIR'S PRETTY WAVY, HUH?
I WANNA BE A GIRL!
ME, TOO! ME, TOO!
Okouchi-san's Fan Club
YOU IDIOT! THINK BEFORE YOU OPEN YOUR MOUTH!
BE A MAN WORTHY OF OKOUCHI-SAN'S FAN CLUB!
pinch
UH, SORRY.
HEY, TADAMI-KUN.

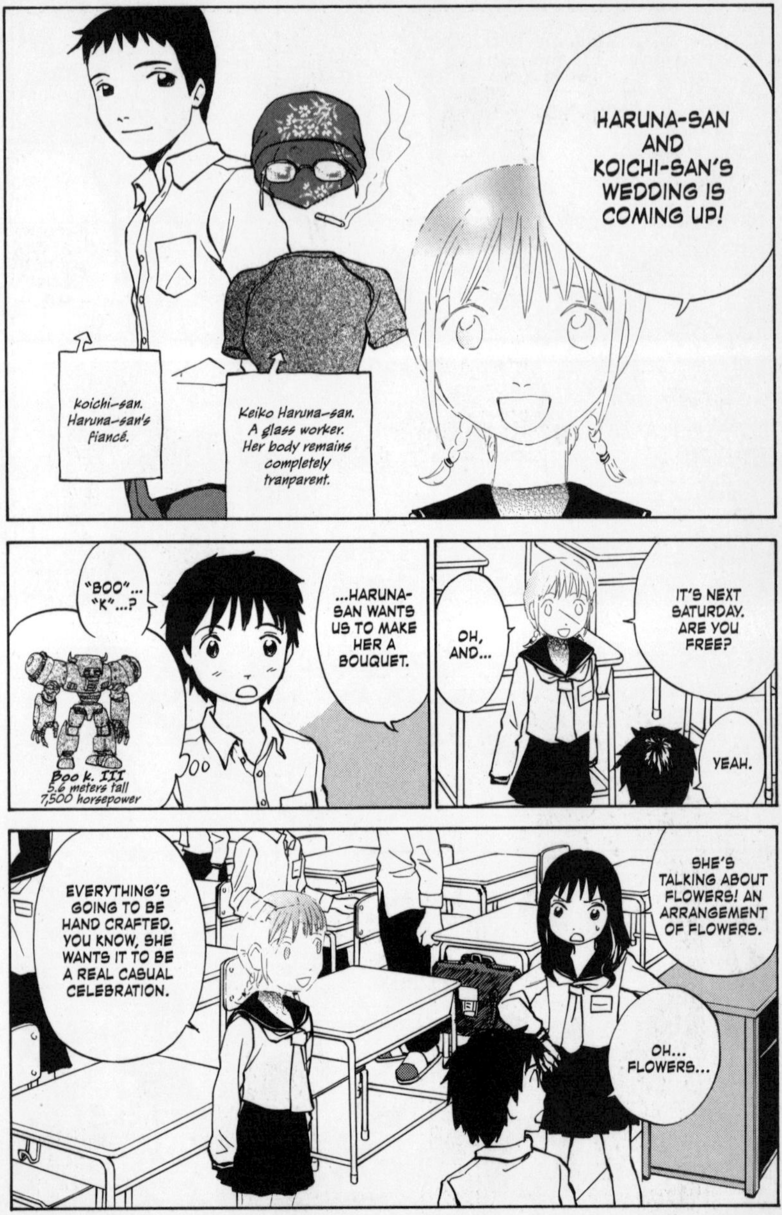
HARUNA-SAN AND KOICHI-SAN'S WEDDING IS COMING UP!
Keiko Haruna-san. A glass worker. Her body remains completely tranparent.
koichi-san. Haruna-san's fiancé.
IT'S NEXT SATURDAY. ARE YOU FREE?
YEAH.
OH, AND...
...HARUNA-SAN WANTS US TO MAKE HER A BOUQUET.
"BOO"... "K"...?
Boo k. III
5.6 meters tall
7,500 horsepower
SHE'S TALKING ABOUT FLOWERS! AN ARRANGEMENT OF FLOWERS.
OH... FLOWERS...
EVERYTHING'S GOING TO BE HAND CRAFTED. YOU KNOW, SHE WANTS IT TO BE A REAL CASUAL CELEBRATION.

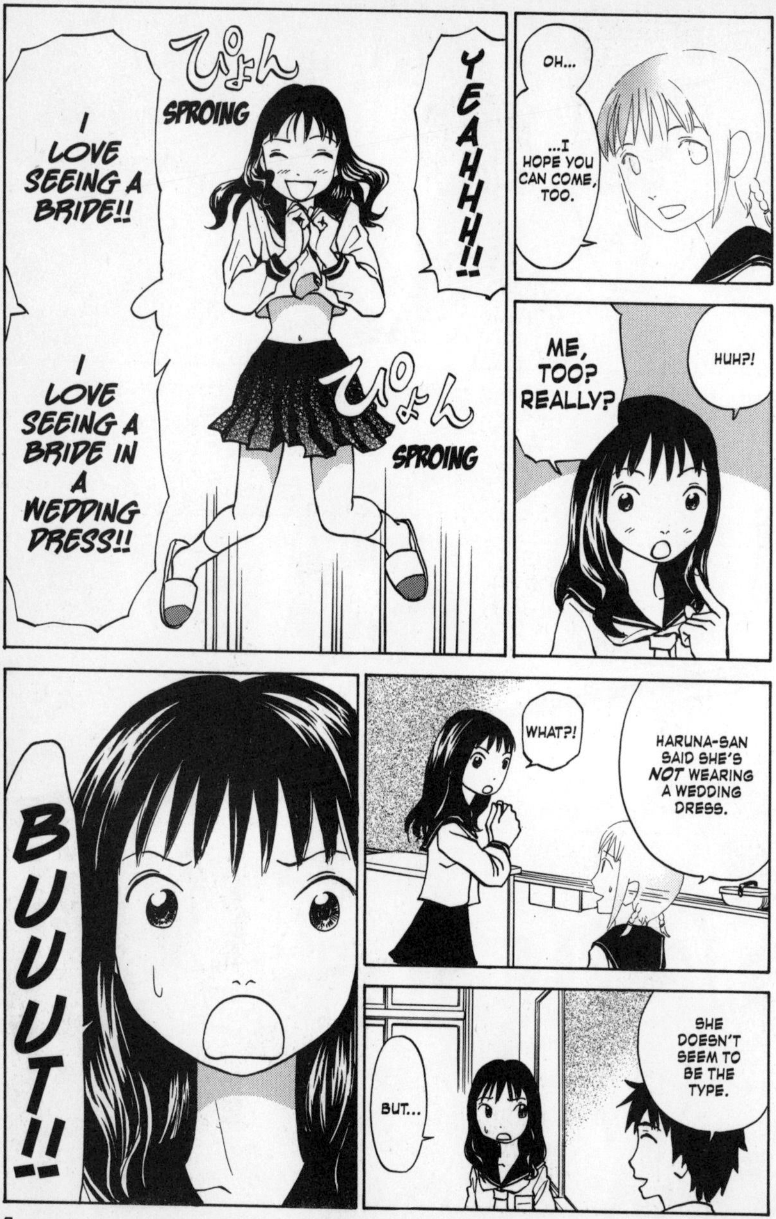
OH...
...I HOPE YOU CAN COME, TOO.
HUH?!
ME, TOO? REALLY?
YEAHHHH!!
ぴょん
SPROING
I LOVE SEEING A BRIDE!!
ぴょん
SPROING
I LOVE SEEING A BRIDE IN A WEDDING DRESS!!
HARUNA-SAN SAID SHE'S *NOT* WEARING A WEDDING DRESS.
WHAT?!
SHE DOESN'T SEEM TO BE THE TYPE.
BUT...
BUUUT!!

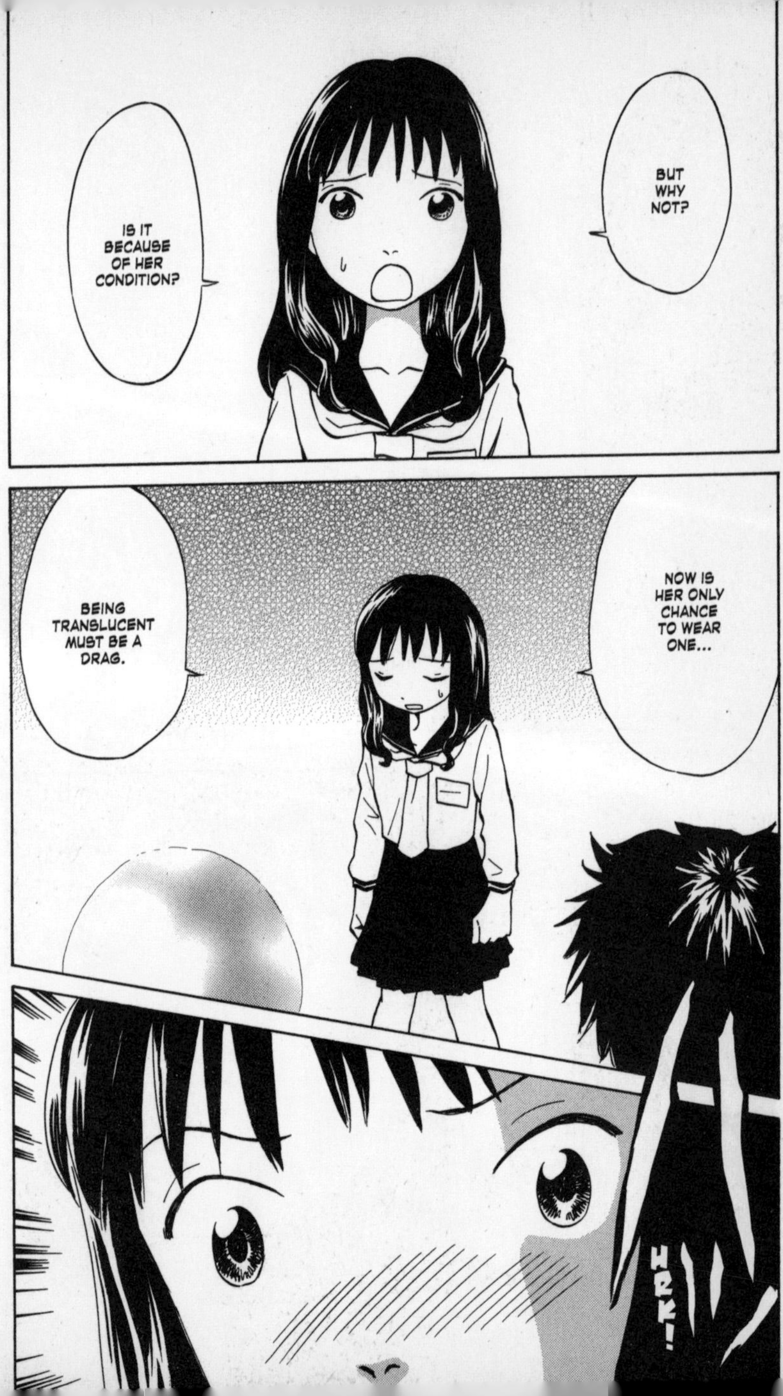
BUT WHY NOT?
IS IT BECAUSE OF HER CONDITION?
NOW IS HER ONLY CHANCE TO WEAR ONE...
BEING TRANSLUCENT MUST BE A DRAG.
HRK!

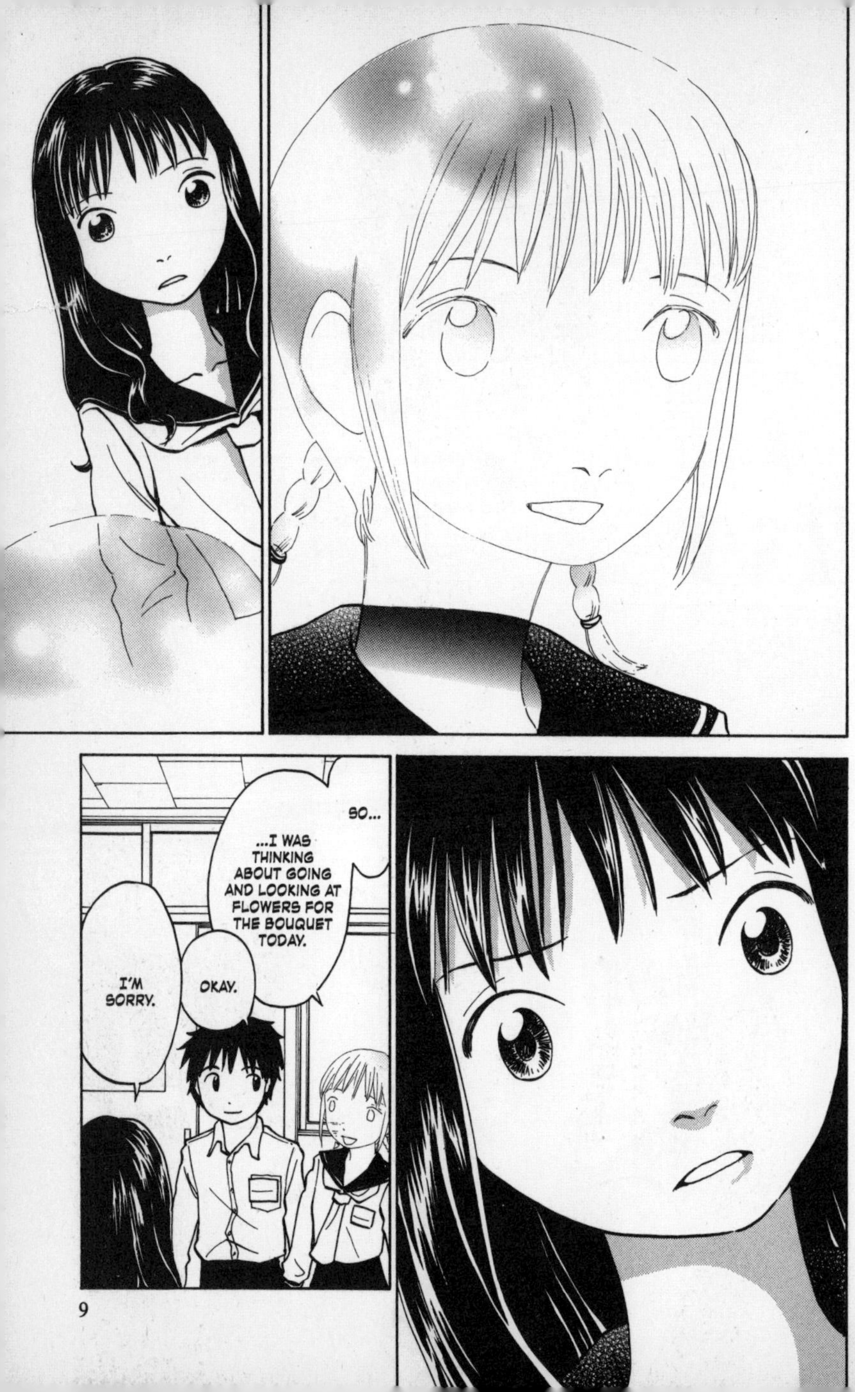
SO...
...I WAS THINKING ABOUT GOING AND LOOKING AT FLOWERS FOR THE BOUQUET TODAY.
OKAY.
I'M SORRY.

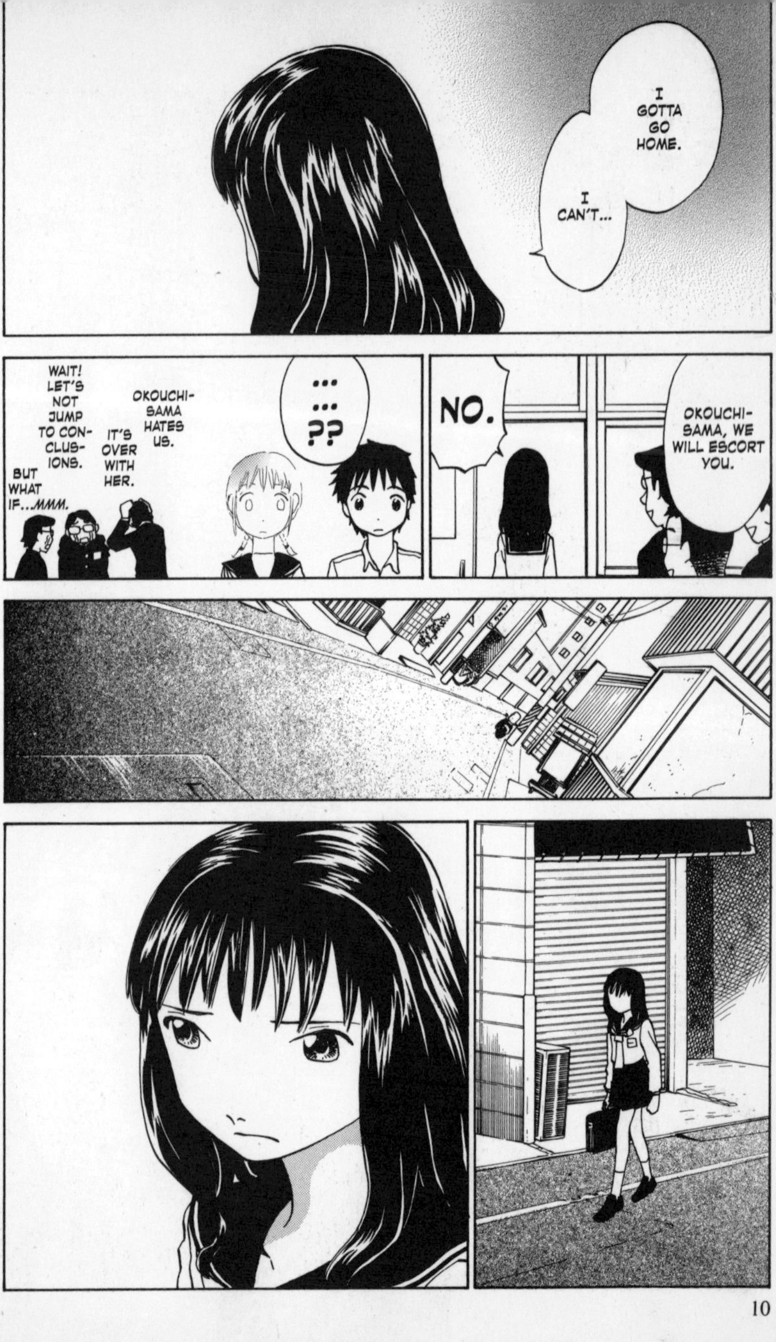
I GOTTA GO HOME.
I CAN'T...
OKOUCHI-SAMA, WE WILL ESCORT YOU.
NO.
... ... ??
OKOUCHI-SAMA HATES US.
IT'S OVER WITH HER.
WAIT! LET'S NOT JUMP TO CONCLUSIONS.
BUT WHAT IF...*MMM.*

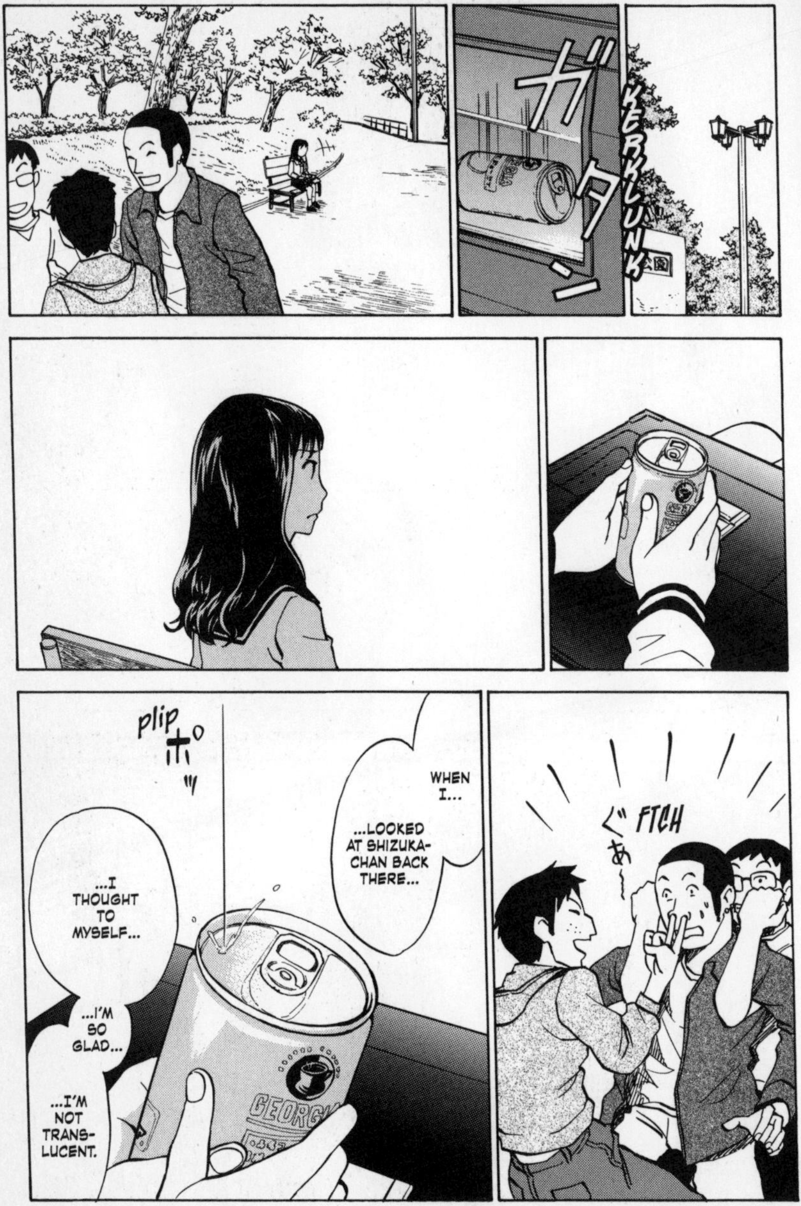

KERKLUNK
公園
ガタ
FTCH
ぐあ～
WHEN I...
...LOOKED AT SHIZUKA-CHAN BACK THERE...
plip
ポッ
...I THOUGHT TO MYSELF...
...I'M SO GLAD...
...I'M NOT TRANS-LUCENT.

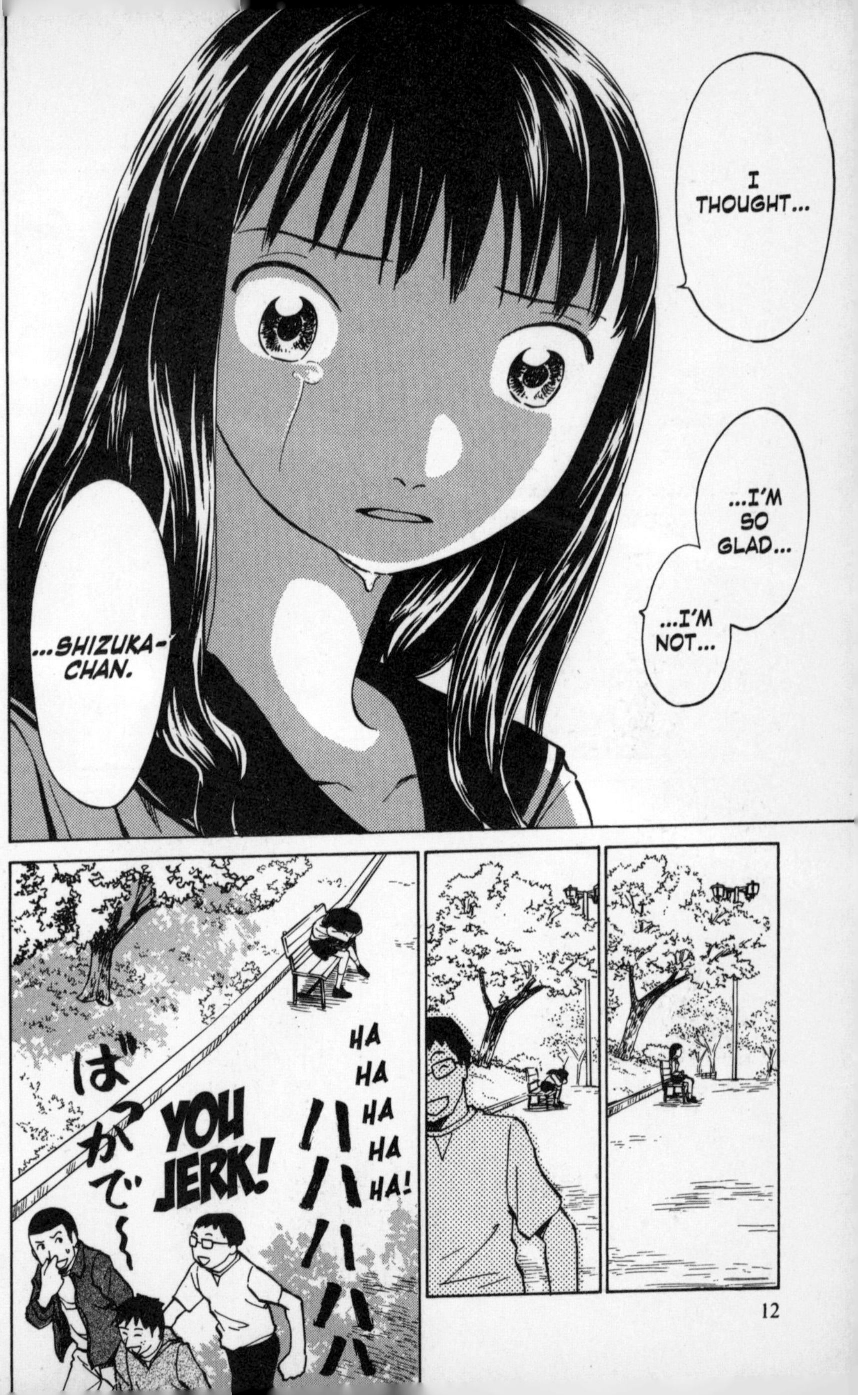
I THOUGHT...
...I'M SO GLAD...
...I'M NOT...
...SHIZUKA-CHAN.
HA HA HA HA HA!
ハハハハ
YOU JERK!
ばっかで～

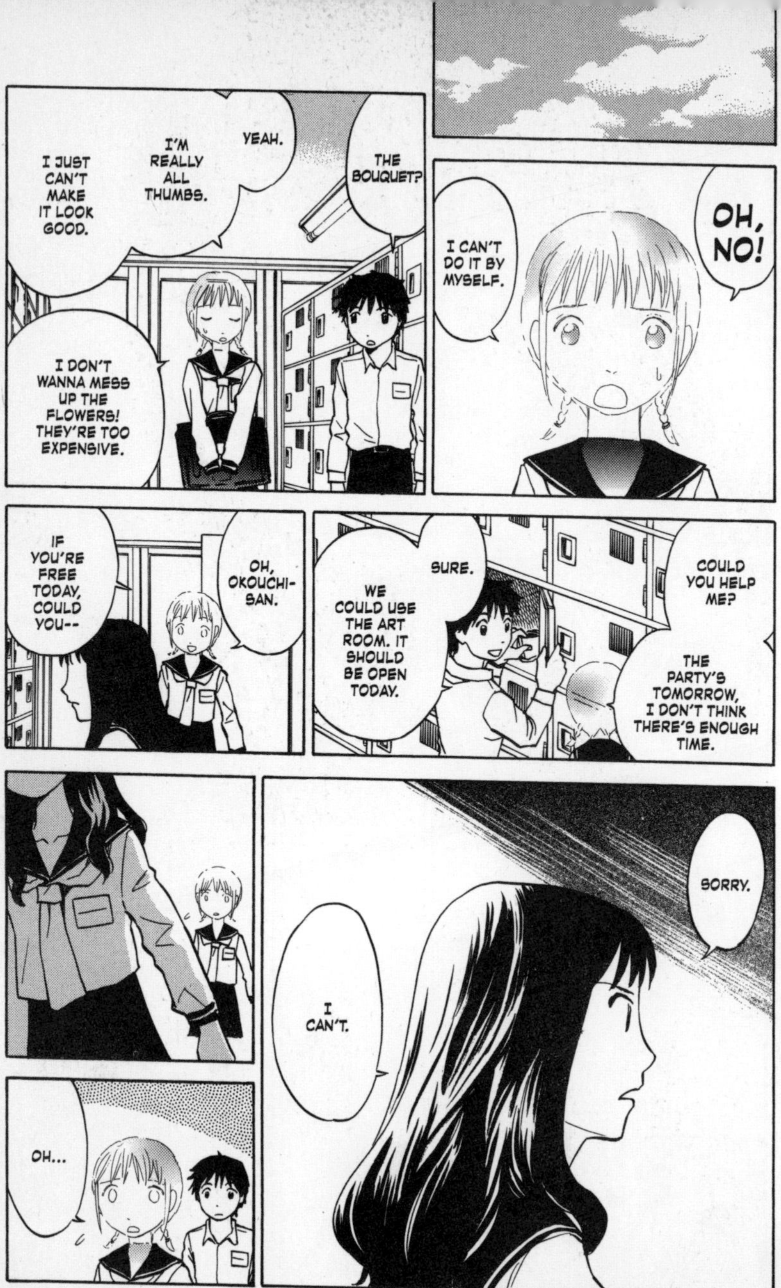
OH, NO!
I CAN'T DO IT BY MYSELF.
THE BOUQUET?
YEAH.
I'M REALLY ALL THUMBS.
I JUST CAN'T MAKE IT LOOK GOOD.
I DON'T WANNA MESS UP THE FLOWERS! THEY'RE TOO EXPENSIVE.
COULD YOU HELP ME?
THE PARTY'S TOMORROW, I DON'T THINK THERE'S ENOUGH TIME.
SURE.
WE COULD USE THE ART ROOM. IT SHOULD BE OPEN TODAY.
OH, OKOUCHI-SAN.
IF YOU'RE FREE TODAY, COULD YOU--
SORRY.
I CAN'T.
OH...

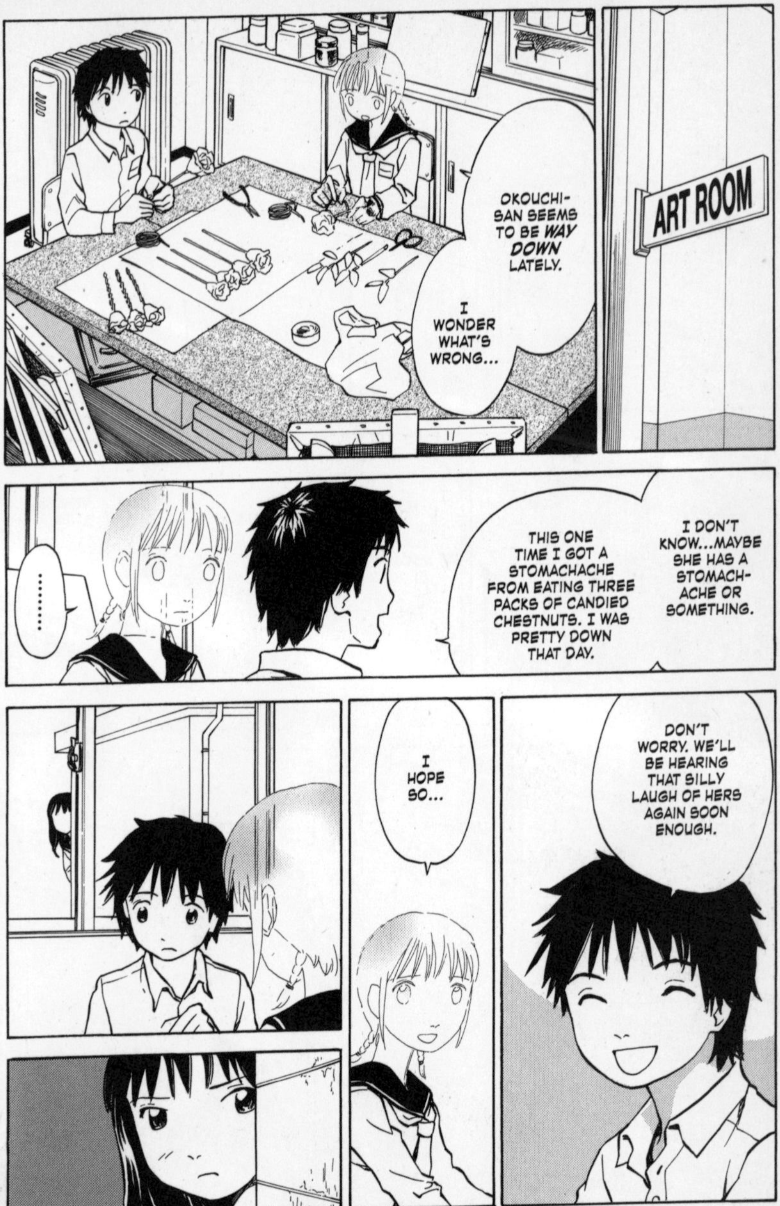
ART ROOM
OKOUCHI-SAN SEEMS TO BE *WAY DOWN* LATELY.
I WONDER WHAT'S WRONG...
I DON'T KNOW...MAYBE SHE HAS A STOMACH-ACHE OR SOMETHING.
THIS ONE TIME I GOT A STOMACHACHE FROM EATING THREE PACKS OF CANDIED CHESTNUTS. I WAS PRETTY DOWN THAT DAY.
....
DON'T WORRY. WE'LL BE HEARING THAT SILLY LAUGH OF HERS AGAIN SOON ENOUGH.
I HOPE SO...

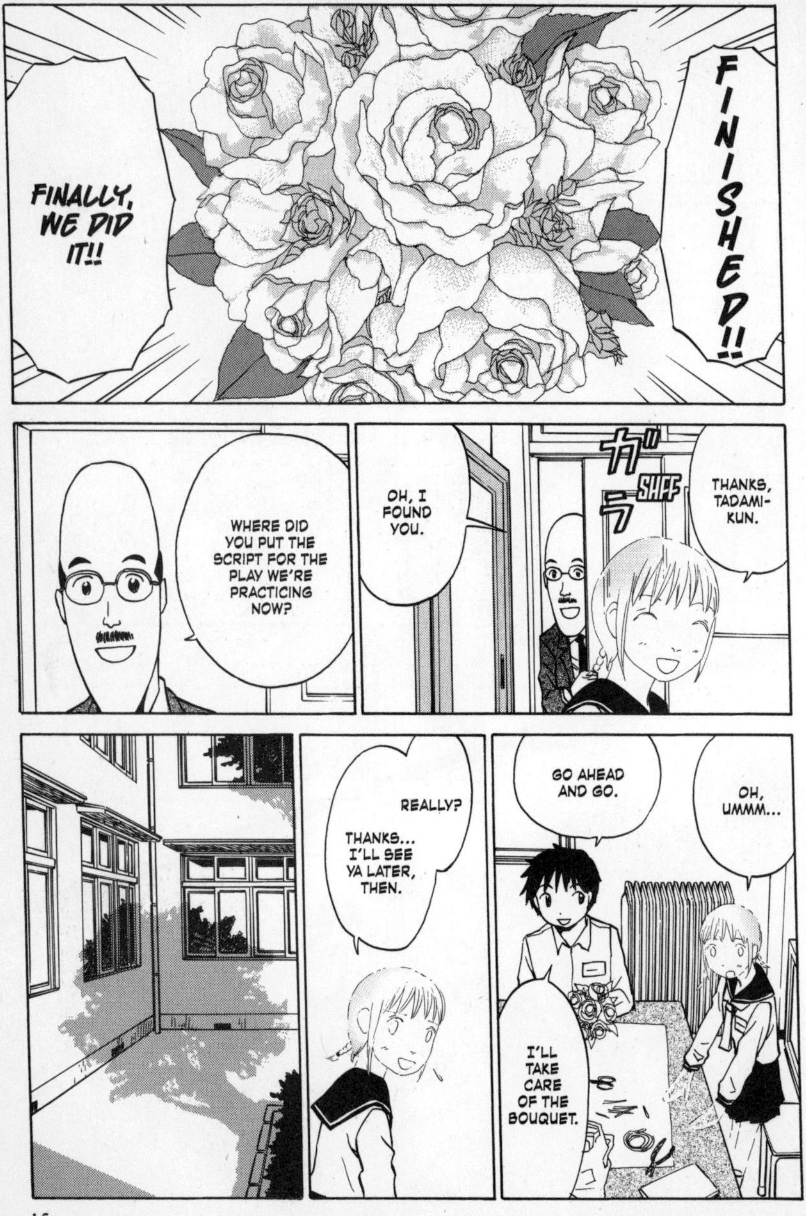
FINISHED!!
FINALLY, WE DID IT!!
THANKS, TADAMI-KUN.
ガラ
SHFF
OH, I FOUND YOU.
WHERE DID YOU PUT THE SCRIPT FOR THE PLAY WE'RE PRACTICING NOW?
OH, UMMM...
GO AHEAD AND GO.
I'LL TAKE CARE OF THE BOUQUET.
REALLY?
THANKS... I'LL SEE YA LATER, THEN.

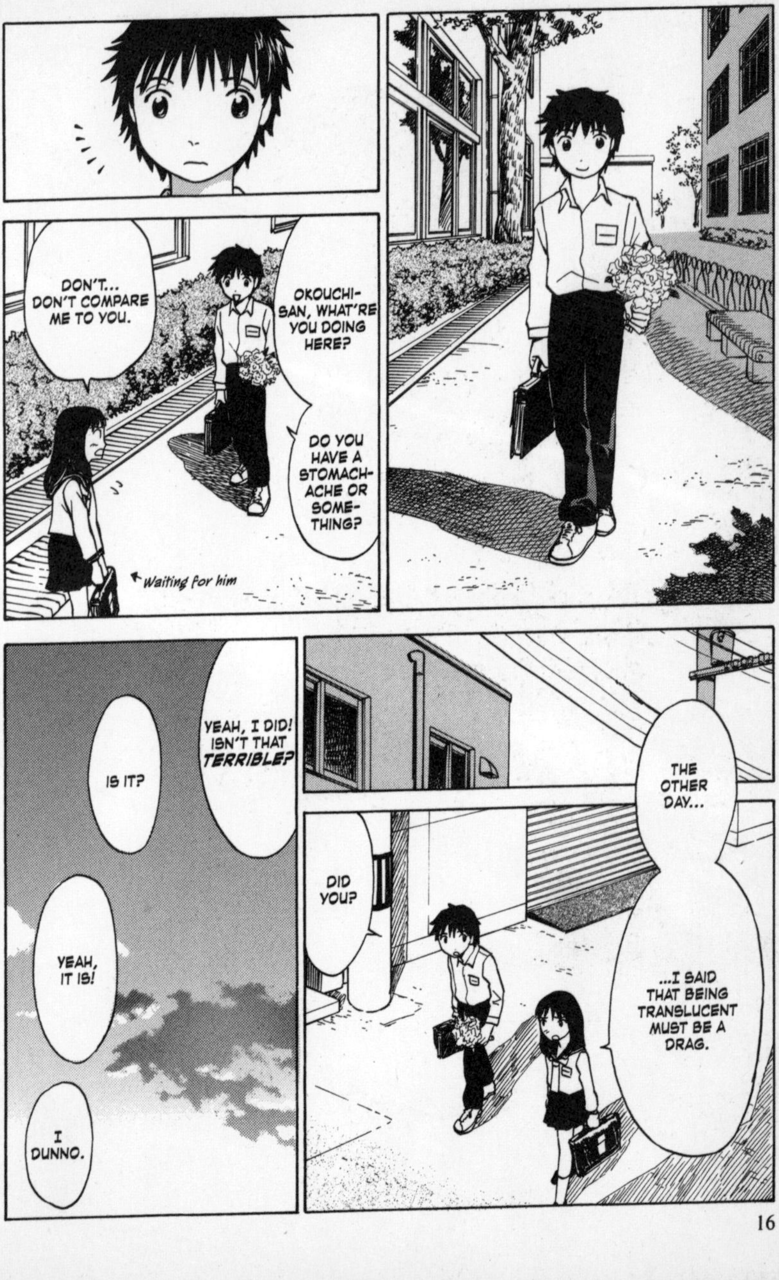
OKOUCHI-SAN, WHAT'RE YOU DOING HERE?
DO YOU HAVE A STOMACHACHE OR SOMETHING?
DON'T... DON'T COMPARE ME TO YOU.
Waiting for him
THE OTHER DAY...
...I SAID THAT BEING TRANSLUCENT MUST BE A DRAG.
DID YOU?
YEAH, I DID! ISN'T THAT *TERRIBLE?*
IS IT?
YEAH, IT IS!
I DUNNO.

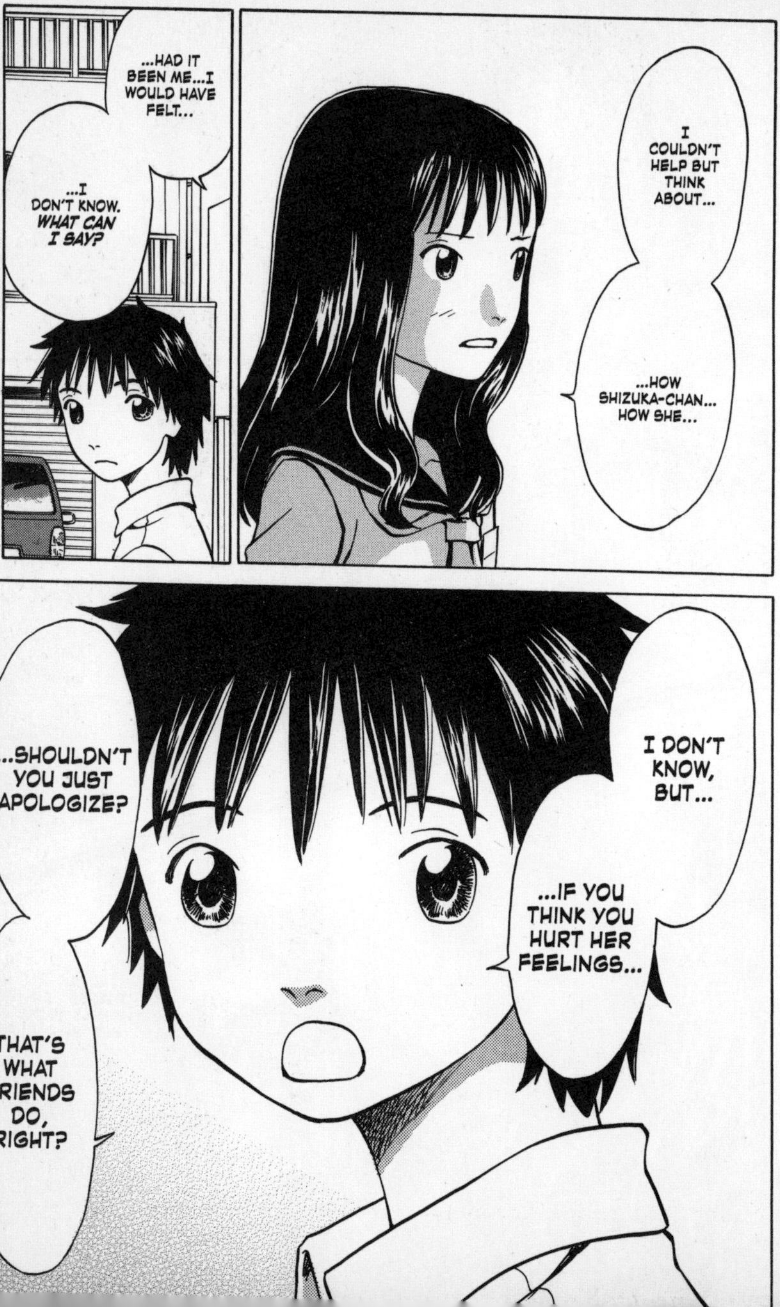
I COULDN'T HELP BUT THINK ABOUT...
...HOW SHIZUKA-CHAN... HOW SHE...
...HAD IT BEEN ME...I WOULD HAVE FELT...
...I DON'T KNOW. *WHAT CAN I SAY?*
I DON'T KNOW, BUT...
...IF YOU THINK YOU HURT HER FEELINGS...
...SHOULDN'T YOU JUST APOLOGIZE?
THAT'S WHAT FRIENDS DO, RIGHT?

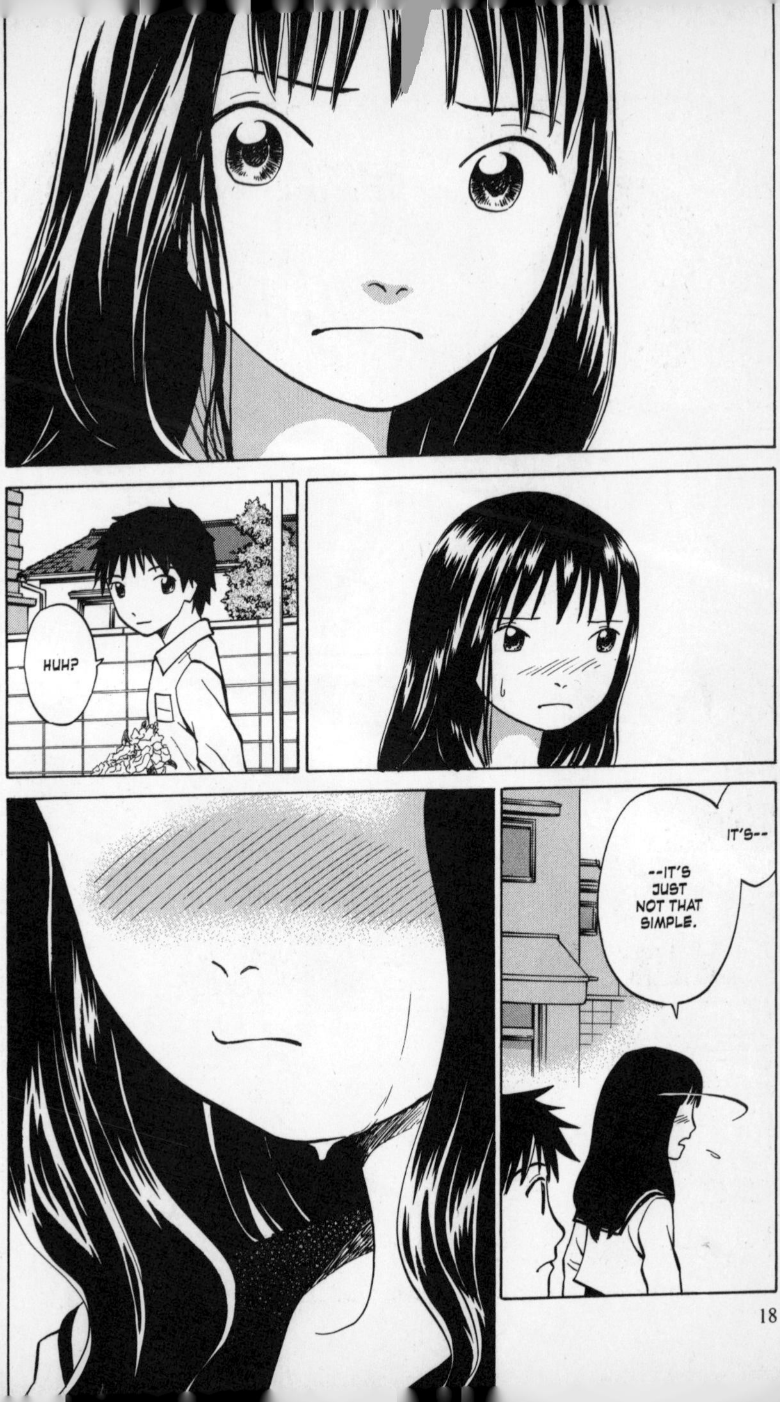
HUH?
IT'S--
--IT'S JUST NOT THAT SIMPLE.

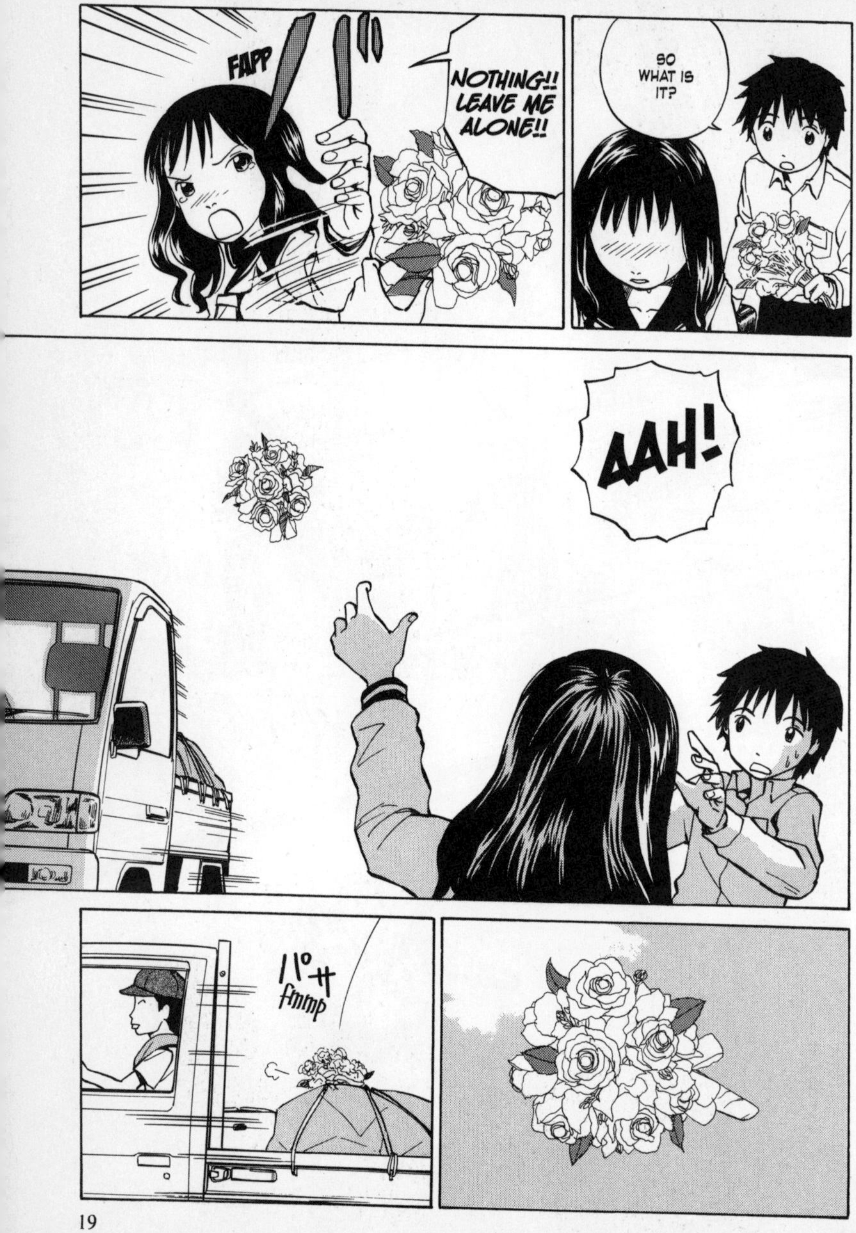
SO WHAT IS IT?
FAPP
NOTHING!! LEAVE ME ALONE!!
AAH!
パサ
fmmp

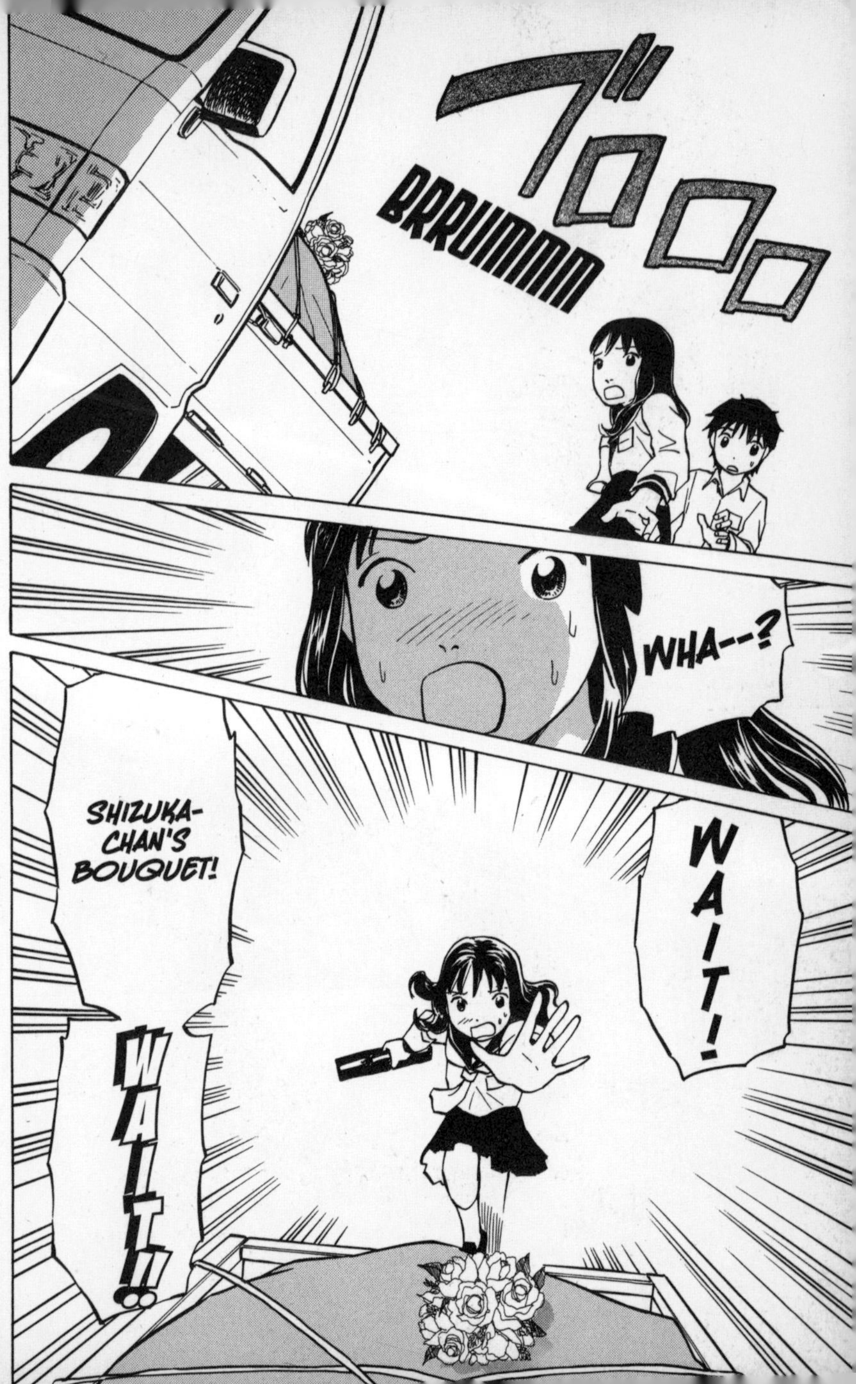
ブロロロ
BRRUMMM
WHA--?
WAIT!
SHIZUKA-CHAN'S BOUQUET!
WAIT!!

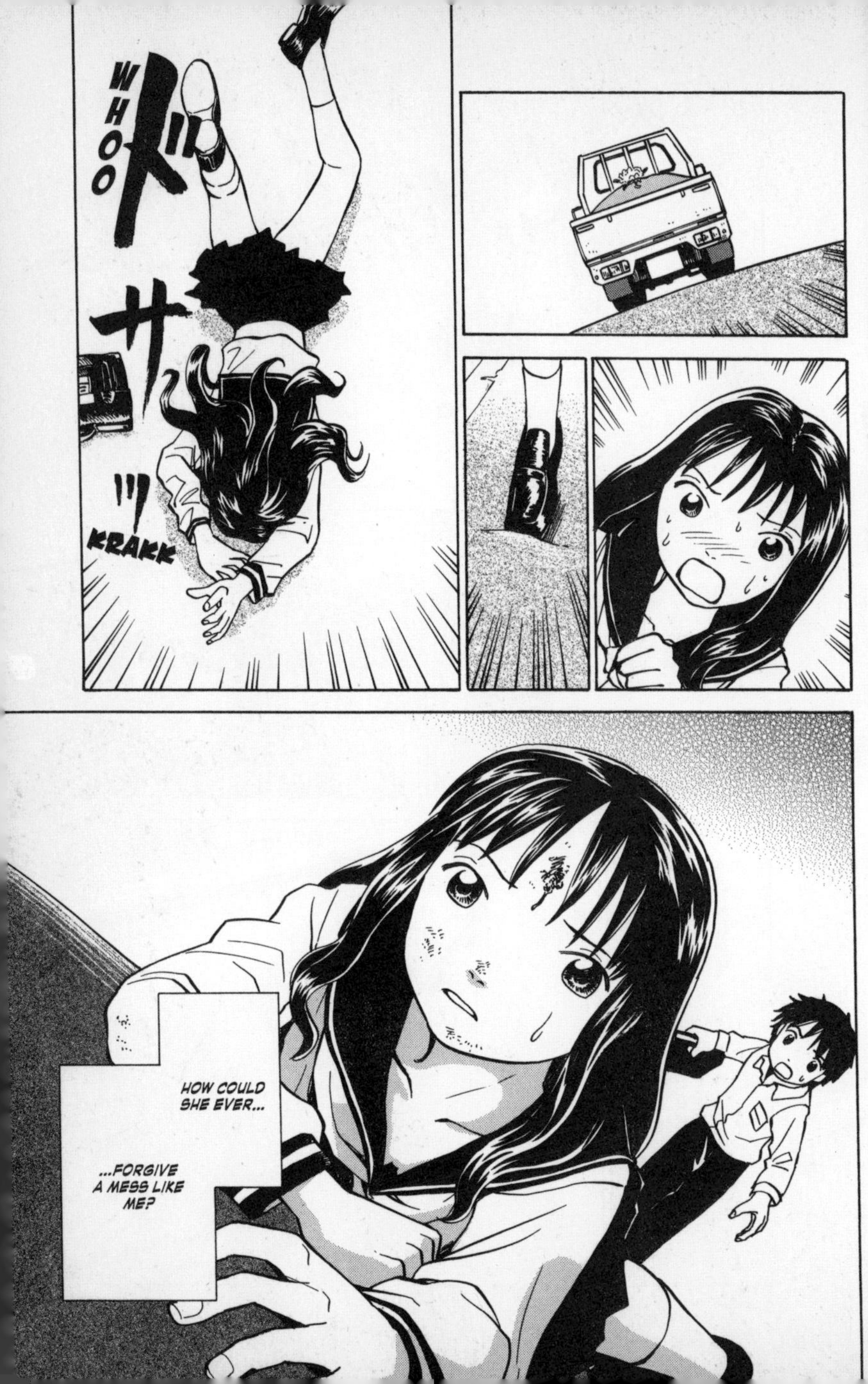
WHOOO
サ
KRAKK
HOW COULD SHE EVER...
...FORGIVE A MESS LIKE ME?

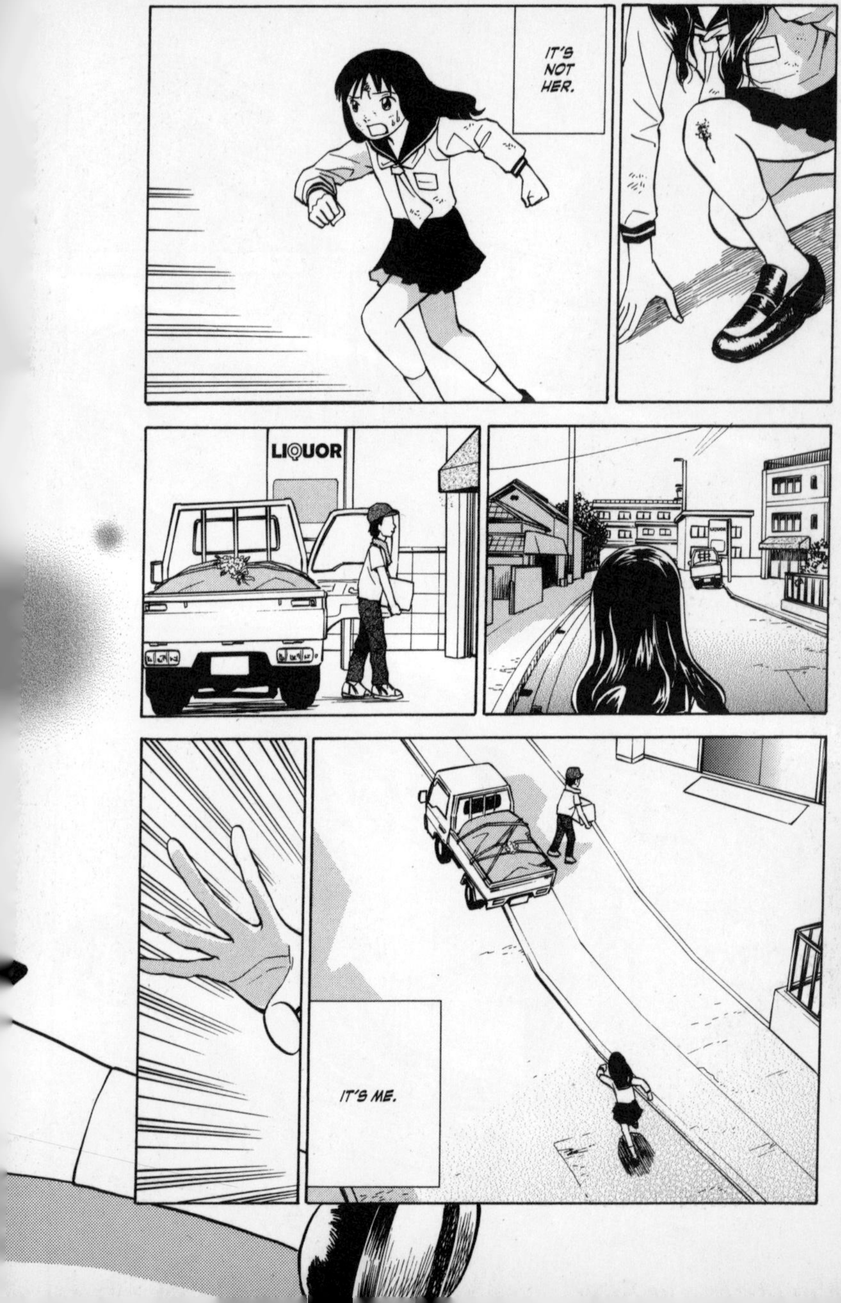
IT'S NOT HER.
LIQUOR
IT'S ME.

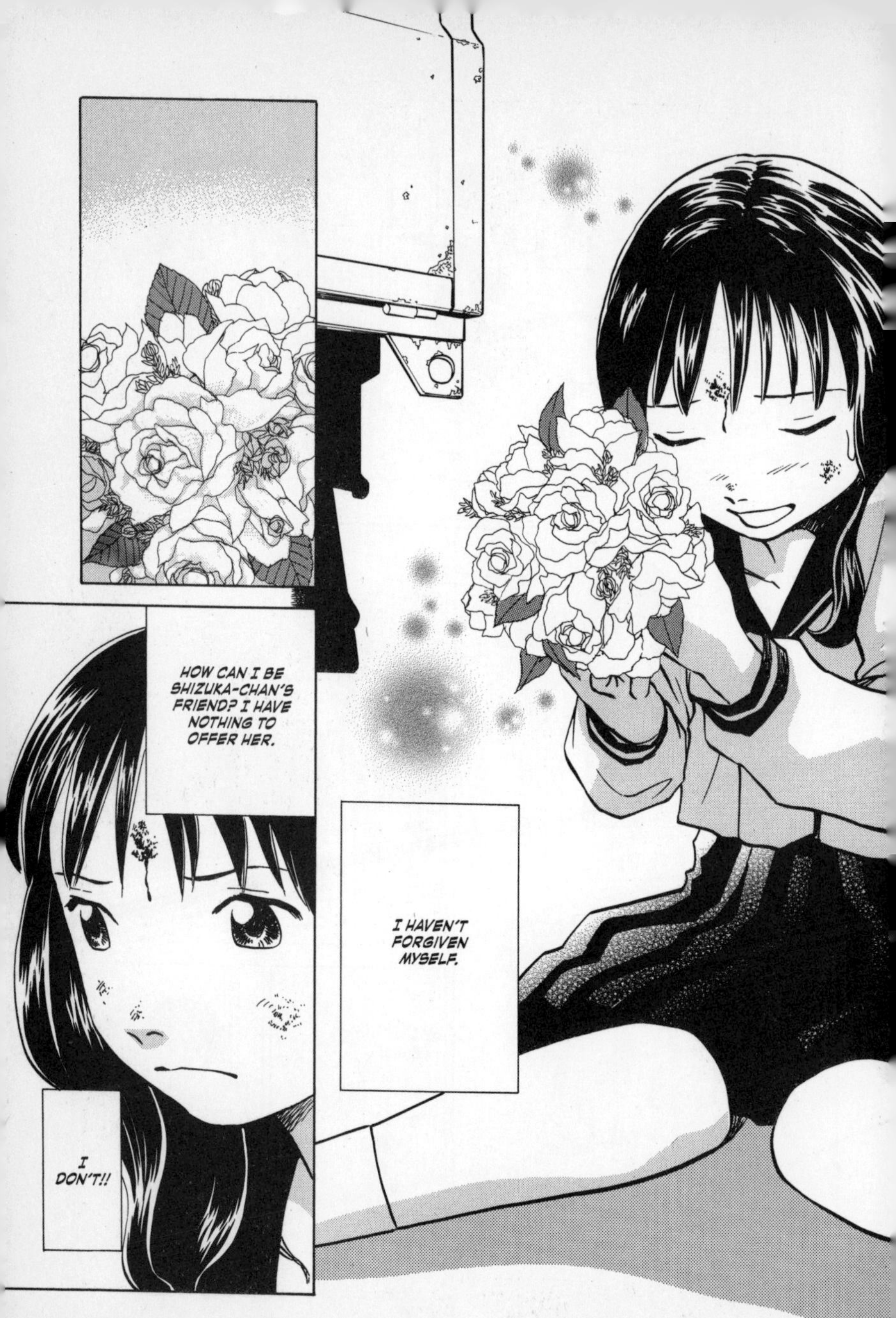
HOW CAN I BE SHIZUKA-CHAN'S FRIEND? I HAVE NOTHING TO OFFER HER.
I HAVEN'T FORGIVEN MYSELF.
I DON'T!!

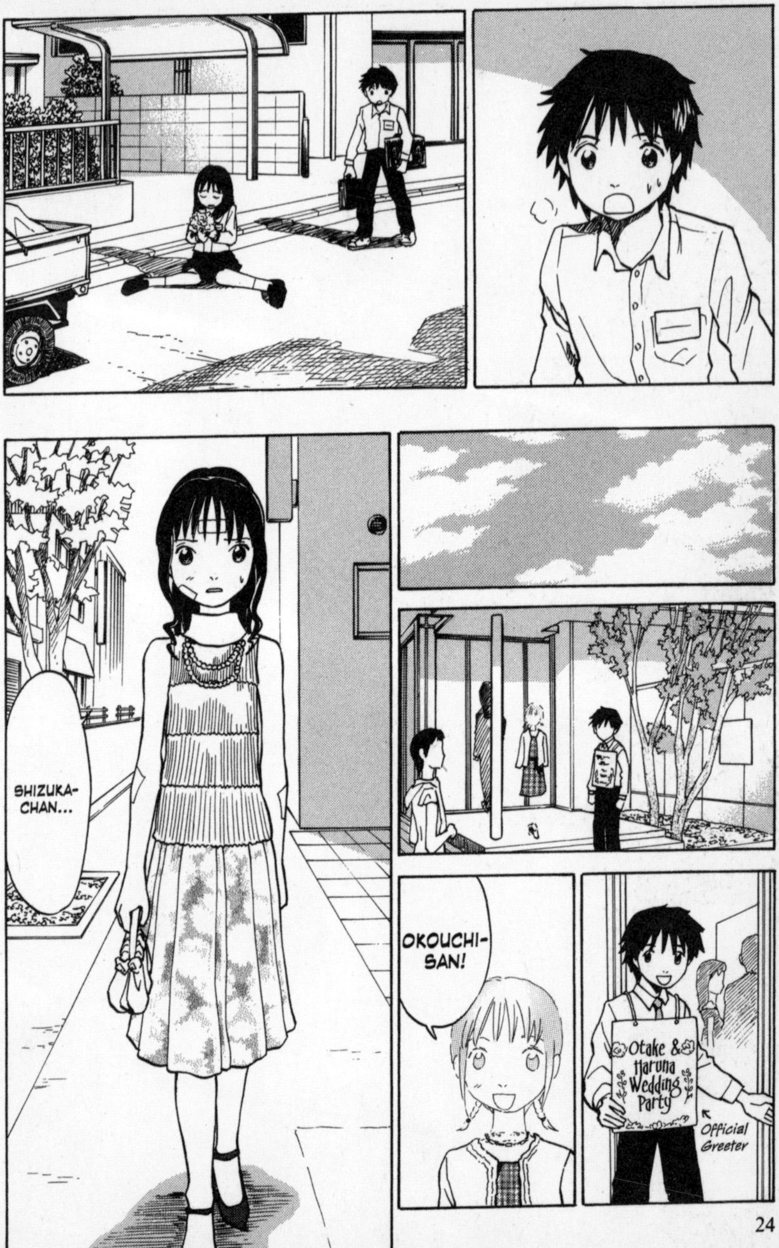
Otake & Haruna Wedding Party
Official Greeter
OKOUCHI-SAN!
SHIZUKA-CHAN...

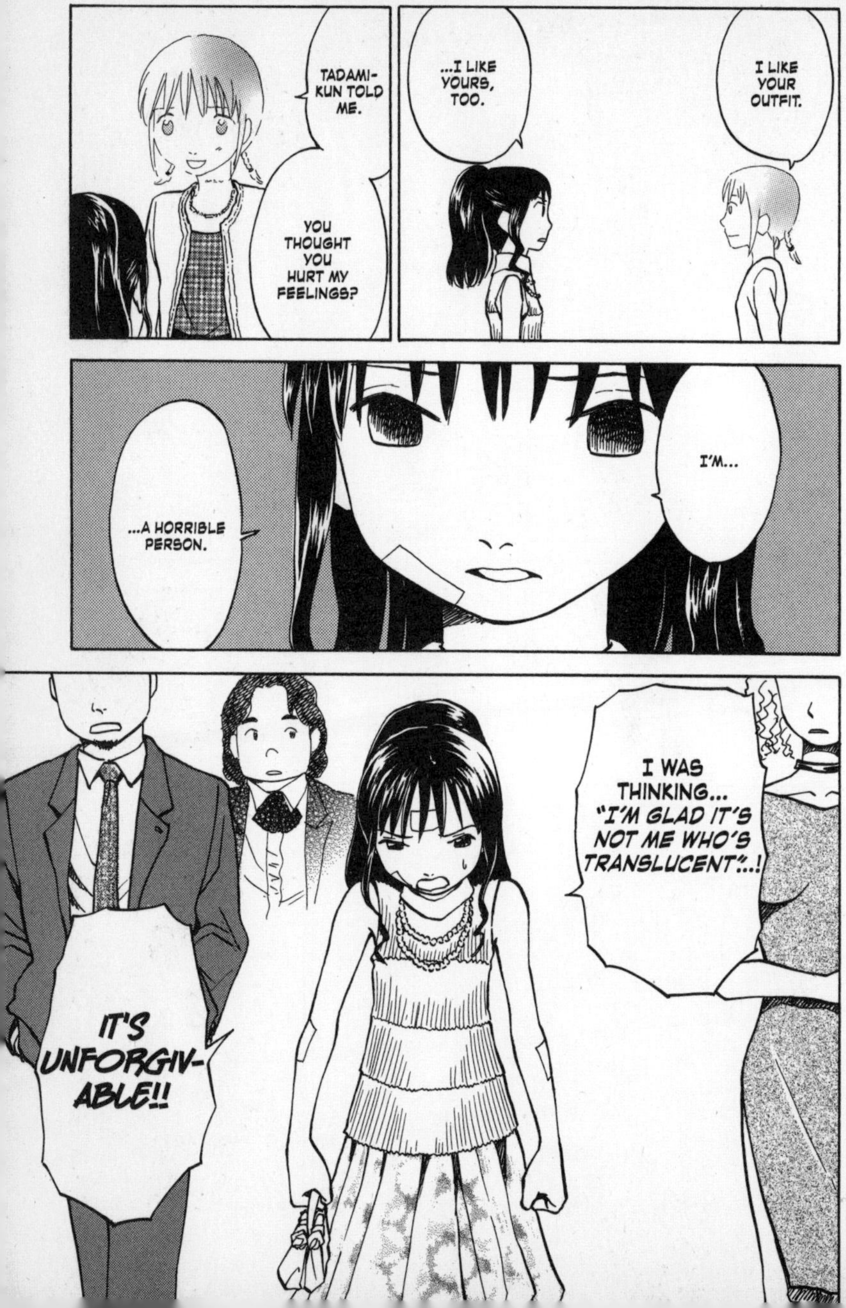
I LIKE YOUR OUTFIT.
...I LIKE YOURS, TOO.
TADAMI-KUN TOLD ME.
YOU THOUGHT YOU HURT MY FEELINGS?
I'M...
...A HORRIBLE PERSON.
I WAS THINKING... "I'M GLAD IT'S NOT ME WHO'S TRANSLUCENT"...!
IT'S UNFORGIV-ABLE!!

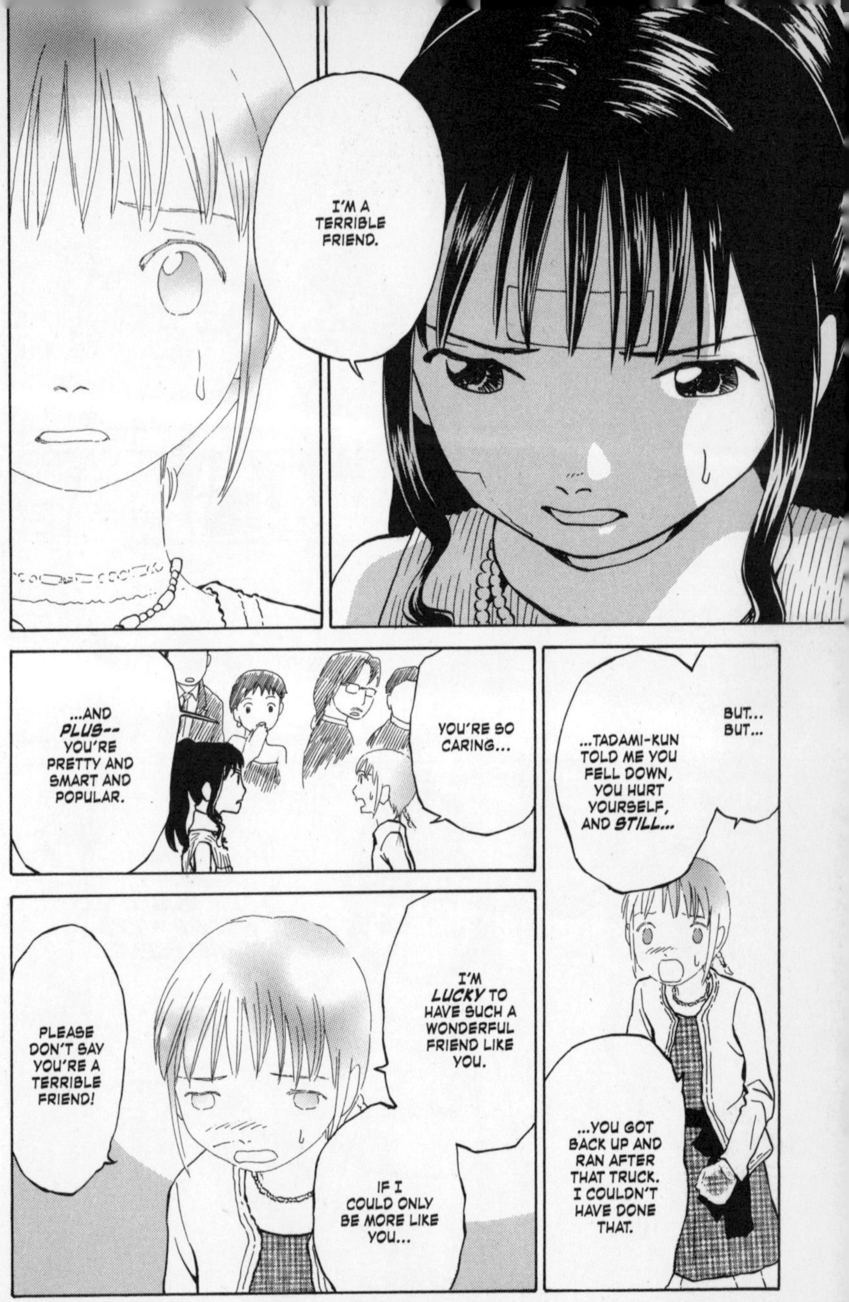
I'M A TERRIBLE FRIEND.
BUT... BUT...
...TADAMI-KUN TOLD ME YOU FELL DOWN, YOU HURT YOURSELF, AND *STILL*...
...YOU GOT BACK UP AND RAN AFTER THAT TRUCK. I COULDN'T HAVE DONE THAT.
YOU'RE SO CARING...
...AND *PLUS*-- YOU'RE PRETTY AND SMART AND POPULAR.
I'M *LUCKY* TO HAVE SUCH A WONDERFUL FRIEND LIKE YOU.
IF I COULD ONLY BE MORE LIKE YOU...
PLEASE DON'T SAY YOU'RE A TERRIBLE FRIEND!

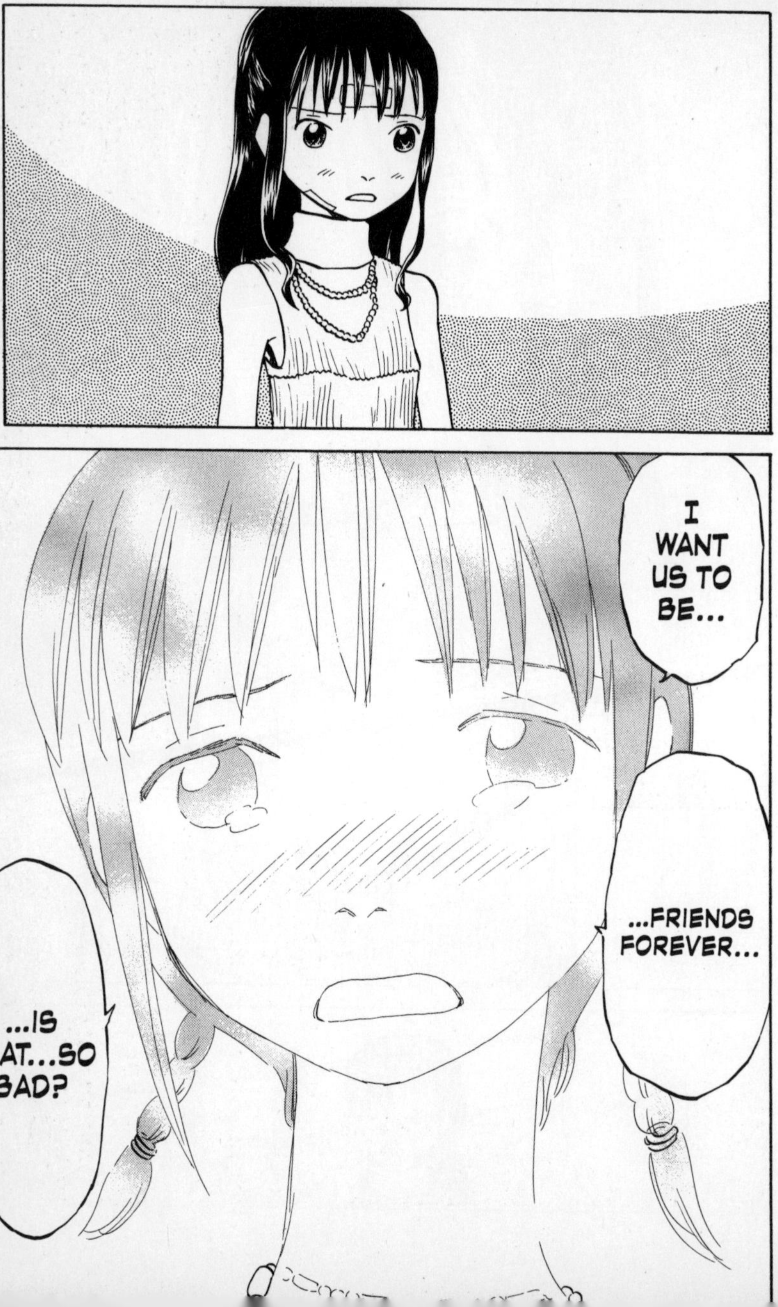
I WANT US TO BE...
...FRIENDS FOREVER...
...IS THAT...SO BAD?

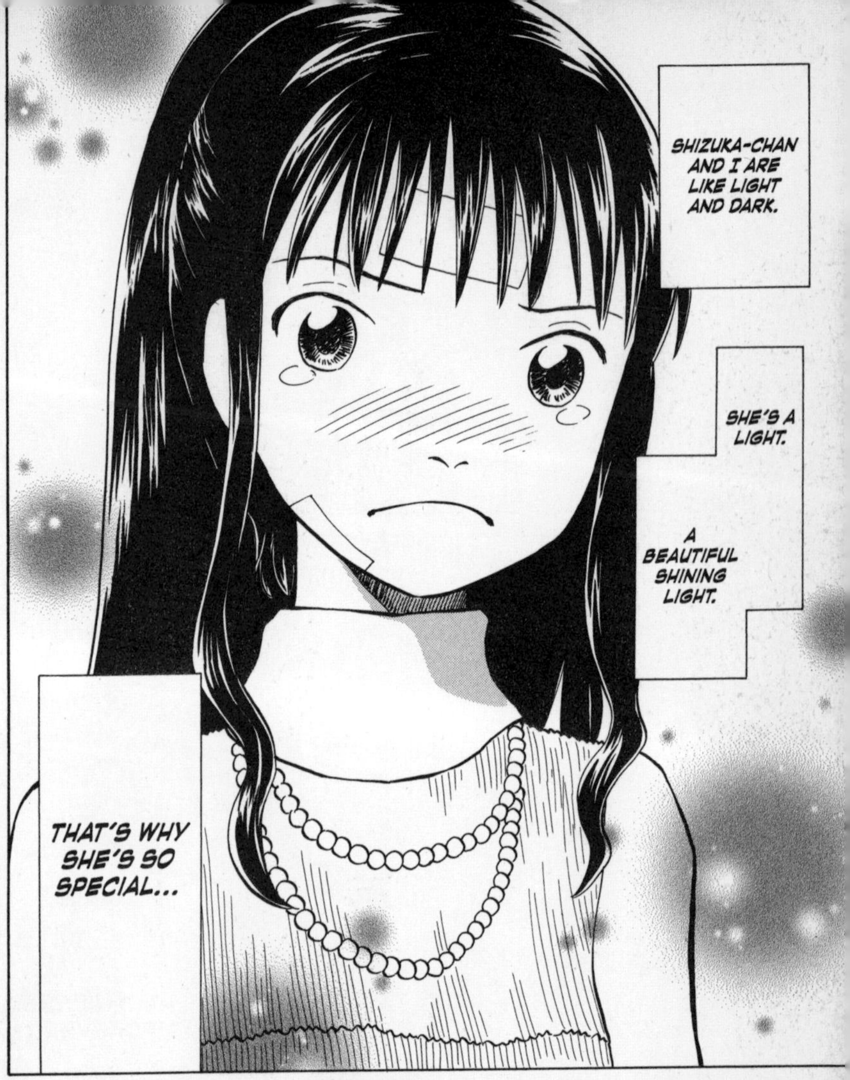
SHIZUKA-CHAN AND I ARE LIKE LIGHT AND DARK.
SHE'S A LIGHT.
A BEAUTIFUL SHINING LIGHT.
THAT'S WHY SHE'S SO SPECIAL...

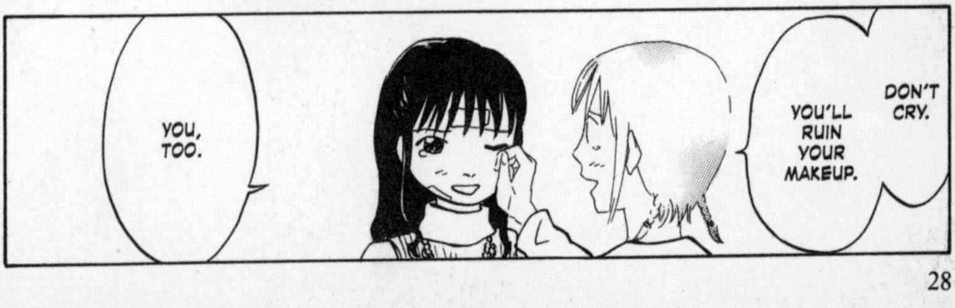
DON'T CRY.
YOU'LL RUIN YOUR MAKEUP.
YOU, TOO.

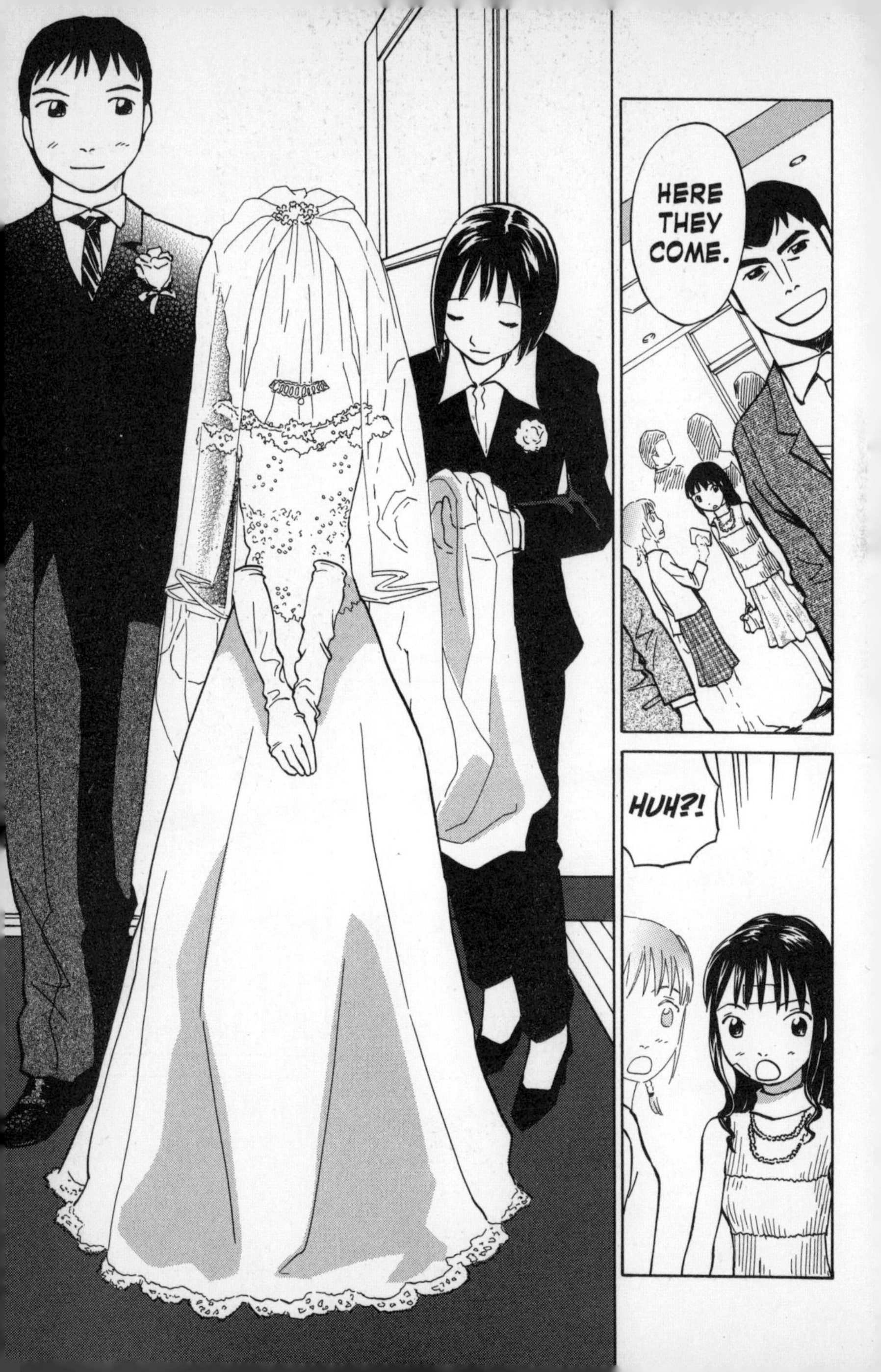
HERE THEY COME.
HUH?!

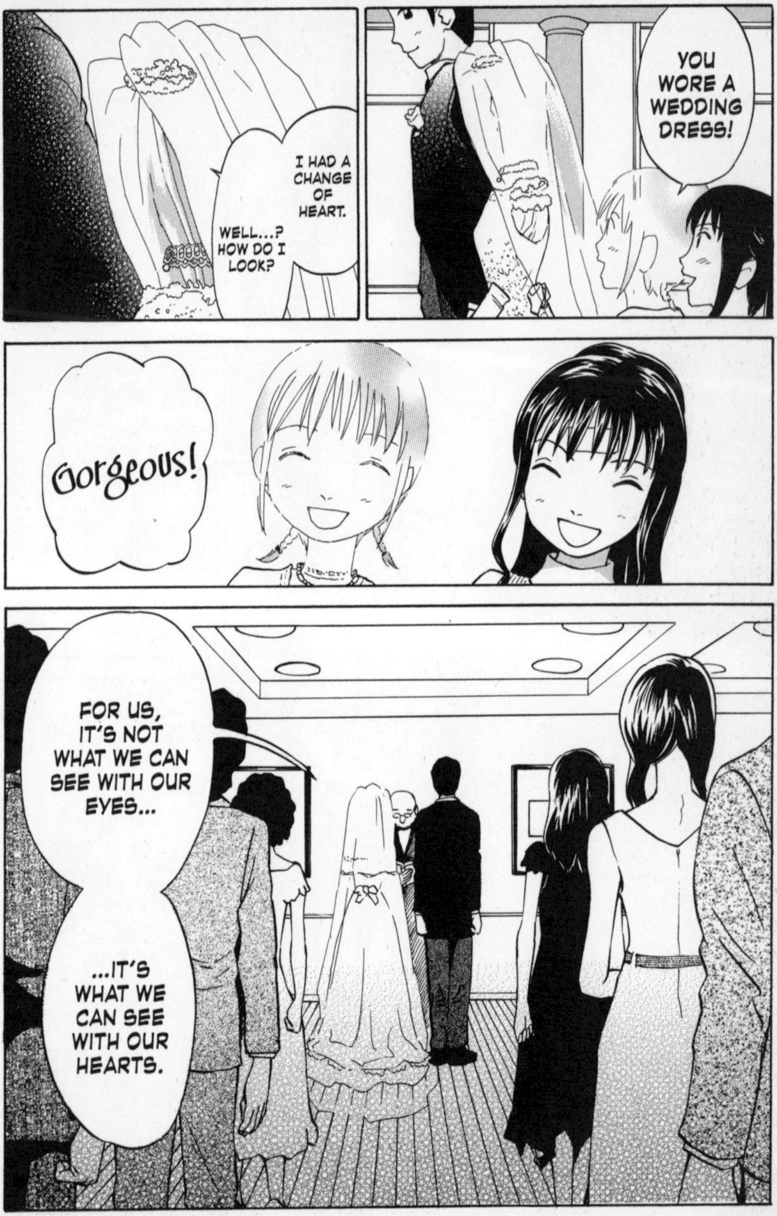
YOU WORE A WEDDING DRESS!
I HAD A CHANGE OF HEART.
WELL...? HOW DO I LOOK?
Gorgeous!
FOR US, IT'S NOT WHAT WE CAN SEE WITH OUR EYES...
...IT'S WHAT WE CAN SEE WITH OUR HEARTS.

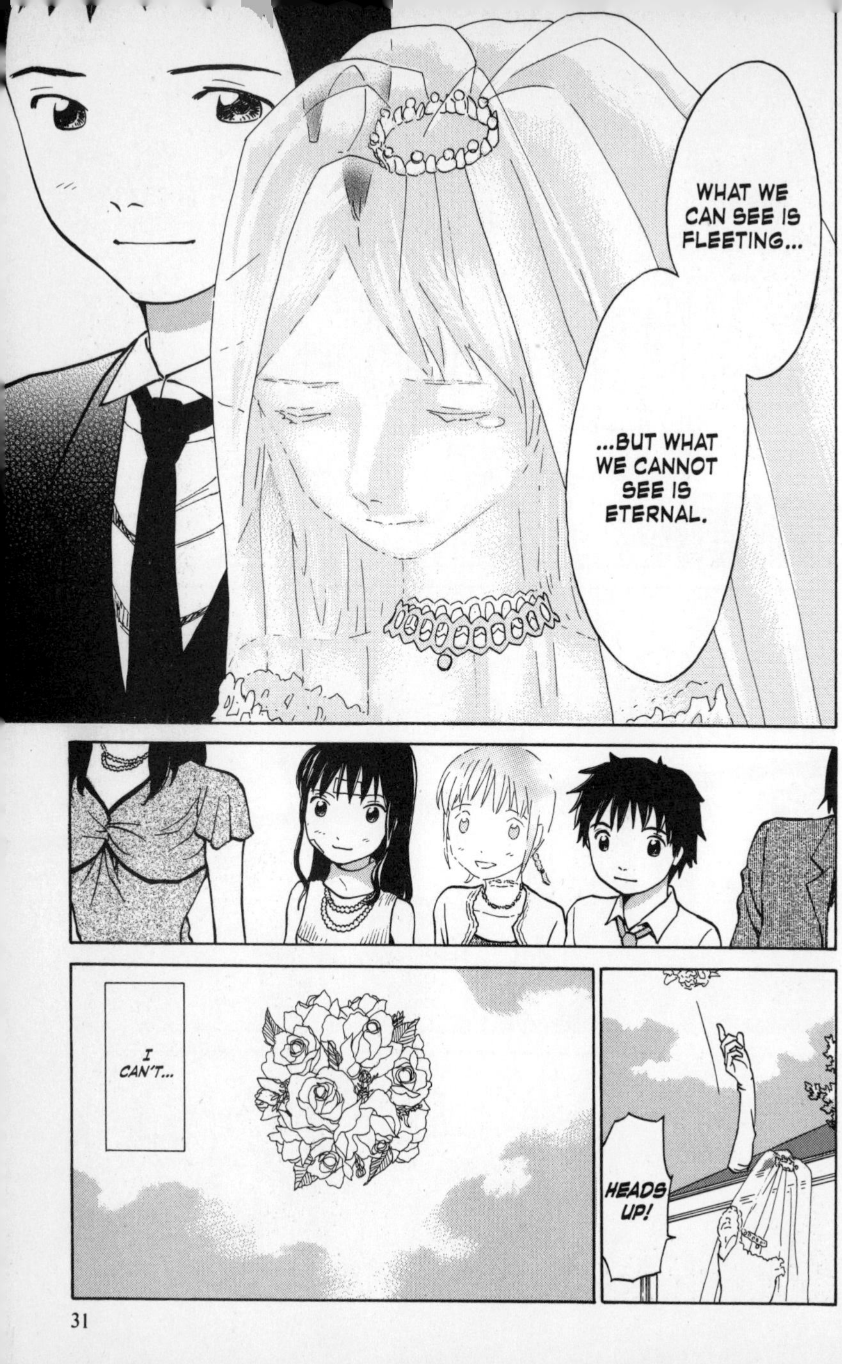
WHAT WE CAN SEE IS FLEETING...
...BUT WHAT WE CANNOT SEE IS ETERNAL.
HEADS UP!
I CAN'T...

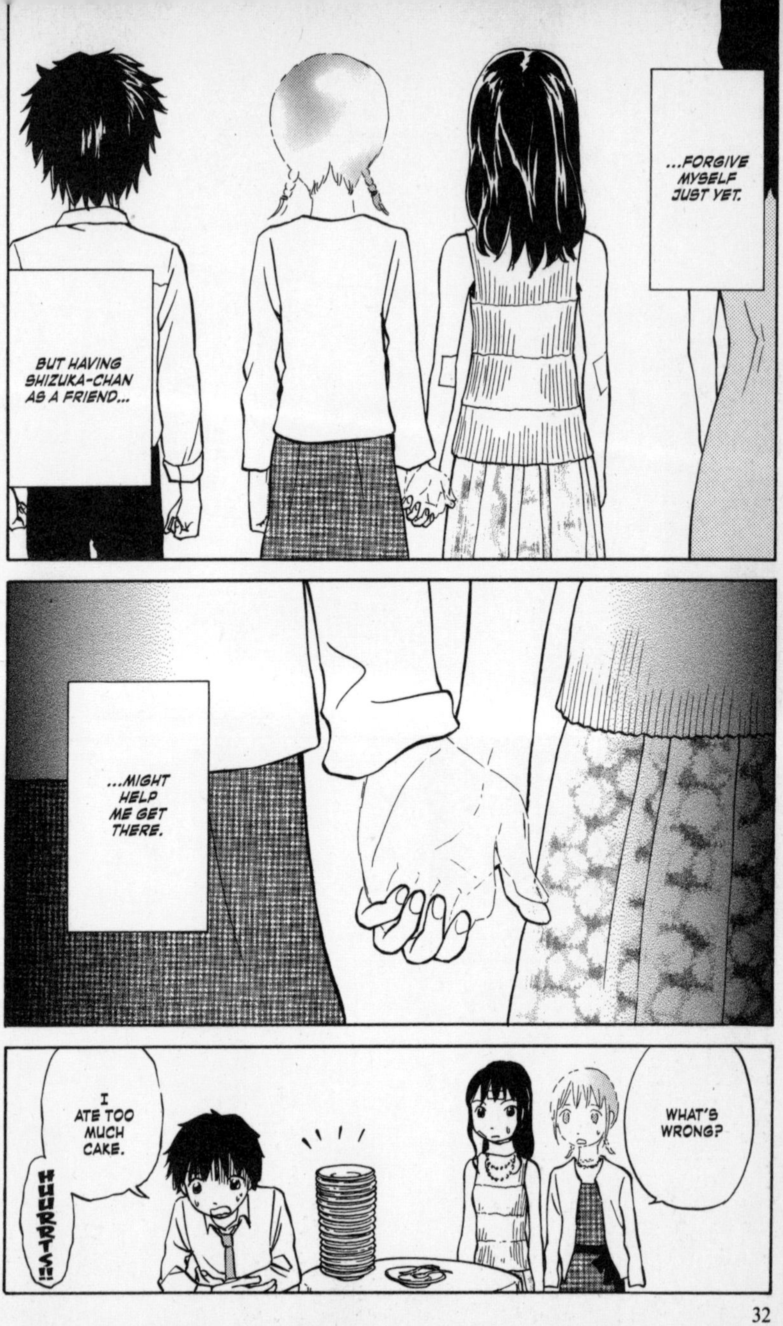
...FORGIVE MYSELF JUST YET.
BUT HAVING SHIZUKA-CHAN AS A FRIEND...
...MIGHT HELP ME GET THERE.
WHAT'S WRONG?
I ATE TOO MUCH CAKE.
HUURRTS!!

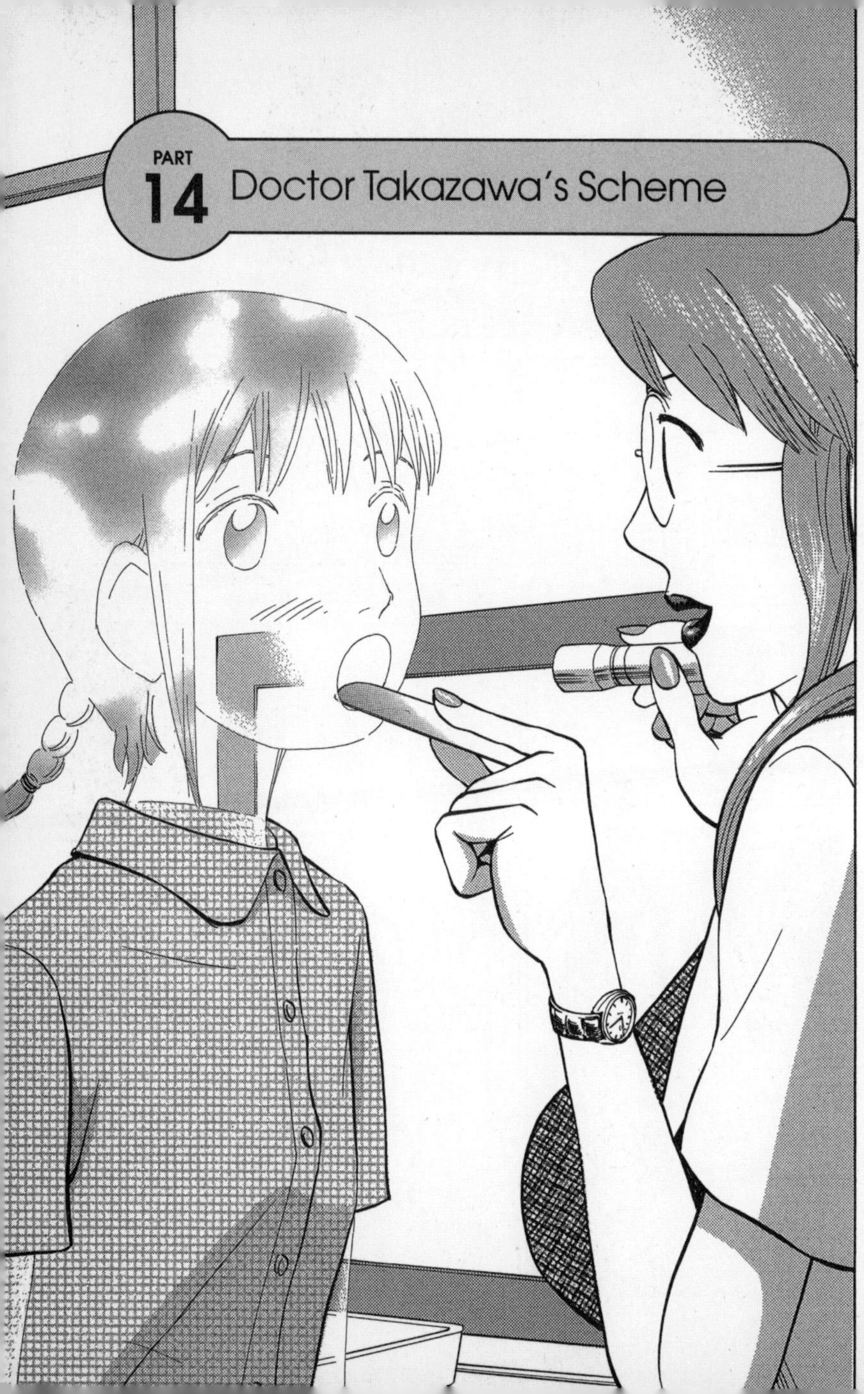
PART
14 Doctor Takazawa's Scheme

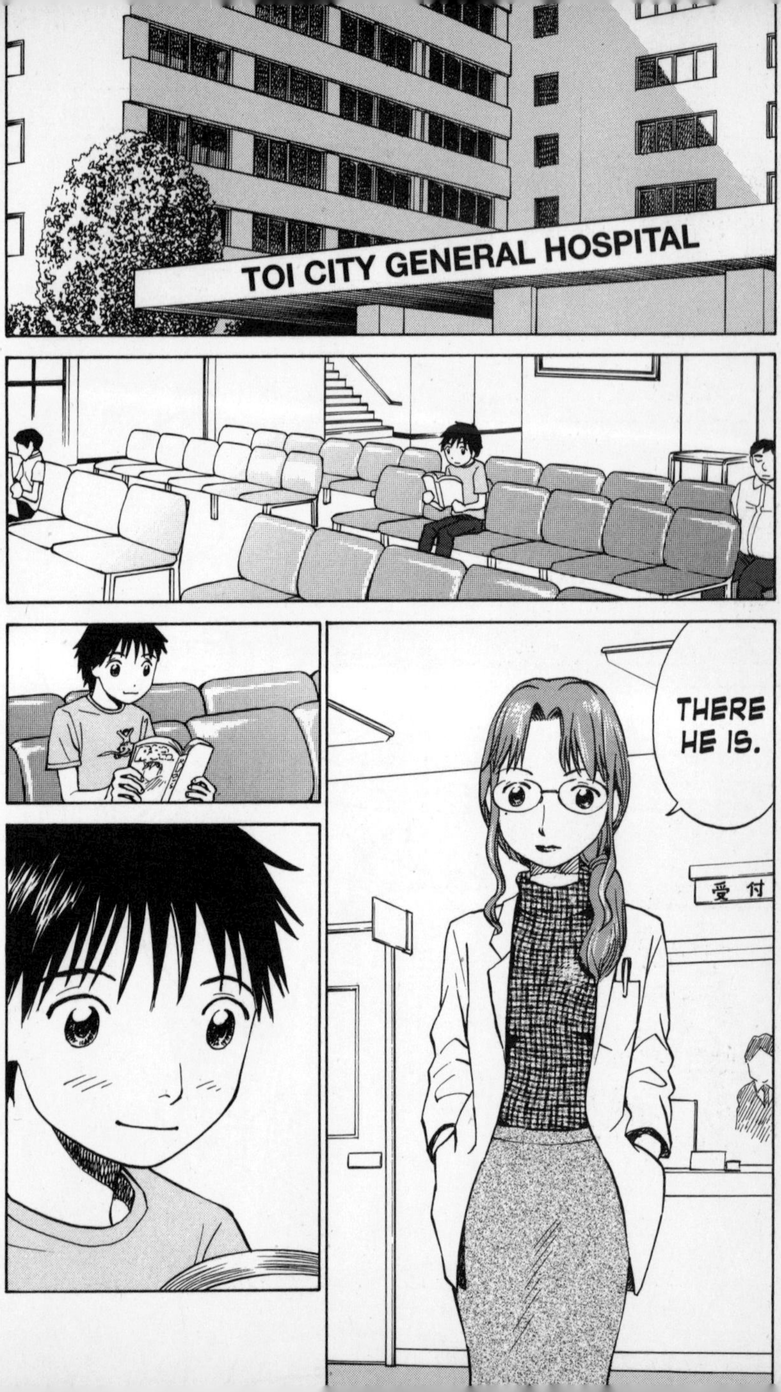
TOI CITY GENERAL HOSPITAL
THERE HE IS.
受付

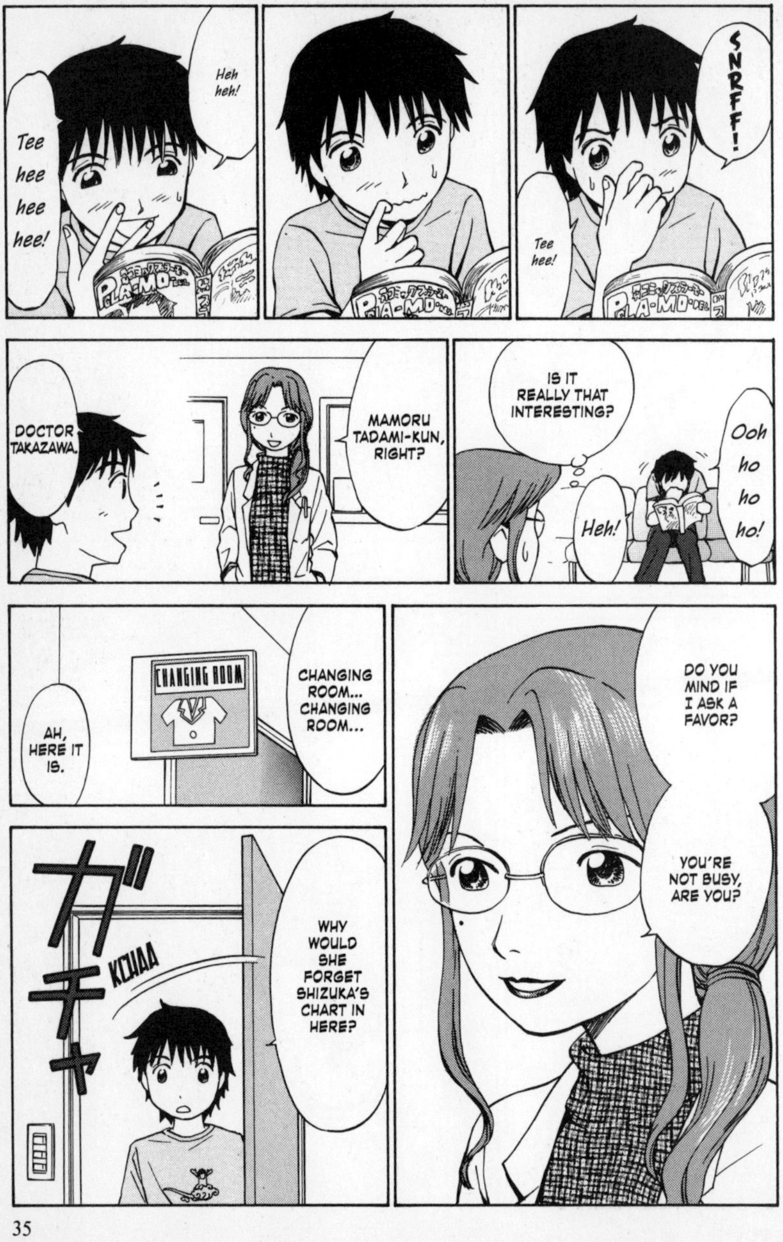
SNRFF!
Tee hee!
Heh heh!
Tee hee hee hee!
IS IT REALLY THAT INTERESTING?
Ooh ho ho ho!
Heh!
MAMORU TADAMI-KUN, RIGHT?
DOCTOR TAKAZAWA.
DO YOU MIND IF I ASK A FAVOR?
YOU'RE NOT BUSY, ARE YOU?
CHANGING ROOM... CHANGING ROOM...
CHANGING ROOM
AH, HERE IT IS.
WHY WOULD SHE FORGET SHIZUKA'S CHART IN HERE?
ガチャ
KCHAA

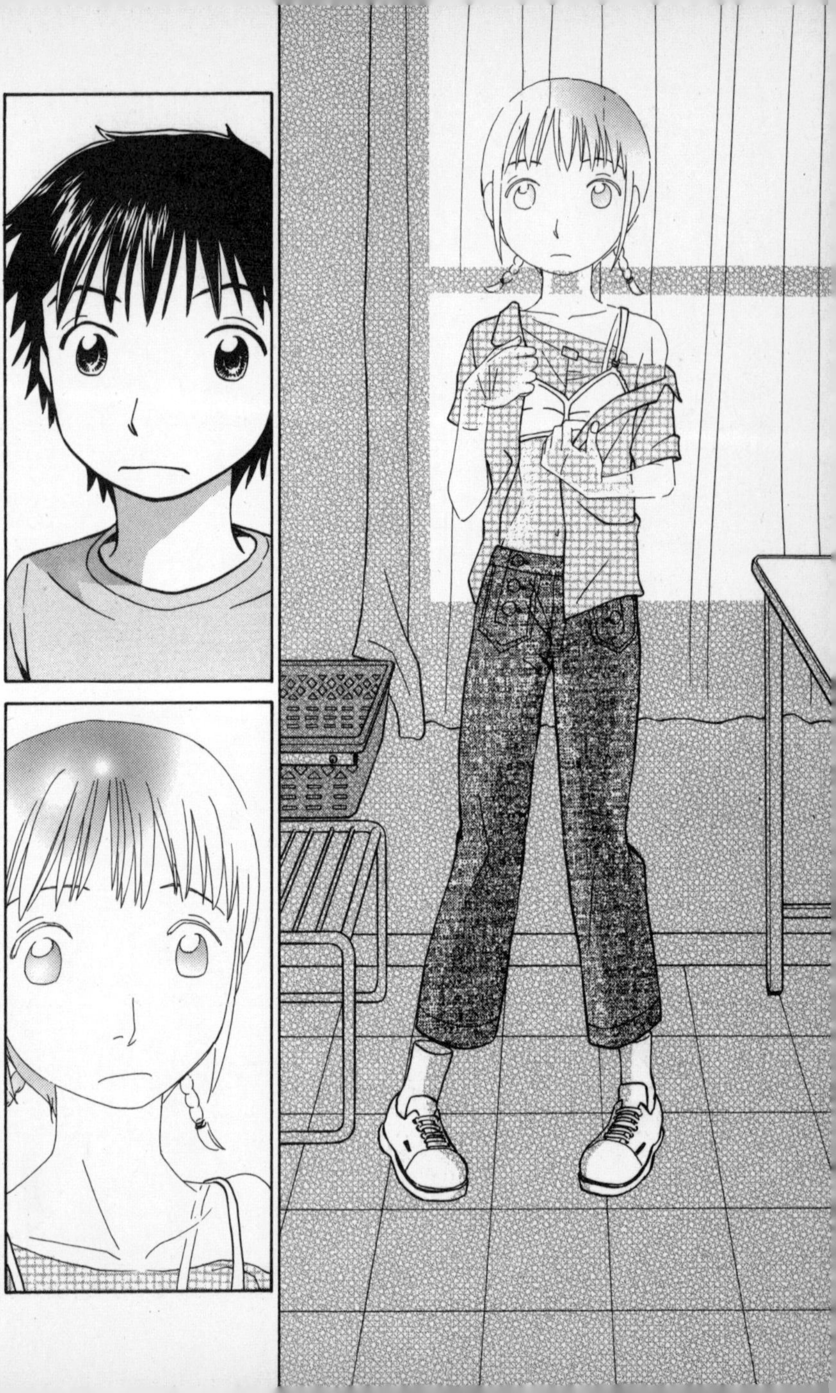

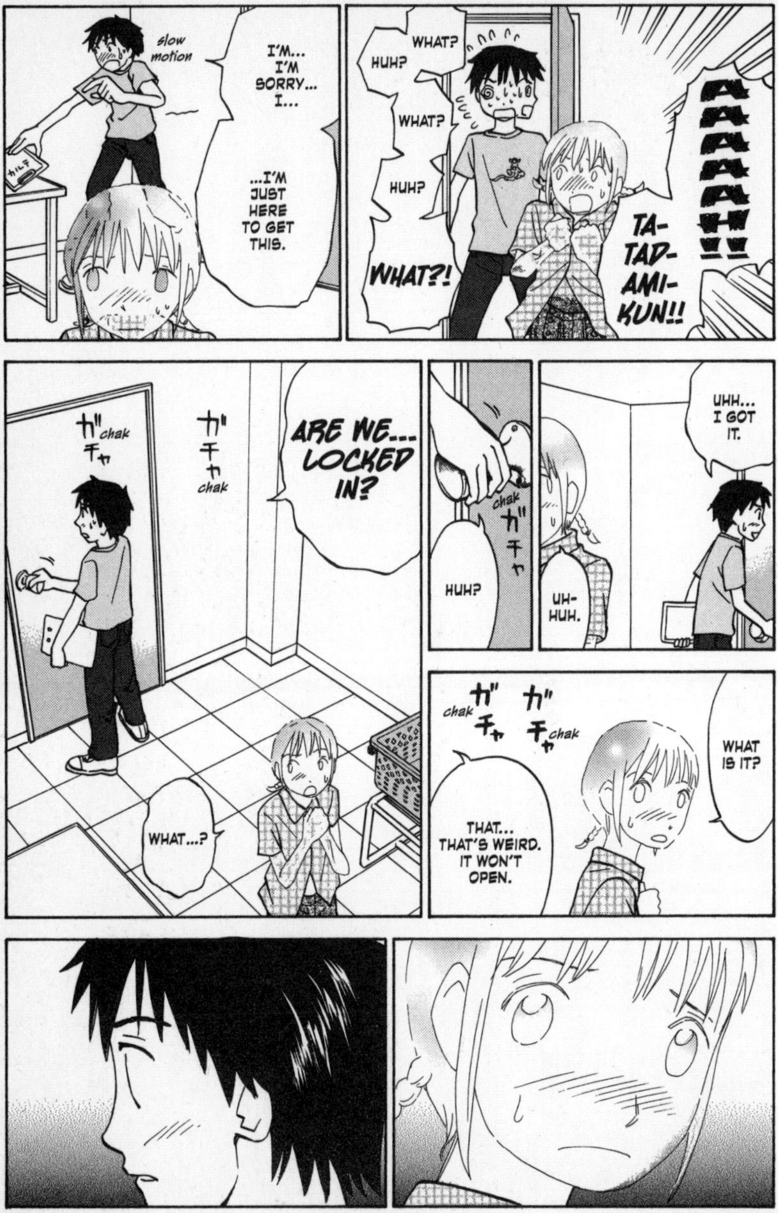
AAAAAH!!
TA-TAD-AMI-KUN!!
WHAT?
HUH?
WHAT?
HUH?
WHAT?!
slow motion
I'M... I'M SORRY... I...
...I'M JUST HERE TO GET THIS.
カルテ
UHH... I GOT IT.
chak ガチャ
UH-HUH.
HUH?
WHAT IS IT?
ガチャ chak
ガチャ chak
THAT... THAT'S WEIRD. IT WON'T OPEN.
ARE WE... LOCKED IN?
ガチャ chak
ガチャ chak
WHAT...?

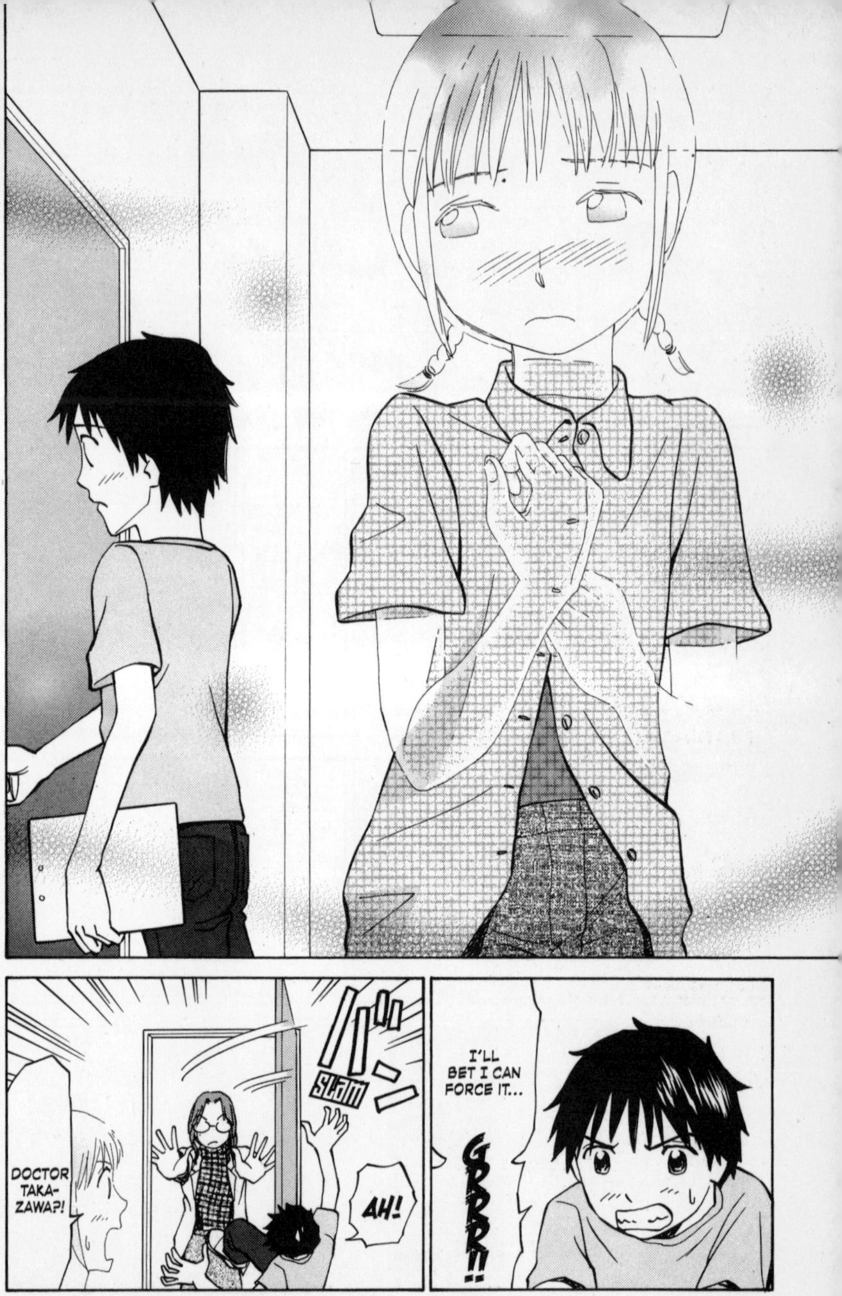
I'LL BET I CAN FORCE IT...
GRRR!!
SLAM
AH!
DOCTOR TAKA-ZAWA?!

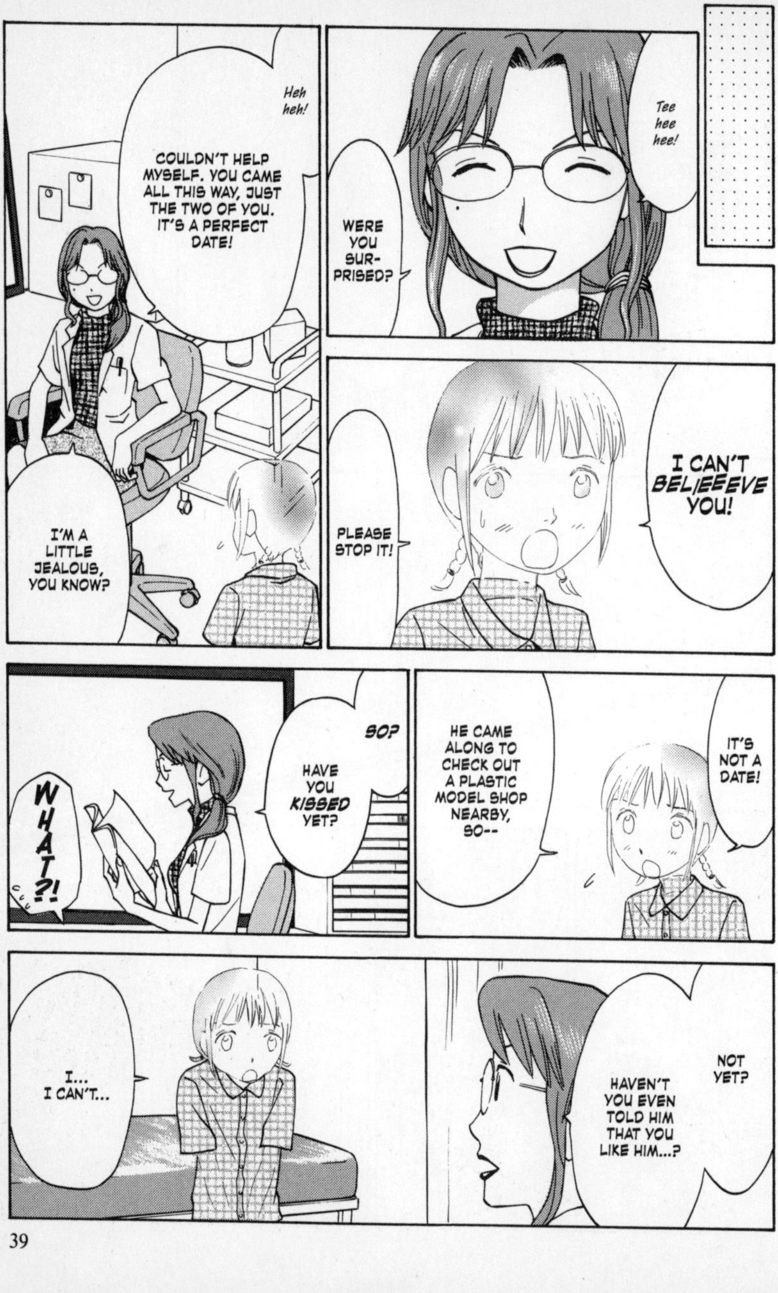
Tee hee hee!
WERE YOU SUR-PRISED?
I CAN'T *BELIEEEVE* YOU!
PLEASE STOP IT!
Heh heh!
COULDN'T HELP MYSELF. YOU CAME ALL THIS WAY, JUST THE TWO OF YOU. IT'S A PERFECT DATE!
I'M A LITTLE JEALOUS, YOU KNOW?
IT'S NOT A DATE!
HE CAME ALONG TO CHECK OUT A PLASTIC MODEL SHOP NEARBY, SO--
SO?
HAVE YOU *KISSED* YET?
WHAT?!
NOT YET?
HAVEN'T YOU EVEN TOLD HIM THAT YOU LIKE HIM...?
I... I CAN'T...

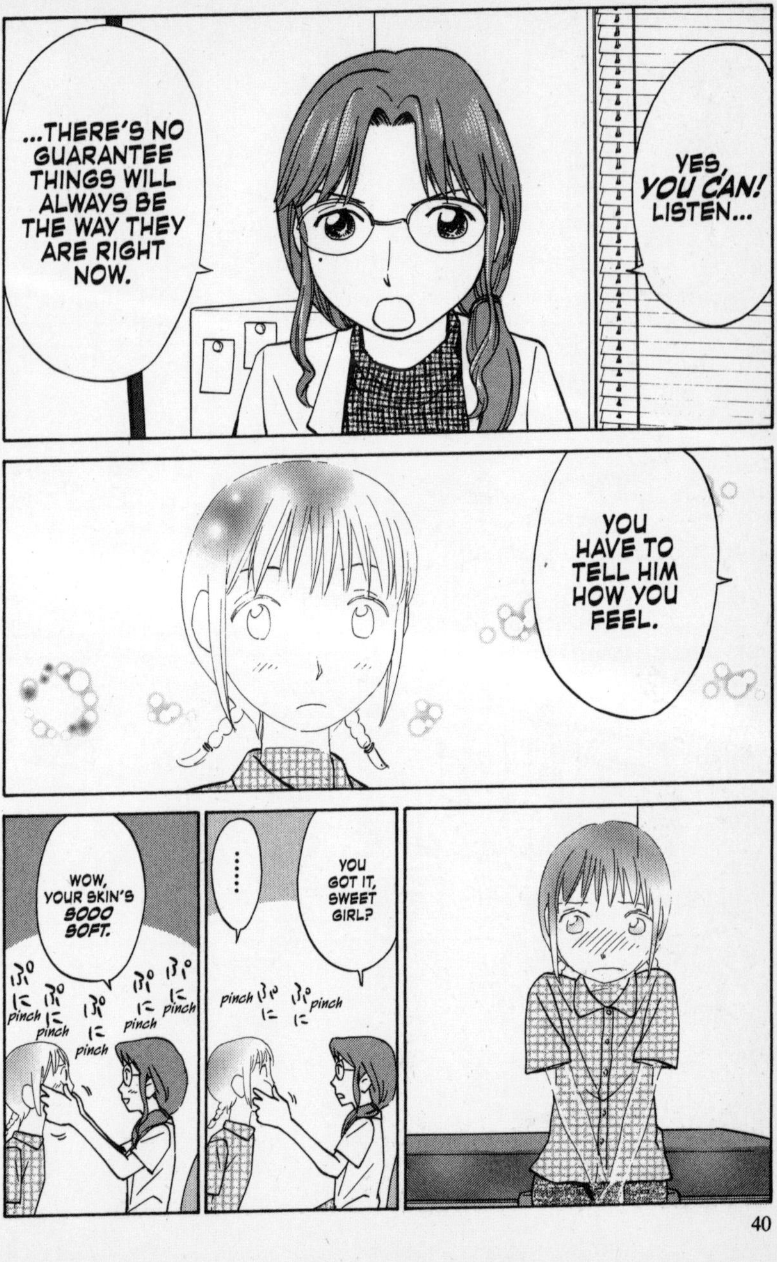
YES, YOU CAN! LISTEN...
...THERE'S NO GUARANTEE THINGS WILL ALWAYS BE THE WAY THEY ARE RIGHT NOW.
YOU HAVE TO TELL HIM HOW YOU FEEL.
YOU GOT IT, SWEET GIRL?
......
ぷに pinch ぷに pinch
WOW, YOUR SKIN'S SOOO SOFT.
ぷに pinch ぷに pinch ぷに pinch ぷに pinch ぷに pinch

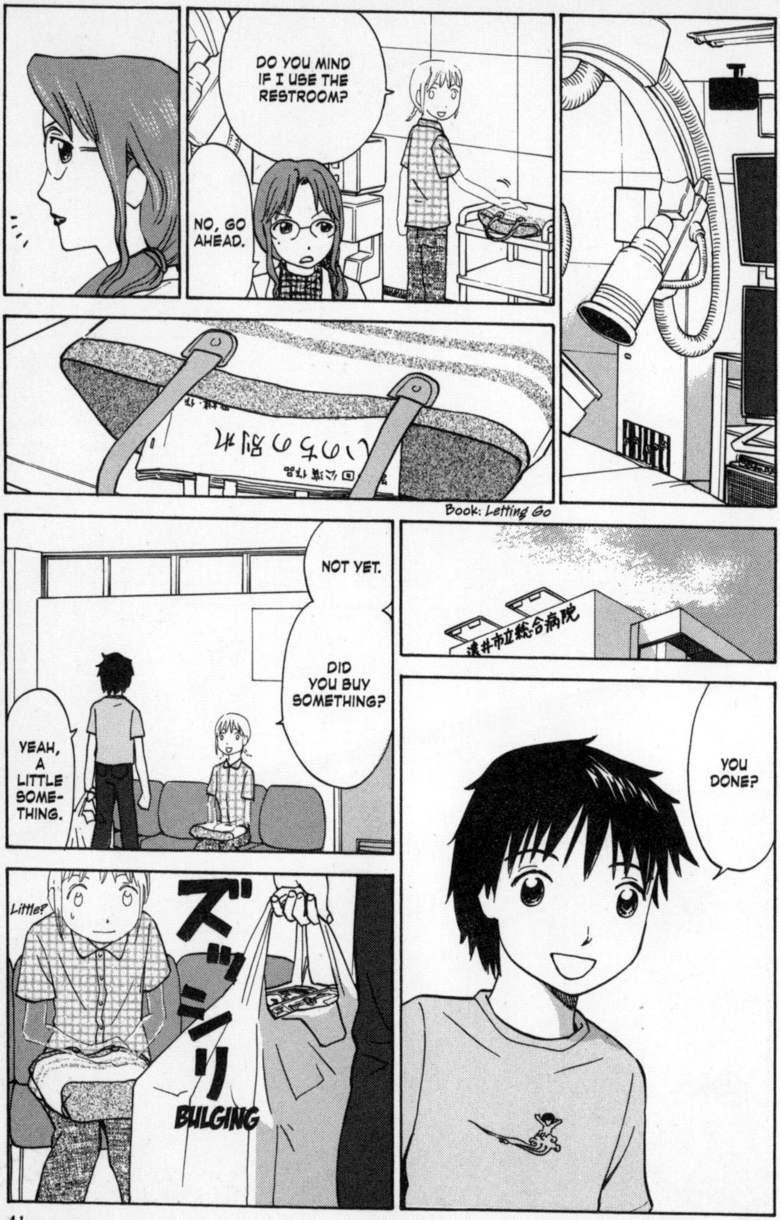
DO YOU MIND IF I USE THE RESTROOM?
NO, GO AHEAD.
Book: Letting Go
YOU DONE?
NOT YET.
DID YOU BUY SOMETHING?
YEAH, A LITTLE SOME-THING.
Little?
BULGING

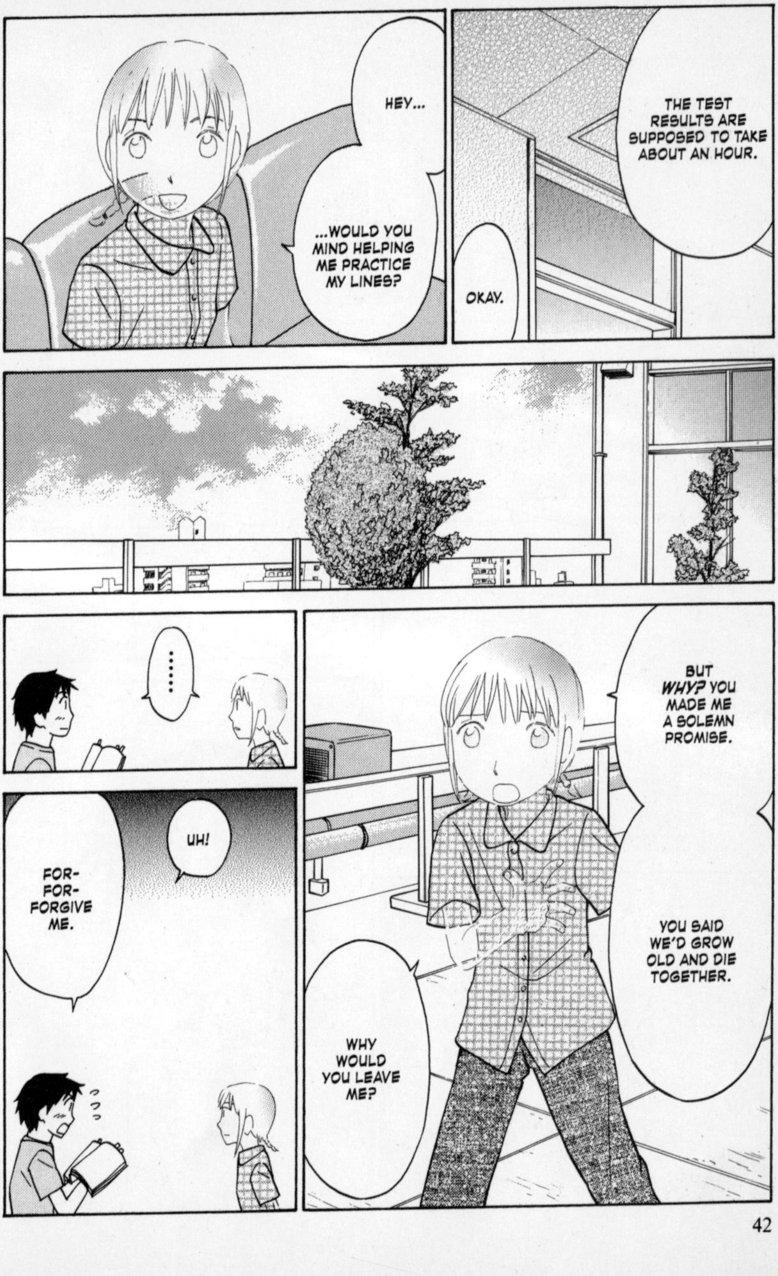
THE TEST RESULTS ARE SUPPOSED TO TAKE ABOUT AN HOUR.
OKAY.
HEY...
...WOULD YOU MIND HELPING ME PRACTICE MY LINES?
BUT *WHY?* YOU MADE ME A SOLEMN PROMISE.
YOU SAID WE'D GROW OLD AND DIE TOGETHER.
WHY WOULD YOU LEAVE ME?
......
UH!
FOR-FOR-FORGIVE ME.

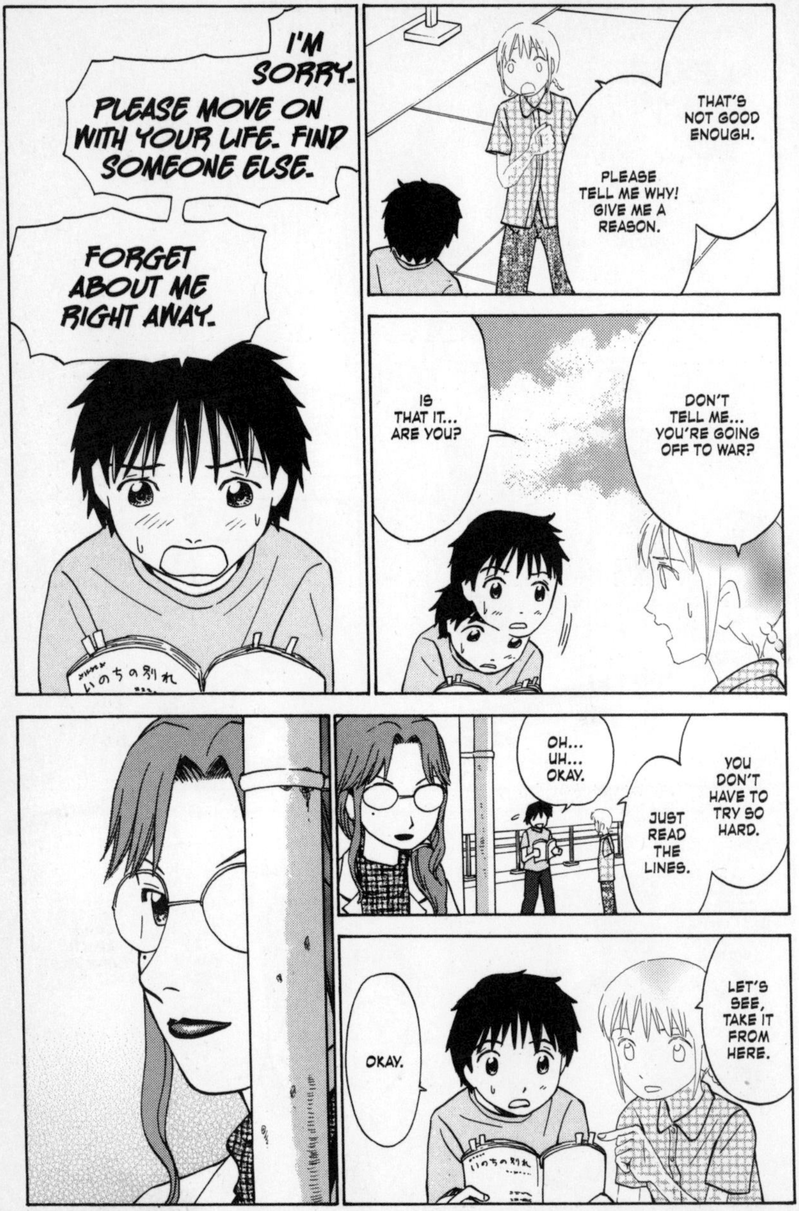
THAT'S NOT GOOD ENOUGH.
PLEASE TELL ME WHY! GIVE ME A REASON.
DON'T TELL ME... YOU'RE GOING OFF TO WAR?
IS THAT IT... ARE YOU?
I'M SORRY.
PLEASE MOVE ON WITH YOUR LIFE. FIND SOMEONE ELSE.
FORGET ABOUT ME RIGHT AWAY.
いのちの別れ
YOU DON'T HAVE TO TRY SO HARD.
JUST READ THE LINES.
OH... UH... OKAY.
LET'S SEE, TAKE IT FROM HERE.
OKAY.
いのちの別れ

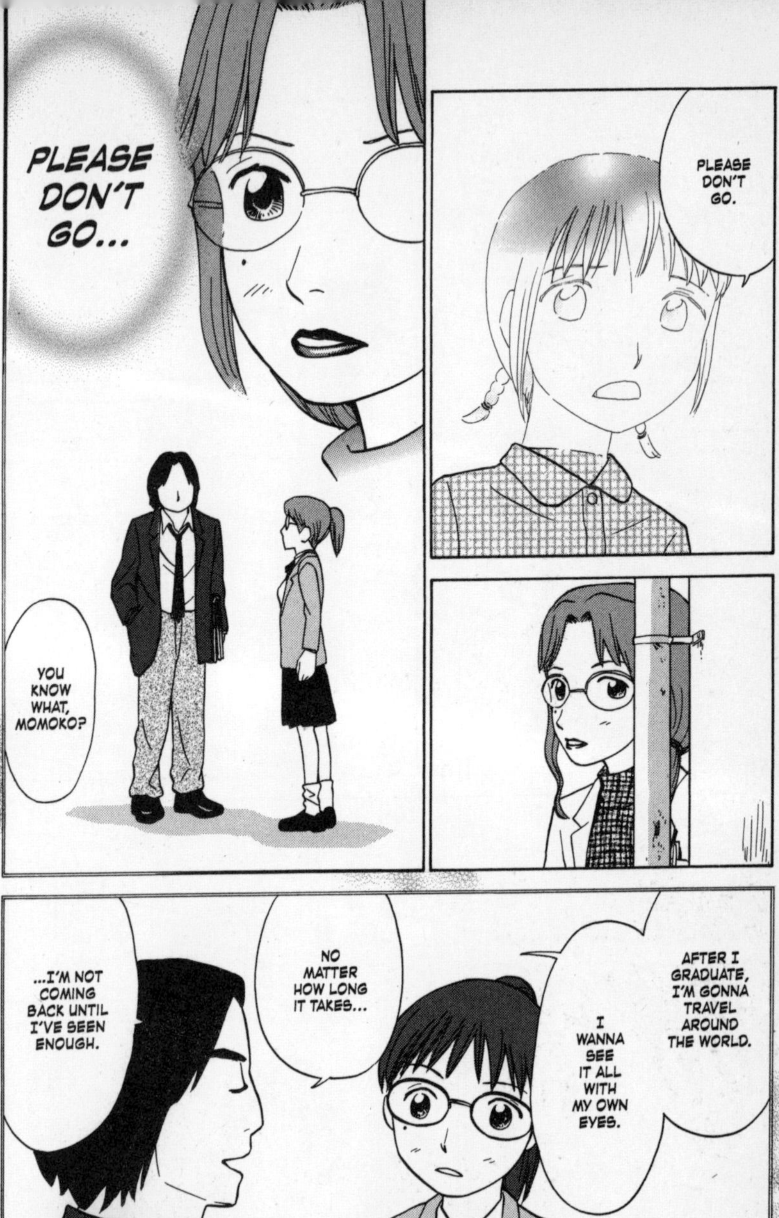
PLEASE DON'T GO.
PLEASE DON'T GO...
YOU KNOW WHAT, MOMOKO?
AFTER I GRADUATE, I'M GONNA TRAVEL AROUND THE WORLD.
I WANNA SEE IT ALL WITH MY OWN EYES.
NO MATTER HOW LONG IT TAKES...
...I'M NOT COMING BACK UNTIL I'VE SEEN ENOUGH.

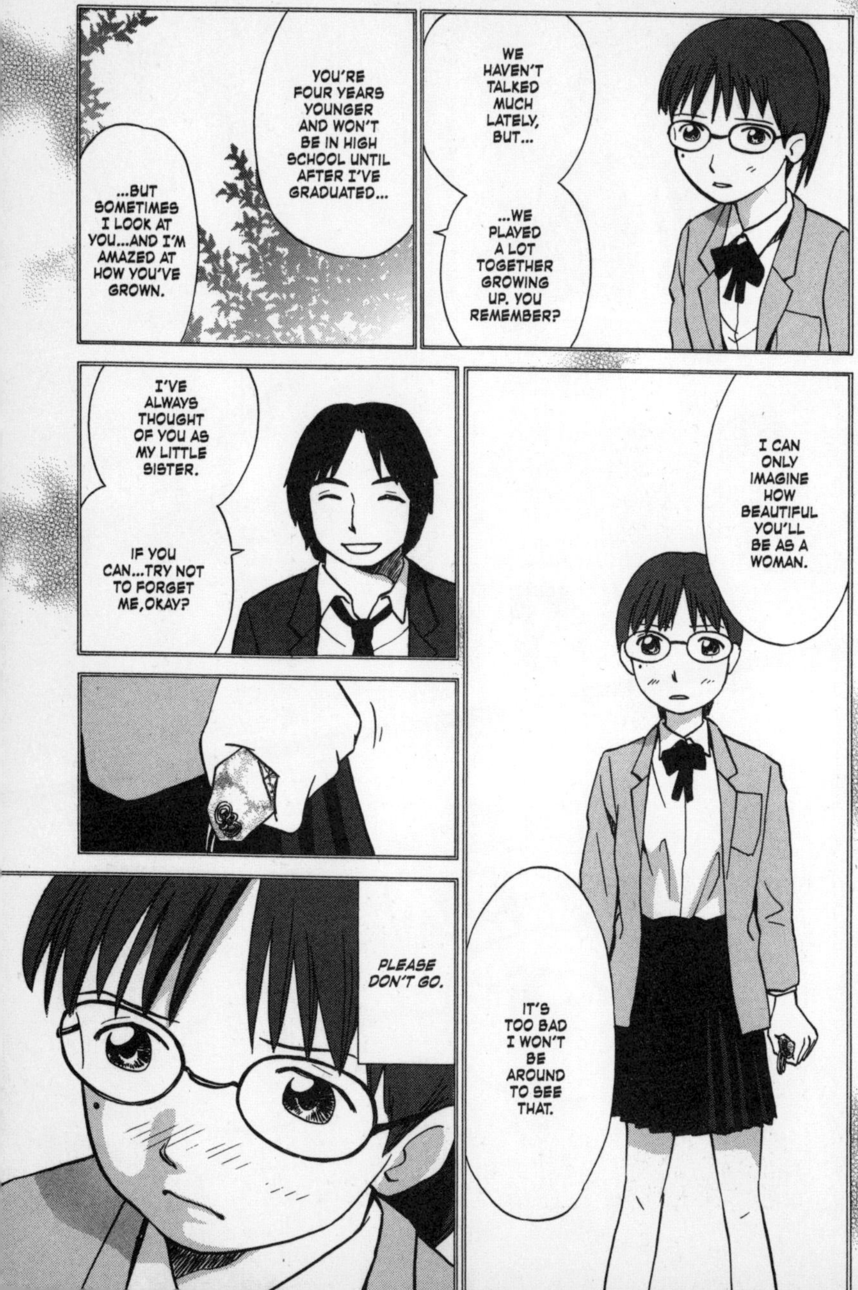
WE HAVEN'T TALKED MUCH LATELY, BUT...
...WE PLAYED A LOT TOGETHER GROWING UP. YOU REMEMBER?
YOU'RE FOUR YEARS YOUNGER AND WON'T BE IN HIGH SCHOOL UNTIL AFTER I'VE GRADUATED...
...BUT SOMETIMES I LOOK AT YOU...AND I'M AMAZED AT HOW YOU'VE GROWN.
I CAN ONLY IMAGINE HOW BEAUTIFUL YOU'LL BE AS A WOMAN.
IT'S TOO BAD I WON'T BE AROUND TO SEE THAT.
I'VE ALWAYS THOUGHT OF YOU AS MY LITTLE SISTER.
IF YOU CAN...TRY NOT TO FORGET ME,OKAY?
PLEASE DON'T GO.

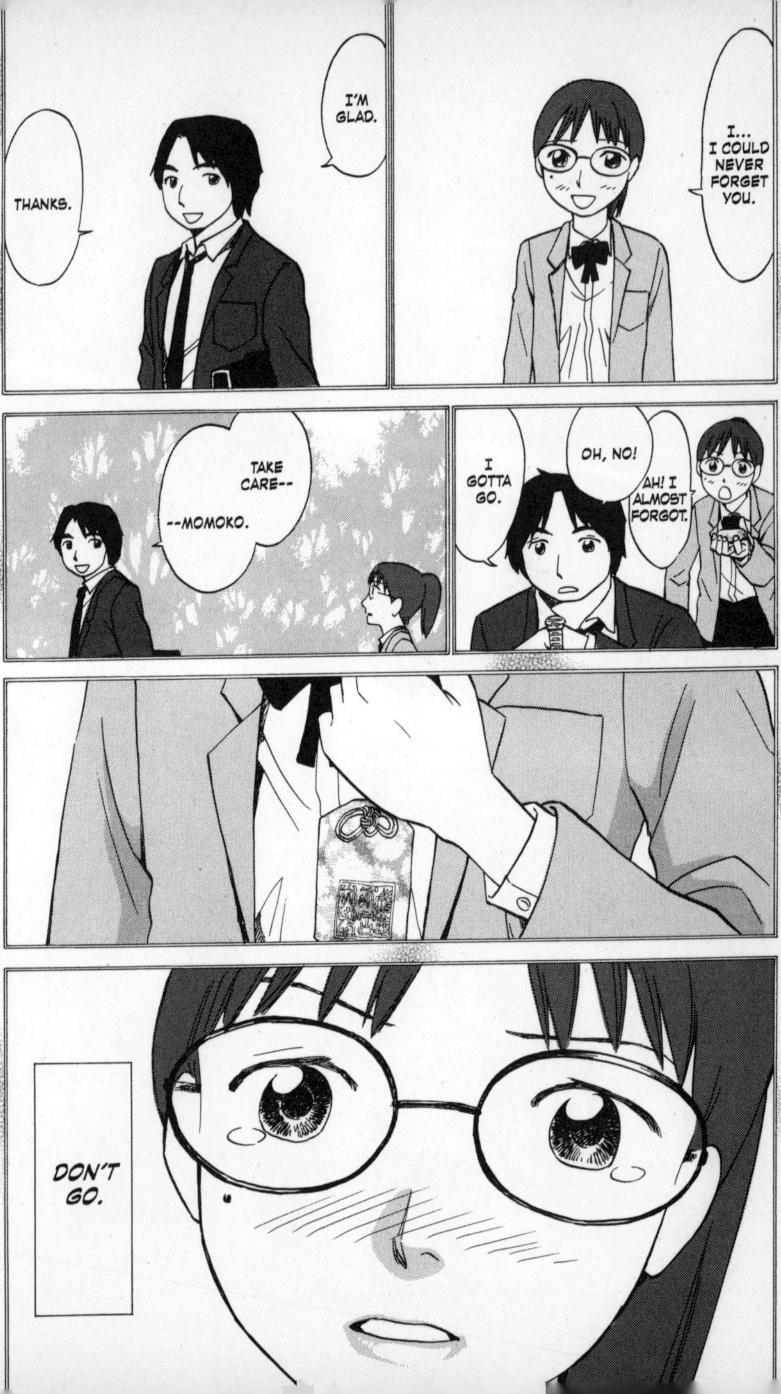
I... I COULD NEVER FORGET YOU.
I'M GLAD.
THANKS.
AH! I ALMOST FORGOT.
OH, NO!
I GOTTA GO.
TAKE CARE--
--MOMOKO.
DON'T GO.

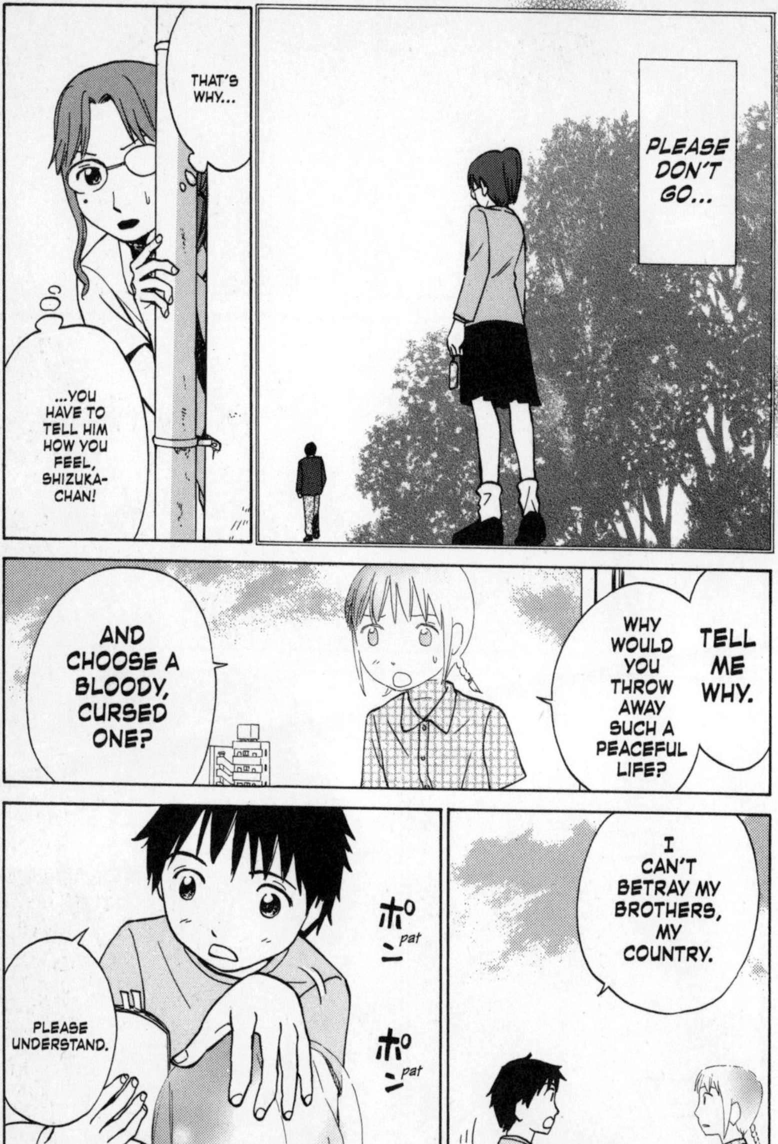
PLEASE DON'T GO...
THAT'S WHY...
...YOU HAVE TO TELL HIM HOW YOU FEEL, SHIZUKA-CHAN!
TELL ME WHY.
WHY WOULD YOU THROW AWAY SUCH A PEACEFUL LIFE?
AND CHOOSE A BLOODY, CURSED ONE?
I CAN'T BETRAY MY BROTHERS, MY COUNTRY.
ポン pat
ポン pat
PLEASE UNDERSTAND.
?

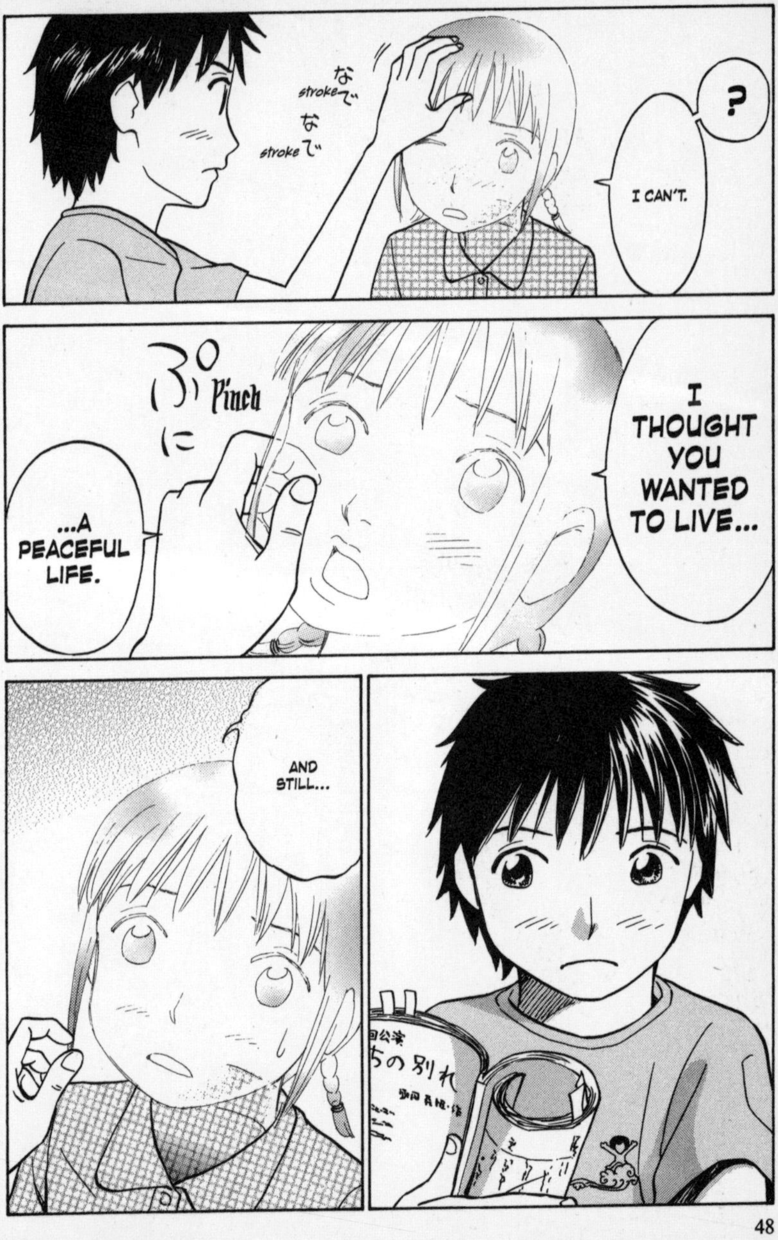
?
I CAN'T.
なで stroke
なで stroke
I THOUGHT YOU WANTED TO LIVE...
ぷに Pinch
...A PEACEFUL LIFE.
回公演
ちの別れ
AND STILL...

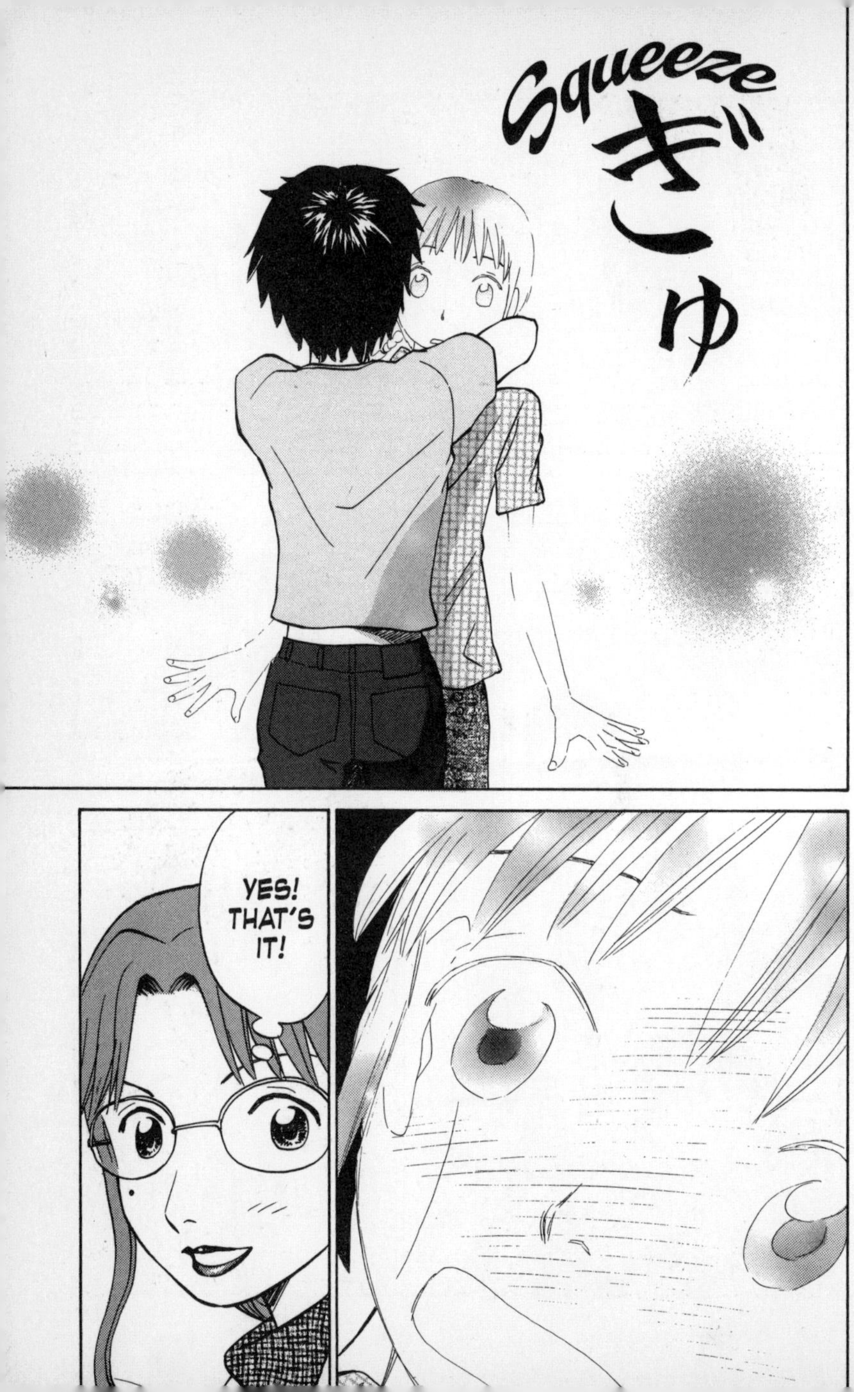
Squeeze
ぎゅ
YES! THAT'S IT!

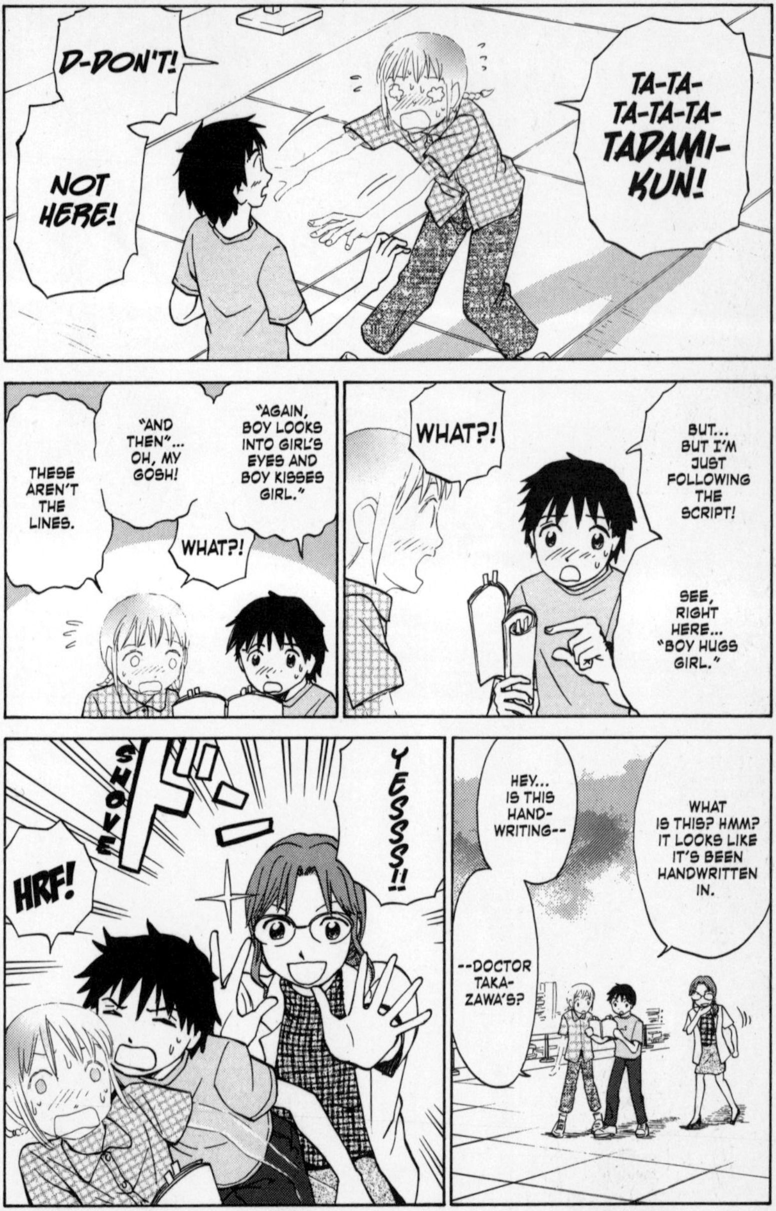
TA-TA-TA-TA-TA-TADAMI-KUN!
D-DON'T!
NOT HERE!
BUT... BUT I'M JUST FOLLOWING THE SCRIPT!
SEE, RIGHT HERE... "BOY HUGS GIRL."
WHAT?!
"AGAIN, BOY LOOKS INTO GIRL'S EYES AND BOY KISSES GIRL."
"AND THEN"... OH, MY GOSH!
WHAT?!
THESE AREN'T THE LINES.
WHAT IS THIS? HMM? IT LOOKS LIKE IT'S BEEN HANDWRITTEN IN.
HEY... IS THIS HAND-WRITING--
--DOCTOR TAKA-ZAWA'S?
YESSS!!
SHOVE
HRF!

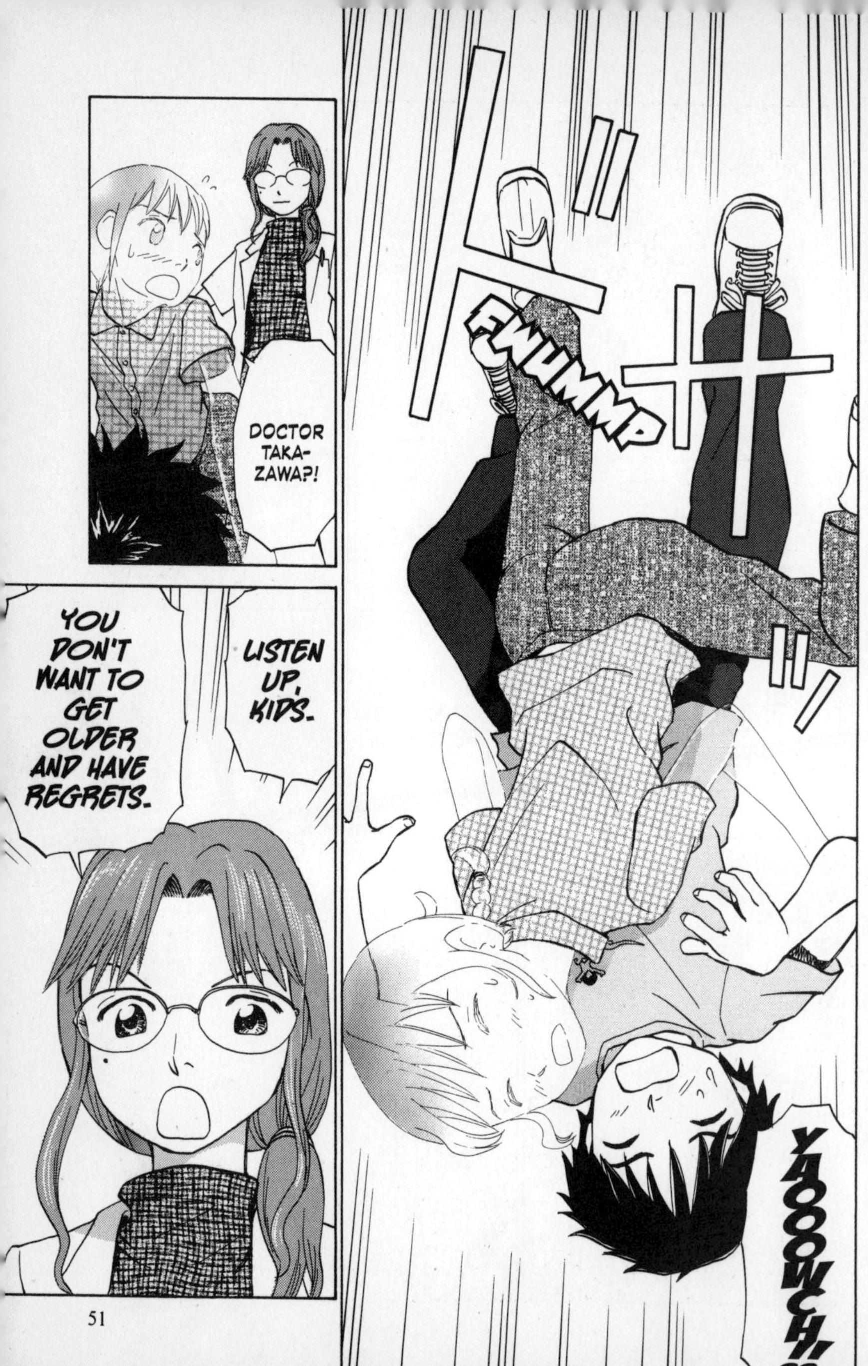
FWUMMP
YAOOOWCH!!
DOCTOR TAKA-ZAWA?!
LISTEN UP, KIDS.
YOU DON'T WANT TO GET OLDER AND HAVE REGRETS.

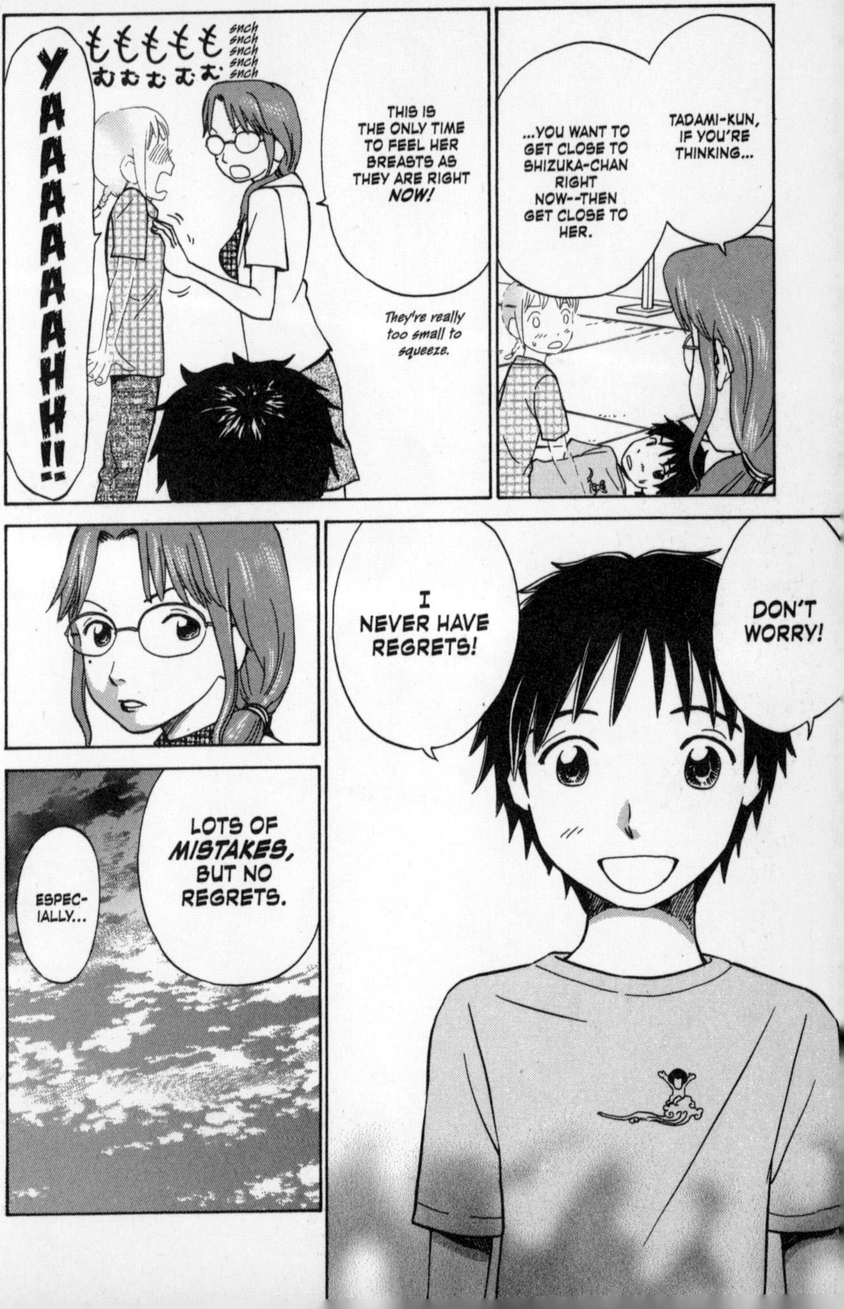
TADAMI-KUN, IF YOU'RE THINKING...
...YOU WANT TO GET CLOSE TO SHIZUKA-CHAN RIGHT NOW--THEN GET CLOSE TO HER.
THIS IS THE ONLY TIME TO FEEL HER BREASTS AS THEY ARE RIGHT *NOW!*
They're really too small to squeeze.
snch snch snch snch snch
ももももも
むむむむむ
YAAAAAAAAAHH!!
DON'T WORRY!
I NEVER HAVE REGRETS!
LOTS OF *MISTAKES,* BUT NO REGRETS.
ESPEC-IALLY...

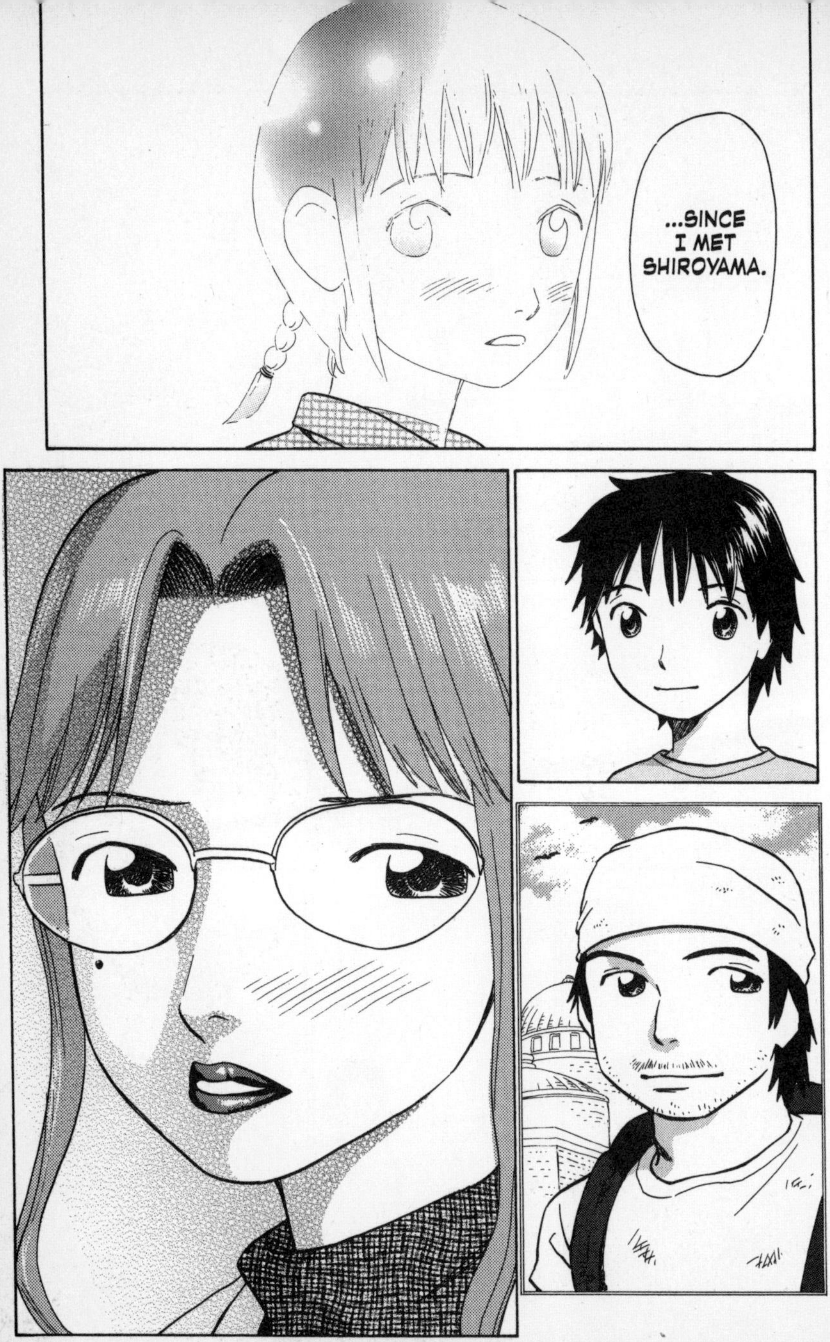
...SINCE I MET SHIROYAMA.

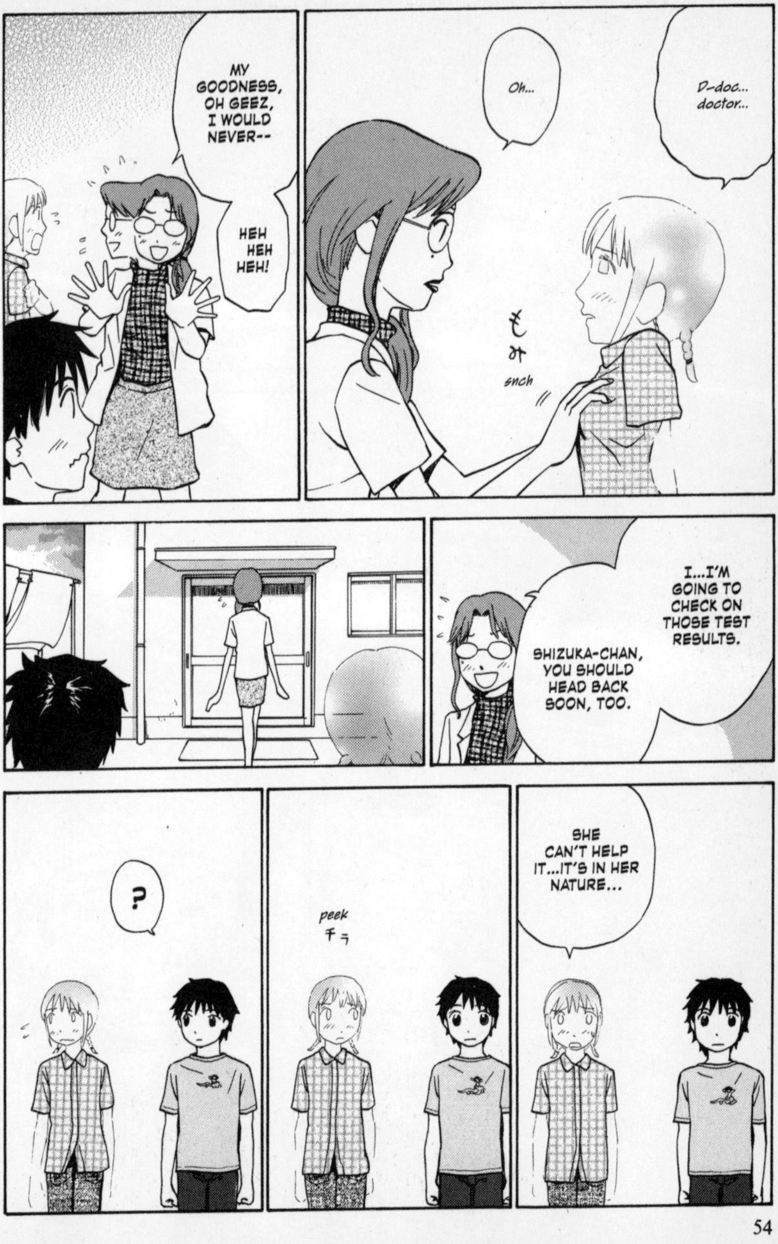
D-doc... doctor...
Oh...
もみ
snch
MY GOODNESS, OH GEEZ, I WOULD NEVER--
HEH HEH HEH!
I...I'M GOING TO CHECK ON THOSE TEST RESULTS.
SHIZUKA-CHAN, YOU SHOULD HEAD BACK SOON, TOO.
SHE CAN'T HELP IT...IT'S IN HER NATURE...
peek
チラ
?

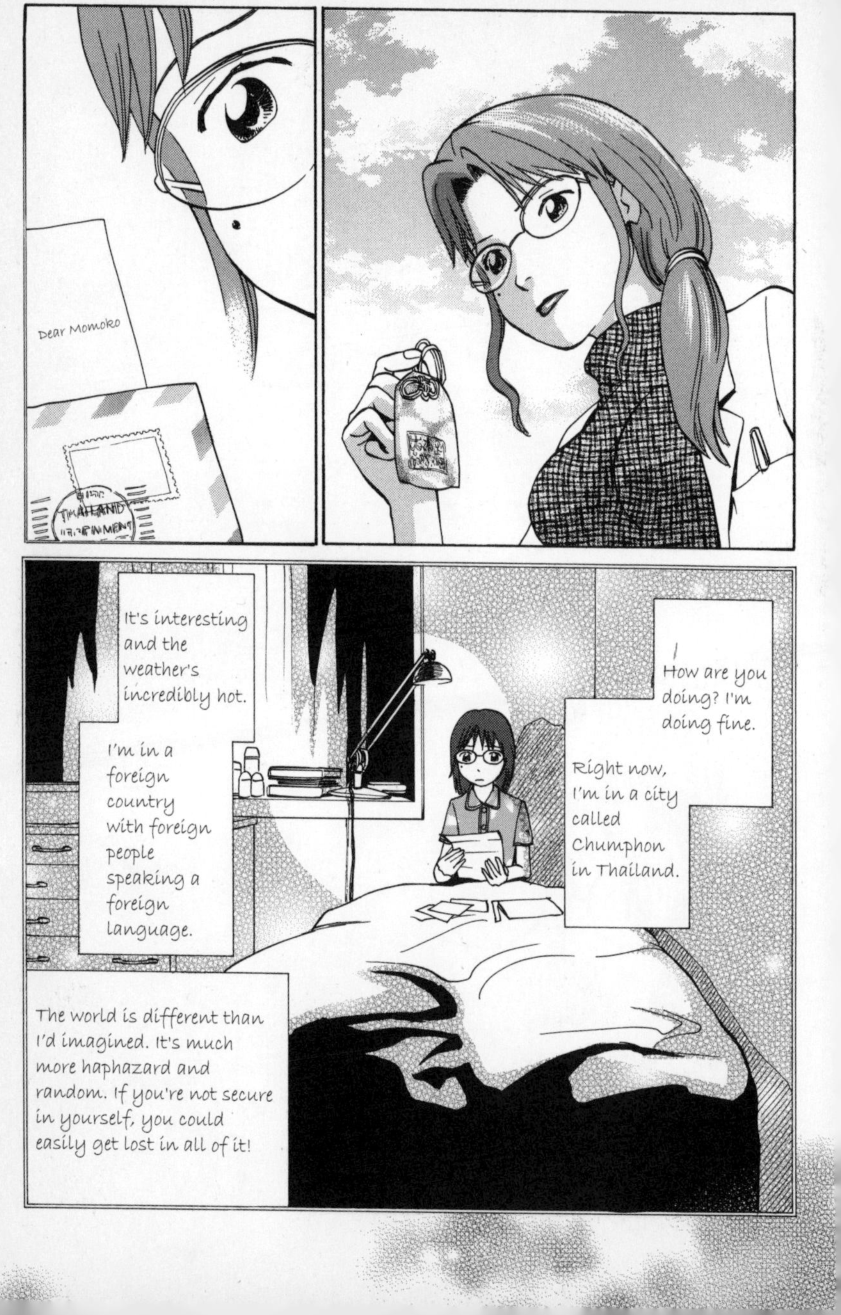
Dear Momoko
THAILAND
How are you doing? I'm doing fine.
Right now, I'm in a city called Chumphon in Thailand.
I'm in a foreign country with foreign people speaking a foreign language.
It's interesting and the weather's incredibly hot.
The world is different than I'd imagined. It's much more haphazard and random. If you're not secure in yourself, you could easily get lost in all of it!

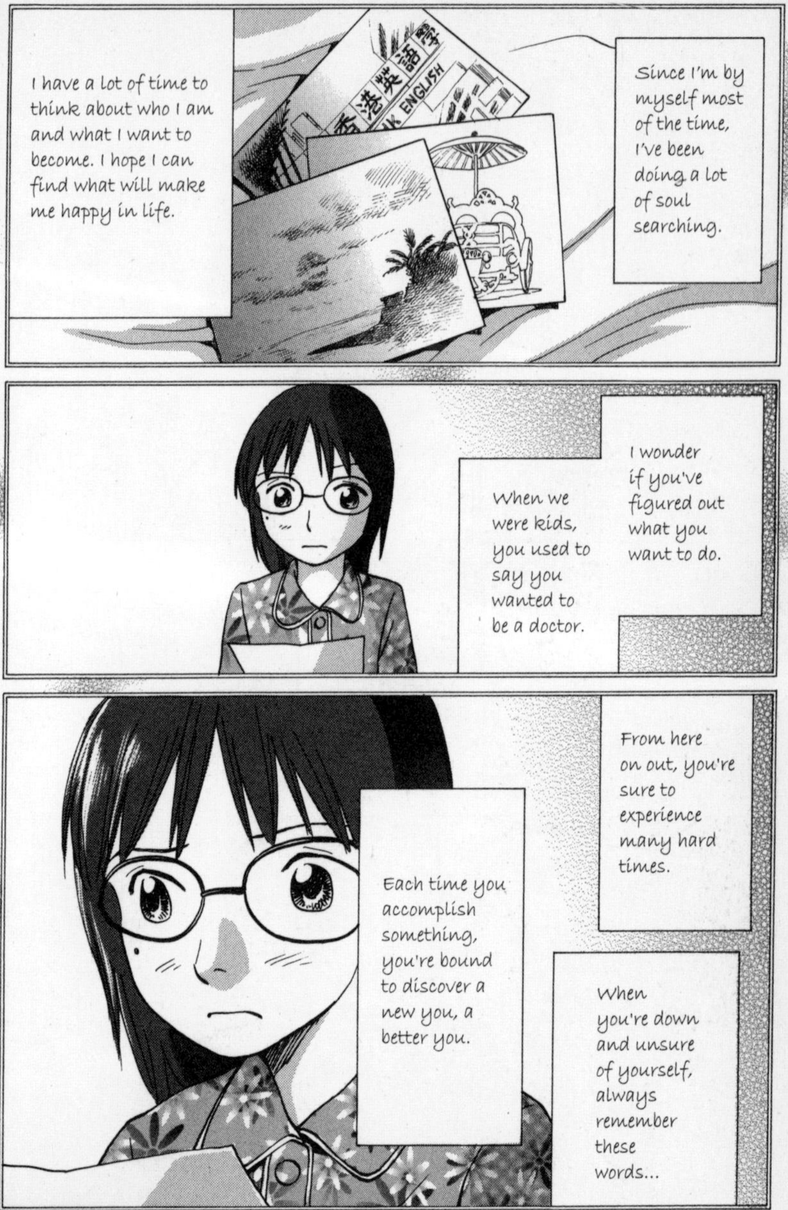
Since I'm by myself most of the time, I've been doing a lot of soul searching.
I have a lot of time to think about who I am and what I want to become. I hope I can find what will make me happy in life.
I wonder if you've figured out what you want to do.
When we were kids, you used to say you wanted to be a doctor.
From here on out, you're sure to experience many hard times.
Each time you accomplish something, you're bound to discover a new you, a better you.
When you're down and unsure of yourself, always remember these words...

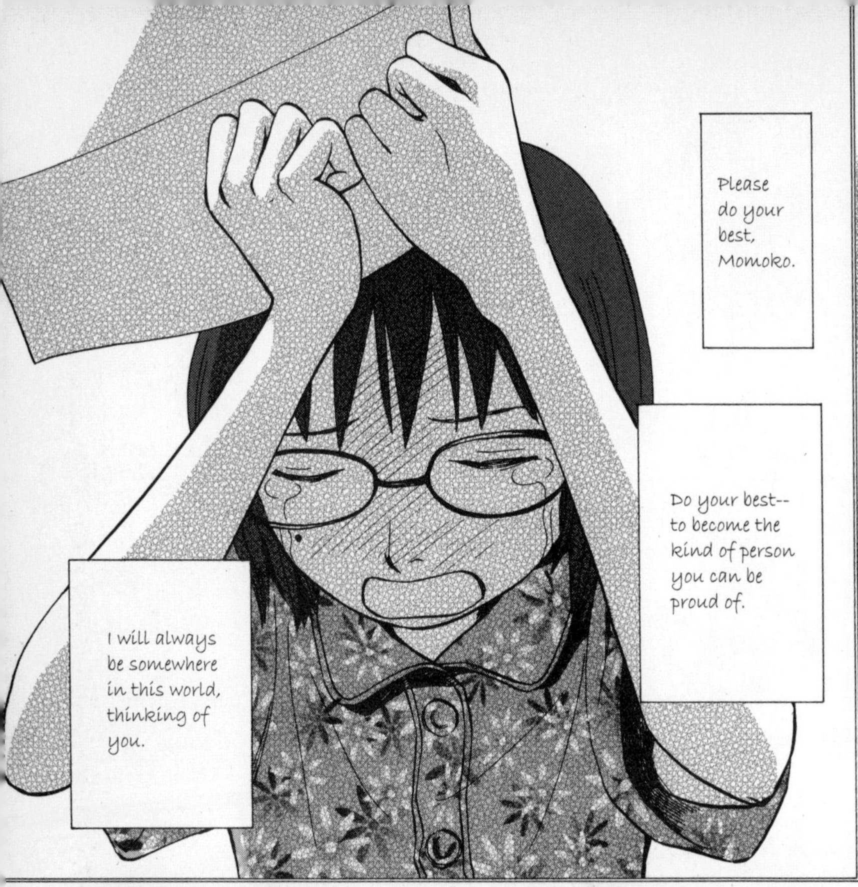
Please do your best, Momoko.
Do your best-- to become the kind of person you can be proud of.
I will always be somewhere in this world, thinking of you.
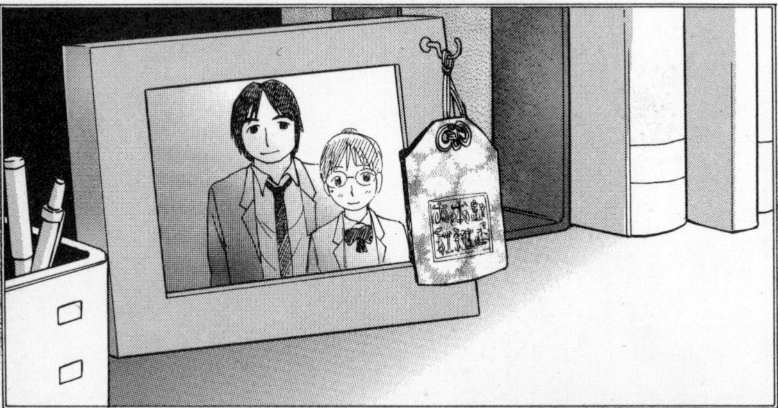

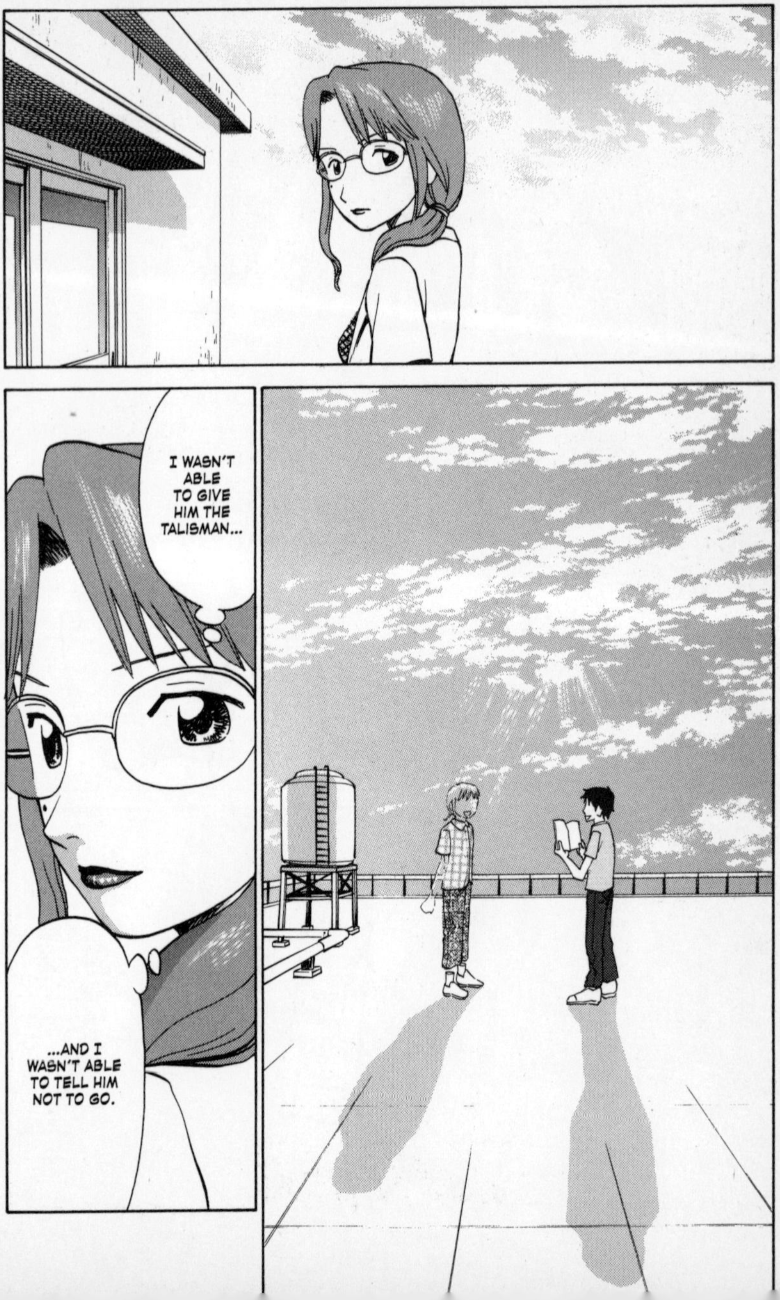
I WASN'T ABLE TO GIVE HIM THE TALISMAN...
...AND I WASN'T ABLE TO TELL HIM NOT TO GO.

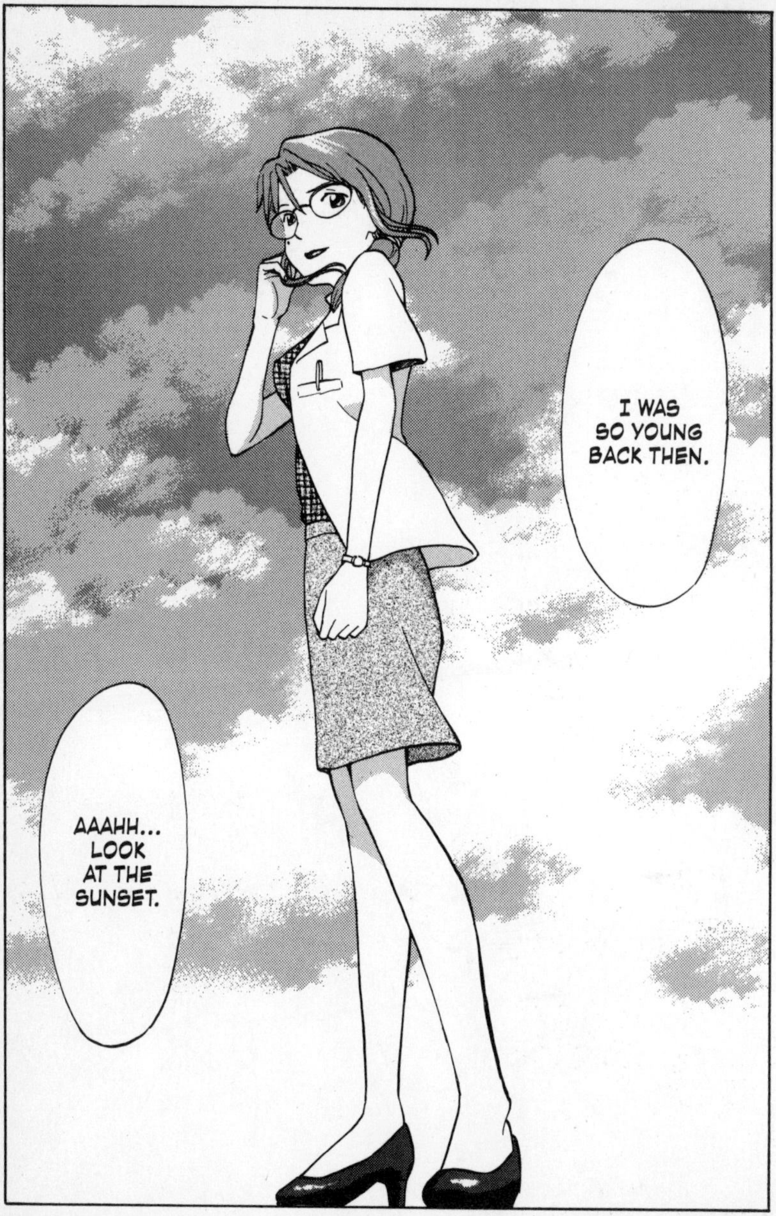
I WAS SO YOUNG BACK THEN.
AAAHH... LOOK AT THE SUNSET.

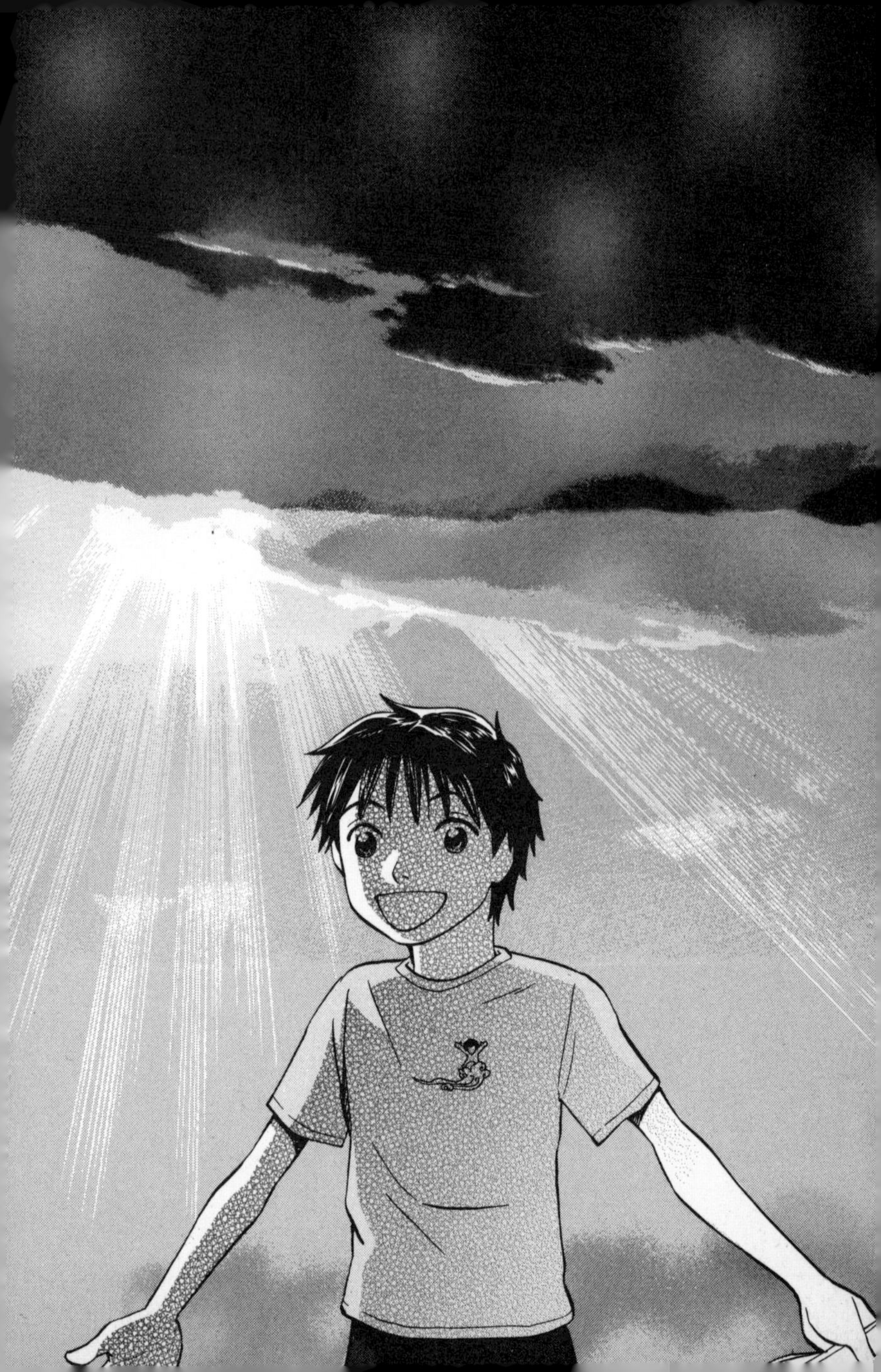

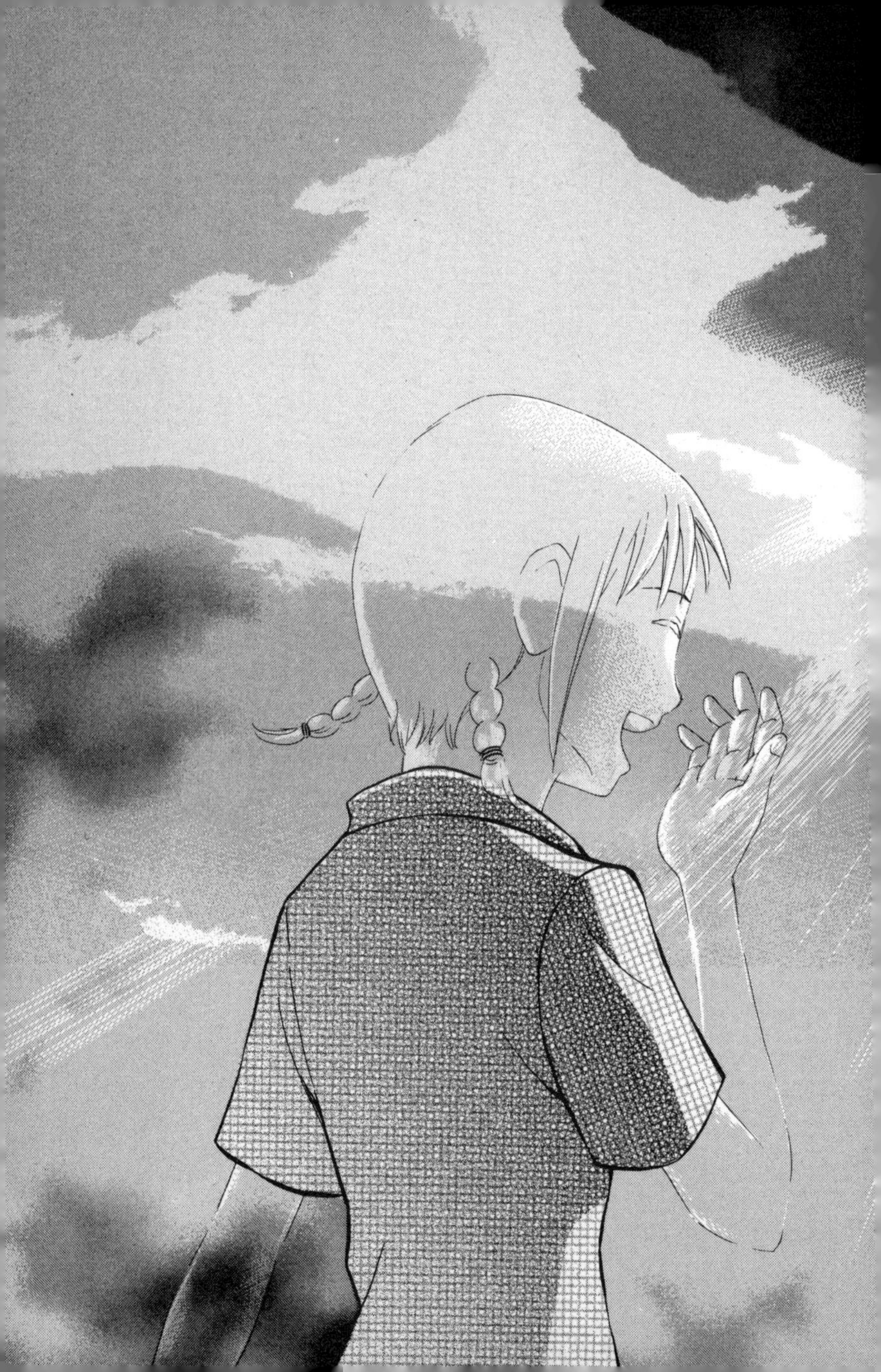

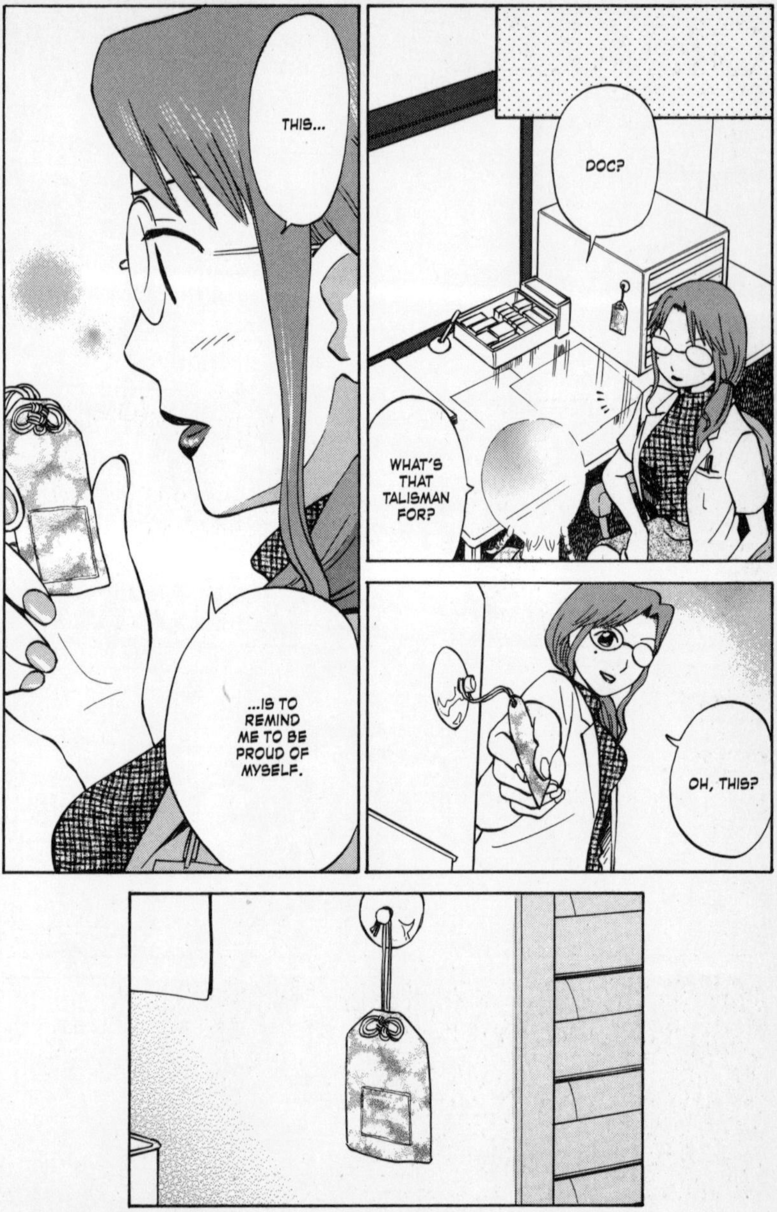
DOC?
WHAT'S THAT TALISMAN FOR?
OH, THIS?
THIS...
...IS TO REMIND ME TO BE PROUD OF MYSELF.

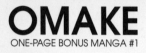

OMAKE

ONE-PAGE BONUS MANGA #1

1

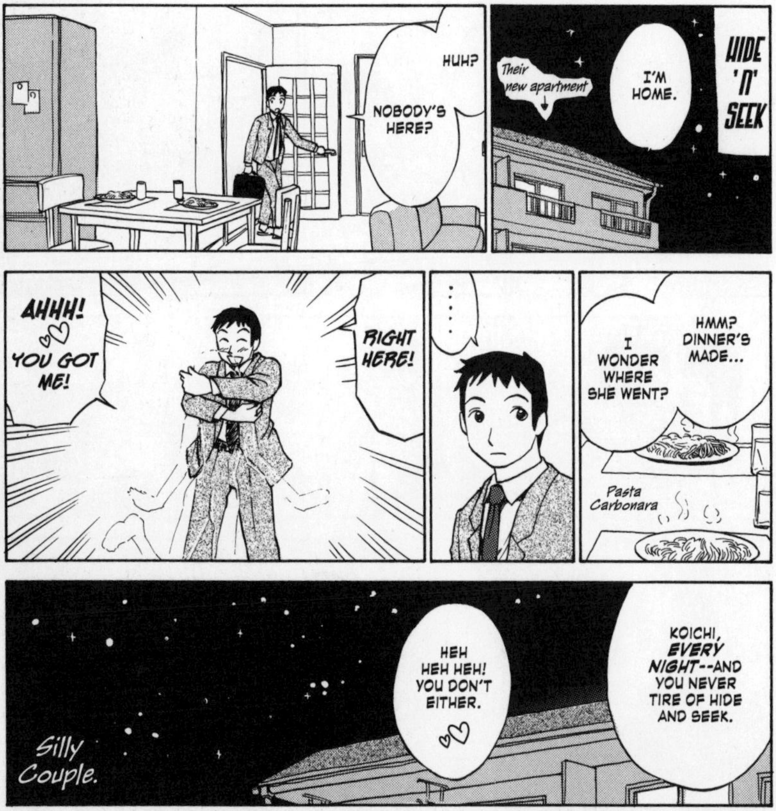
HIDE 'N' SEEK
Their new apartment
I'M HOME.
HUH?
NOBODY'S HERE?
HMM? DINNER'S MADE...
I WONDER WHERE SHE WENT?
Pasta Carbonara
......
RIGHT HERE!
AHHH! YOU GOT ME!
KOICHI, EVERY NIGHT--AND YOU NEVER TIRE OF HIDE AND SEEK.
HEH HEH HEH! YOU DON'T EITHER.
Silly Couple.

OMAKE

ONE-PAGE BONUS MANGA #2

2

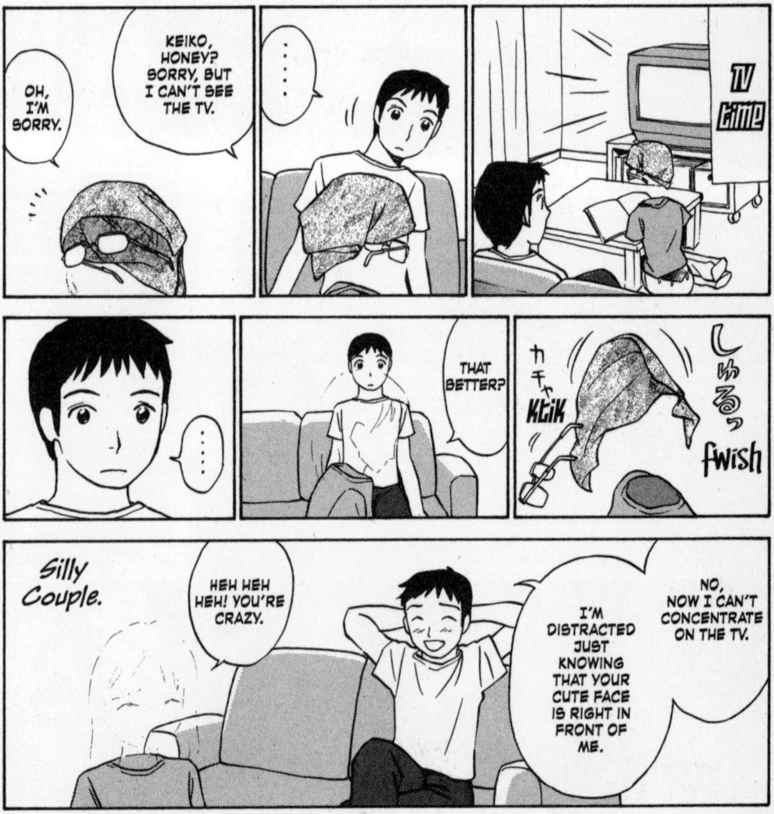

TV time
.....
KEIKO, HONEY? SORRY, BUT I CAN'T SEE THE TV.
OH, I'M SORRY.
しゅるっ
fwish
カチャ
Ktik
THAT BETTER?
.....
NO, NOW I CAN'T CONCENTRATE ON THE TV.
I'M DISTRACTED JUST KNOWING THAT YOUR CUTE FACE IS RIGHT IN FRONT OF ME.
HEH HEH HEH! YOU'RE CRAZY.
Silly Couple.

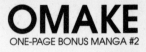

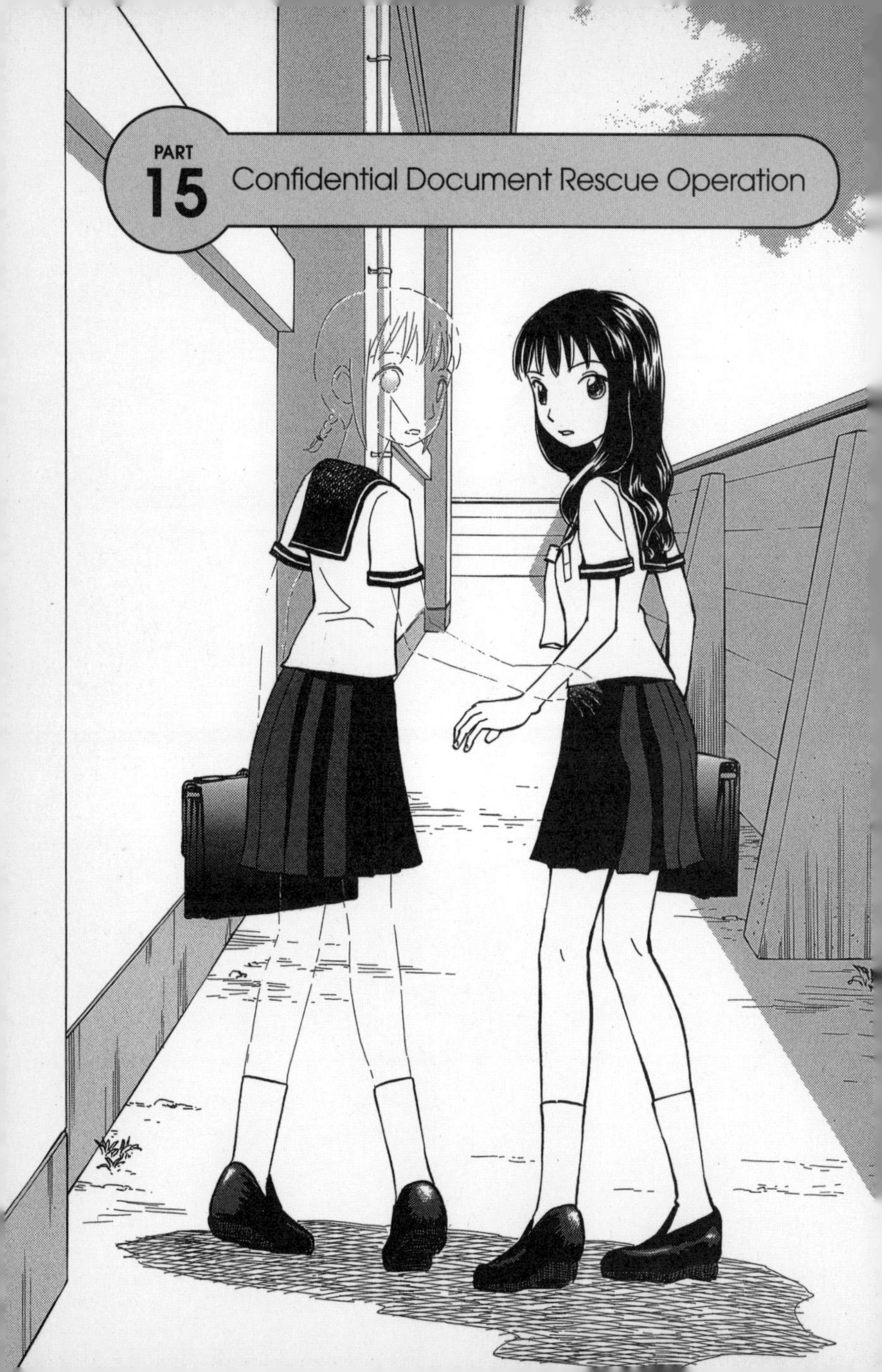
PART
15
Confidential Document Rescue Operation

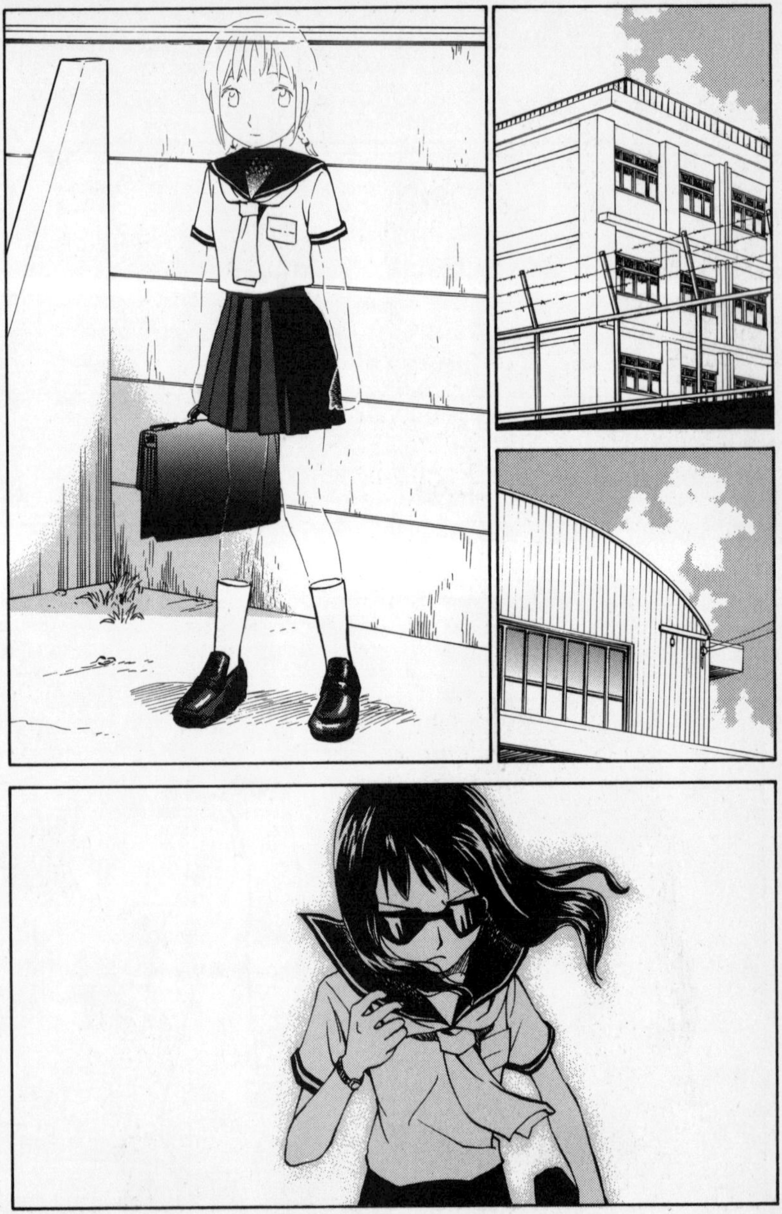

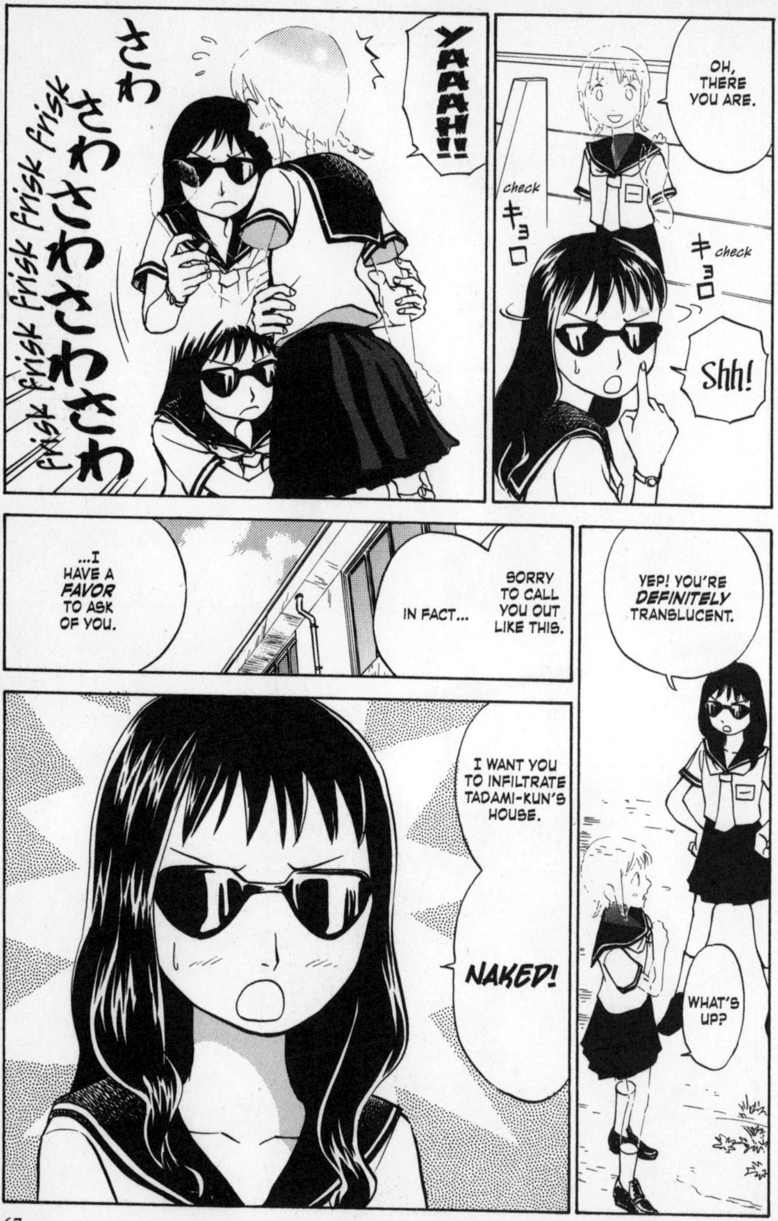
OH, THERE YOU ARE.
check
キョロ
check
キョロ
Shh!
YAAAAH!!
さわ
さわさわさわさわ
frisk frisk frisk frisk
frisk frisk
YEP! YOU'RE *DEFINITELY* TRANSLUCENT.
WHAT'S UP?
SORRY TO CALL YOU OUT LIKE THIS.
IN FACT...
...I HAVE A *FAVOR* TO ASK OF YOU.
I WANT YOU TO INFILTRATE TADAMI-KUN'S HOUSE.
NAKED!

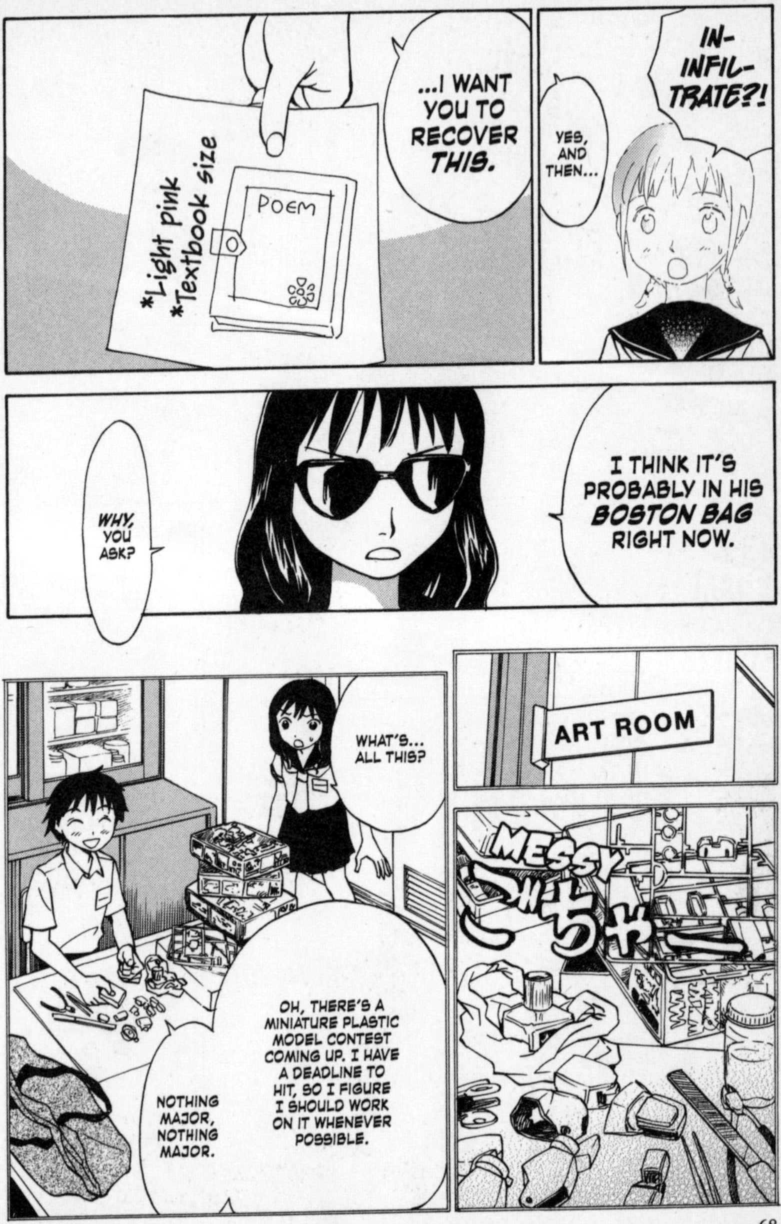
IN-INFILTRATE?!
YES, AND THEN...
...I WANT YOU TO RECOVER THIS.
*Light pink
*Textbook size
POEM
I THINK IT'S PROBABLY IN HIS BOSTON BAG RIGHT NOW.
WHY, YOU ASK?
ART ROOM
MESSY
ごちゃ
WHAT'S... ALL THIS?
OH, THERE'S A MINIATURE PLASTIC MODEL CONTEST COMING UP. I HAVE A DEADLINE TO HIT, SO I FIGURE I SHOULD WORK ON IT WHENEVER POSSIBLE.
NOTHING MAJOR, NOTHING MAJOR.

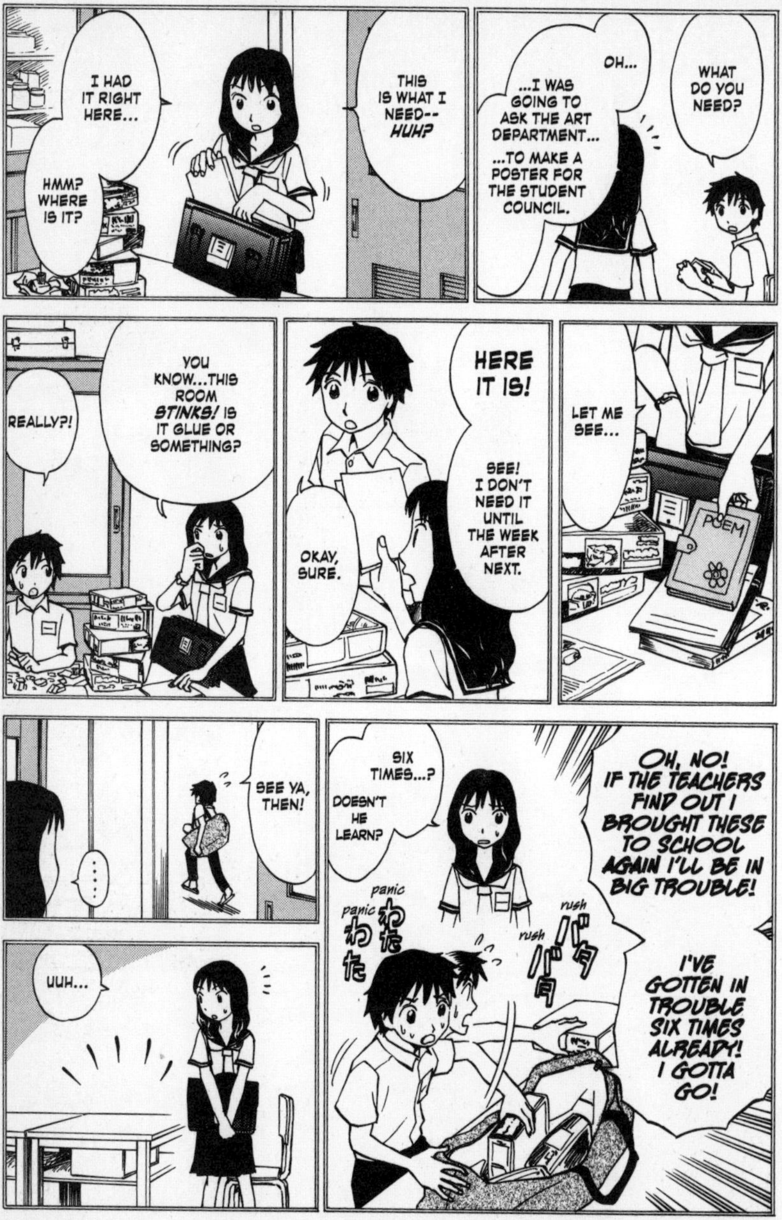
WHAT DO YOU NEED?
OH...
...I WAS GOING TO ASK THE ART DEPARTMENT...
...TO MAKE A POSTER FOR THE STUDENT COUNCIL.
THIS IS WHAT I NEED-- *HUH?*
I HAD IT RIGHT HERE...
HMM? WHERE IS IT?
LET ME SEE...
HERE IT IS!
SEE! I DON'T NEED IT UNTIL THE WEEK AFTER NEXT.
OKAY, SURE.
YOU KNOW...THIS ROOM *STINKS!* IS IT GLUE OR SOMETHING?
REALLY?!
OH, NO! IF THE TEACHERS FIND OUT I BROUGHT THESE TO SCHOOL AGAIN I'LL BE IN BIG TROUBLE!
I'VE GOTTEN IN TROUBLE SIX TIMES ALREADY! I GOTTA GO!
バタ rush
バタ rush
わた panic
わた panic
SIX TIMES...?
DOESN'T HE LEARN?
SEE YA, THEN!
.....
UUH...

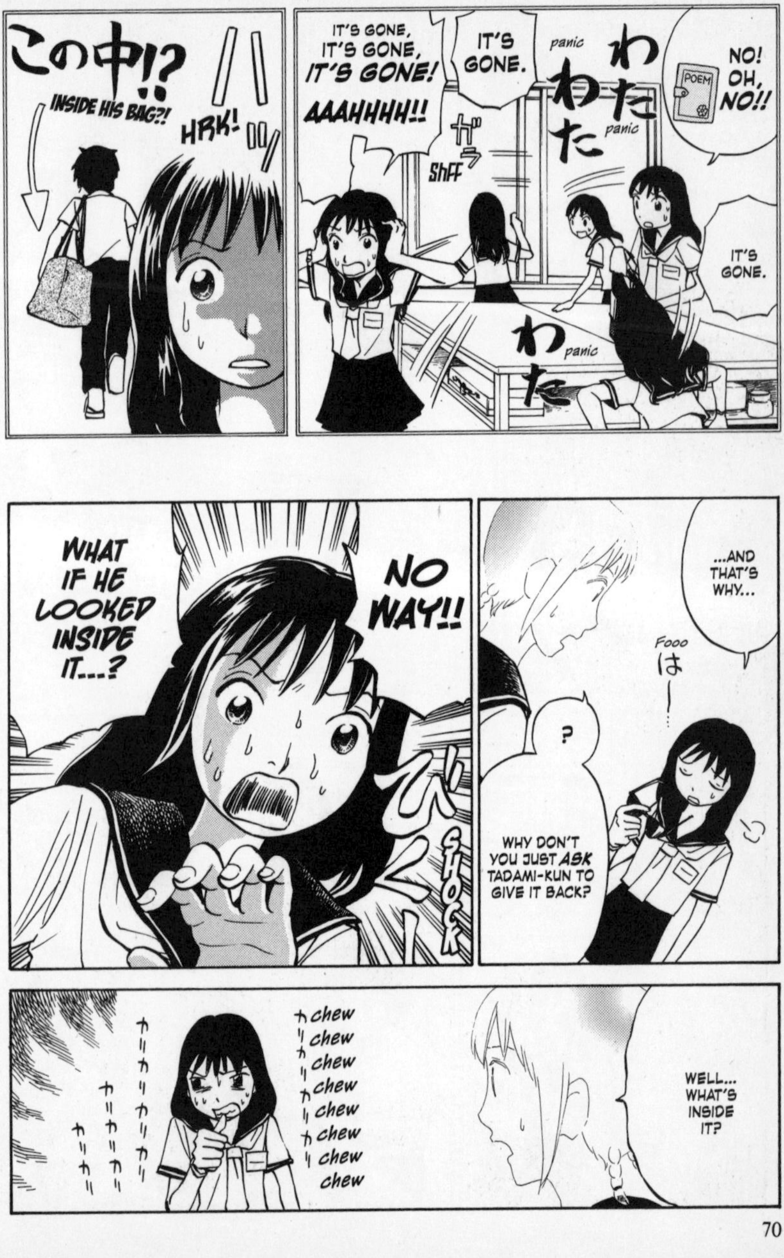
NO! OH, NO!!
POEM
IT'S GONE.
わた panic わた panic
IT'S GONE.
わた panic
IT'S GONE, IT'S GONE, IT'S GONE!
AAAHHHH!!
ガラ ShFF
この中!?
INSIDE HIS BAG?!
HRK!
...AND THAT'S WHY...
はー Fooo
?
WHY DON'T YOU JUST ASK TADAMI-KUN TO GIVE IT BACK?
NO WAY!!
WHAT IF HE LOOKED INSIDE IT...?
SHOCK
WELL... WHAT'S INSIDE IT?
chew chew chew chew chew chew chew chew
カリカリカリカリ カリカリカリ カリカリ

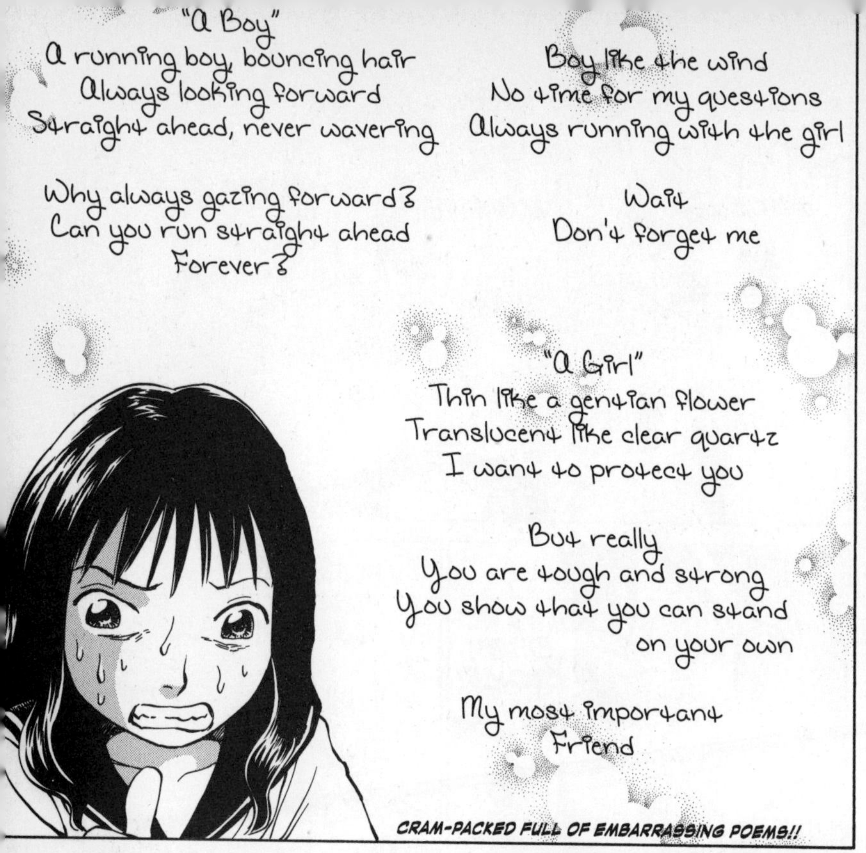
"A Boy"
A running boy, bouncing hair
Always looking forward
Straight ahead, never wavering
Boy like the wind
No time for my questions
Always running with the girl
Why always gazing forward?
Can you run straight ahead
Forever?
Wait
Don't forget me
"A Girl"
Thin like a gentian flower
Translucent like clear quartz
I want to protect you
But really
You are tough and strong
You show that you can stand
on your own
My most important
Friend
CRAM-PACKED FULL OF EMBARRASSING POEMS!!
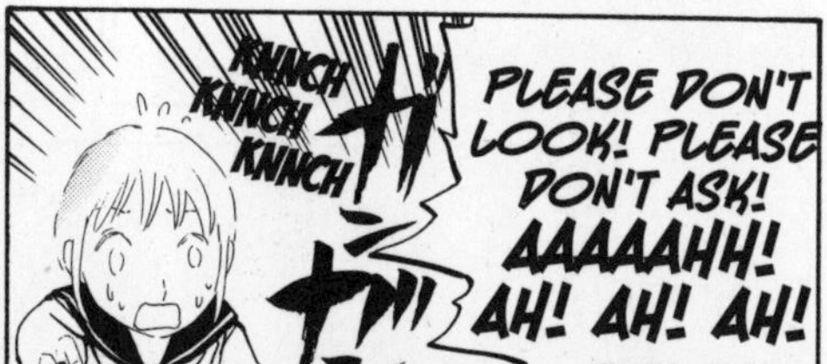
PLEASE DON'T LOOK! PLEASE DON'T ASK! AAAAAHH! AH! AH! AH!
KNNCH KNNCH KNNCH
OKOUCHI-SAN!!
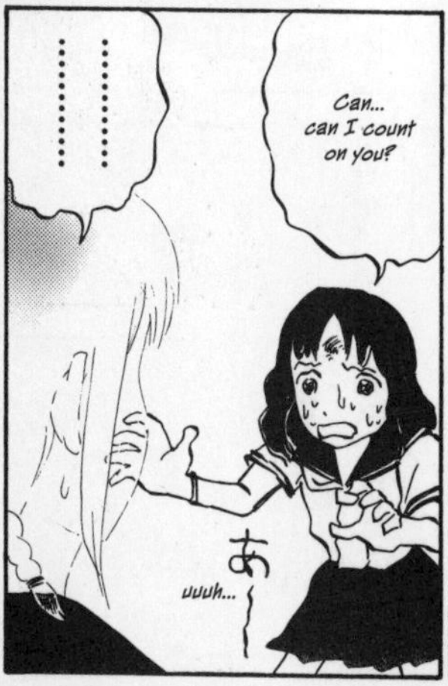
Can... can I count on you?
......
あ
uuuh...

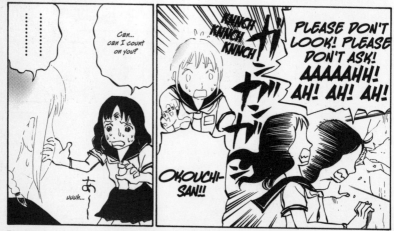

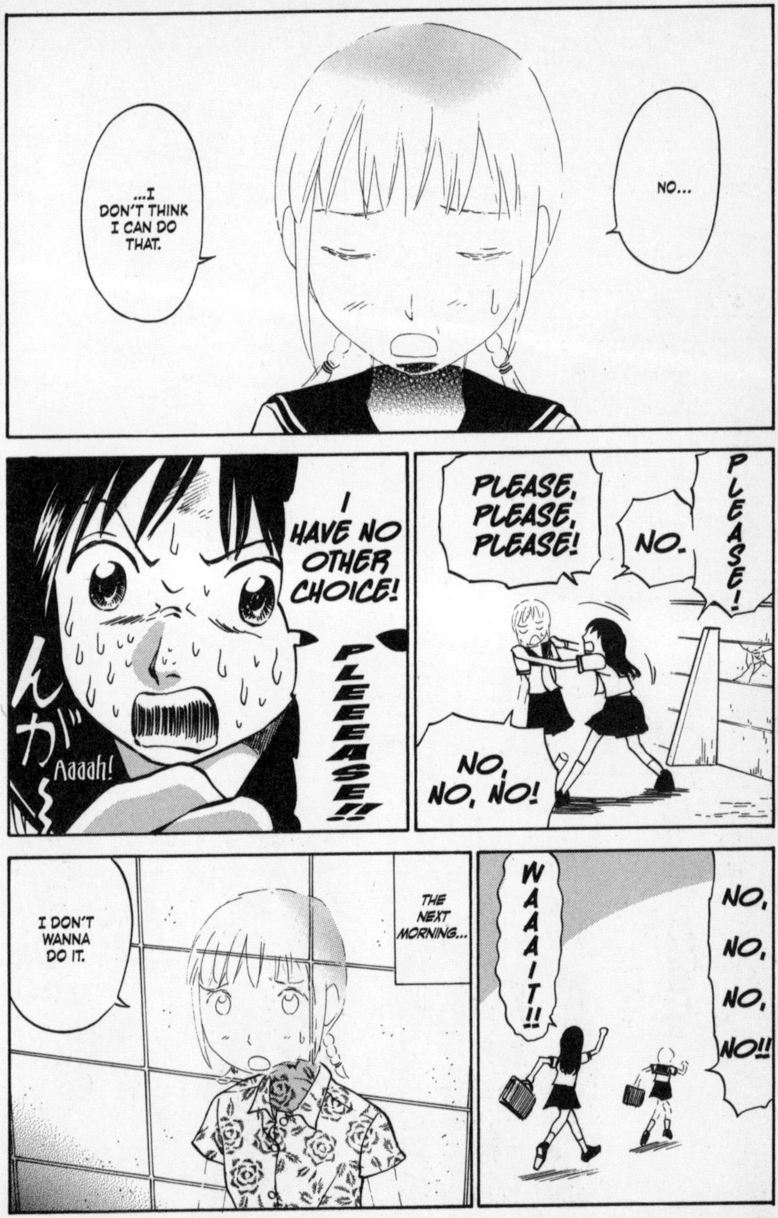
NO...
...I DON'T THINK I CAN DO THAT.
PLEASE!
NO.
PLEASE, PLEASE, PLEASE!
NO, NO, NO!
I HAVE NO OTHER CHOICE!
PLEEEEASE!!
んが～
Aaaah!
NO, NO, NO, NO!!
WAAAAIT!!
THE NEXT MORNING...
I DON'T WANNA DO IT.

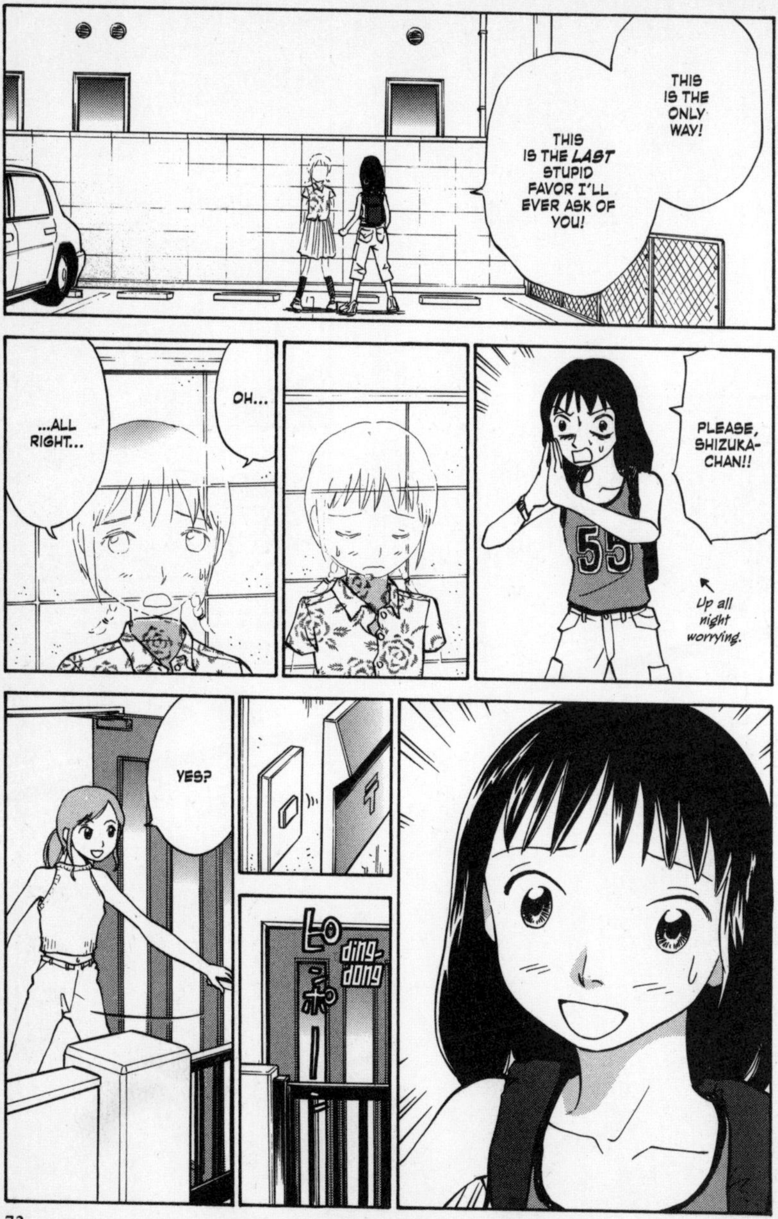

THIS IS THE ONLY WAY!
THIS IS THE *LAST* STUPID FAVOR I'LL EVER ASK OF YOU!
PLEASE, SHIZUKA-CHAN!!
Up all night worrying.
OH...
...ALL RIGHT...
ding-dong
YES?

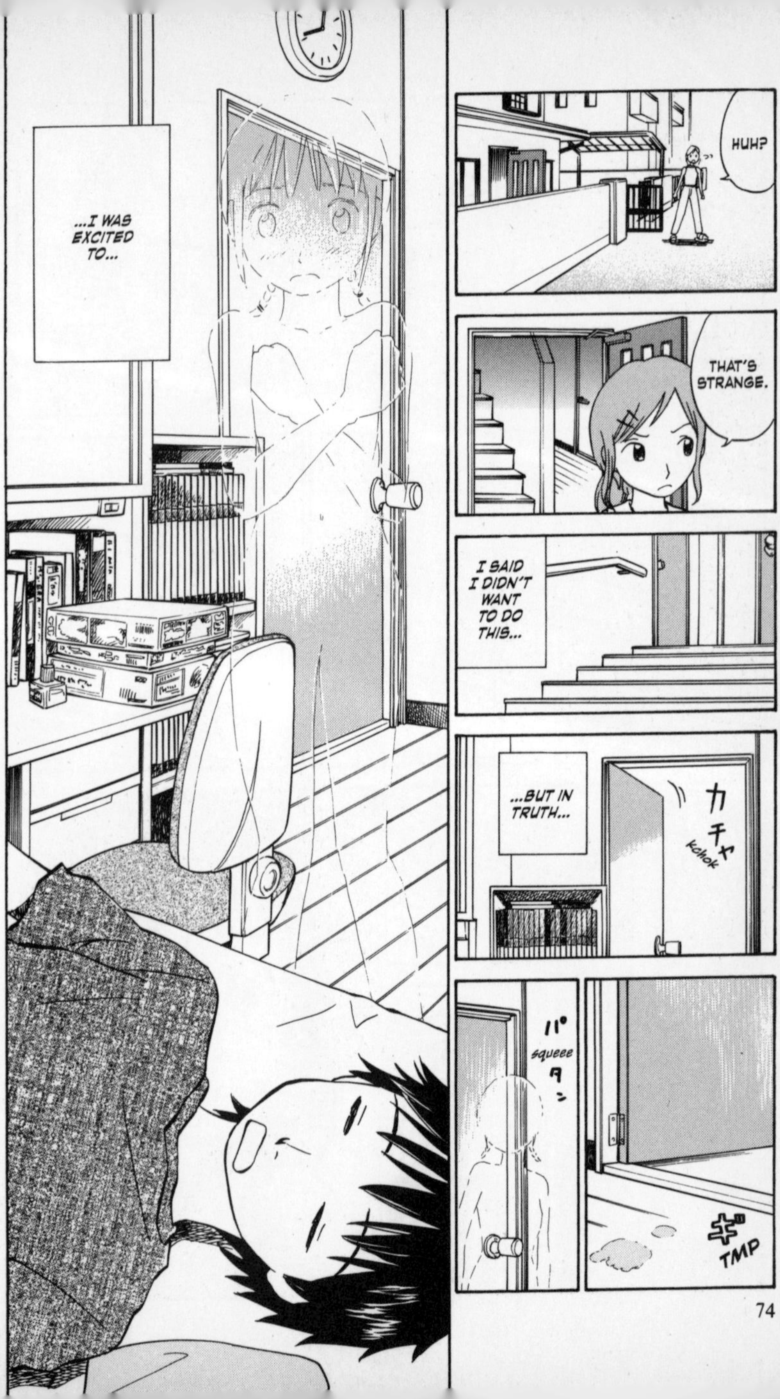
HUH?
THAT'S STRANGE.
I SAID I DIDN'T WANT TO DO THIS...
...BUT IN TRUTH...
カチャ
kchok
ギ
TMP
パタン
squeee
...I WAS EXCITED TO...

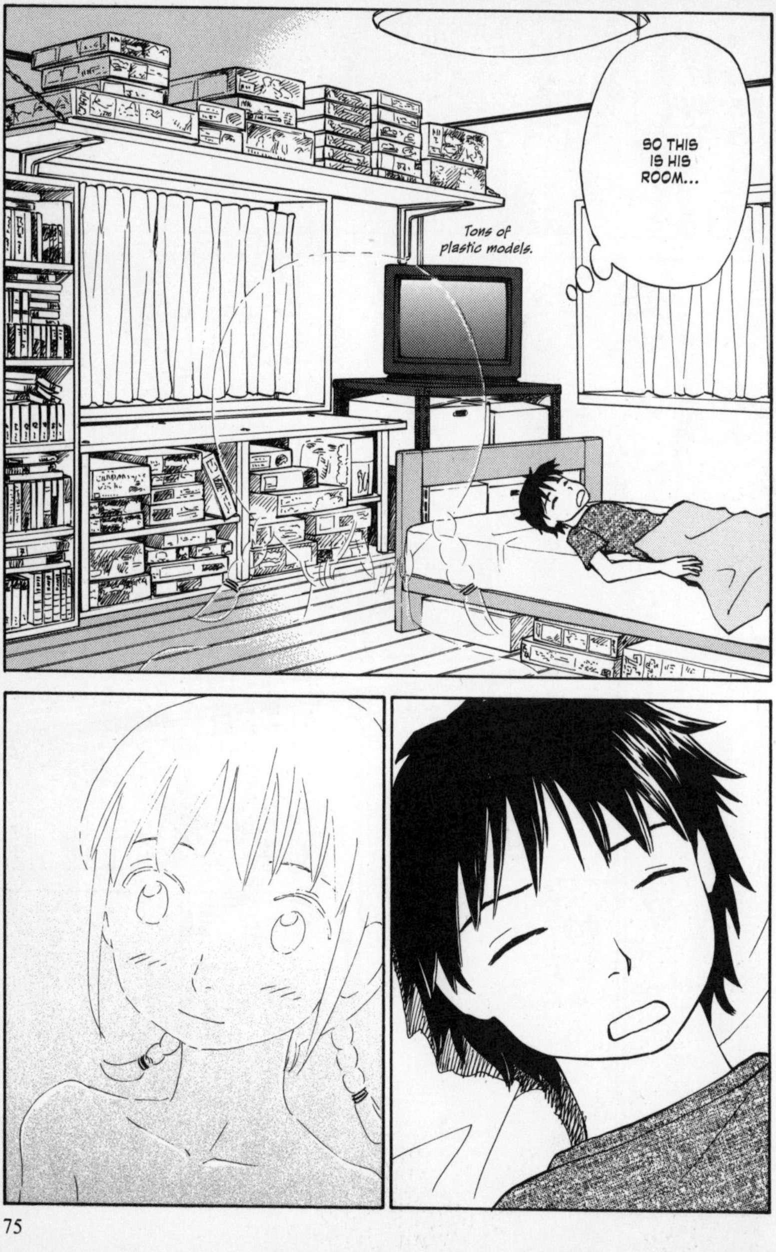
SO THIS IS HIS ROOM...
Tons of plastic models.

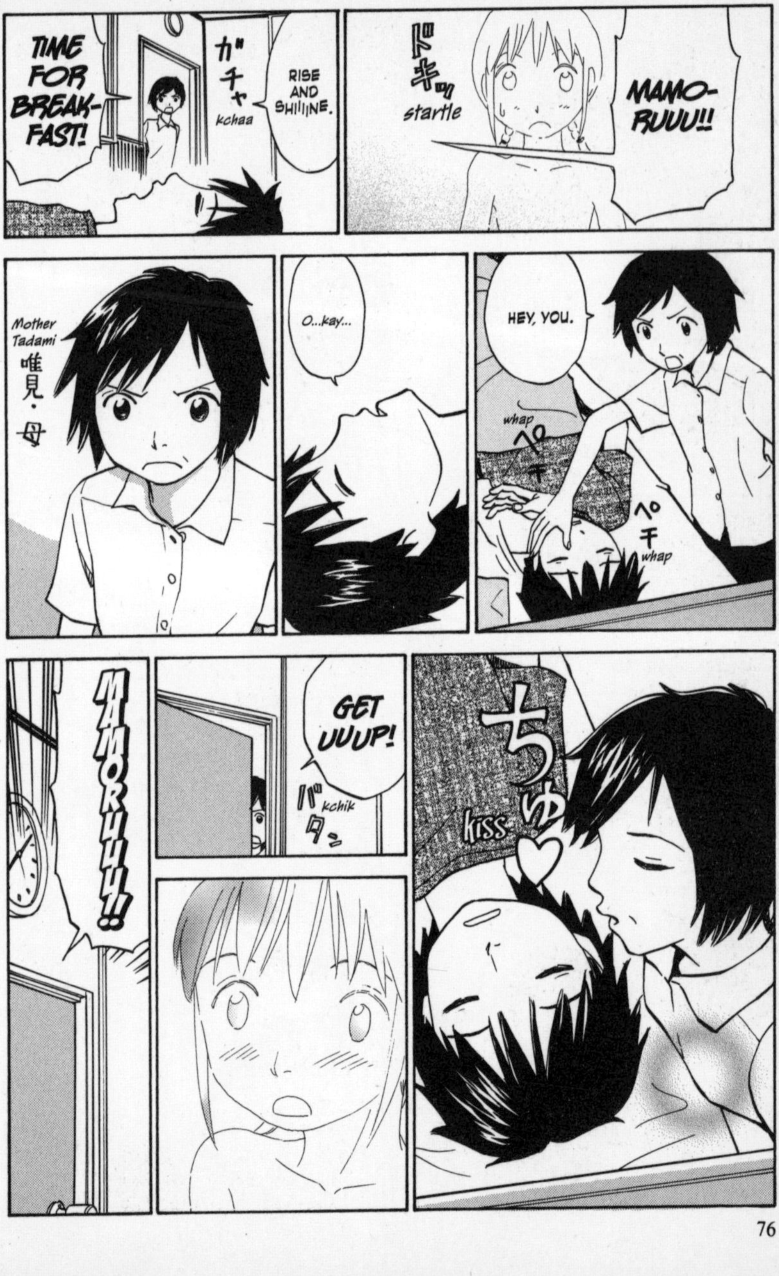
ドキッ
startle
MAMO-RUUU!!
RISE AND SHIIIINE.
ガチャ
kchaa
TIME FOR BREAK-FAST!
HEY, YOU.
ペチ
whap
ペチ
whap
O...kay...
Mother Tadami
唯見・母
ちゅ
kiss
GET UUUP!
バタン
kchik
MAMORUUUU!!

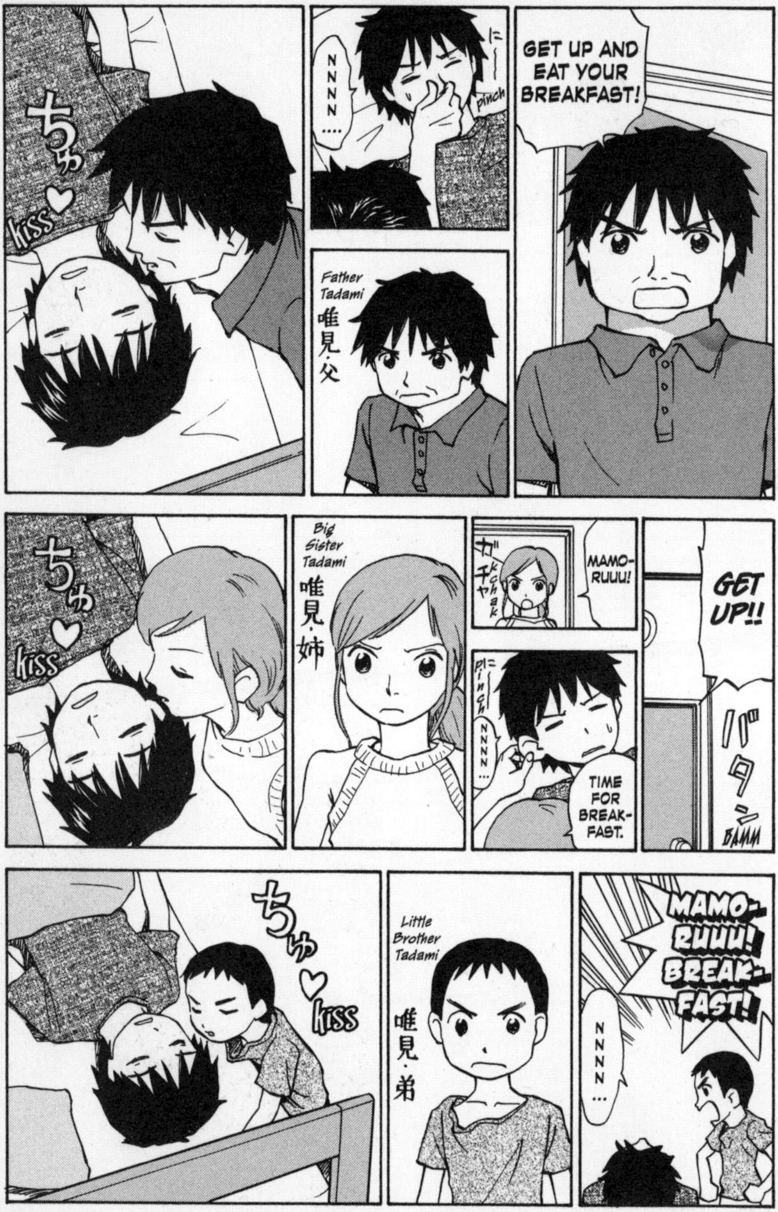
GET UP AND EAT YOUR BREAKFAST!
に~~
pinch
NNNN .....
Father Tadami
唯見・父
ちゅ♥
kiss
GET UP!!
バタン
BAMM
ガチャ
kchak
MAMO-RUUU!
TIME FOR BREAK-FAST.
に~
pinch
NNNN ...
Big Sister Tadami
唯見・姉
ちゅ♥
kiss
MAMO-RUUU! BREAK-FAST!
NNNN ...
Little Brother Tadami
唯見・弟
ちゅ♥
kiss

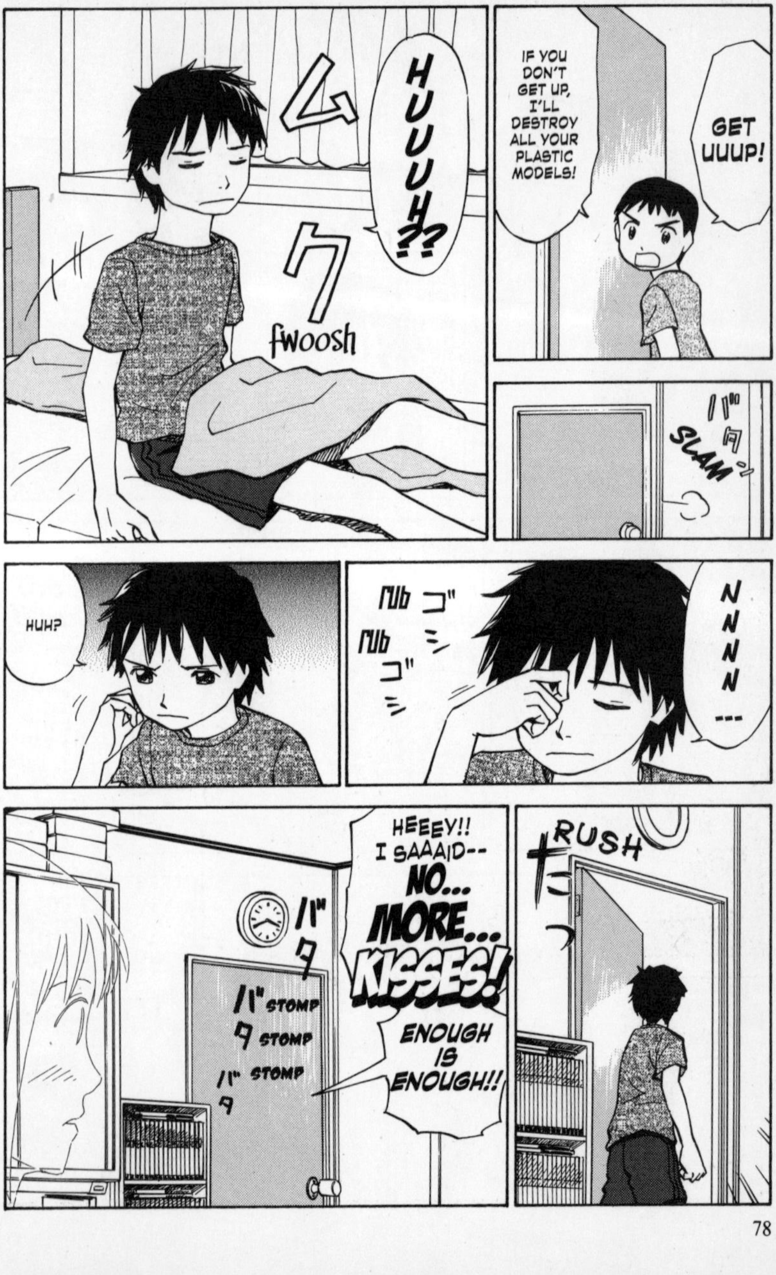
GET UUUP!
IF YOU DON'T GET UP, I'LL DESTROY ALL YOUR PLASTIC MODELS!
バタン
SLAM
HUUUUH??
ムク
fwoosh
NNNN---
ゴシ rub
ゴシ rub
HUH?
ダッ
RUSH
HEEEY!! I SAAAID-- NO... MORE... KISSES!
ENOUGH IS ENOUGH!!
バタ
バタ STOMP
バタ STOMP
STOMP

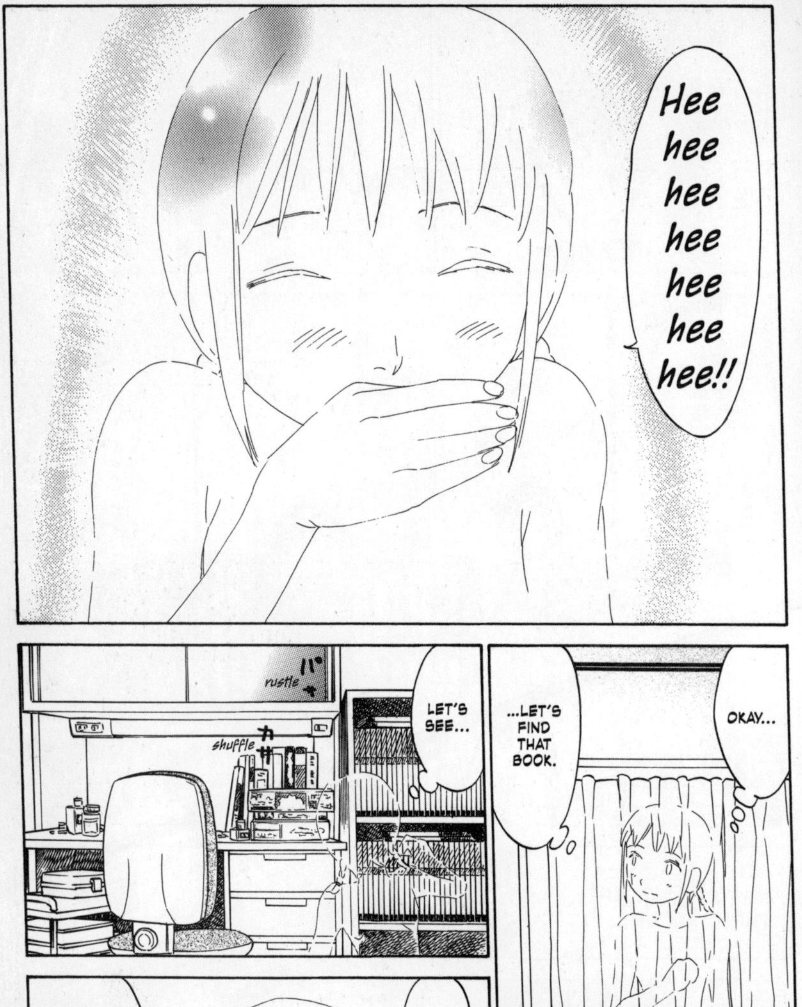
Hee hee hee hee hee hee hee!!
OKAY...
...LET'S FIND THAT BOOK.
rustle
shuffle
LET'S SEE...
HUH...?
I DON'T SEE IT, OKOUCHI-SAN...

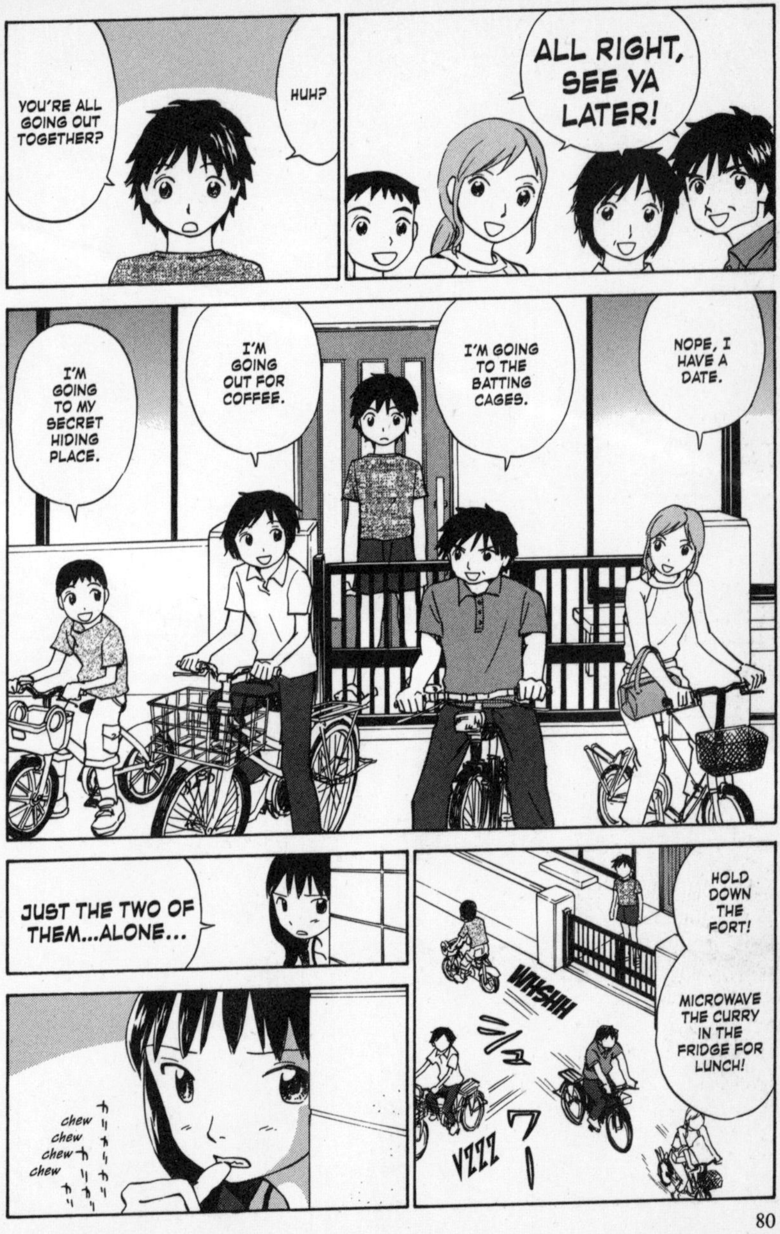
ALL RIGHT, SEE YA LATER!
HUH?
YOU'RE ALL GOING OUT TOGETHER?
NOPE, I HAVE A DATE.
I'M GOING TO THE BATTING CAGES.
I'M GOING OUT FOR COFFEE.
I'M GOING TO MY SECRET HIDING PLACE.
HOLD DOWN THE FORT!
MICROWAVE THE CURRY IN THE FRIDGE FOR LUNCH!
WHSHH
シュ
ワー
VZZZ
JUST THE TWO OF THEM...ALONE...
chew chew chew chew

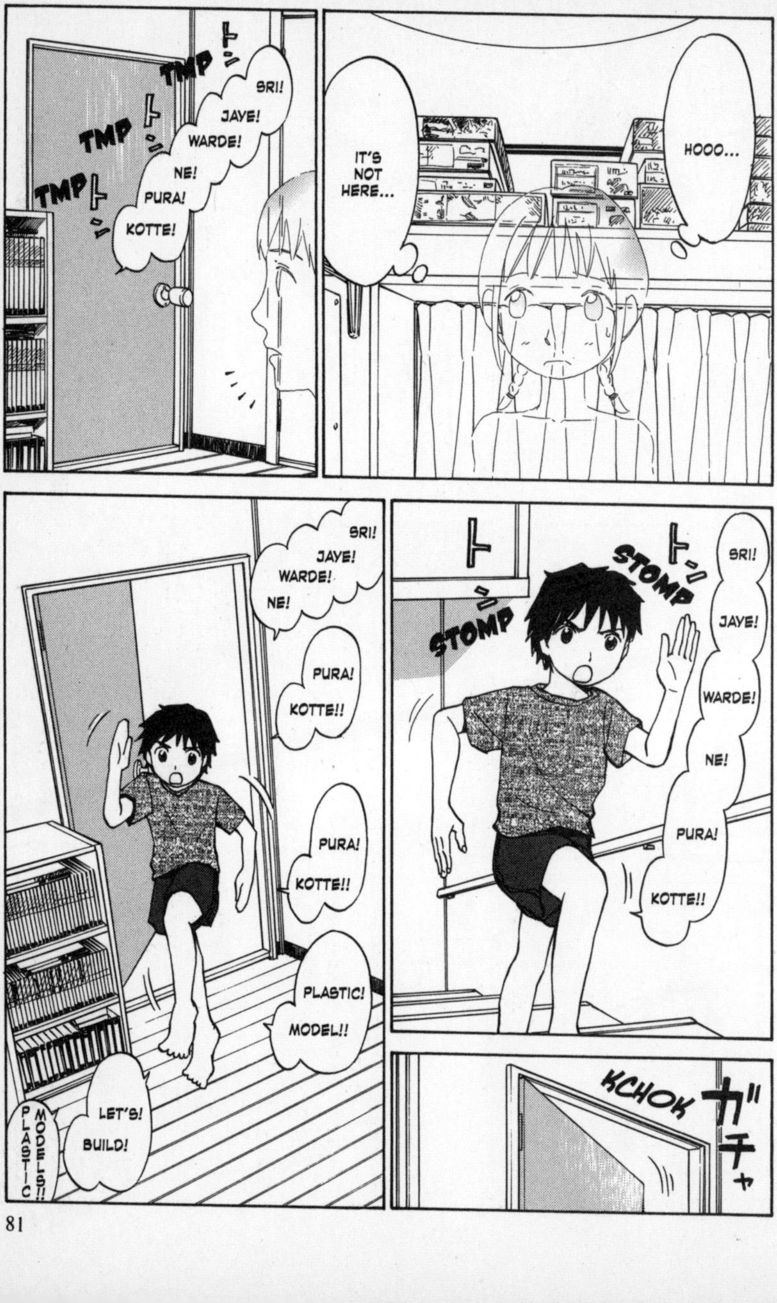
HOOO...
IT'S NOT HERE...
TMP ト
TMP ト
TMP ト
SRI! JAYE! WARDE! NE! PURA! KOTTE!
ト
STOMP ト
SRI! JAYE! WARDE! NE! PURA! KOTTE!!
STOMP
KCHOK ガチャ
SRI! JAYE! WARDE! NE!
PURA! KOTTE!!
PURA! KOTTE!!
PLASTIC! MODEL!!
LET'S! BUILD!
PLASTIC MODELS!!

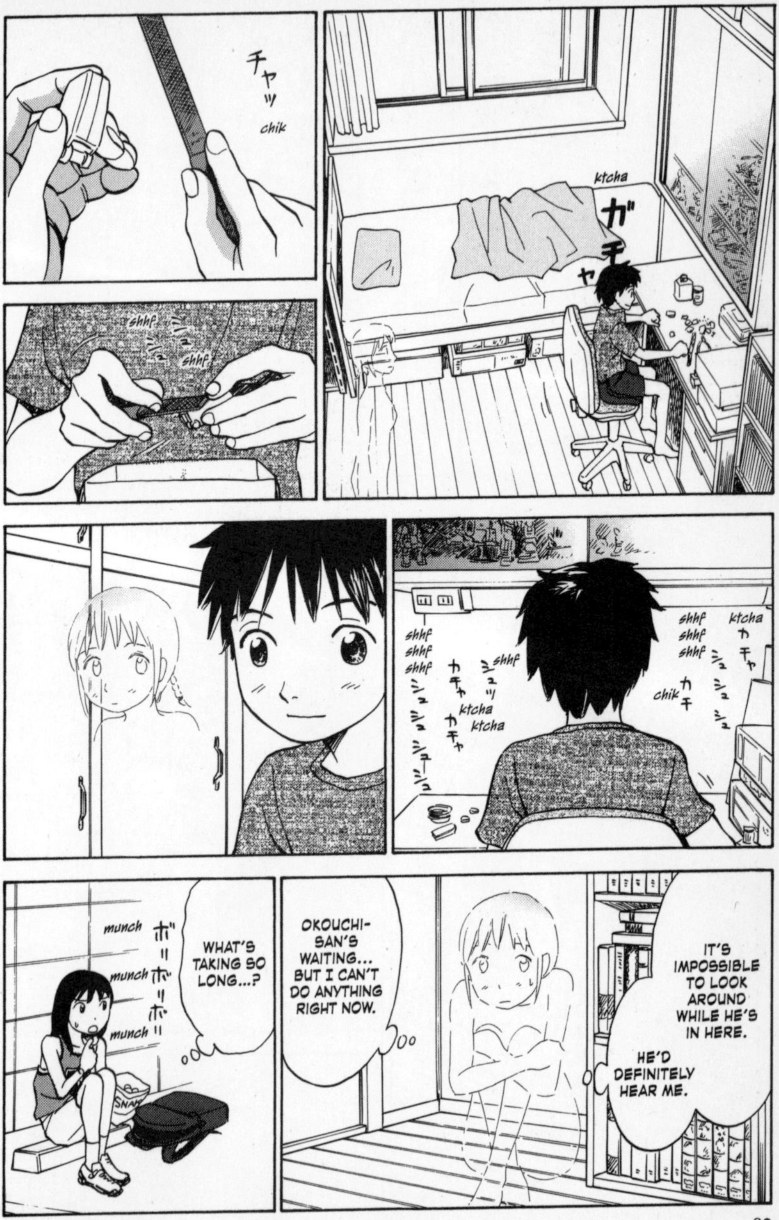
ktcha
ガチャ
チャッ
chik
shhf
シュ
shhf
シュ
shhf
shhf
shhf
ktcha
カチャ
シュシュシュ
chik
カチ
shhf
シュッ
カチャ
ktcha
ktcha
カチャ
shhf
shhf
shhf
シュシュシュー
IT'S IMPOSSIBLE TO LOOK AROUND WHILE HE'S IN HERE.
HE'D DEFINITELY HEAR ME.
OKOUCHI-SAN'S WAITING... BUT I CAN'T DO ANYTHING RIGHT NOW.
WHAT'S TAKING SO LONG...?
munch
munch
munch
ボリボリボリ

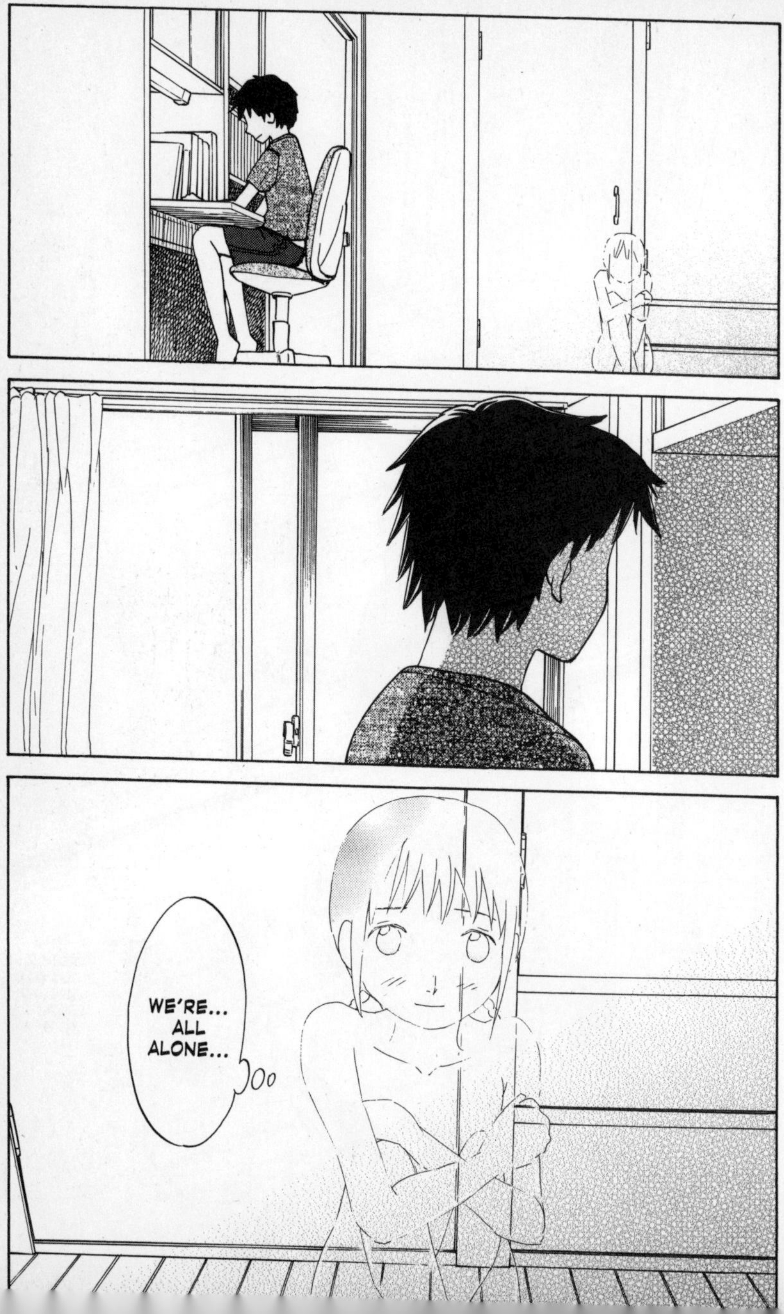
WE'RE... ALL ALONE...

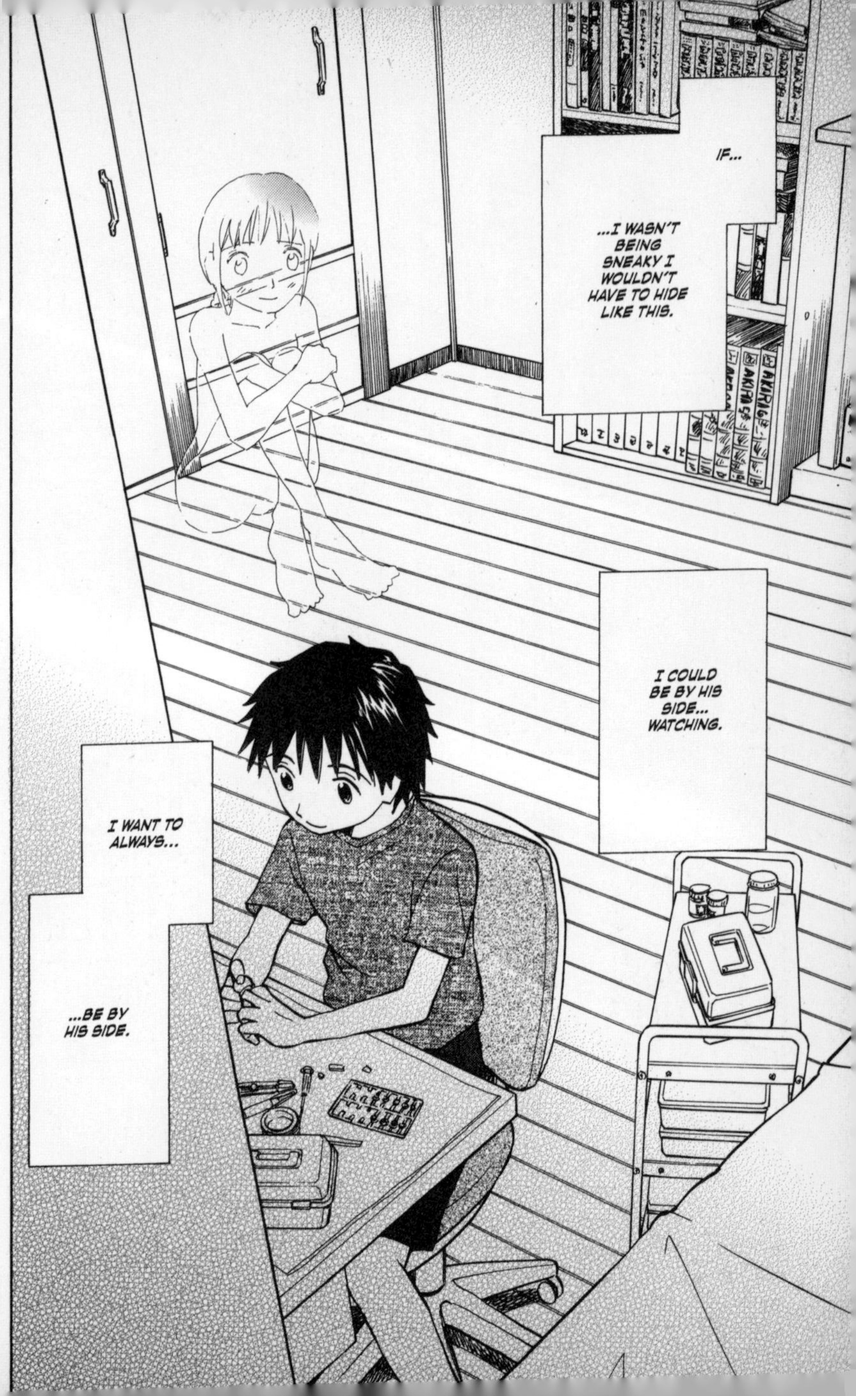
IF...
...I WASN'T BEING SNEAKY I WOULDN'T HAVE TO HIDE LIKE THIS.
I COULD BE BY HIS SIDE... WATCHING.
I WANT TO ALWAYS...
...BE BY HIS SIDE.

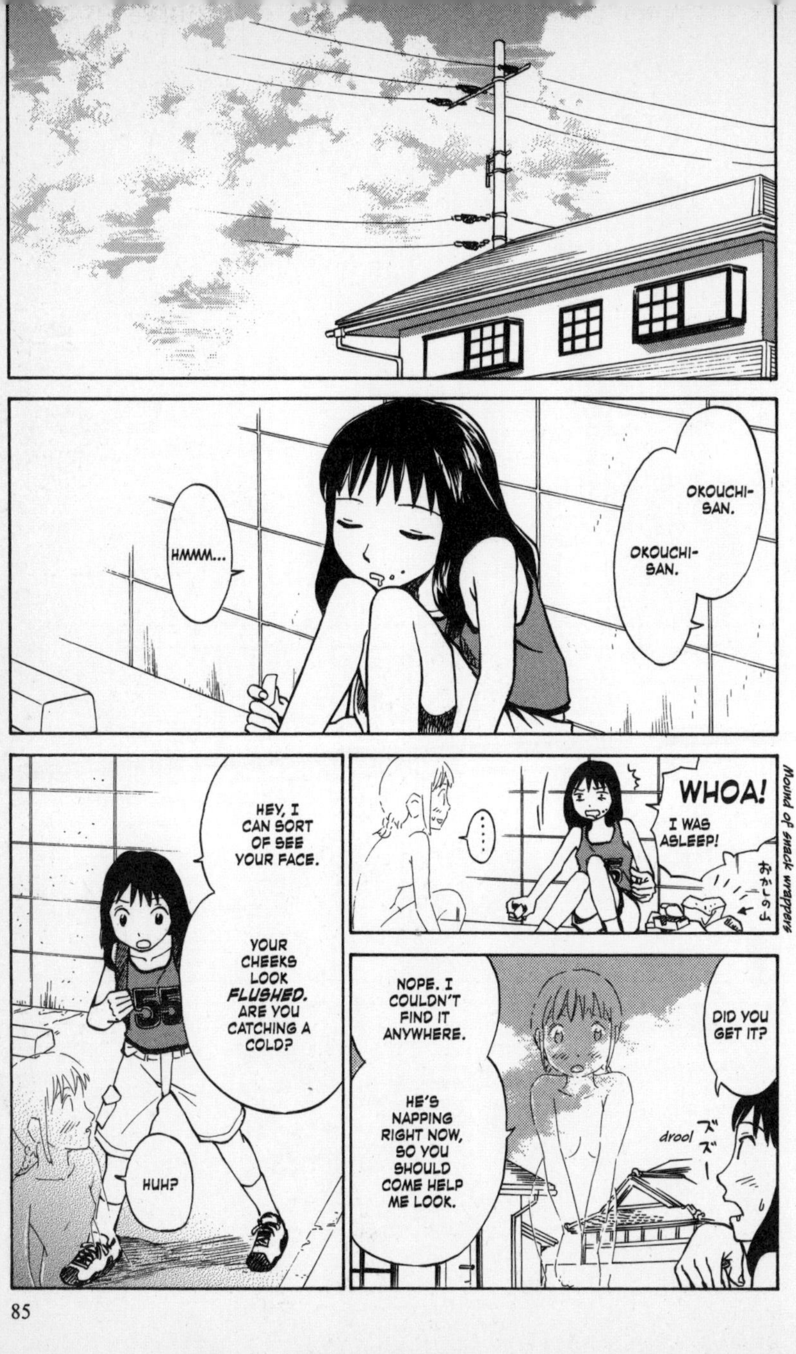
OKOUCHI-SAN.
OKOUCHI-SAN.
HMMM...
WHOA!
I WAS ASLEEP!
おかしの山
Mound of snack wrappers
......
DID YOU GET IT?
ズズー
drool
NOPE. I COULDN'T FIND IT ANYWHERE.
HE'S NAPPING RIGHT NOW, SO YOU SHOULD COME HELP ME LOOK.
HEY, I CAN SORT OF SEE YOUR FACE.
YOUR CHEEKS LOOK *FLUSHED.* ARE YOU CATCHING A COLD?
HUH?

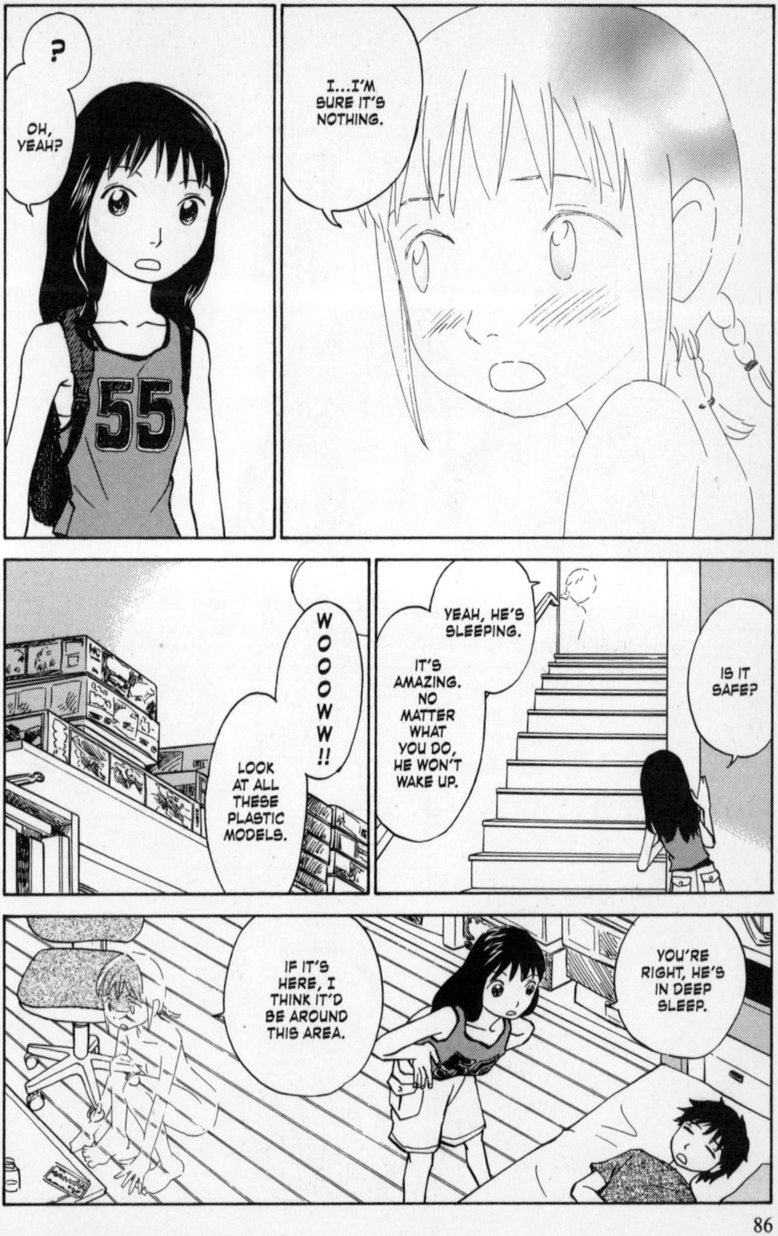
I...I'M SURE IT'S NOTHING.
?
OH, YEAH?
IS IT SAFE?
YEAH, HE'S SLEEPING.
IT'S AMAZING. NO MATTER WHAT YOU DO, HE WON'T WAKE UP.
WOOOOWW!!
LOOK AT ALL THESE PLASTIC MODELS.
YOU'RE RIGHT, HE'S IN DEEP SLEEP.
IF IT'S HERE, I THINK IT'D BE AROUND THIS AREA.

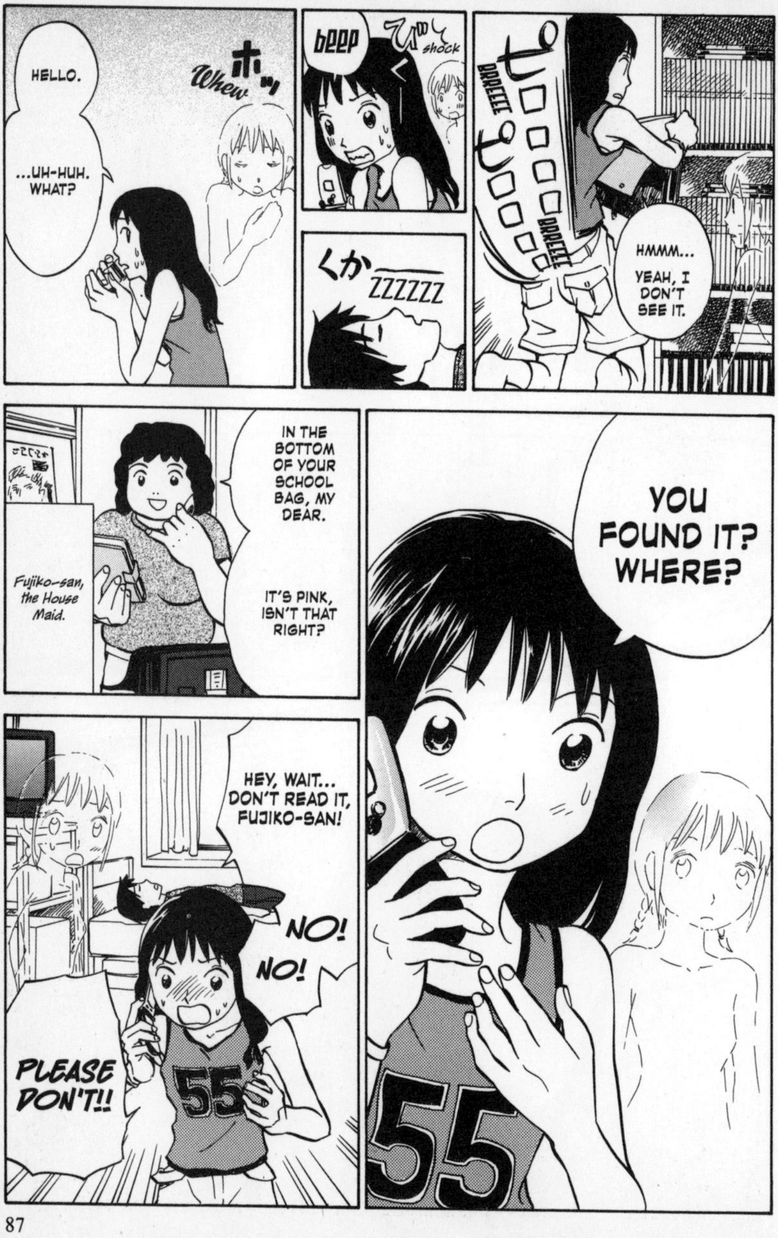
BREEEE
BREEEE
HMMM... YEAH, I DON'T SEE IT.
beep
shock
くか
ZZZZZZ
ホッ
Whew
HELLO.
...UH-HUH. WHAT?
YOU FOUND IT? WHERE?
IN THE BOTTOM OF YOUR SCHOOL BAG, MY DEAR.
IT'S PINK, ISN'T THAT RIGHT?
Fujiko-san, the House Maid.
HEY, WAIT... DON'T READ IT, FUJIKO-SAN!
NO!
NO!
PLEASE DON'T!!

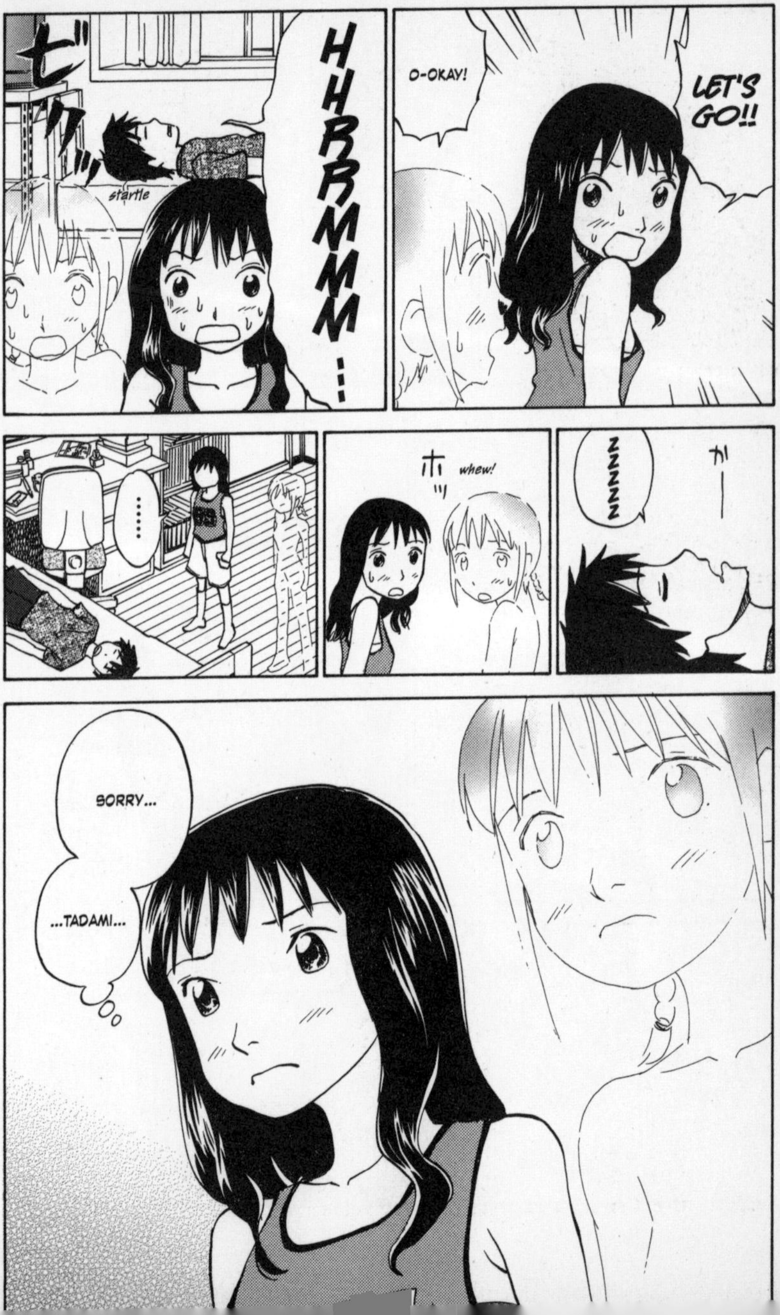
LET'S GO!!
O-OKAY!
HHRRMMMM...
ビクッ
startle
ZZZZZ
ガー
ホッ
whew!
......
SORRY...
...TADAMI...

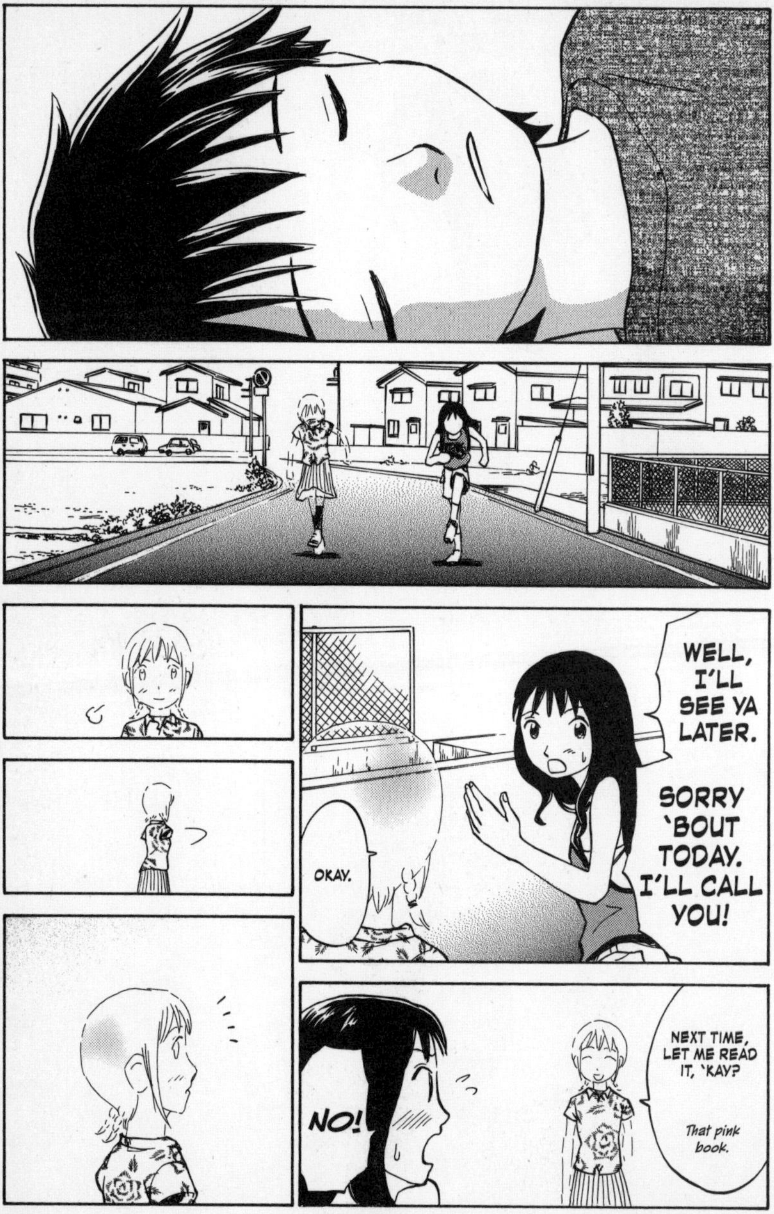
WELL, I'LL SEE YA LATER.
SORRY 'BOUT TODAY. I'LL CALL YOU!
OKAY.
NEXT TIME, LET ME READ IT, 'KAY?
That pink book.
NO!

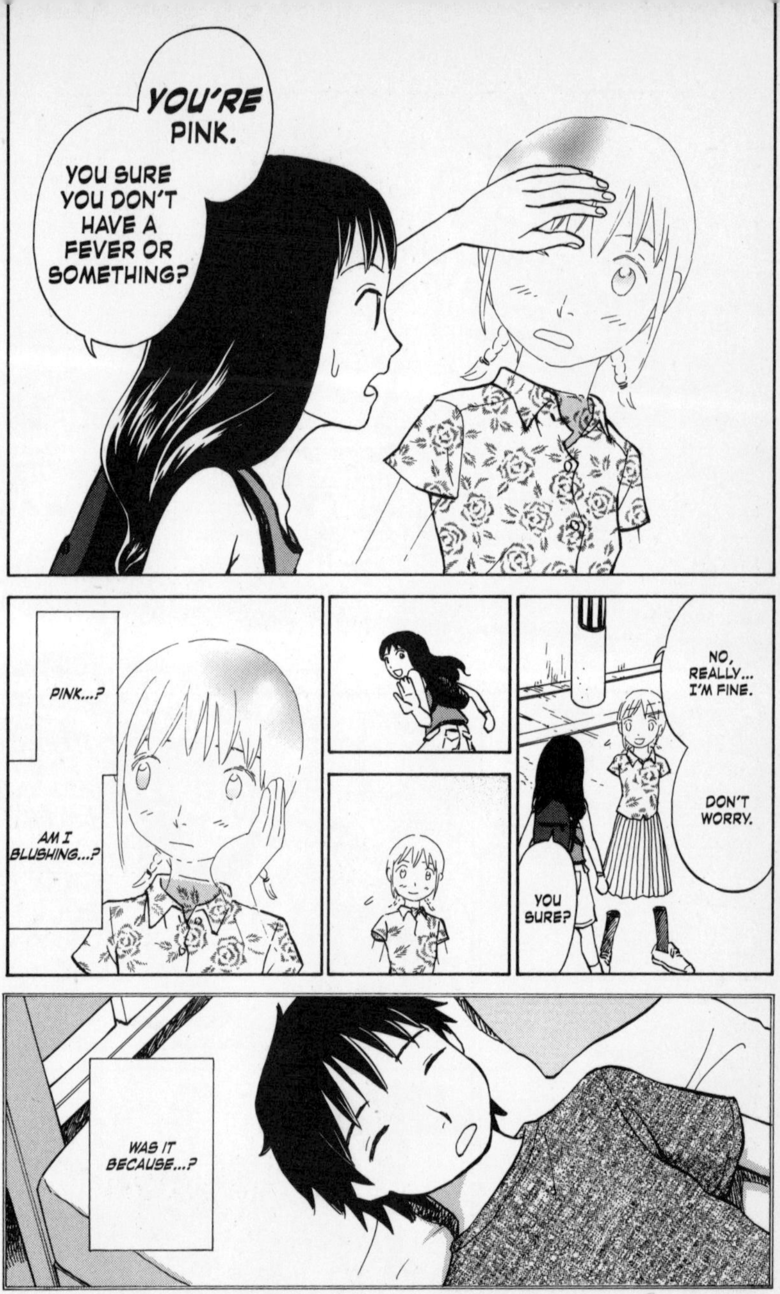
YOU'RE PINK.
YOU SURE YOU DON'T HAVE A FEVER OR SOMETHING?
NO, REALLY... I'M FINE.
DON'T WORRY.
YOU SURE?
PINK...?
AM I BLUSHING...?
WAS IT BECAUSE...?

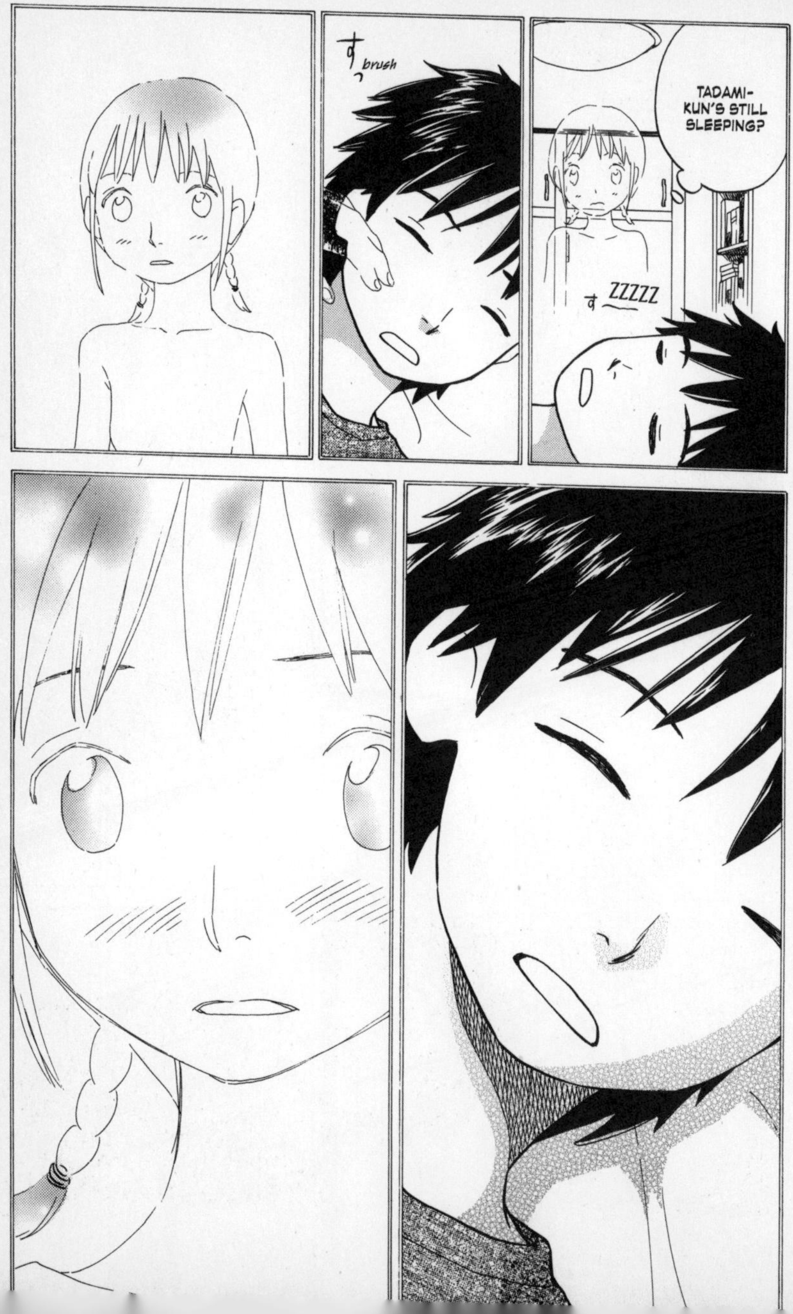
TADAMI-KUN'S STILL SLEEPING?
す ZZZZZ
すっ brush

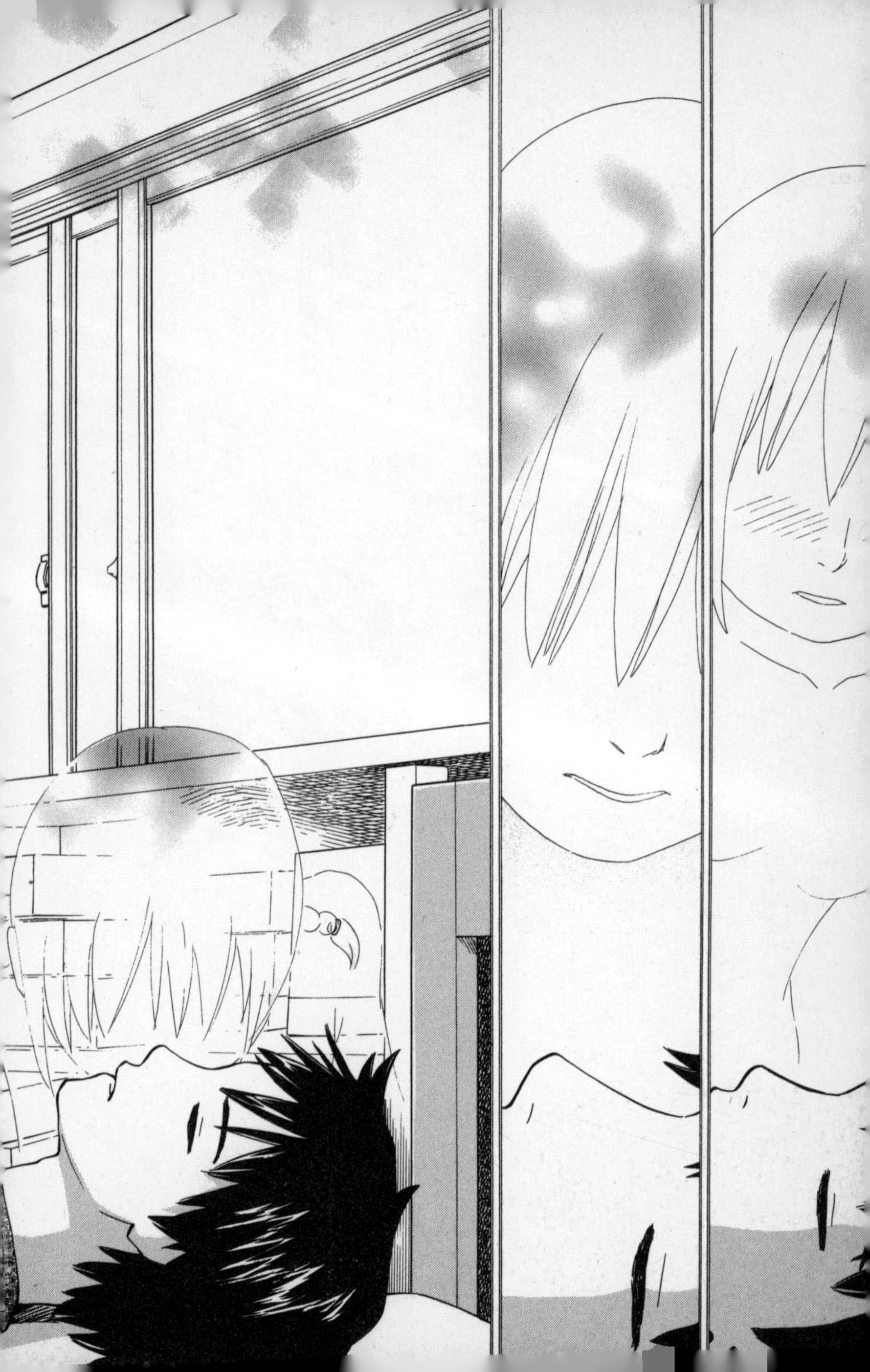

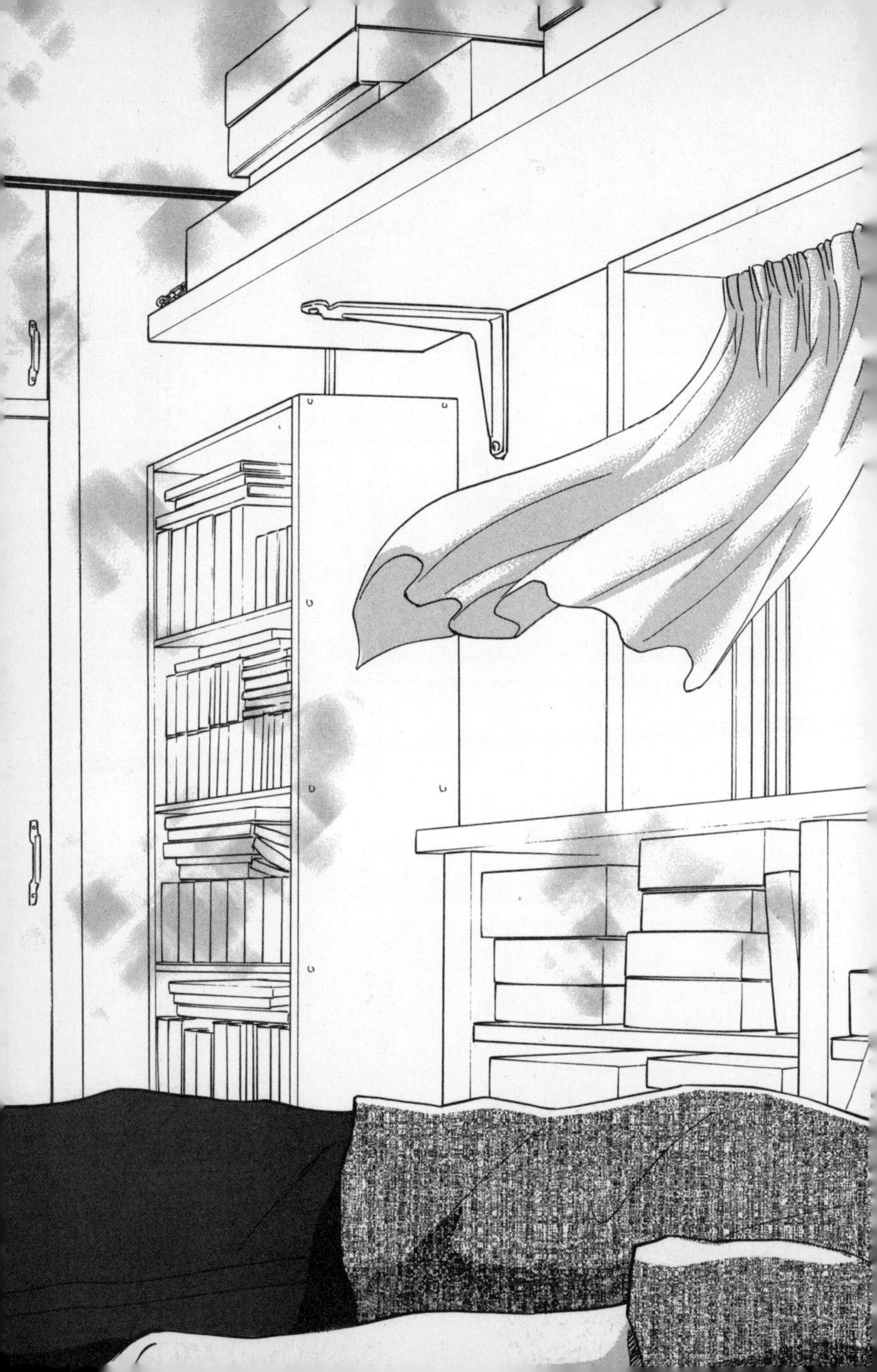

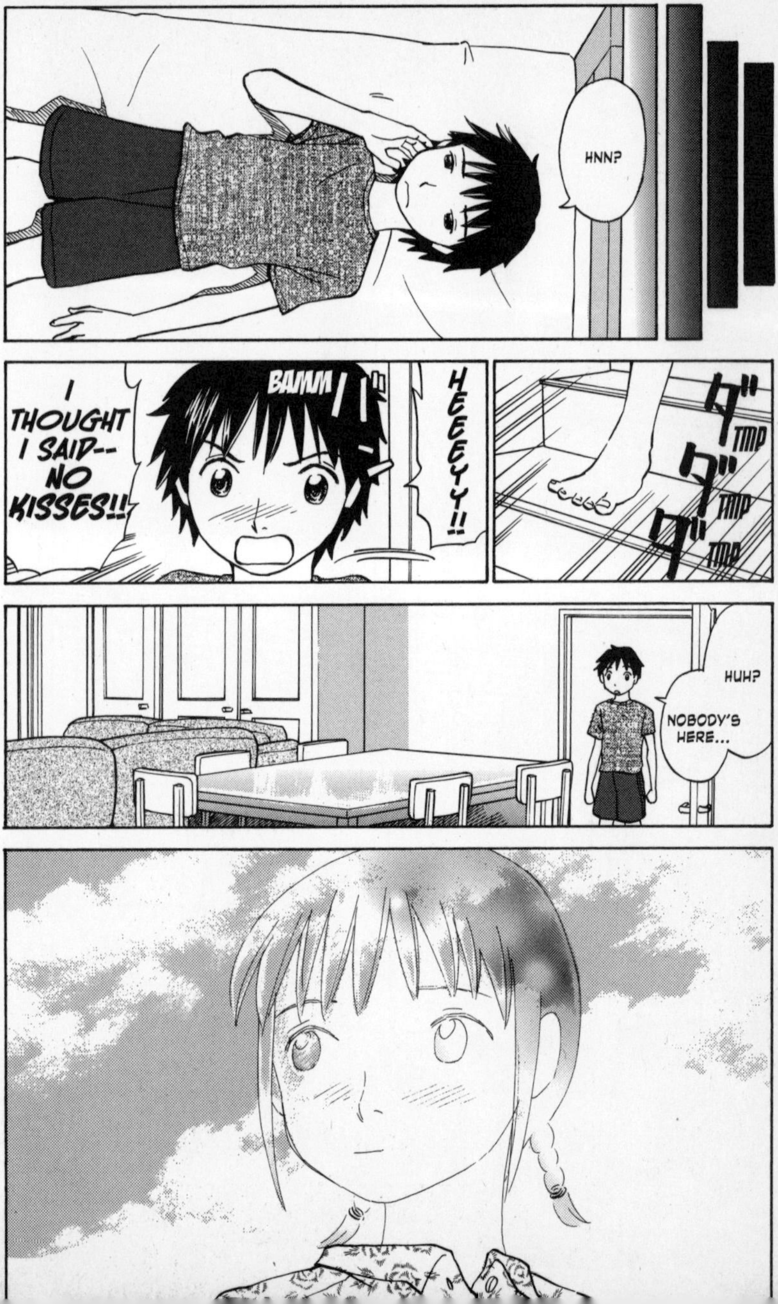
HNN?
ダ
TMP
ダ
TMP
ダ
TMP
HEEEEYYY!!
BAMM
I THOUGHT I SAID-- NO KISSES!!!
HUH?
NOBODY'S HERE...

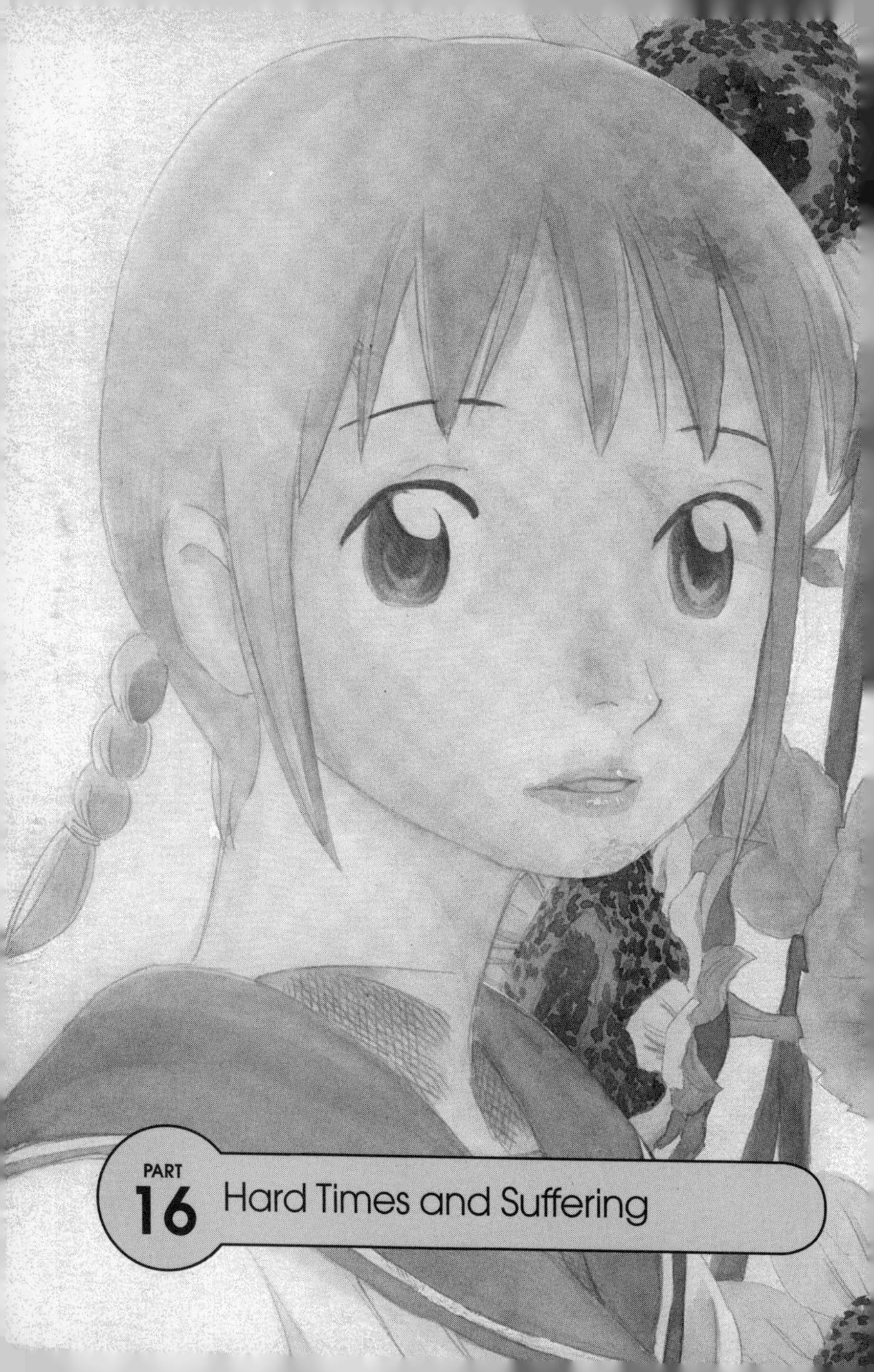

PART 16 Hard Times and Suffering

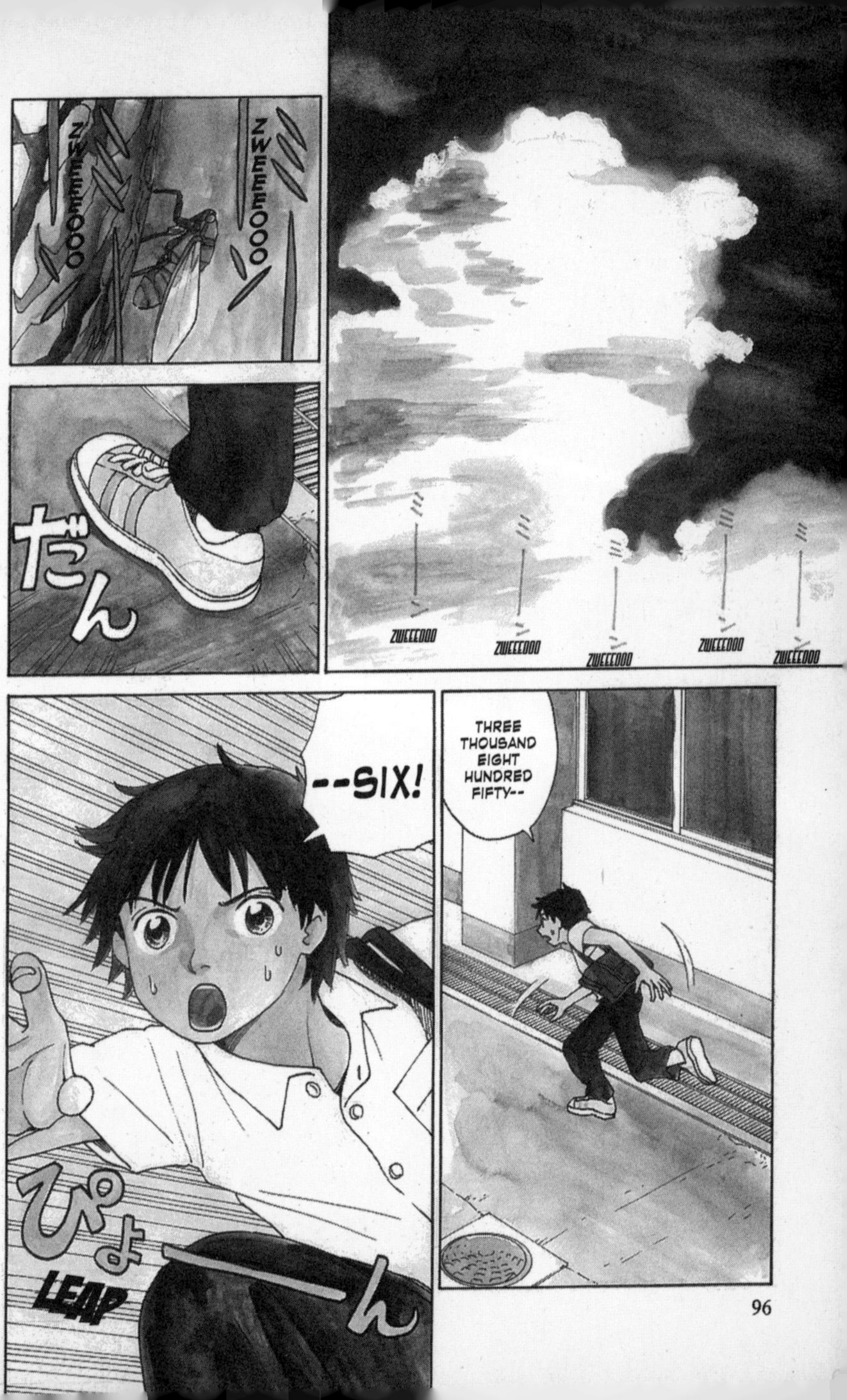
ZWEEEOOO
ZWEEEOOO
ZWEEEOOO
ZWEEEOOO
ZWEEEOOO
ZWEEEOOO
ZWEEEOOO
だん
THREE THOUSAND EIGHT HUNDRED FIFTY--
--SIX!
ぴょーん
LEAP

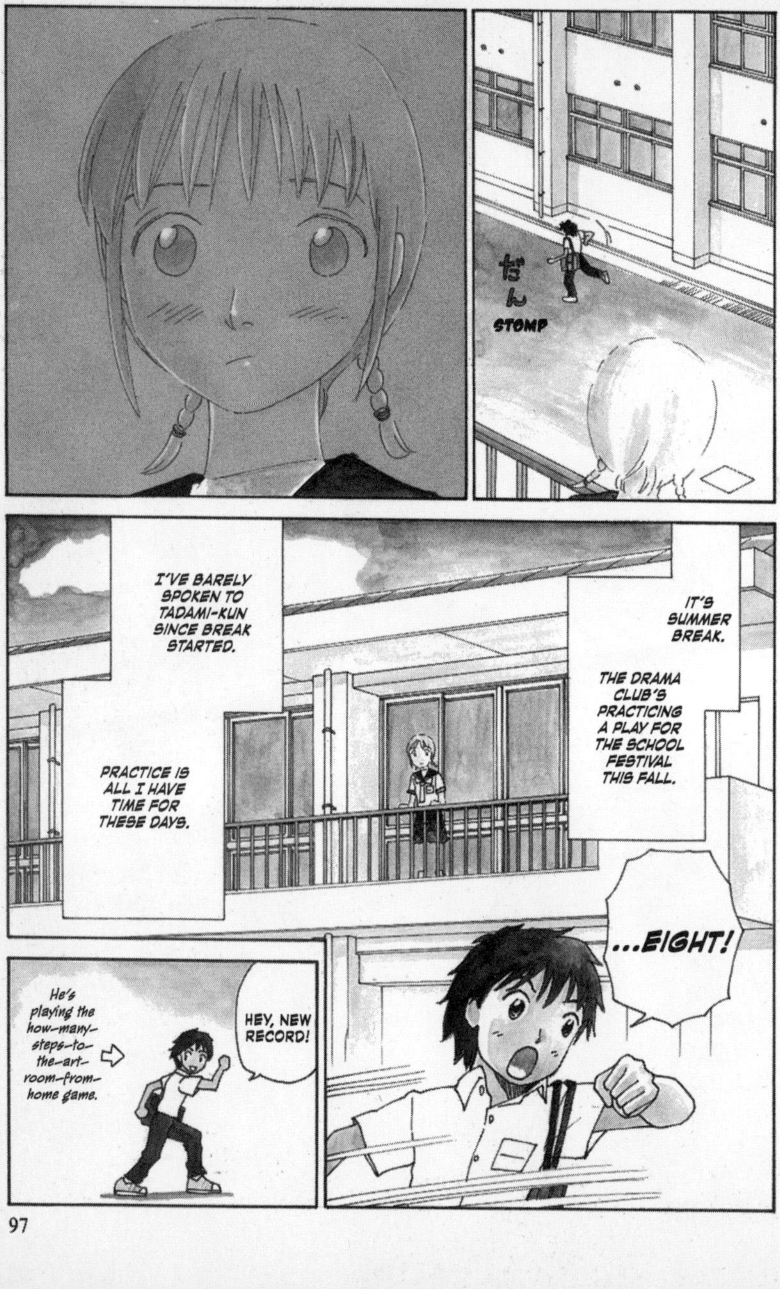
だん
STOMP
IT'S SUMMER BREAK.
THE DRAMA CLUB'S PRACTICING A PLAY FOR THE SCHOOL FESTIVAL THIS FALL.
I'VE BARELY SPOKEN TO TADAMI-KUN SINCE BREAK STARTED.
PRACTICE IS ALL I HAVE TIME FOR THESE DAYS.
...EIGHT!
HEY, NEW RECORD!
He's playing the how-many-steps-to-the-art-room-from-home game.

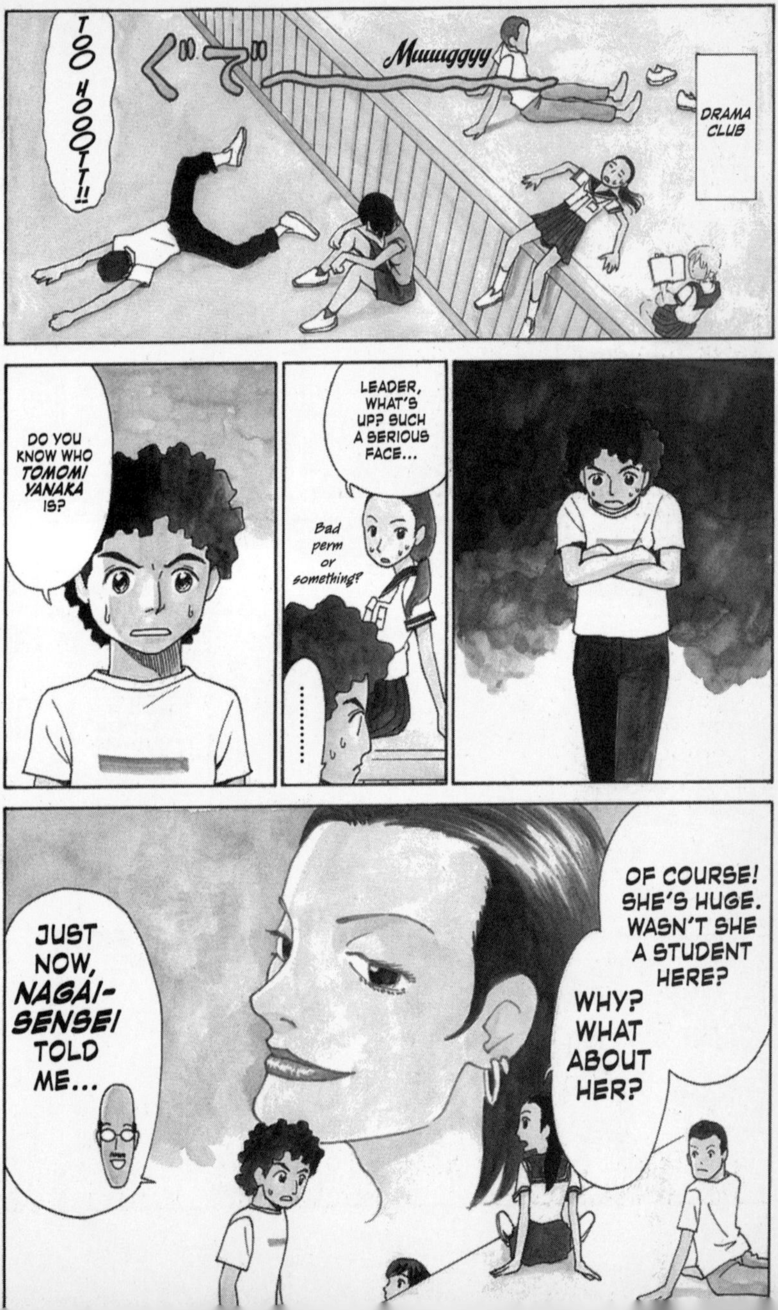
DRAMA CLUB
Muuuggyy
TOO HOOOOTT!!
LEADER, WHAT'S UP? SUCH A SERIOUS FACE...
Bad perm or something?
......
DO YOU KNOW WHO TOMOMI YANAKA IS?
OF COURSE! SHE'S HUGE. WASN'T SHE A STUDENT HERE?
WHY? WHAT ABOUT HER?
JUST NOW, NAGAI-SENSEI TOLD ME...

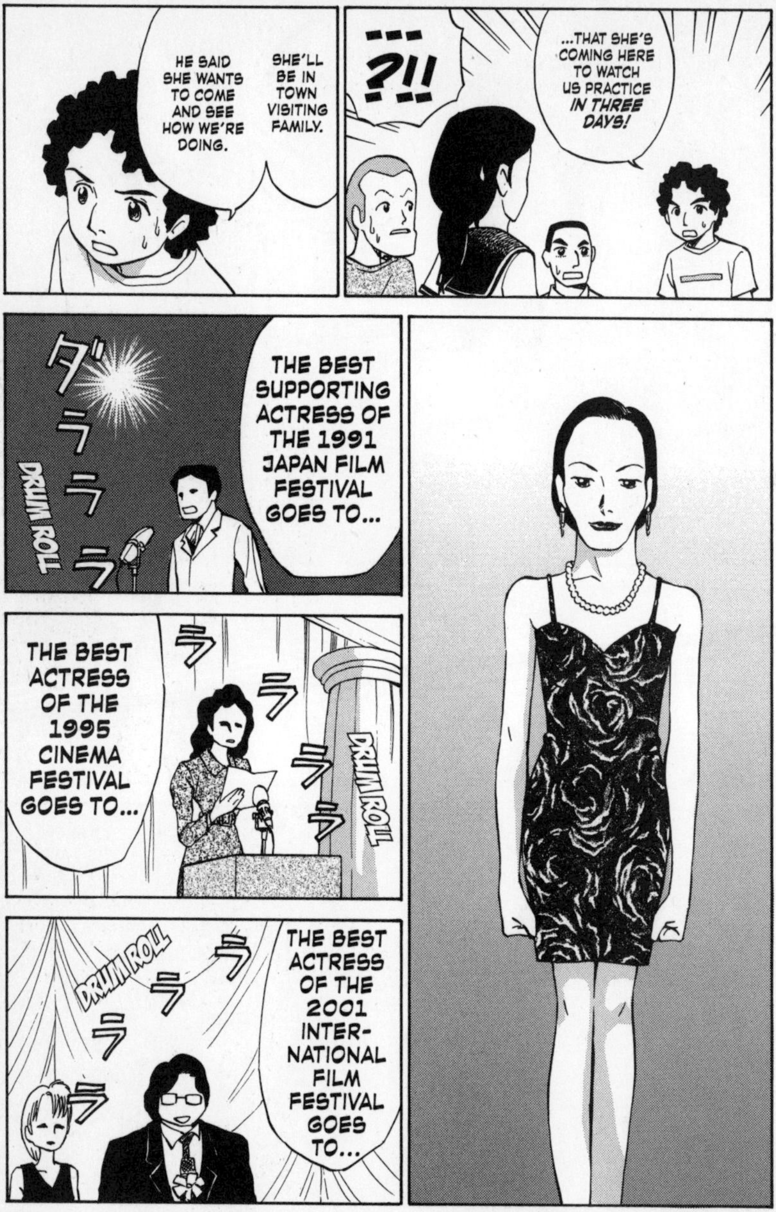
HE SAID SHE WANTS TO COME AND SEE HOW WE'RE DOING.
SHE'LL BE IN TOWN VISITING FAMILY.
?!!
...THAT SHE'S COMING HERE TO WATCH US PRACTICE IN THREE DAYS!
ダ ラ ラ ラ
DRUM ROLL
THE BEST SUPPORTING ACTRESS OF THE 1991 JAPAN FILM FESTIVAL GOES TO...
THE BEST ACTRESS OF THE 1995 CINEMA FESTIVAL GOES TO...
ラ ラ ラ ラ
DRUM ROLL
DRUM ROLL
ラ ラ ラ ラ
THE BEST ACTRESS OF THE 2001 INTER-NATIONAL FILM FESTIVAL GOES TO...

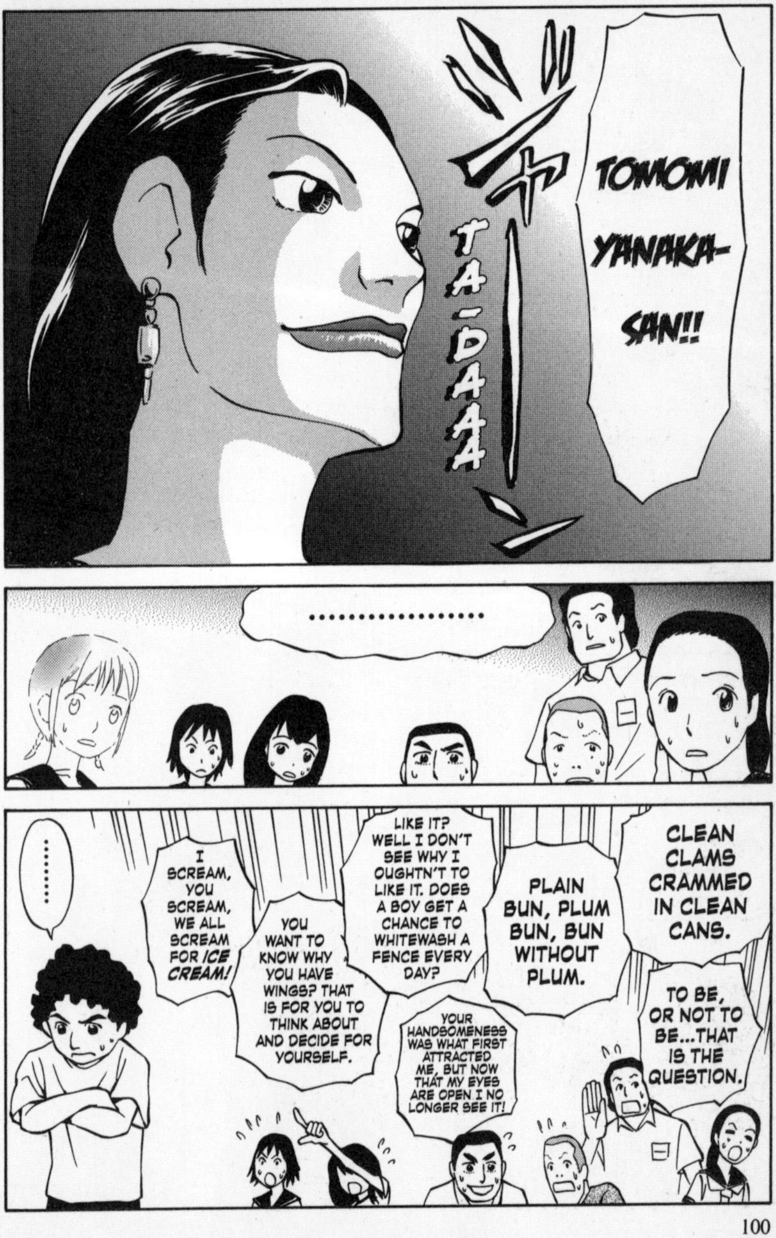

TOMOMI YANAKA-SAN!!
TA-DAAAA
....
CLEAN CLAMS CRAMMED IN CLEAN CANS.
TO BE, OR NOT TO BE...THAT IS THE QUESTION.
PLAIN BUN, PLUM BUN, BUN WITHOUT PLUM.
LIKE IT? WELL I DON'T SEE WHY I OUGHTN'T TO LIKE IT. DOES A BOY GET A CHANCE TO WHITEWASH A FENCE EVERY DAY?
YOUR HANDSOMENESS WAS WHAT FIRST ATTRACTED ME, BUT NOW THAT MY EYES ARE OPEN I NO LONGER SEE IT!
YOU WANT TO KNOW WHY YOU HAVE WINGS? THAT IS FOR YOU TO THINK ABOUT AND DECIDE FOR YOURSELF.
I SCREAM, YOU SCREAM, WE ALL SCREAM FOR *ICE CREAM!*
....

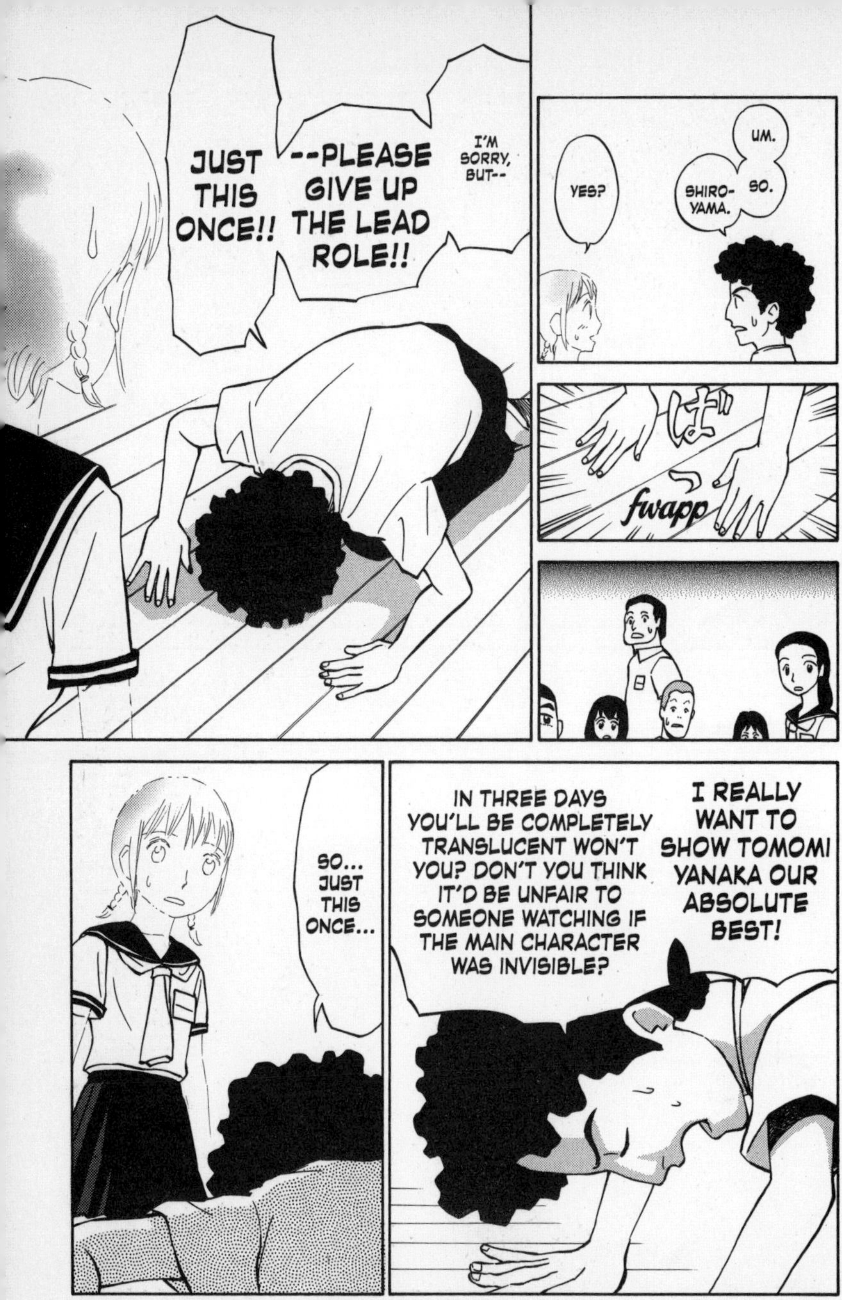
UM.
SO.
SHIRO-YAMA.
YES?
ばっ
fwapp
I'M SORRY, BUT--
--PLEASE GIVE UP THE LEAD ROLE!!
JUST THIS ONCE!!
I REALLY WANT TO SHOW TOMOMI YANAKA OUR ABSOLUTE BEST!
IN THREE DAYS YOU'LL BE COMPLETELY TRANSLUCENT WON'T YOU? DON'T YOU THINK IT'D BE UNFAIR TO SOMEONE WATCHING IF THE MAIN CHARACTER WAS INVISIBLE?
SO... JUST THIS ONCE...

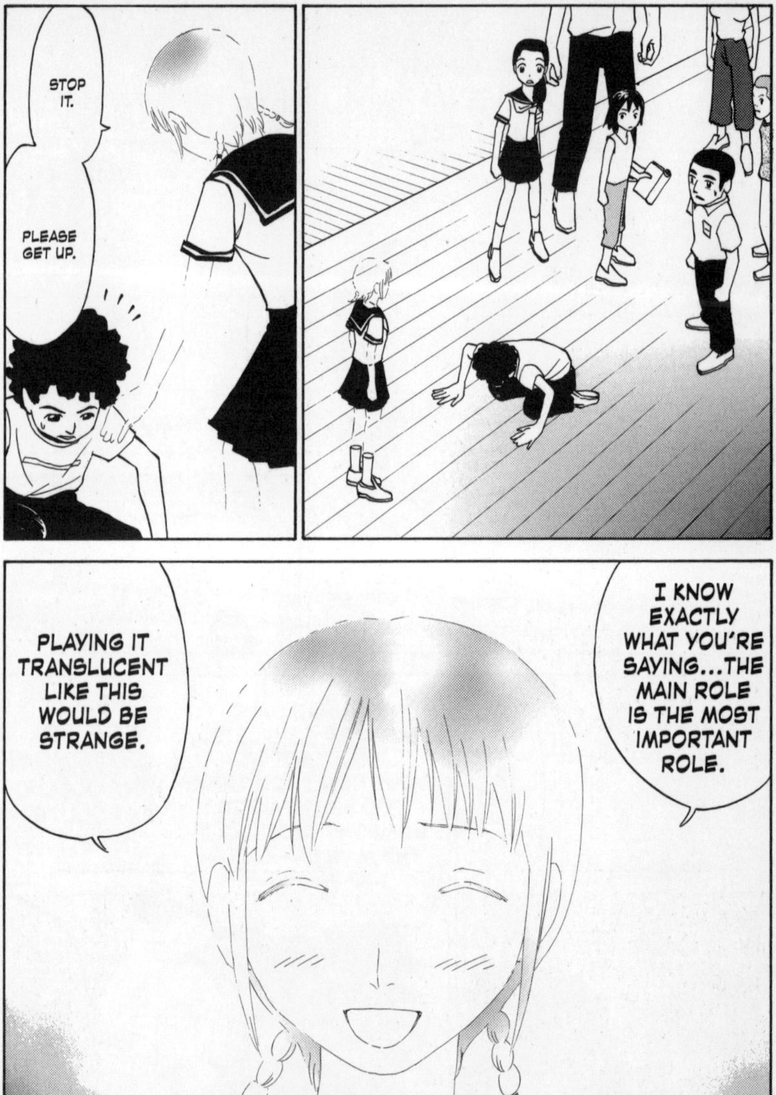
STOP IT.
PLEASE GET UP.
I KNOW EXACTLY WHAT YOU'RE SAYING...THE MAIN ROLE IS THE MOST IMPORTANT ROLE.
PLAYING IT TRANSLUCENT LIKE THIS WOULD BE STRANGE.

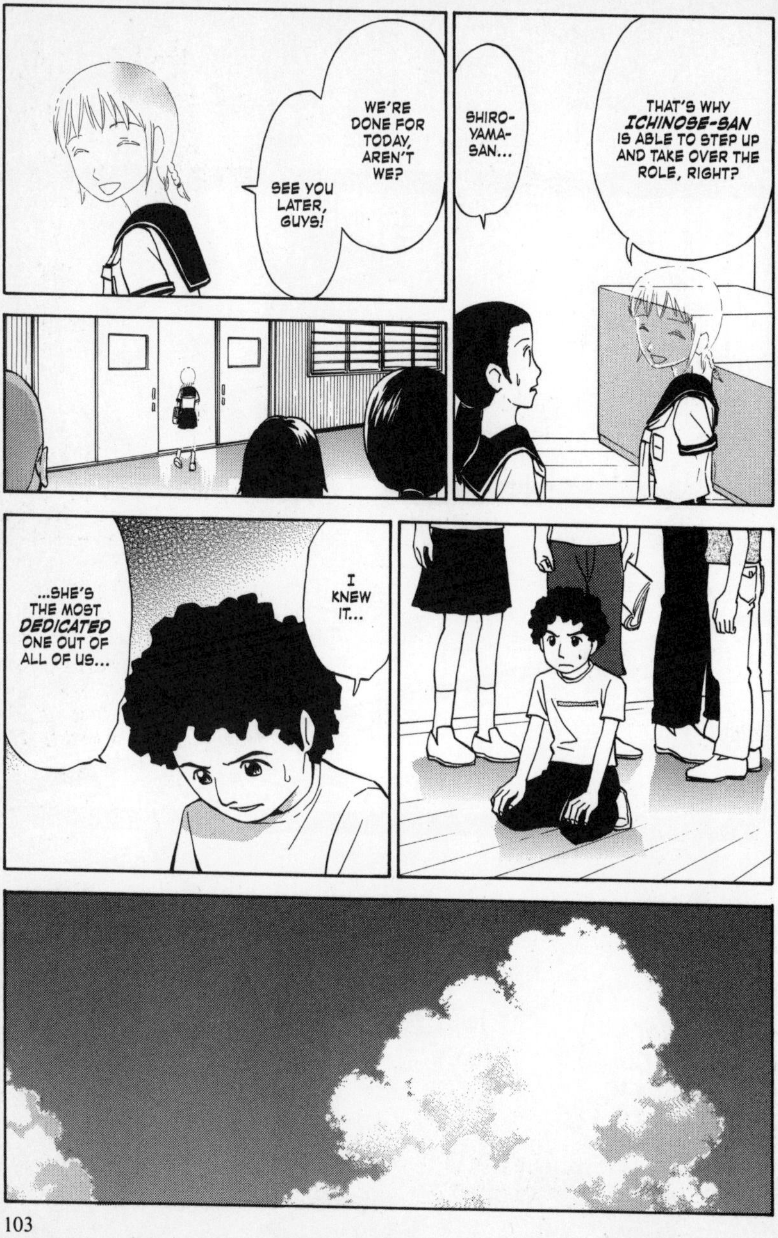
THAT'S WHY *ICHINOSE-SAN* IS ABLE TO STEP UP AND TAKE OVER THE ROLE, RIGHT?
SHIRO-YAMA-SAN...
WE'RE DONE FOR TODAY, AREN'T WE?
SEE YOU LATER, GUYS!
I KNEW IT...
...SHE'S THE MOST *DEDICATED* ONE OUT OF ALL OF US...

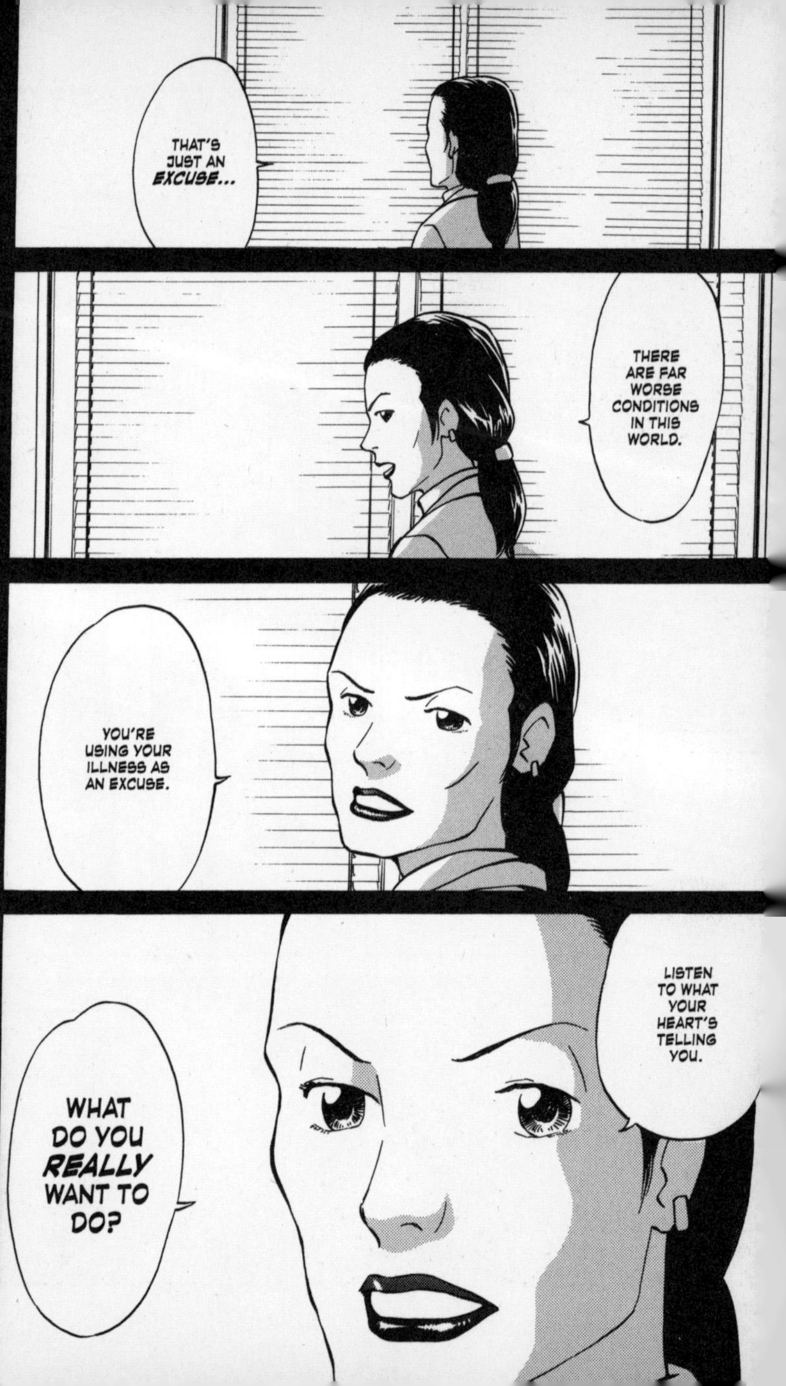
THAT'S JUST AN *EXCUSE...*
THERE ARE FAR WORSE CONDITIONS IN THIS WORLD.
YOU'RE USING YOUR ILLNESS AS AN EXCUSE.
LISTEN TO WHAT YOUR HEART'S TELLING YOU.
WHAT DO YOU *REALLY* WANT TO DO?

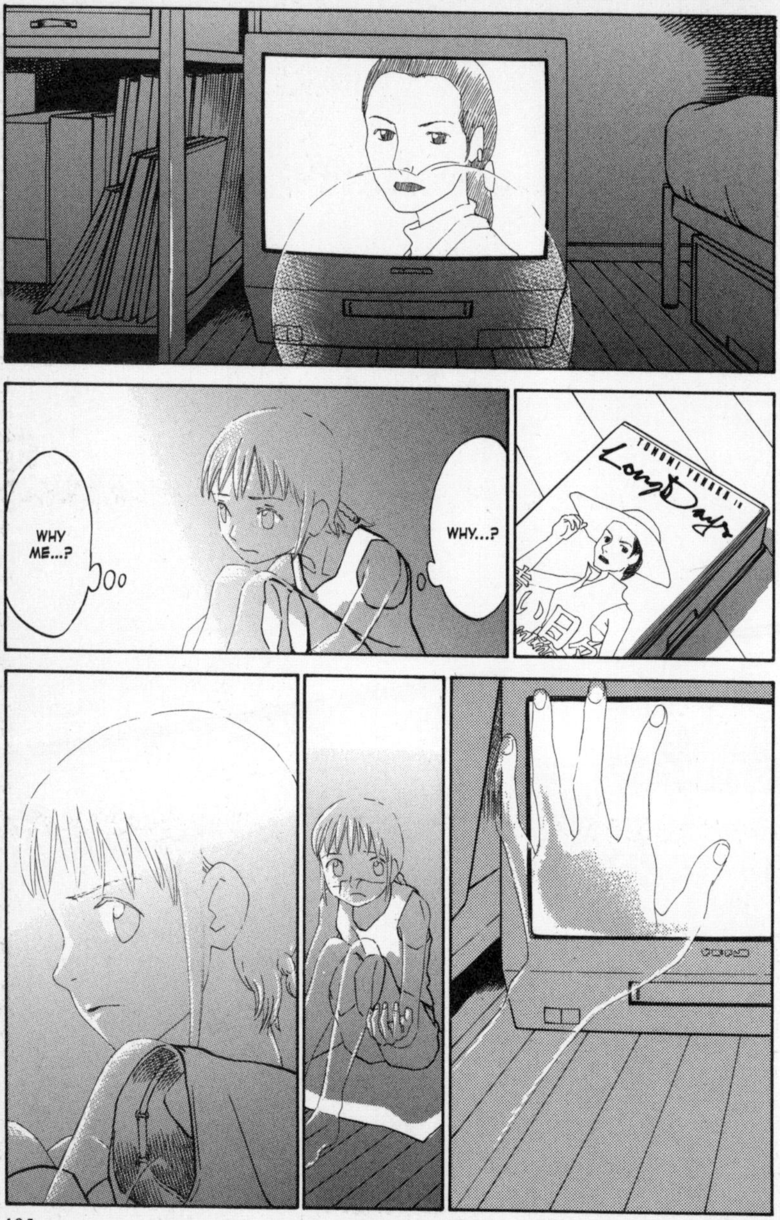
TOMOMI YANAKA in
Long Days
WHY...?
WHY ME...?

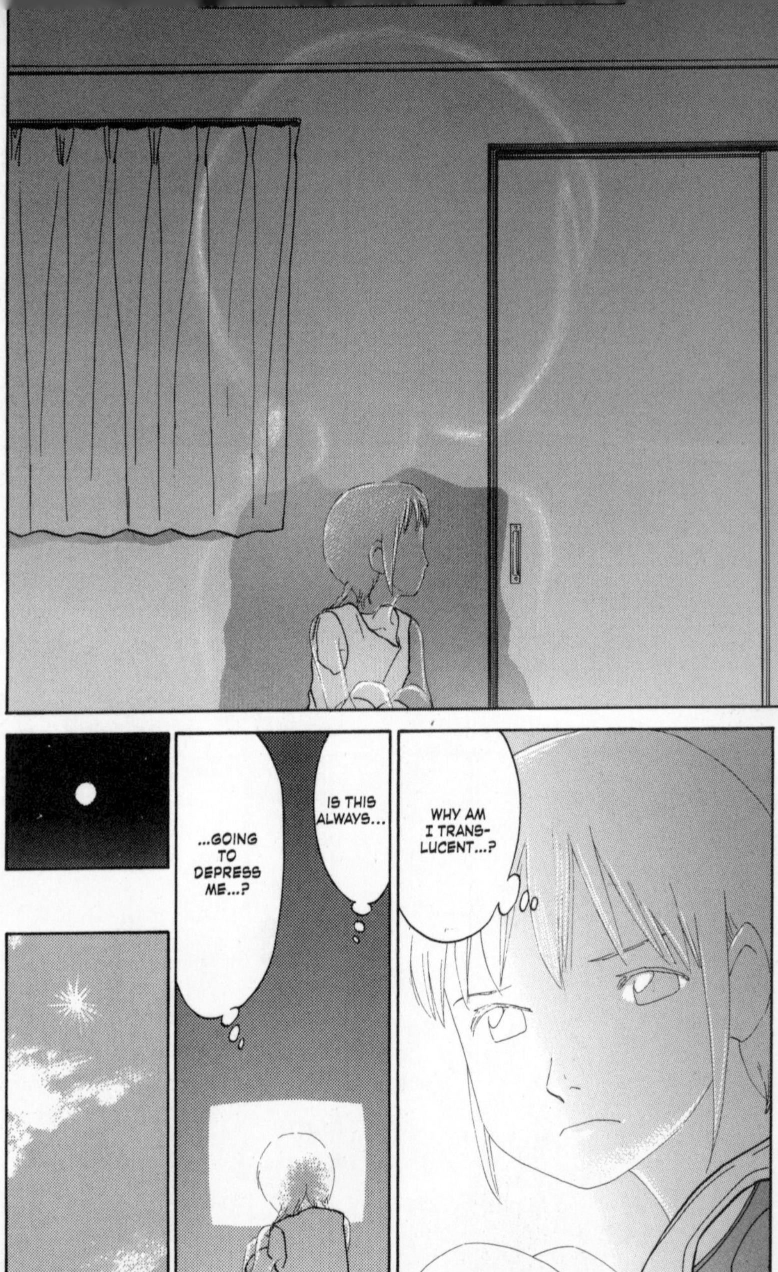
WHY AM I TRANS- LUCENT...?
IS THIS ALWAYS...
...GOING TO DEPRESS ME...?

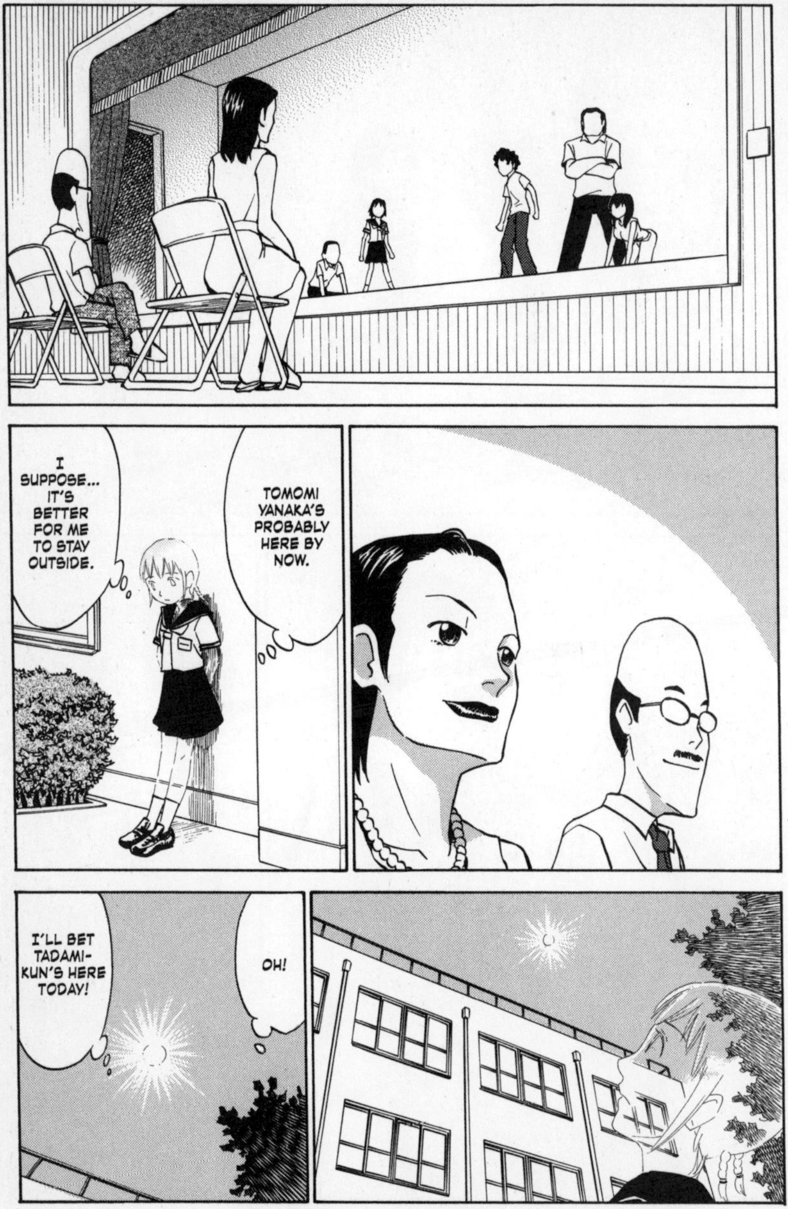
TOMOMI YANAKA'S PROBABLY HERE BY NOW.
I SUPPOSE... IT'S BETTER FOR ME TO STAY OUTSIDE.
OH!
I'LL BET TADAMI-KUN'S HERE TODAY!

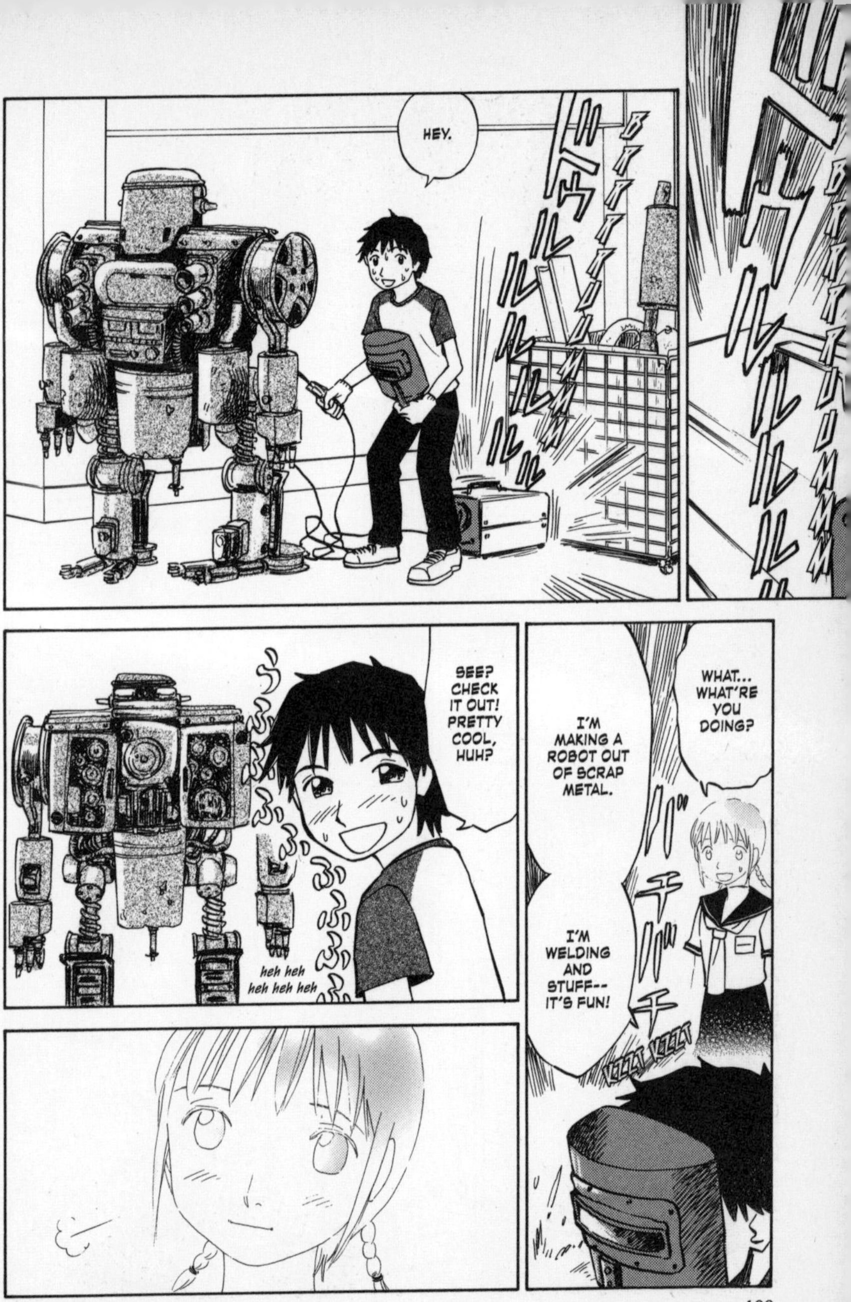
BRRRRUUMMM
HEY.
BRRRRRUUMMMM
WHAT... WHAT'RE YOU DOING?
I'M MAKING A ROBOT OUT OF SCRAP METAL.
I'M WELDING AND STUFF-- IT'S FUN!
KZZZT KZZZT
SEE? CHECK IT OUT! PRETTY COOL, HUH?
heh heh heh heh heh

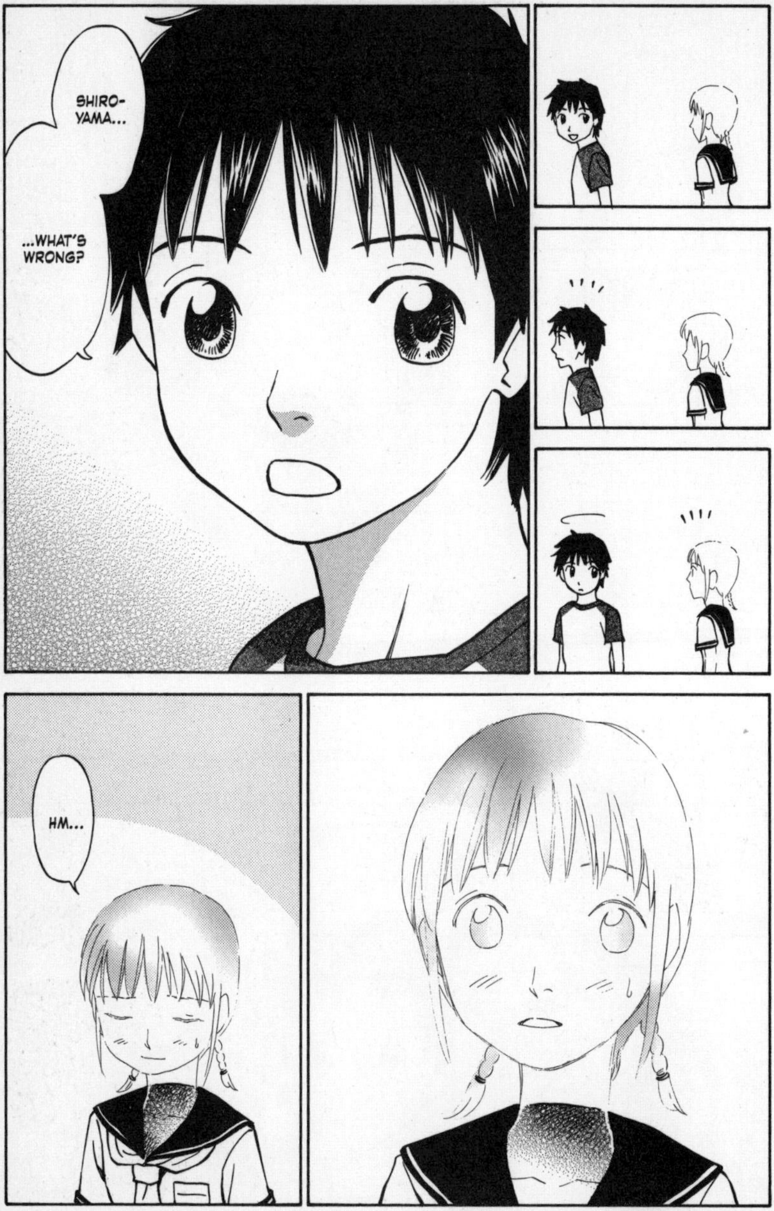
SHIRO-YAMA...
...WHAT'S WRONG?
HM...

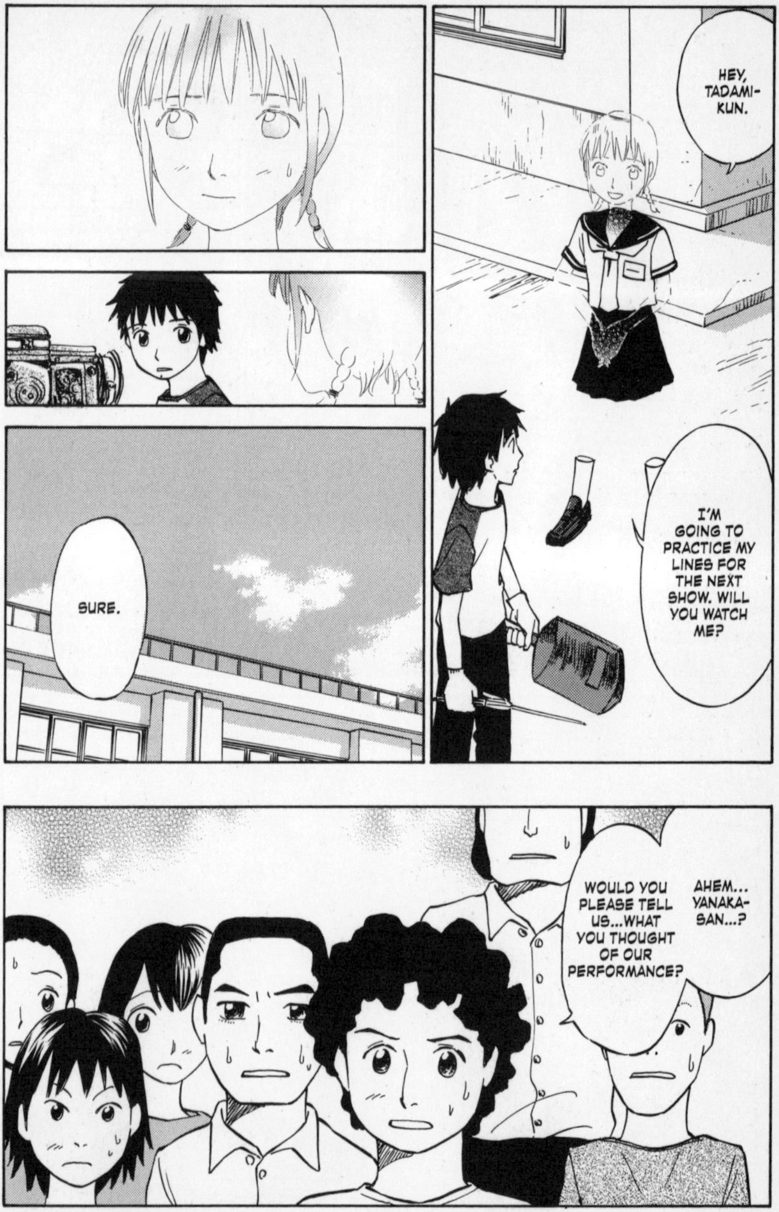
HEY, TADAMI-KUN.
I'M GOING TO PRACTICE MY LINES FOR THE NEXT SHOW. WILL YOU WATCH ME?
SURE.
AHEM... YANAKA-SAN...?
WOULD YOU PLEASE TELL US...WHAT YOU THOUGHT OF OUR PERFORMANCE?

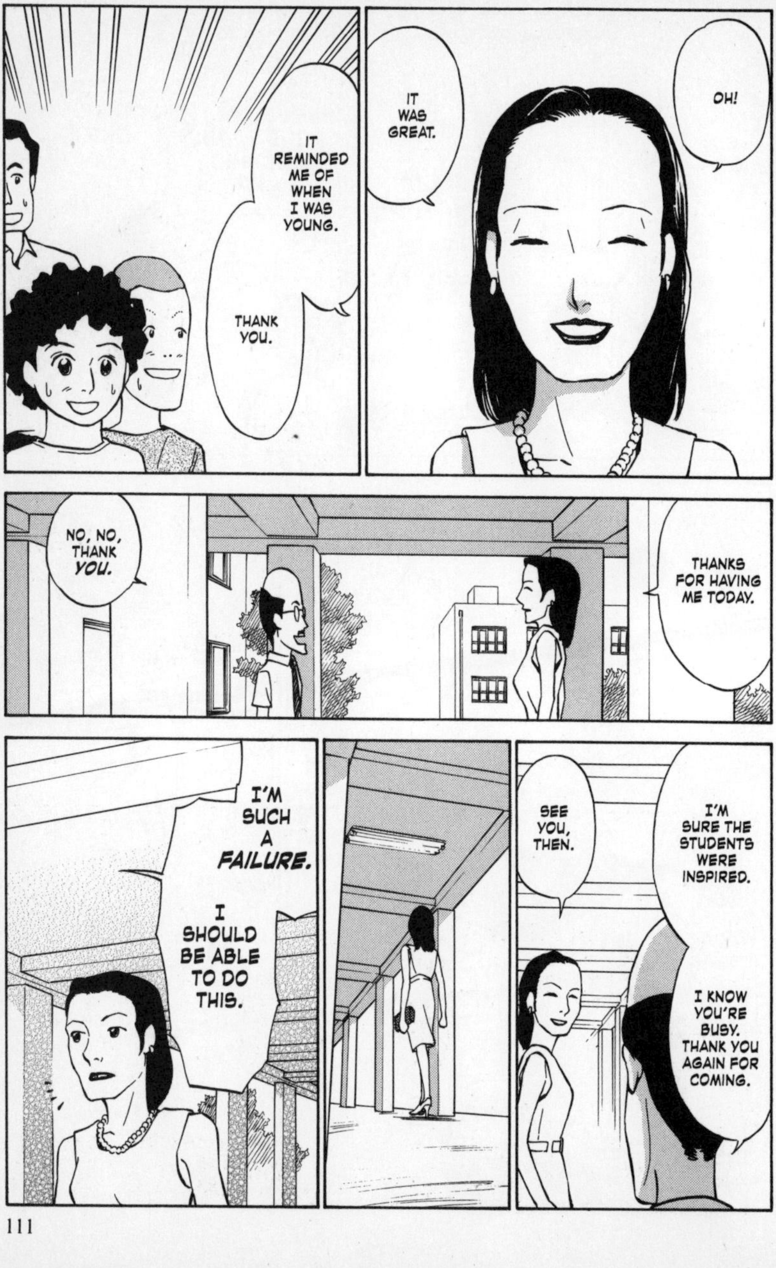
OH!
IT WAS GREAT.
IT REMINDED ME OF WHEN I WAS YOUNG.
THANK YOU.
THANKS FOR HAVING ME TODAY.
NO, NO, THANK *YOU.*
I'M SURE THE STUDENTS WERE INSPIRED.
I KNOW YOU'RE BUSY. THANK YOU AGAIN FOR COMING.
SEE YOU, THEN.
I'M SUCH A *FAILURE.*
I SHOULD BE ABLE TO DO THIS.

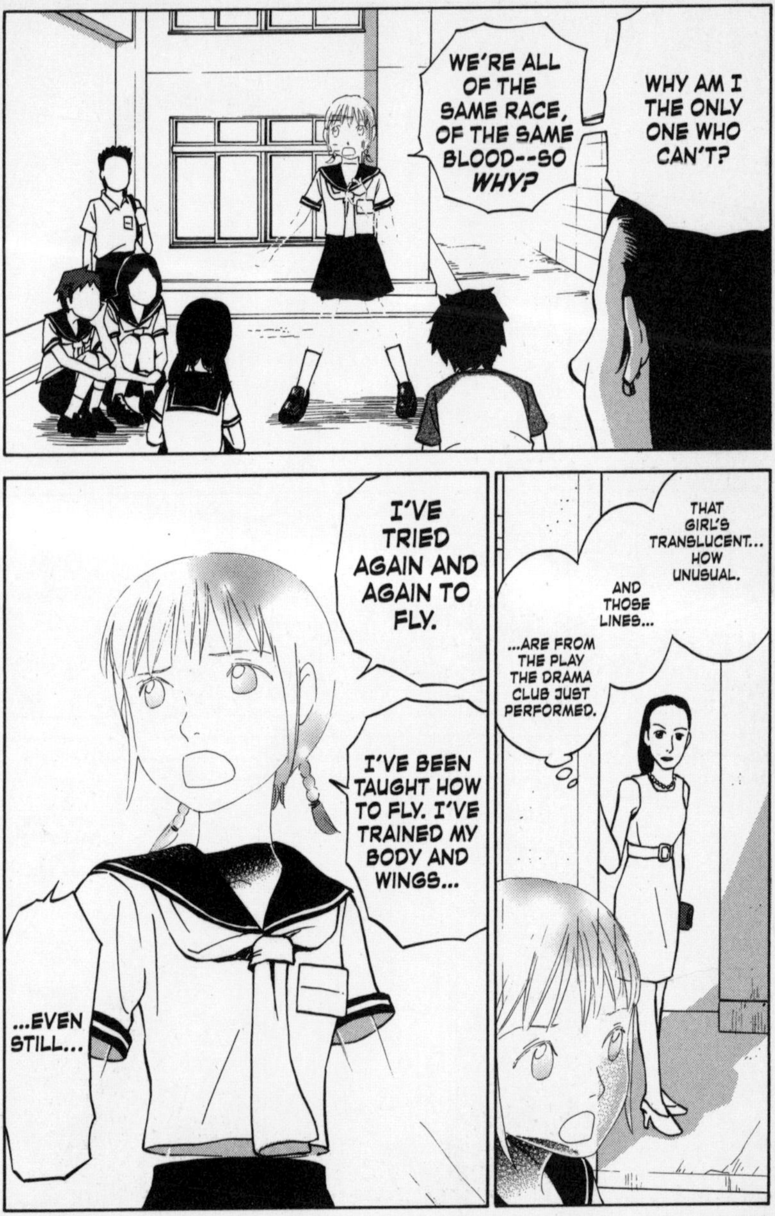
WE'RE ALL OF THE SAME RACE, OF THE SAME BLOOD--SO *WHY?*
WHY AM I THE ONLY ONE WHO CAN'T?
THAT GIRL'S TRANSLUCENT... HOW UNUSUAL.
AND THOSE LINES...
...ARE FROM THE PLAY THE DRAMA CLUB JUST PERFORMED.
I'VE TRIED AGAIN AND AGAIN TO FLY.
I'VE BEEN TAUGHT HOW TO FLY. I'VE TRAINED MY BODY AND WINGS...
...EVEN STILL...

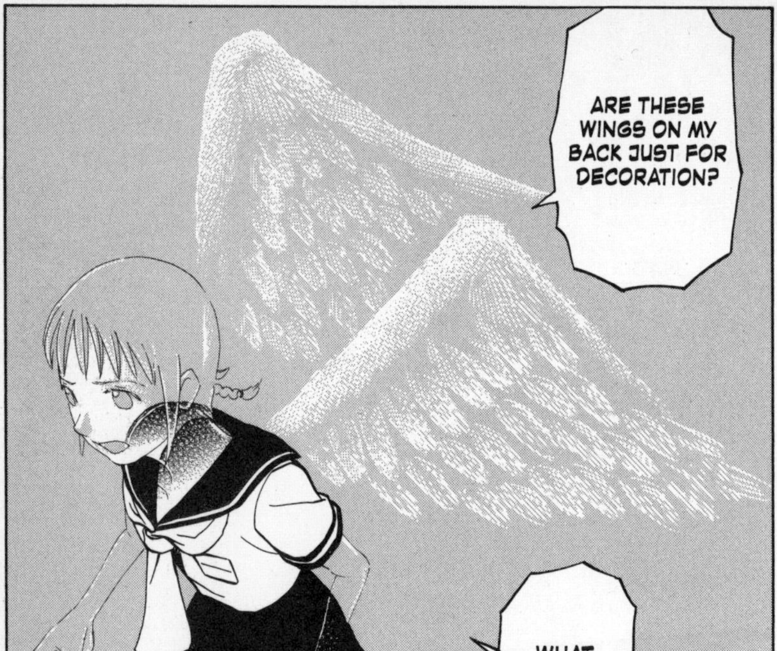
ARE THESE WINGS ON MY BACK JUST FOR DECORATION?
WHAT ARE THEY FOR?

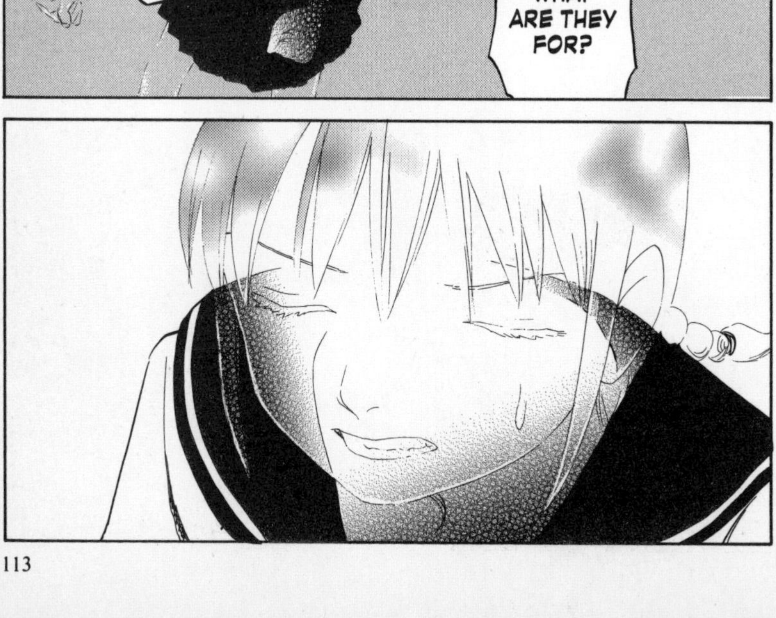

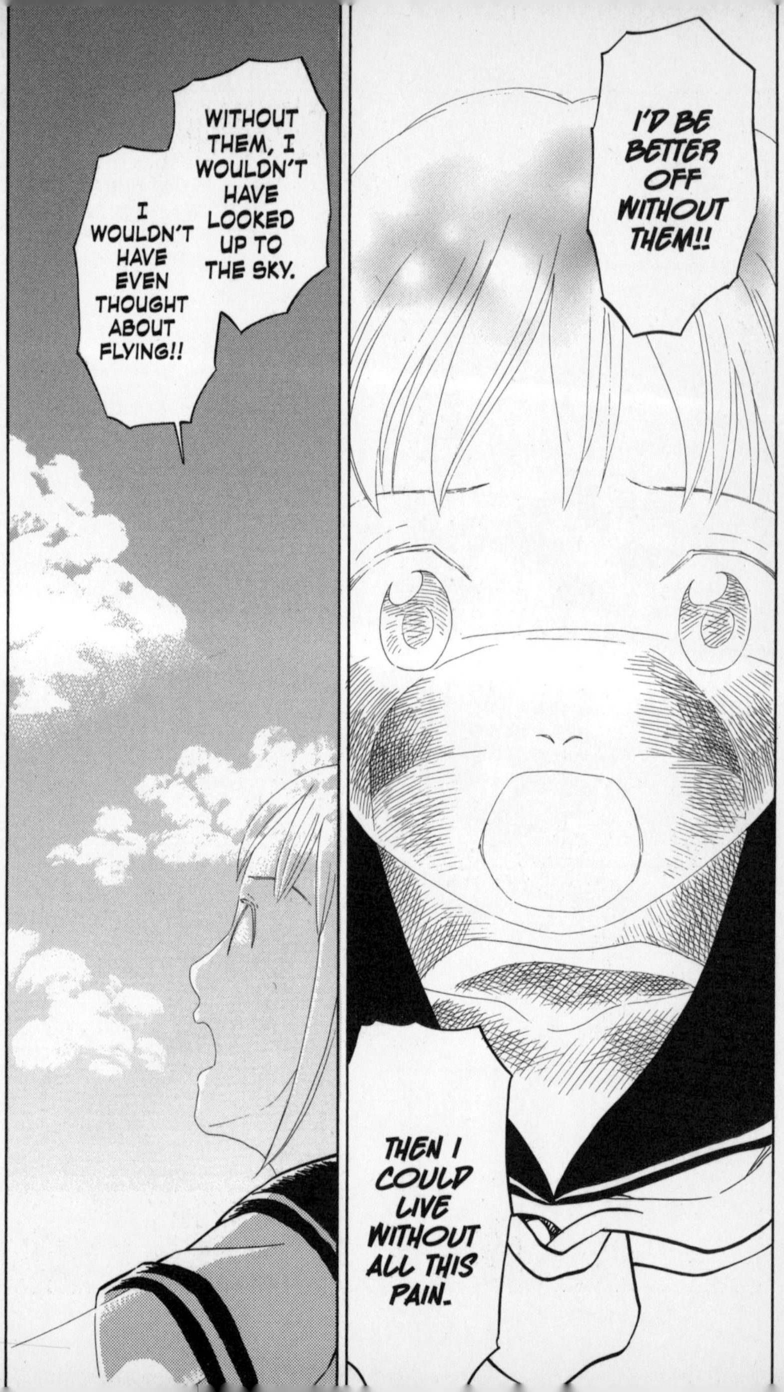
I'D BE BETTER OFF WITHOUT THEM!!
THEN I COULD LIVE WITHOUT ALL THIS PAIN.
WITHOUT THEM, I WOULDN'T HAVE LOOKED UP TO THE SKY.
I WOULDN'T HAVE EVEN THOUGHT ABOUT FLYING!!

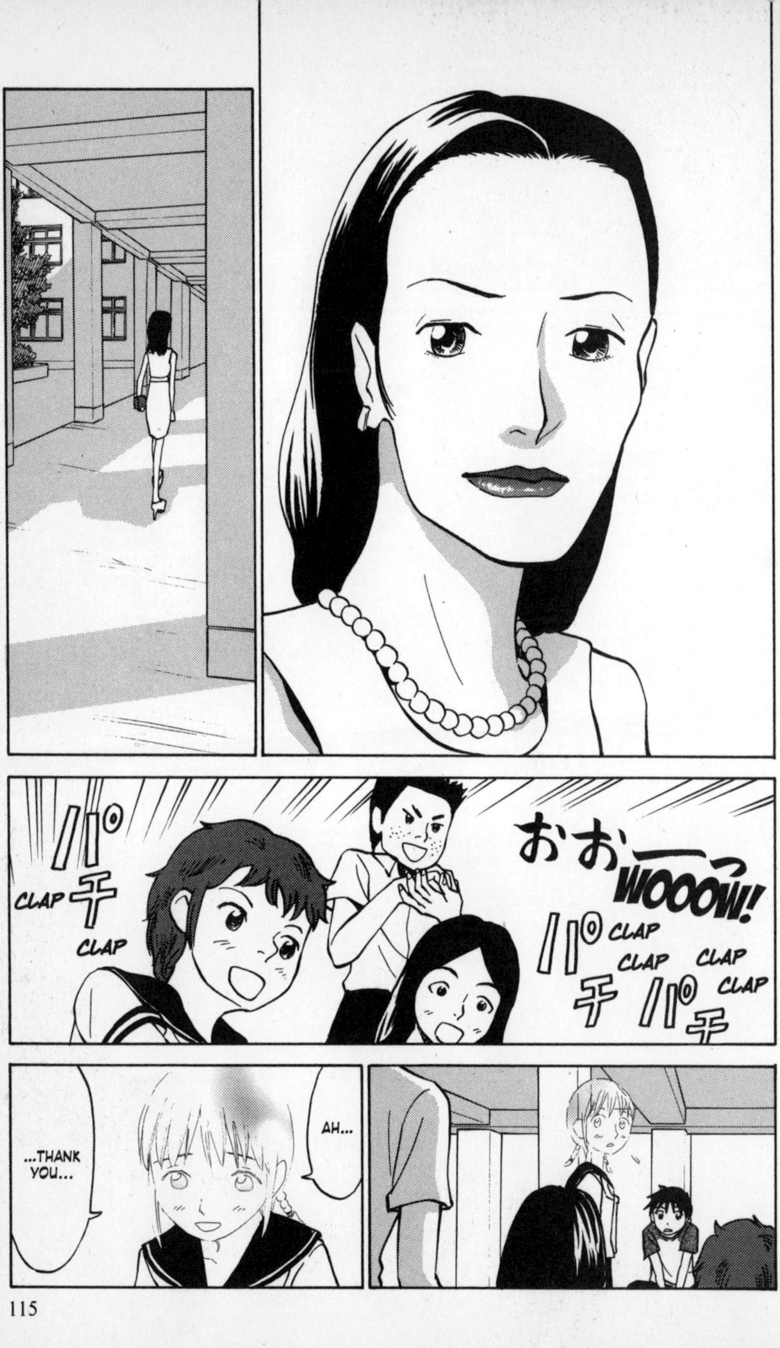
おおーーっ
WOOOW!
パチパチ
CLAP
CLAP
CLAP
CLAP
パチ
CLAP
CLAP
AH...
...THANK YOU...

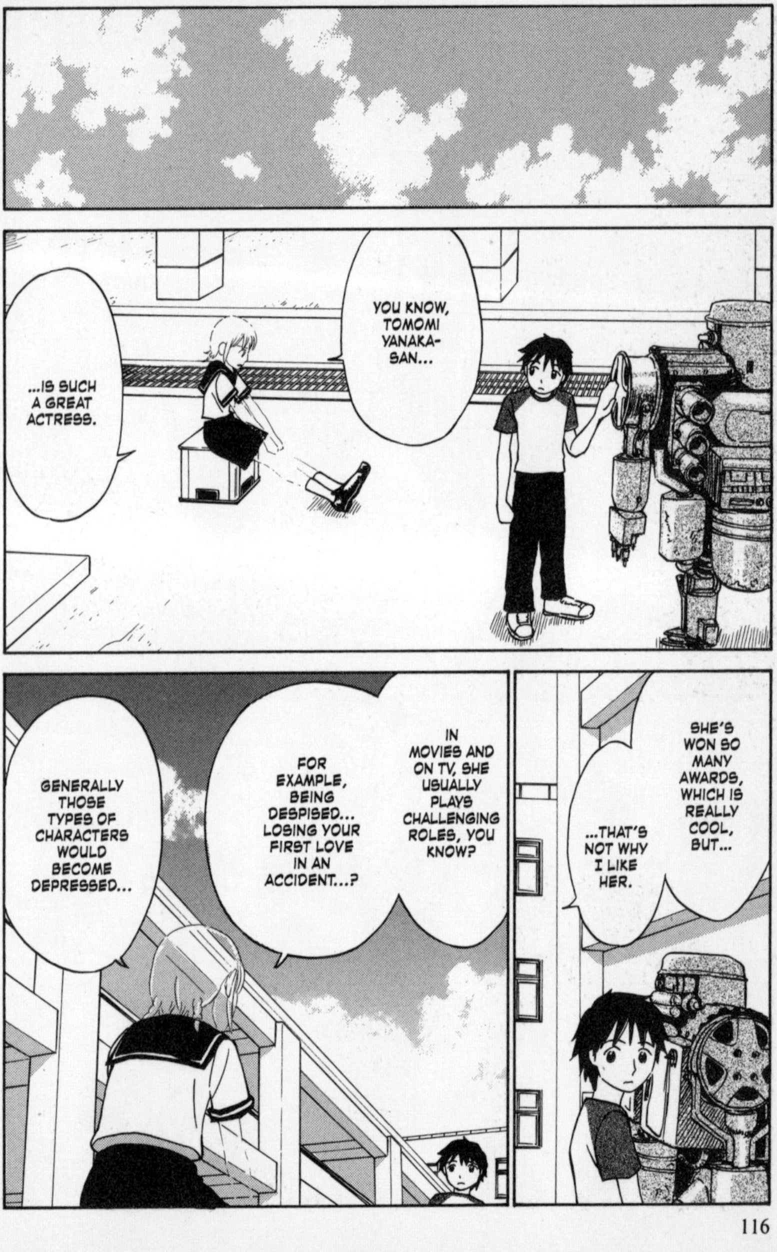
YOU KNOW, TOMOMI YANAKA-SAN...
...IS SUCH A GREAT ACTRESS.
SHE'S WON SO MANY AWARDS, WHICH IS REALLY COOL, BUT...
...THAT'S NOT WHY I LIKE HER.
IN MOVIES AND ON TV, SHE USUALLY PLAYS CHALLENGING ROLES, YOU KNOW?
FOR EXAMPLE, BEING DESPISED... LOSING YOUR FIRST LOVE IN AN ACCIDENT...?
GENERALLY THOSE TYPES OF CHARACTERS WOULD BECOME DEPRESSED...

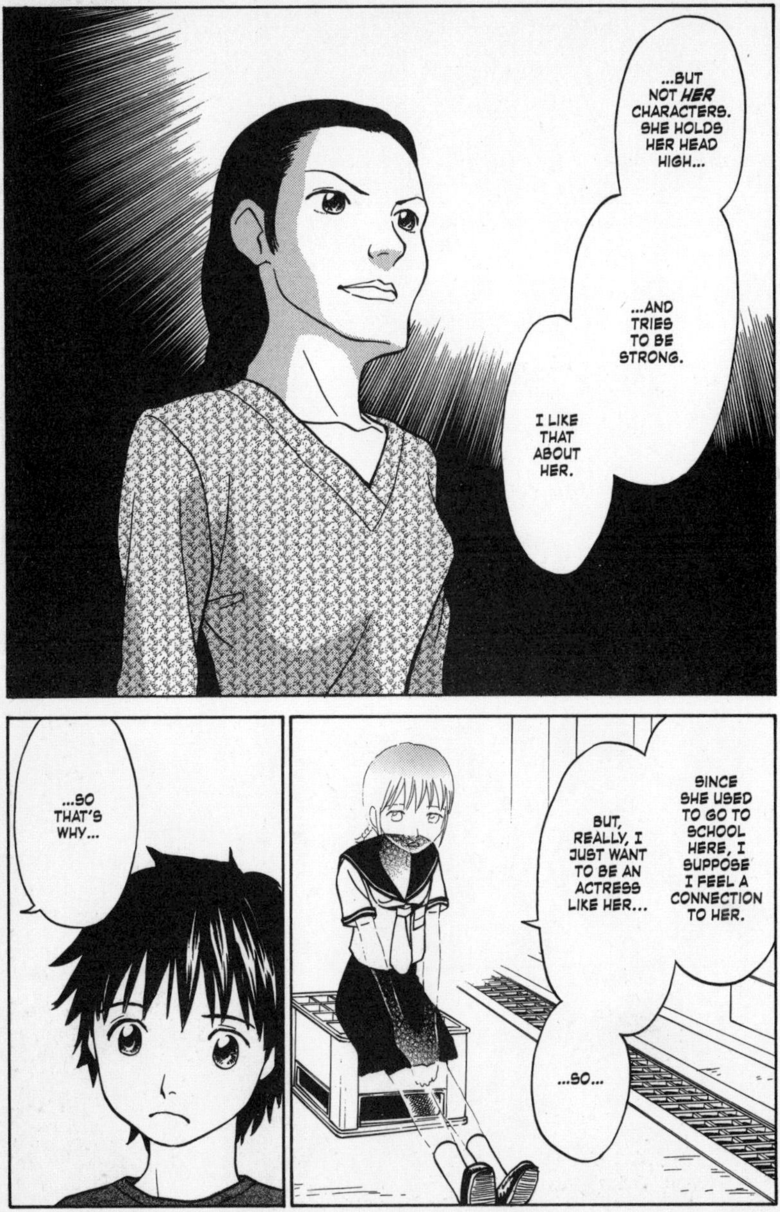
...BUT NOT *HER* CHARACTERS. SHE HOLDS HER HEAD HIGH...
...AND TRIES TO BE STRONG.
I LIKE THAT ABOUT HER.
SINCE SHE USED TO GO TO SCHOOL HERE, I SUPPOSE I FEEL A CONNECTION TO HER.
BUT, REALLY, I JUST WANT TO BE AN ACTRESS LIKE HER...
...SO...
...SO THAT'S WHY...

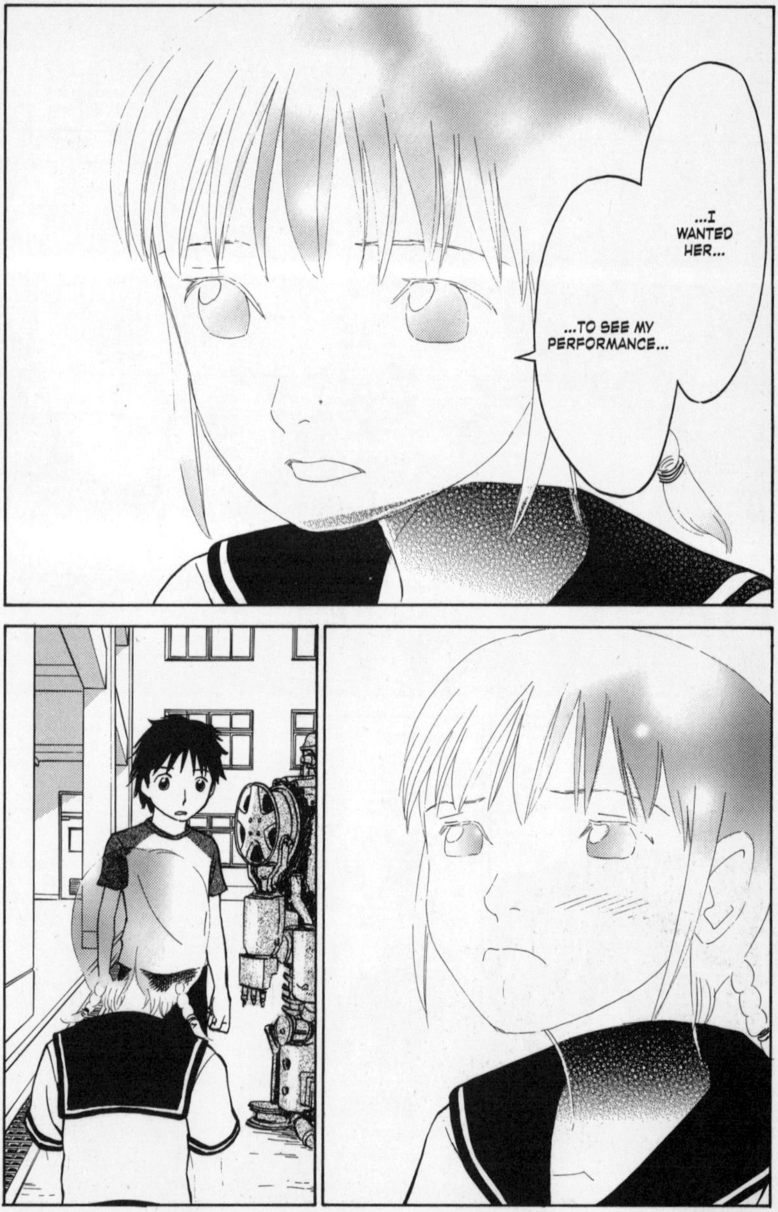
...I WANTED HER...
...TO SEE MY PERFORMANCE...

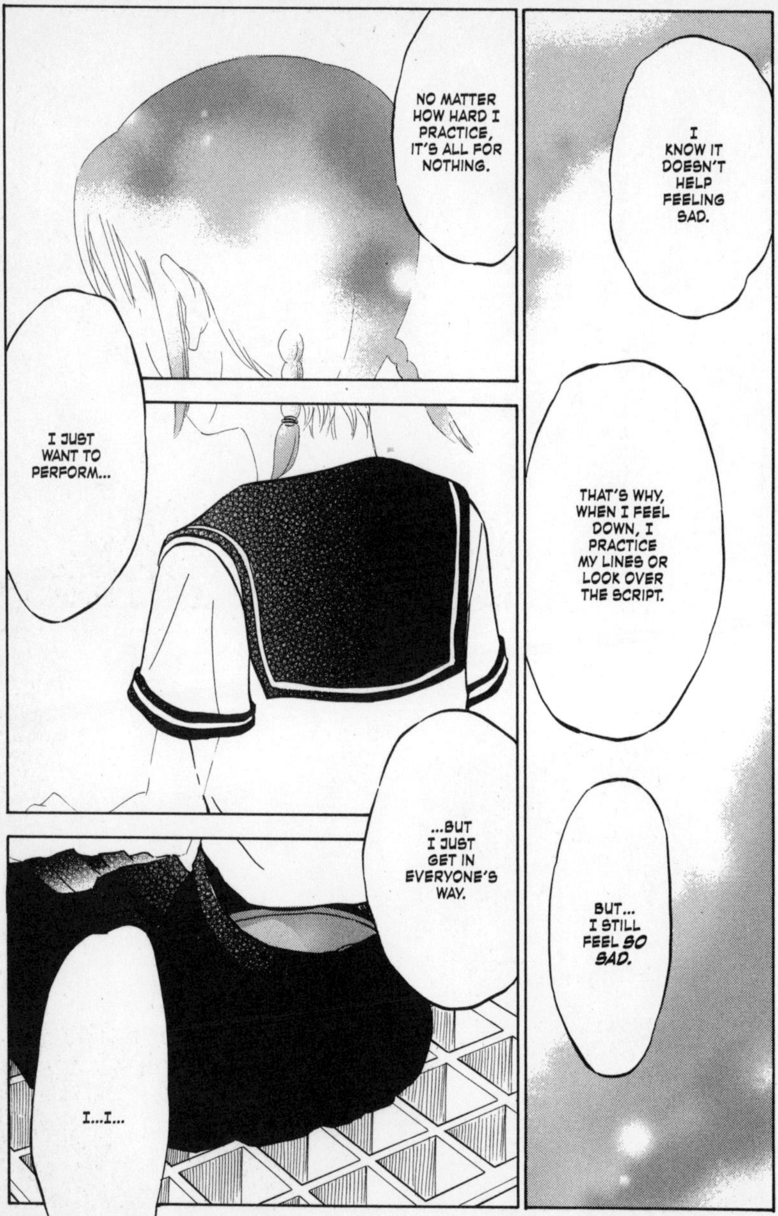
I KNOW IT DOESN'T HELP FEELING SAD.
THAT'S WHY, WHEN I FEEL DOWN, I PRACTICE MY LINES OR LOOK OVER THE SCRIPT.
BUT... I STILL FEEL *SO SAD.*
NO MATTER HOW HARD I PRACTICE, IT'S ALL FOR NOTHING.
I JUST WANT TO PERFORM...
...BUT I JUST GET IN EVERYONE'S WAY.
I...I...

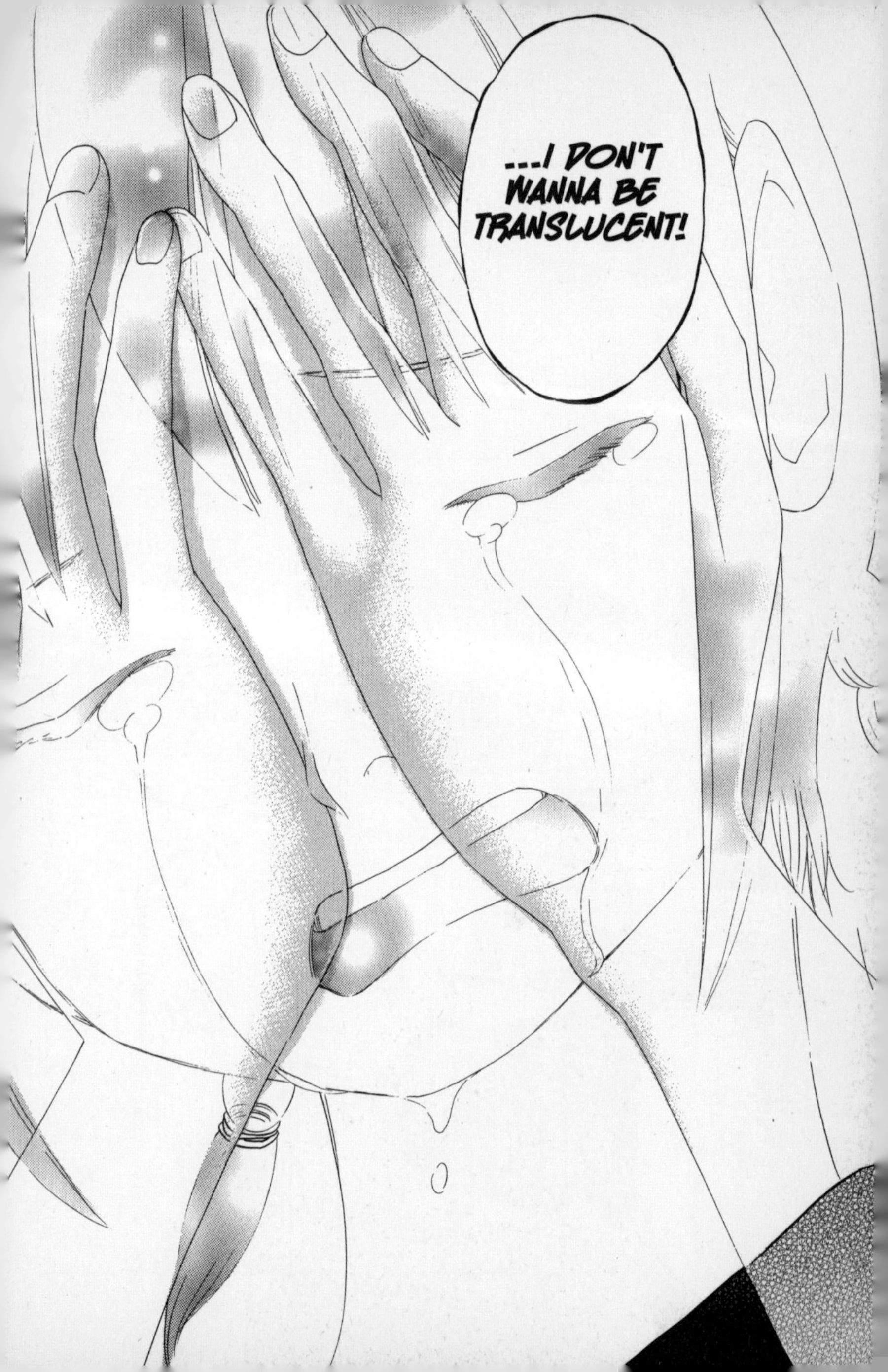
...I DON'T WANNA BE TRANSLUCENT!

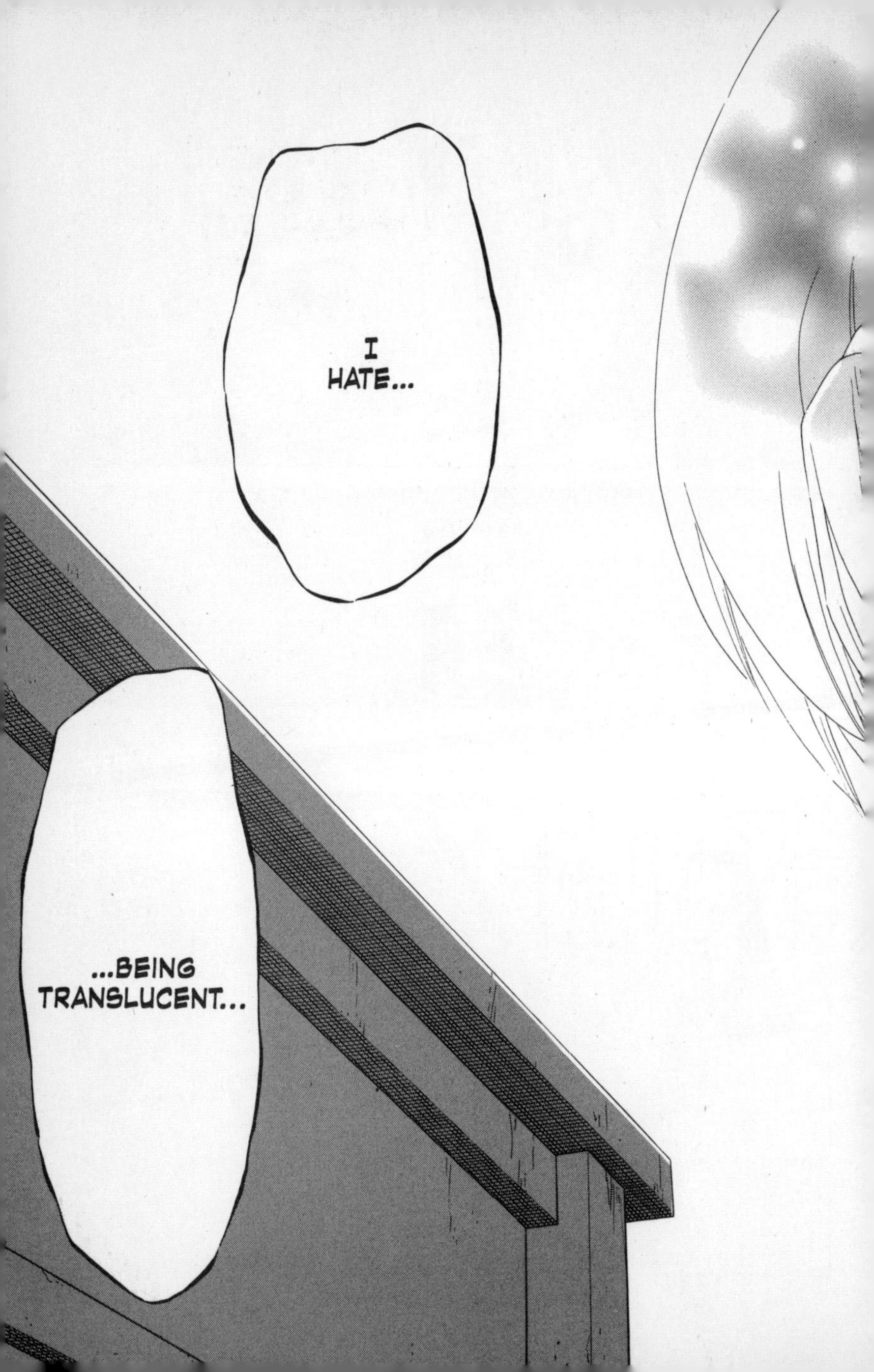
I HATE...
...BEING TRANSLUCENT...

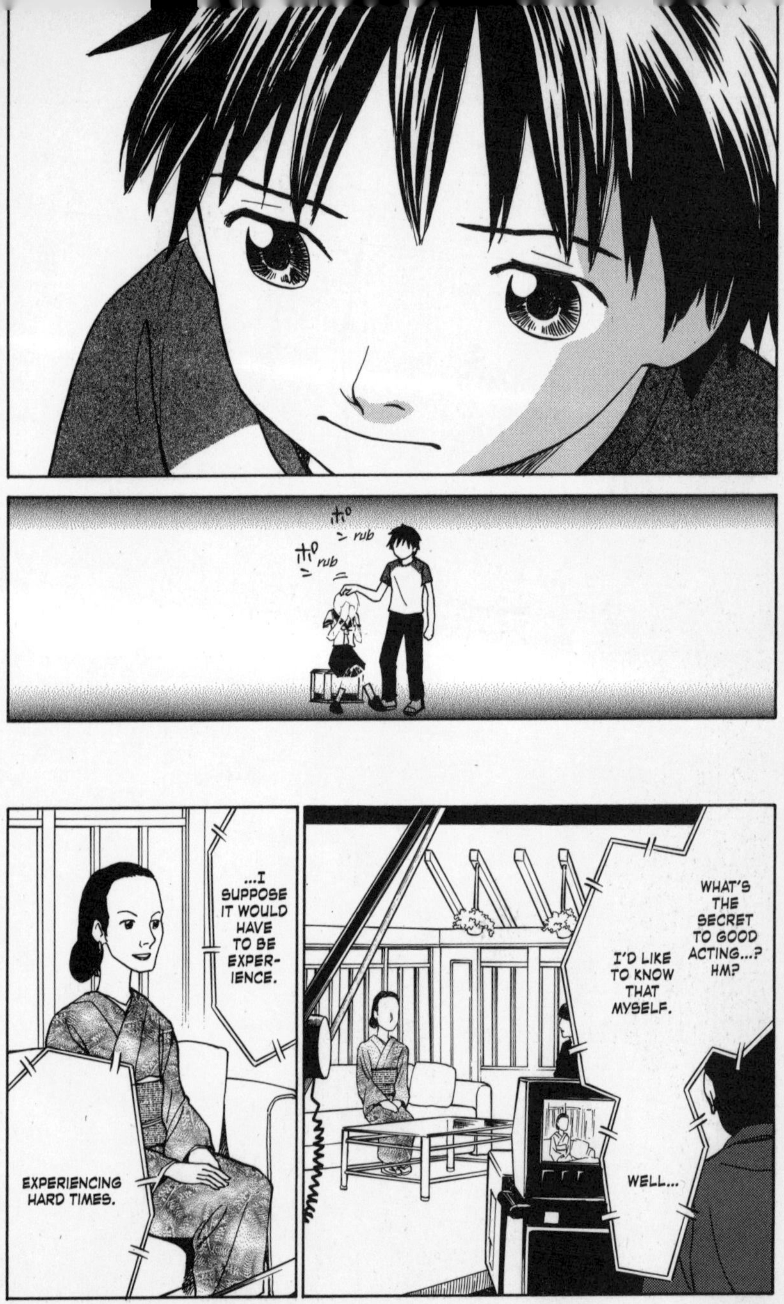
ポ rub
ポ rub
WHAT'S THE SECRET TO GOOD ACTING...? HM?
I'D LIKE TO KNOW THAT MYSELF.
WELL...
...I SUPPOSE IT WOULD HAVE TO BE EXPERIENCE.
EXPERIENCING HARD TIMES.

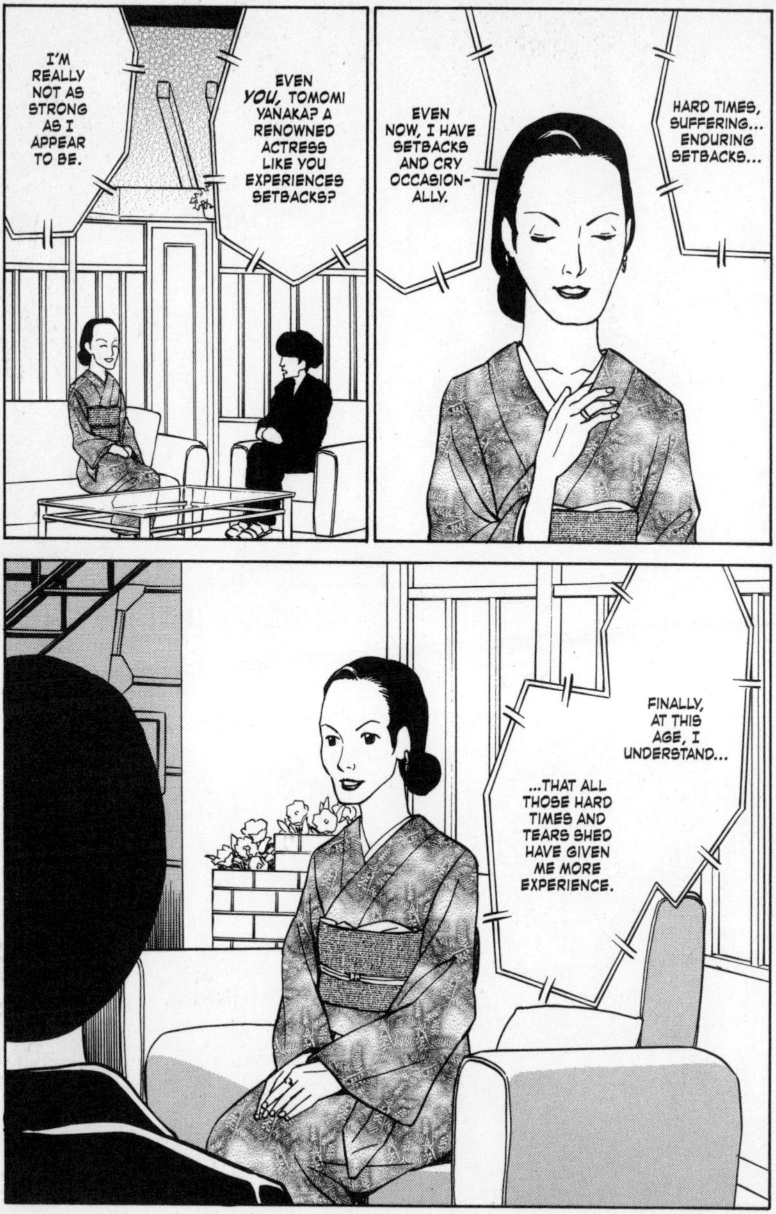
I'M REALLY NOT AS STRONG AS I APPEAR TO BE.
EVEN *YOU,* TOMOMI YANAKA? A RENOWNED ACTRESS LIKE YOU EXPERIENCES SETBACKS?
EVEN NOW, I HAVE SETBACKS AND CRY OCCASION-ALLY.
HARD TIMES, SUFFERING... ENDURING SETBACKS...
FINALLY, AT THIS AGE, I UNDERSTAND...
...THAT ALL THOSE HARD TIMES AND TEARS SHED HAVE GIVEN ME MORE EXPERIENCE.

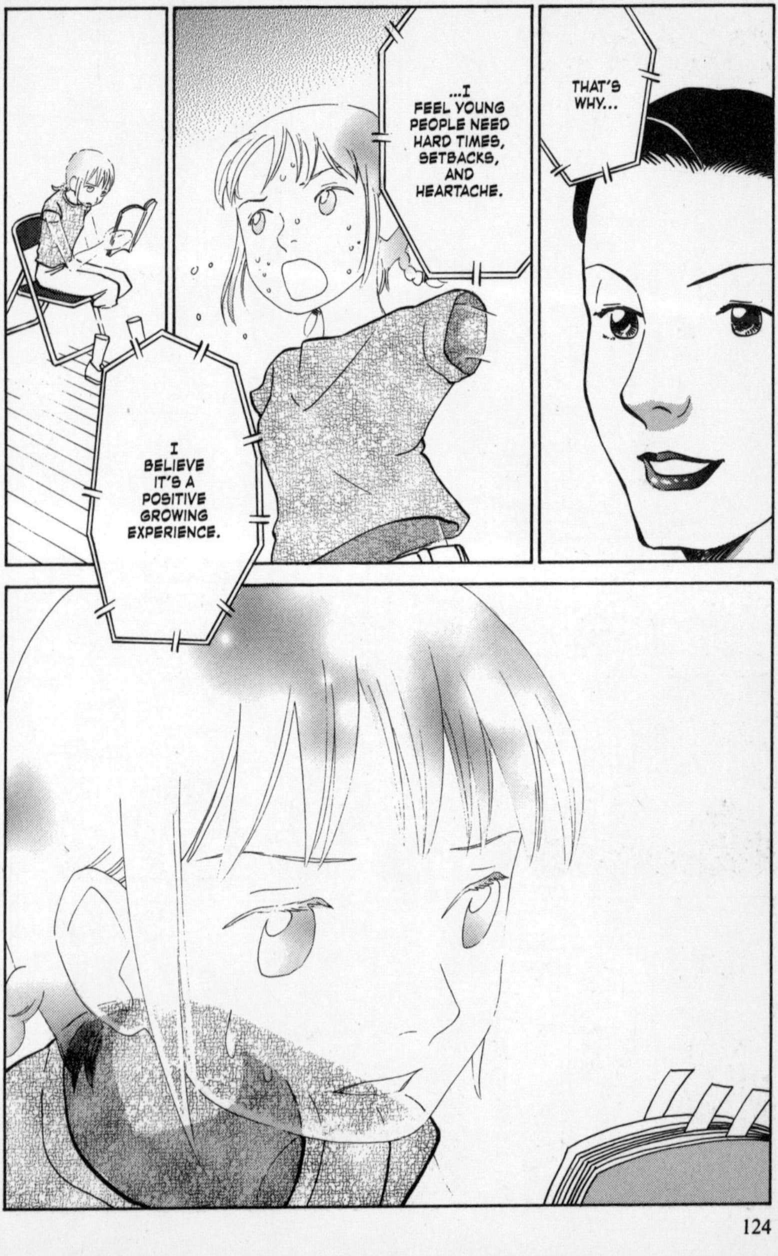
THAT'S WHY...
...I FEEL YOUNG PEOPLE NEED HARD TIMES, SETBACKS, AND HEARTACHE.
I BELIEVE IT'S A POSITIVE GROWING EXPERIENCE.

OMAKE

ONE-PAGE BONUS MANGA #3

3

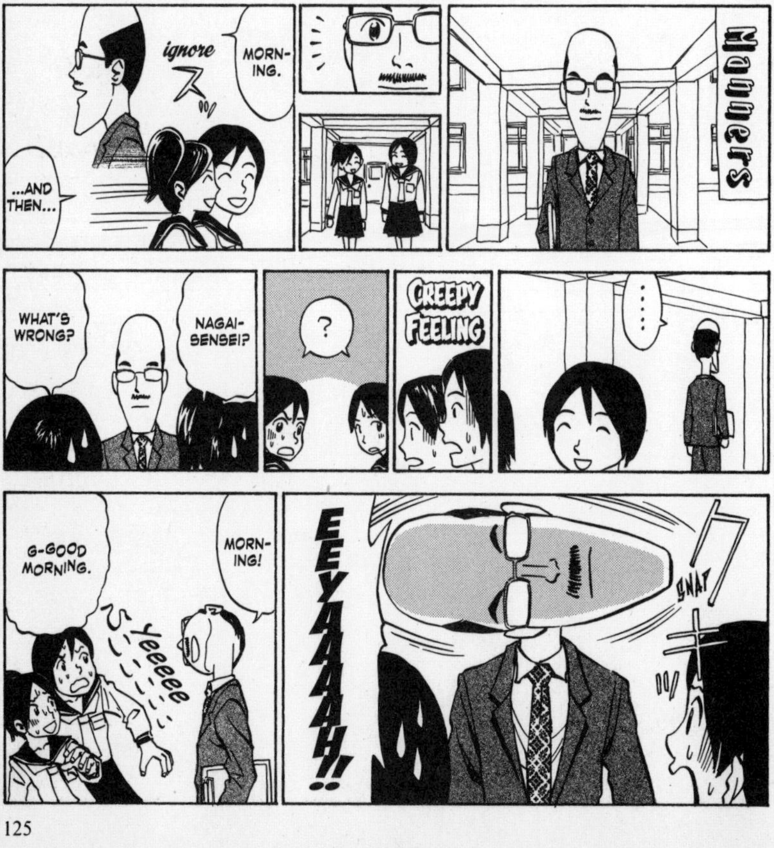

Manners
MORN-ING.
ignore
...AND THEN...
.....
CREEPY FEELING
?
NAGAI-SENSEI?
WHAT'S WRONG?
EEYAAAAAH!!
SNAP
MORN-ING!
G-GOOD MORNING.
Yeeeeee

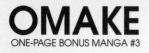

OMAKE

ONE-PAGE BONUS MANGA #4

4

Made with Love
MOR... NING...
ふあ～
Aaahh!
HEY, YOU'RE UP EARLY.
IS THAT DAD'S BENTO LUNCH?
IT IS.
WOULD YOU SPRINKLE ON SOME *FURIKAKE* AND WRAP IT UP?
YEAH, SURE.
......
FURI-KAKE ISN'T VERY CREA-TIVE.
チャッ
snip
Seaweed
会社
HEY, TADAMI-SAN? IS THAT A BENTO MADE WITH *LOVE?*
HEH HEH!
びくっ
startle
WHAT'S THIS?
ROASTED SEAWEED ART?

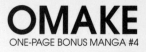

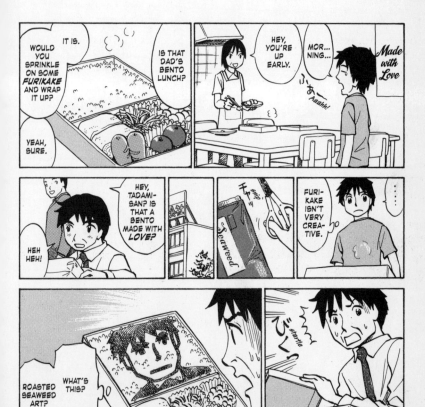

PART 17 Shizuka Becomes a Ghost

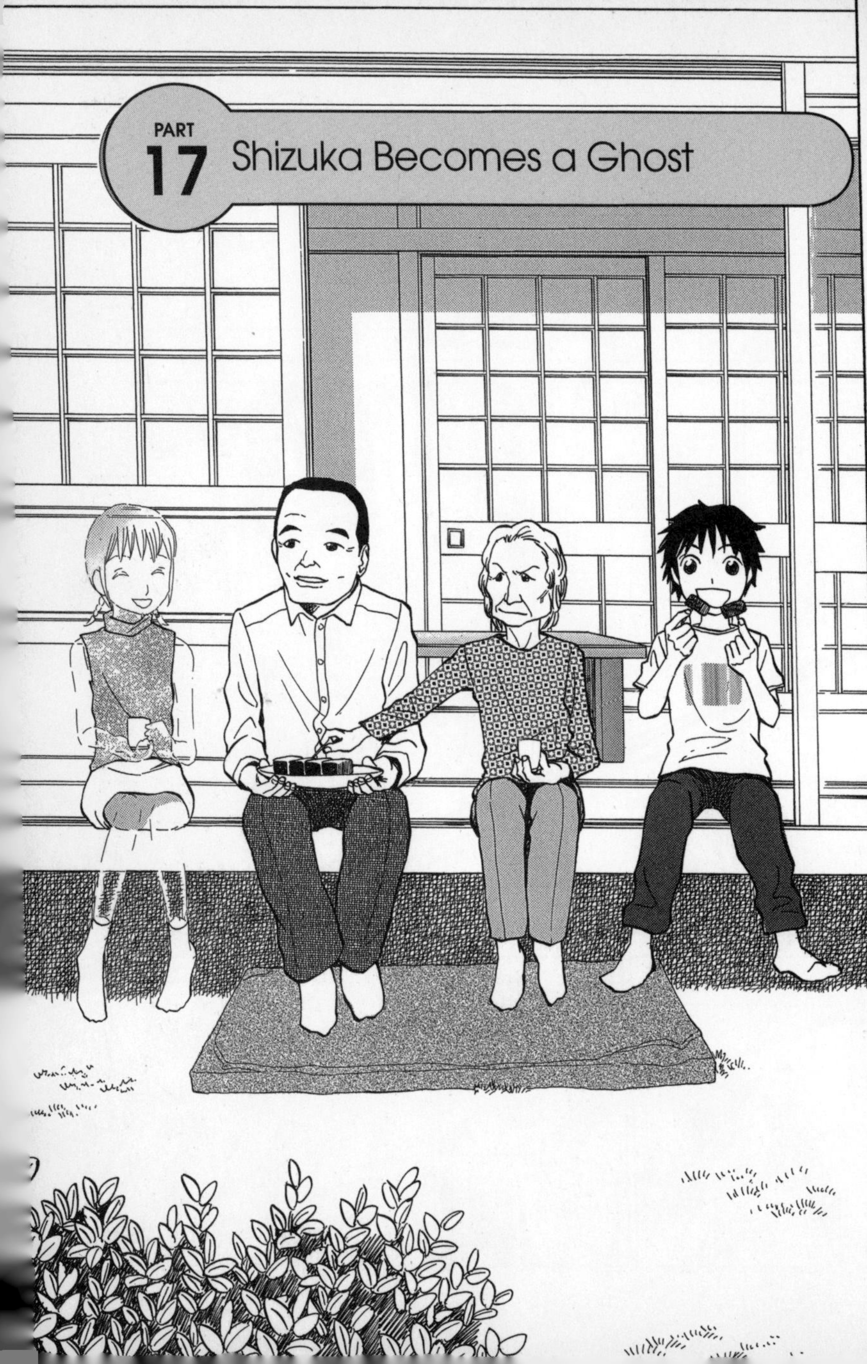

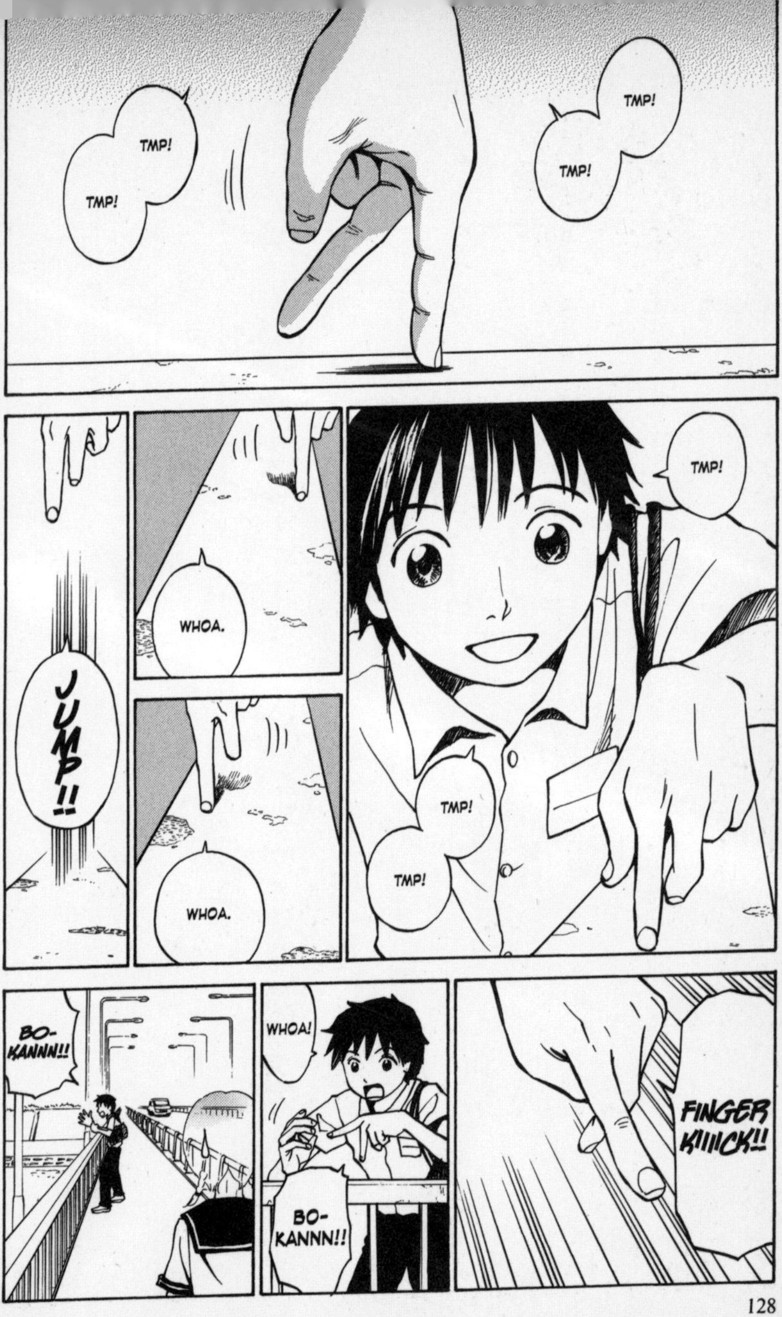
TMP! TMP!
TMP! TMP!
TMP!
TMP! TMP!
WHOA.
WHOA.
JUMP!!
FINGER KIIIICK!!
WHOA!
BO-KANNN!!
BO-KANNN!!

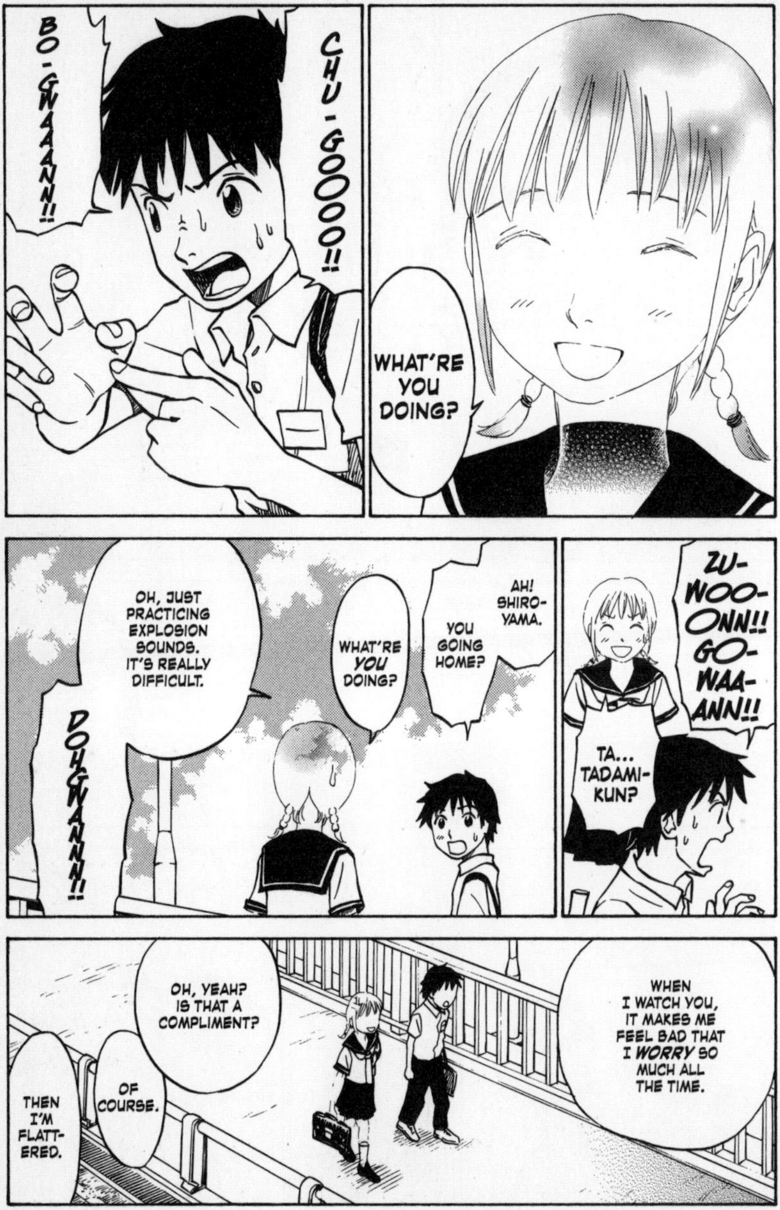
WHAT'RE YOU DOING?
CHU-GOOOOO!!
BO-GWAAAANN!!
ZU-WOOO-ONN!! GO-WAA-ANN!!
TA... TADAMI-KUN?
AH! SHIRO-YAMA.
YOU GOING HOME?
WHAT'RE *YOU* DOING?
OH, JUST PRACTICING EXPLOSION SOUNDS. IT'S REALLY DIFFICULT.
DOHGWANNN!!
WHEN I WATCH YOU, IT MAKES ME FEEL BAD THAT I *WORRY* SO MUCH ALL THE TIME.
OH, YEAH? IS THAT A COMPLIMENT?
OF COURSE.
THEN I'M FLATT-ERED.

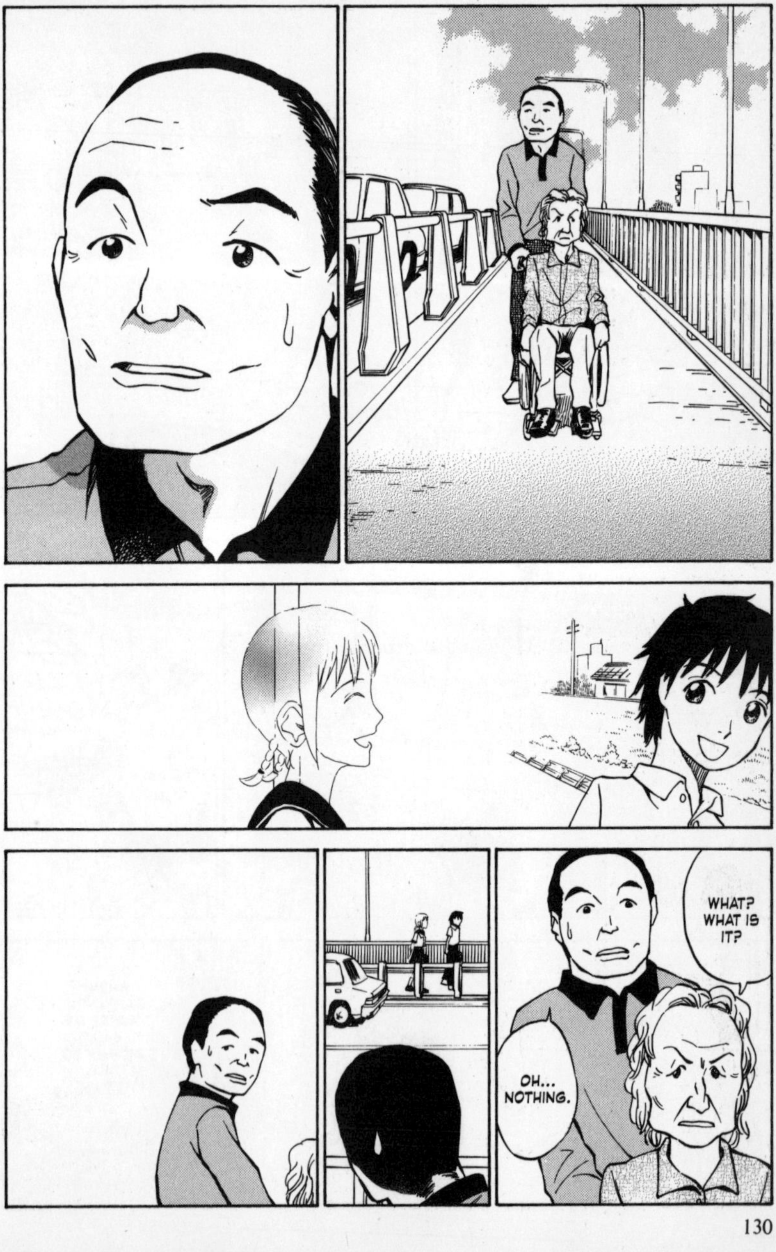
WHAT? WHAT IS IT?
OH... NOTHING.

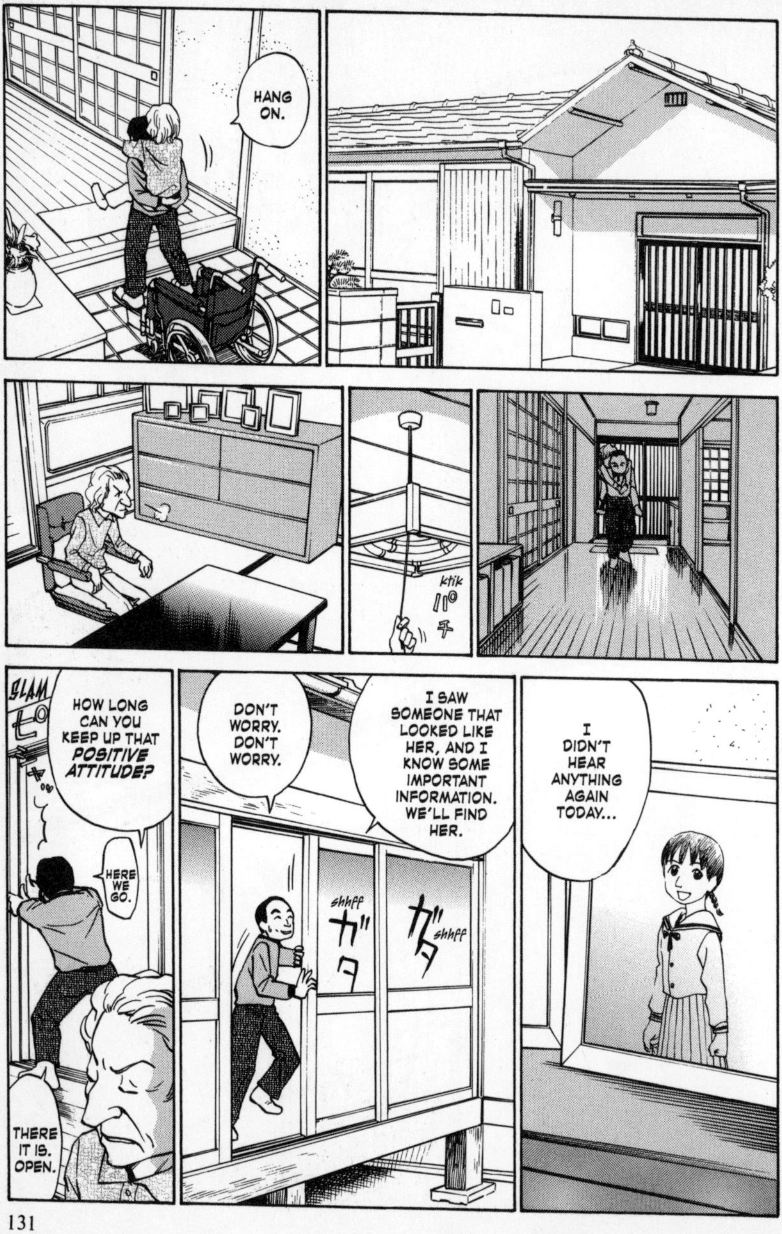
HANG ON.
ktik
パチ
I DIDN'T HEAR ANYTHING AGAIN TODAY...
I SAW SOMEONE THAT LOOKED LIKE HER, AND I KNOW SOME IMPORTANT INFORMATION. WE'LL FIND HER.
DON'T WORRY. DON'T WORRY.
shhff
ガタ
shhff
ガタ
SLAM
HOW LONG CAN YOU KEEP UP THAT *POSITIVE ATTITUDE?*
HERE WE GO.
THERE IT IS. OPEN.

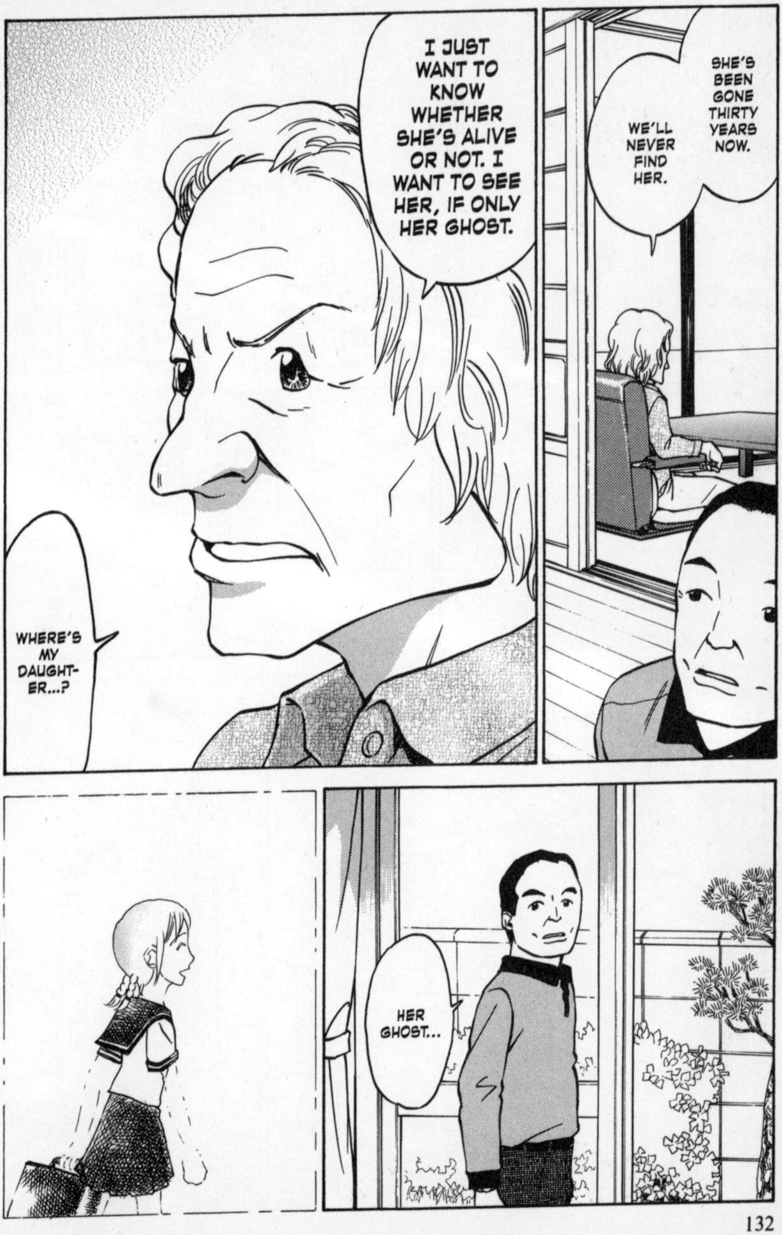
SHE'S BEEN GONE THIRTY YEARS NOW.
WE'LL NEVER FIND HER.
I JUST WANT TO KNOW WHETHER SHE'S ALIVE OR NOT. I WANT TO SEE HER, IF ONLY HER GHOST.
WHERE'S MY DAUGHTER...?
HER GHOST...

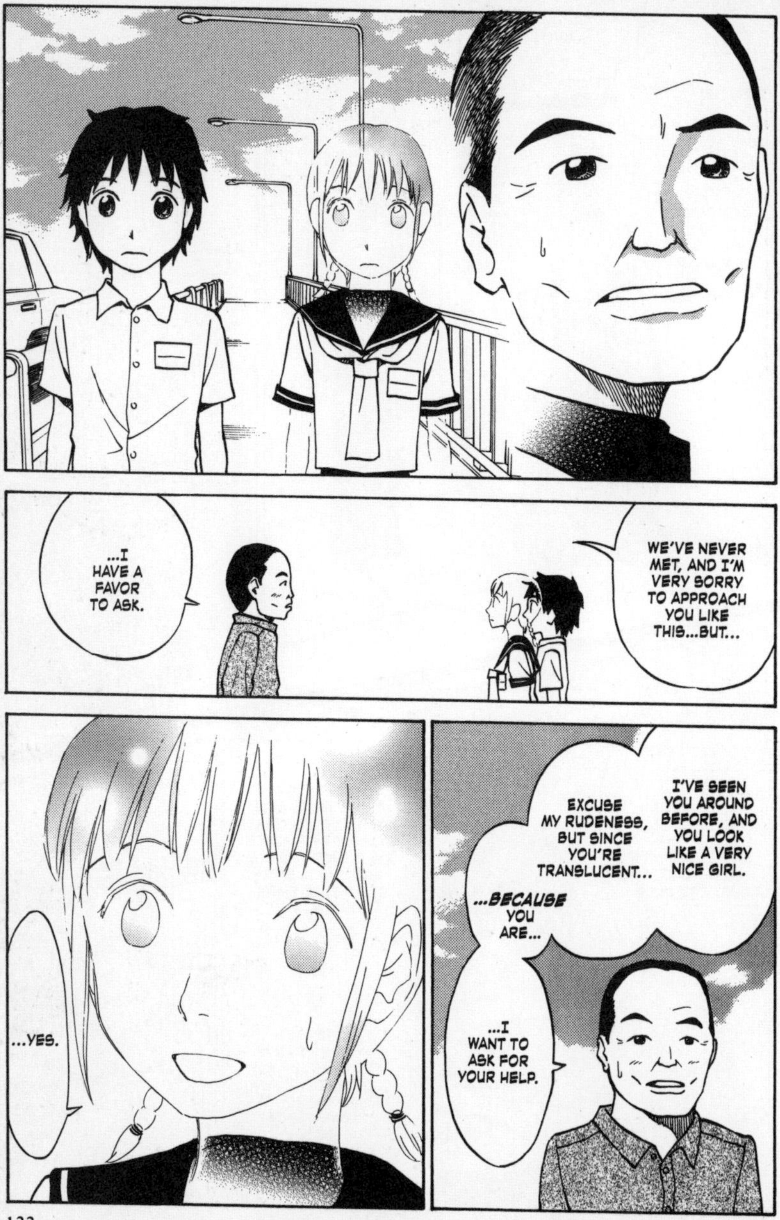
WE'VE NEVER MET, AND I'M VERY SORRY TO APPROACH YOU LIKE THIS...BUT...
...I HAVE A FAVOR TO ASK.
I'VE SEEN YOU AROUND BEFORE, AND YOU LOOK LIKE A VERY NICE GIRL.
EXCUSE MY RUDENESS, BUT SINCE YOU'RE TRANSLUCENT...
...*BECAUSE* YOU ARE...
...I WANT TO ASK FOR YOUR HELP.
...YES.

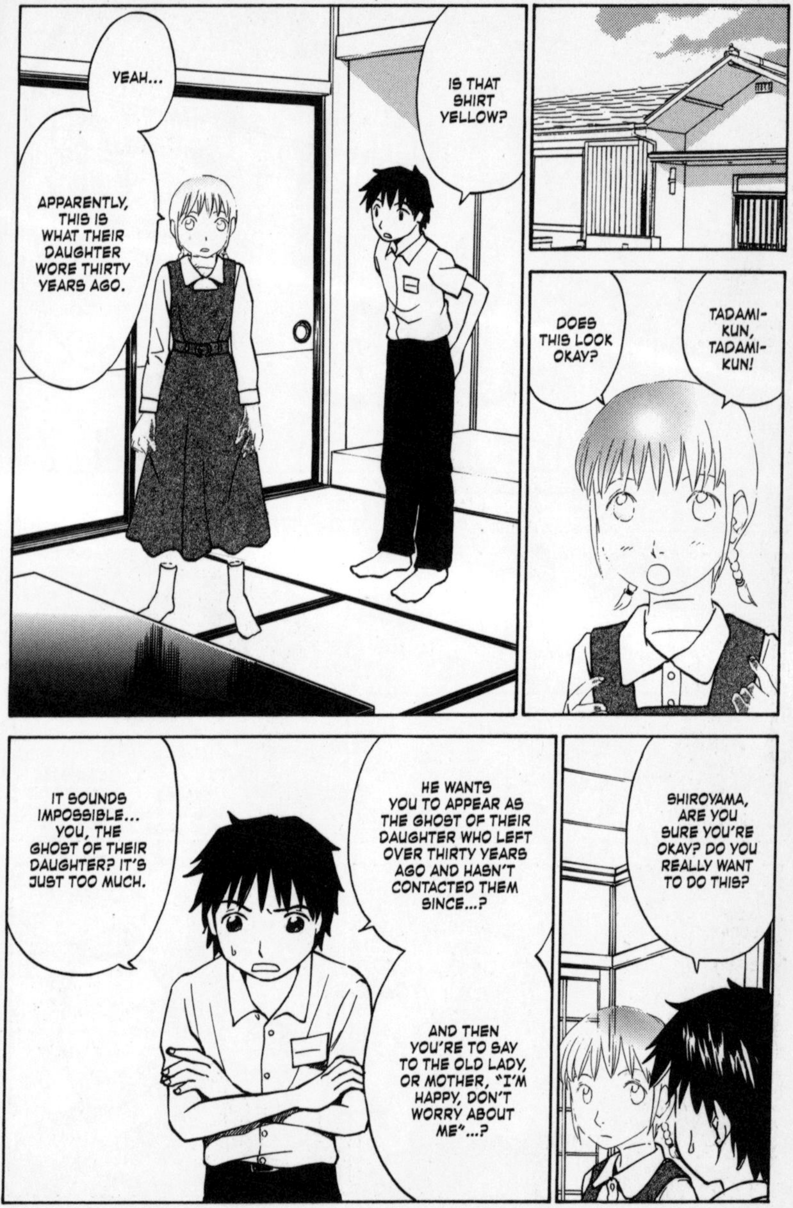
TADAMI-KUN, TADAMI-KUN!
DOES THIS LOOK OKAY?
IS THAT SHIRT YELLOW?
YEAH...
APPARENTLY, THIS IS WHAT THEIR DAUGHTER WORE THIRTY YEARS AGO.
SHIROYAMA, ARE YOU SURE YOU'RE OKAY? DO YOU REALLY WANT TO DO THIS?
HE WANTS YOU TO APPEAR AS THE GHOST OF THEIR DAUGHTER WHO LEFT OVER THIRTY YEARS AGO AND HASN'T CONTACTED THEM SINCE...?
AND THEN YOU'RE TO SAY TO THE OLD LADY, OR MOTHER, "I'M HAPPY, DON'T WORRY ABOUT ME"...?
IT SOUNDS IMPOSSIBLE... YOU, THE GHOST OF THEIR DAUGHTER? IT'S JUST TOO MUCH.

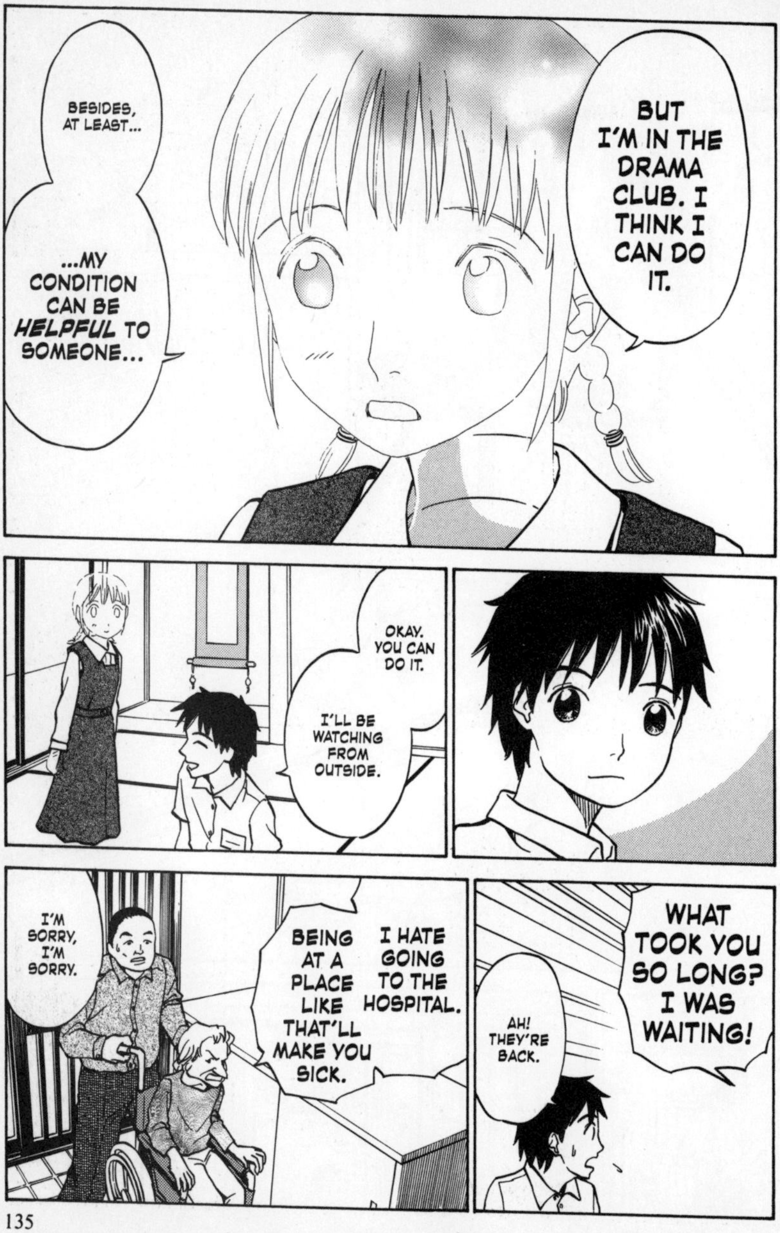
BUT I'M IN THE DRAMA CLUB. I THINK I CAN DO IT.
BESIDES, AT LEAST...
...MY CONDITION CAN BE *HELPFUL* TO SOMEONE...
OKAY. YOU CAN DO IT.
I'LL BE WATCHING FROM OUTSIDE.
WHAT TOOK YOU SO LONG? I WAS WAITING!
AH! THEY'RE BACK.
I HATE GOING TO THE HOSPITAL.
BEING AT A PLACE LIKE THAT'LL MAKE YOU SICK.
I'M SORRY, I'M SORRY.

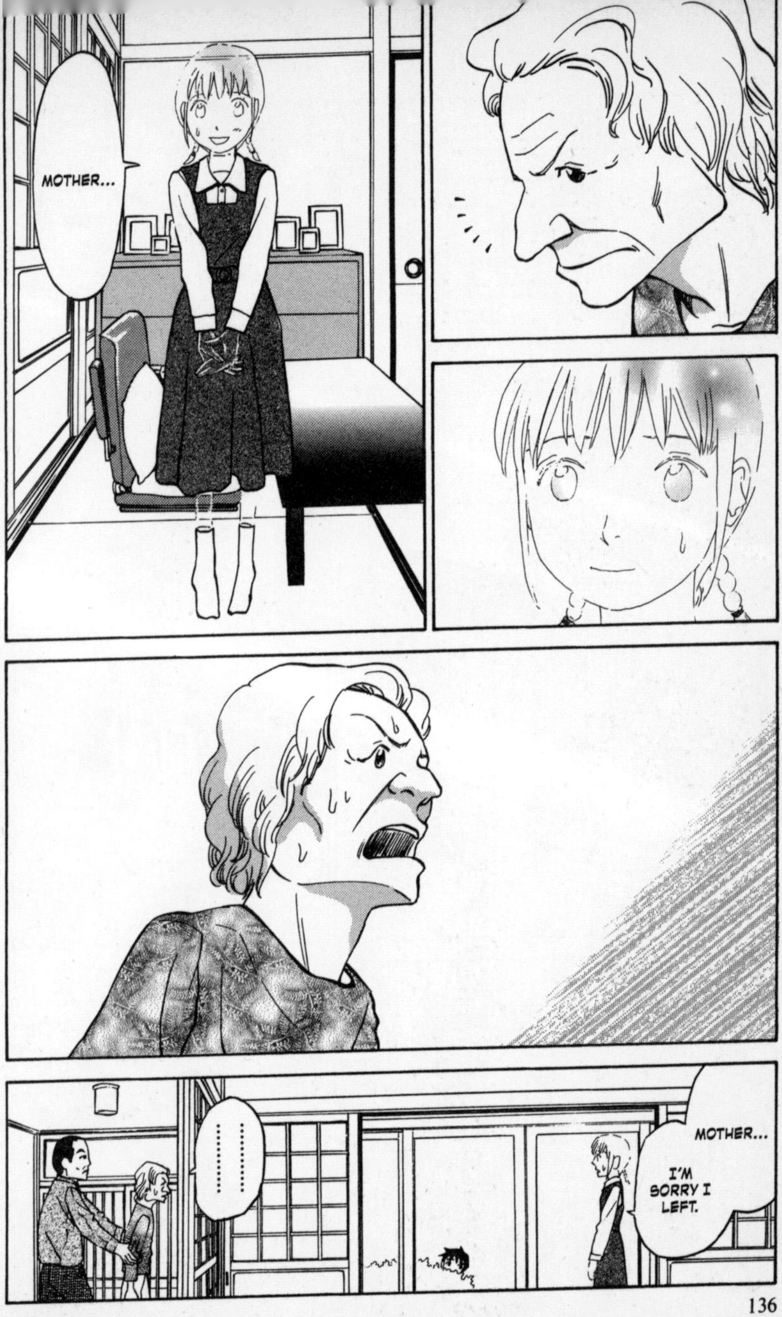
MOTHER...
MOTHER...
I'M SORRY I LEFT.
......

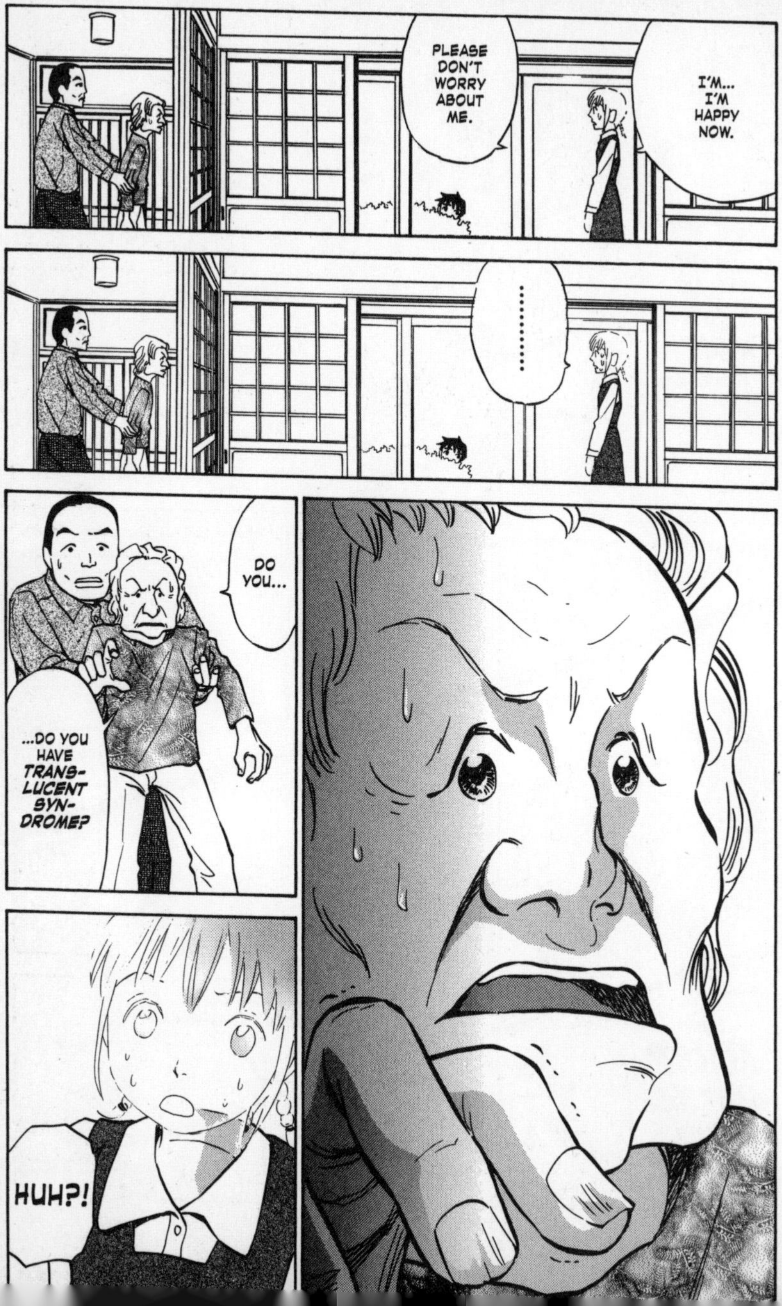
I'M... I'M HAPPY NOW.
PLEASE DON'T WORRY ABOUT ME.
......
DO YOU...
...DO YOU HAVE *TRANSLUCENT SYNDROME?*
HUH?!

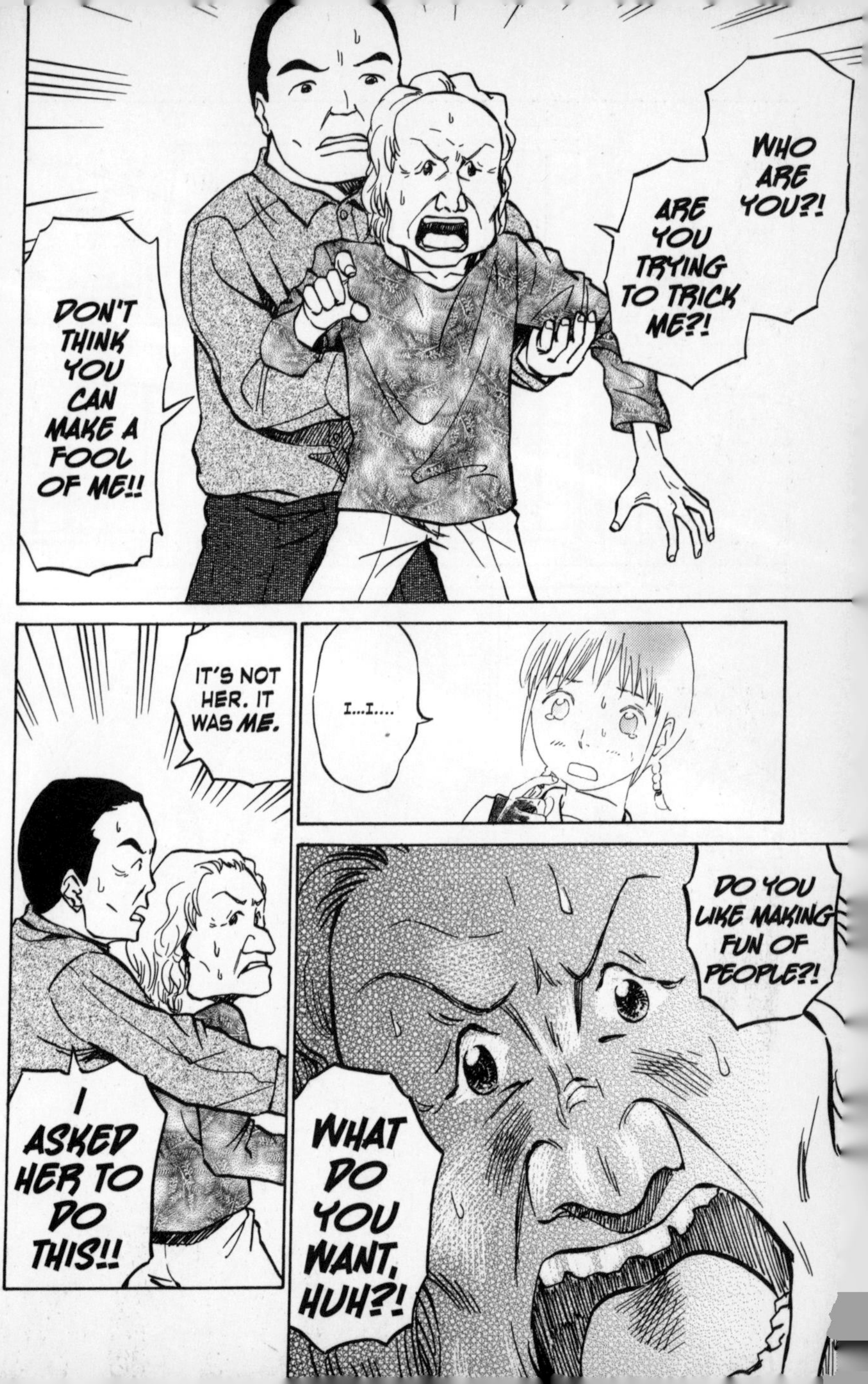
WHO ARE YOU?!
ARE YOU TRYING TO TRICK ME?!
DON'T THINK YOU CAN MAKE A FOOL OF ME!!
I...I....
DO YOU LIKE MAKING FUN OF PEOPLE?!
WHAT DO YOU WANT, HUH?!
IT'S NOT HER. IT WAS ME.
I ASKED HER TO DO THIS!!

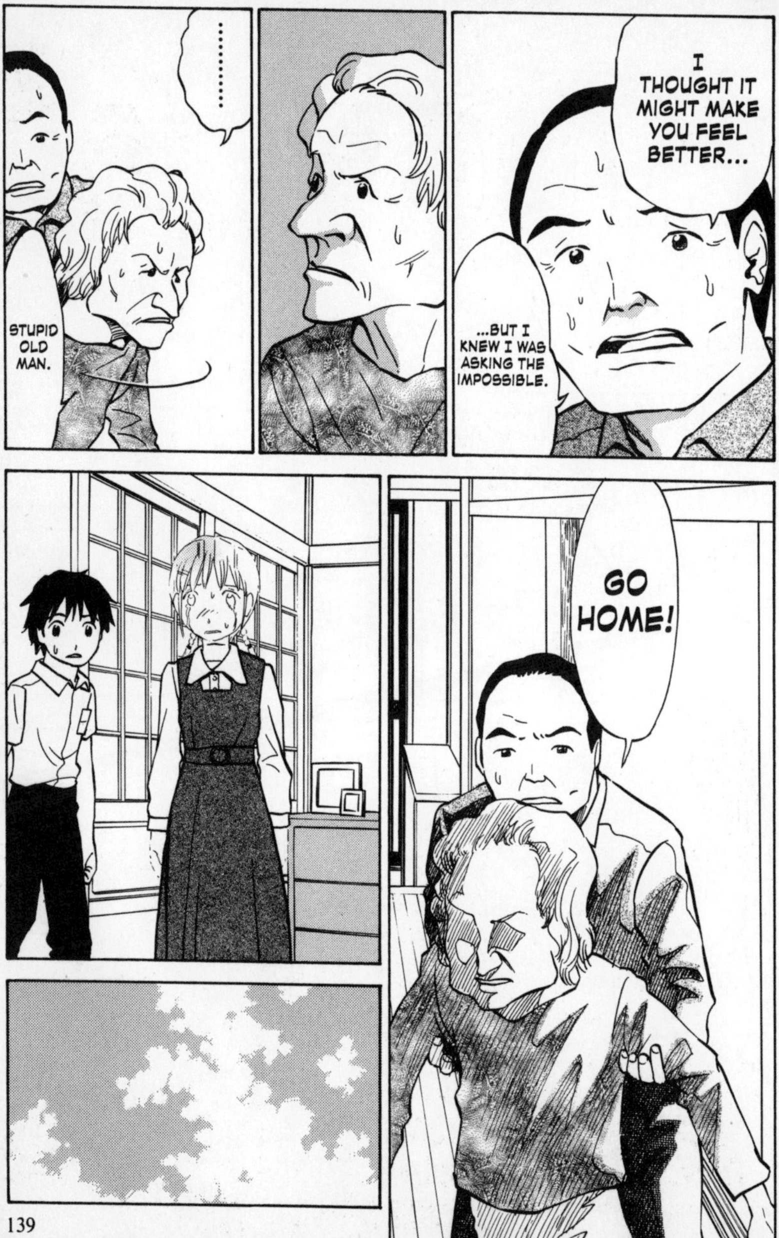
I THOUGHT IT MIGHT MAKE YOU FEEL BETTER...
...BUT I KNEW I WAS ASKING THE IMPOSSIBLE.
......
STUPID OLD MAN.
GO HOME!

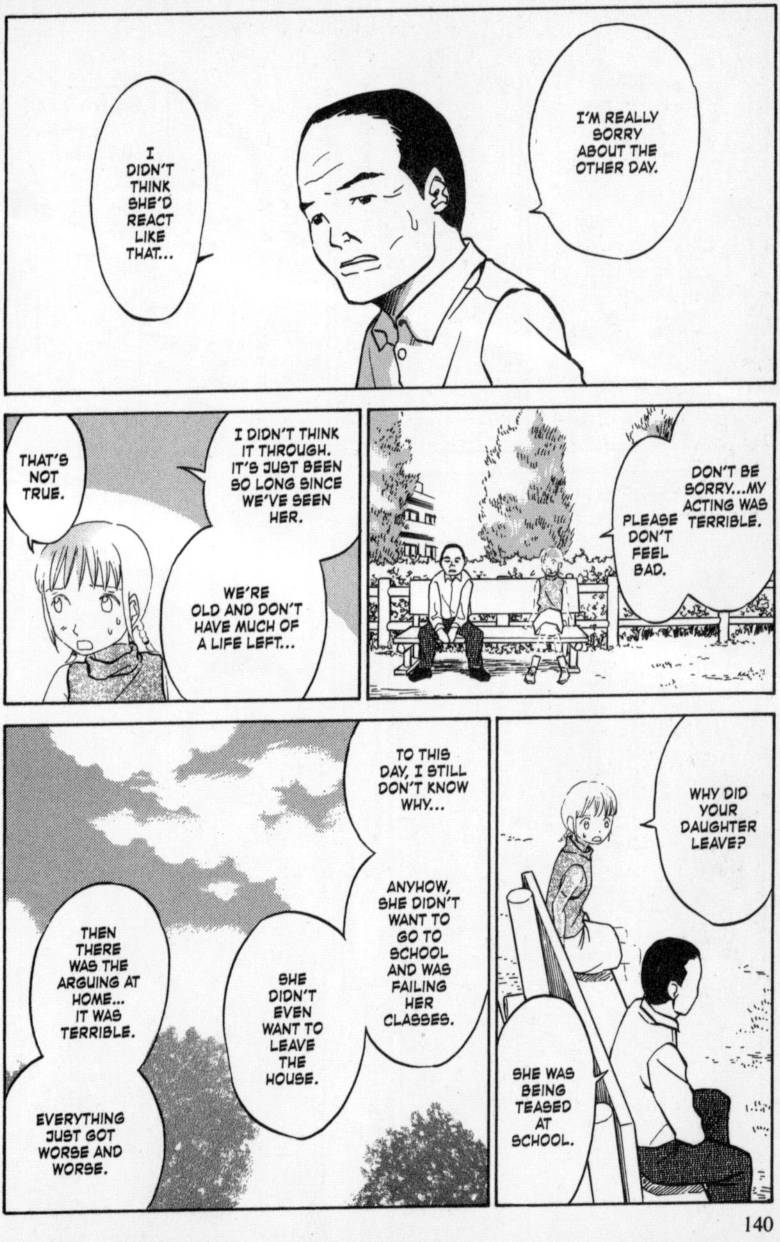
I'M REALLY SORRY ABOUT THE OTHER DAY.
I DIDN'T THINK SHE'D REACT LIKE THAT...
DON'T BE SORRY...MY ACTING WAS TERRIBLE.
PLEASE DON'T FEEL BAD.
I DIDN'T THINK IT THROUGH. IT'S JUST BEEN SO LONG SINCE WE'VE SEEN HER.
THAT'S NOT TRUE.
WE'RE OLD AND DON'T HAVE MUCH OF A LIFE LEFT...
WHY DID YOUR DAUGHTER LEAVE?
SHE WAS BEING TEASED AT SCHOOL.
TO THIS DAY, I STILL DON'T KNOW WHY...
ANYHOW, SHE DIDN'T WANT TO GO TO SCHOOL AND WAS FAILING HER CLASSES.
SHE DIDN'T EVEN WANT TO LEAVE THE HOUSE.
THEN THERE WAS THE ARGUING AT HOME... IT WAS TERRIBLE.
EVERYTHING JUST GOT WORSE AND WORSE.

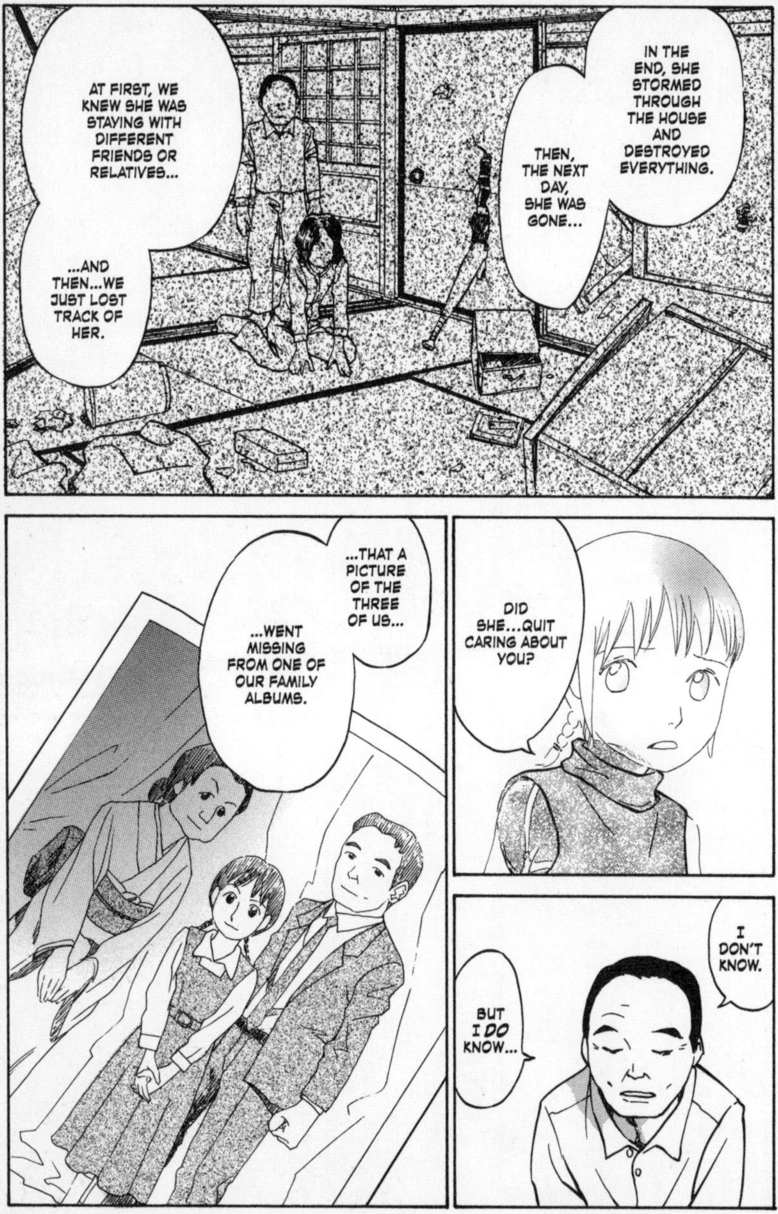
IN THE END, SHE STORMED THROUGH THE HOUSE AND DESTROYED EVERYTHING.
THEN, THE NEXT DAY, SHE WAS GONE...
AT FIRST, WE KNEW SHE WAS STAYING WITH DIFFERENT FRIENDS OR RELATIVES...
...AND THEN...WE JUST LOST TRACK OF HER.
DID SHE...QUIT CARING ABOUT YOU?
I DON'T KNOW.
BUT I *DO* KNOW...
...THAT A PICTURE OF THE THREE OF US...
...WENT MISSING FROM ONE OF OUR FAMILY ALBUMS.

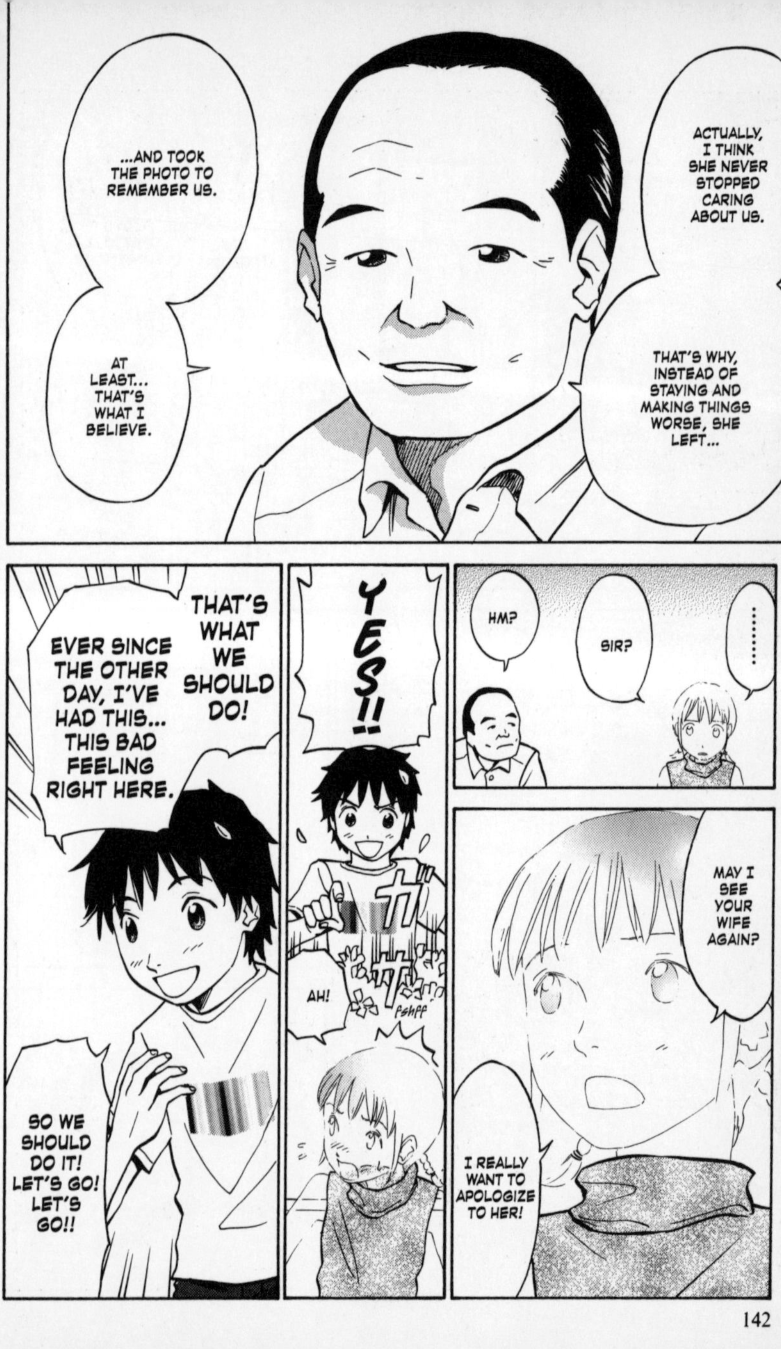
ACTUALLY, I THINK SHE NEVER STOPPED CARING ABOUT US.
THAT'S WHY, INSTEAD OF STAYING AND MAKING THINGS WORSE, SHE LEFT...
...AND TOOK THE PHOTO TO REMEMBER US.
AT LEAST... THAT'S WHAT I BELIEVE.
....
SIR?
HM?
MAY I SEE YOUR WIFE AGAIN?
I REALLY WANT TO APOLOGIZE TO HER!
YES!!
AH!
fshff
THAT'S WHAT WE SHOULD DO!
EVER SINCE THE OTHER DAY, I'VE HAD THIS... THIS BAD FEELING RIGHT HERE.
SO WE SHOULD DO IT! LET'S GO! LET'S GO!!

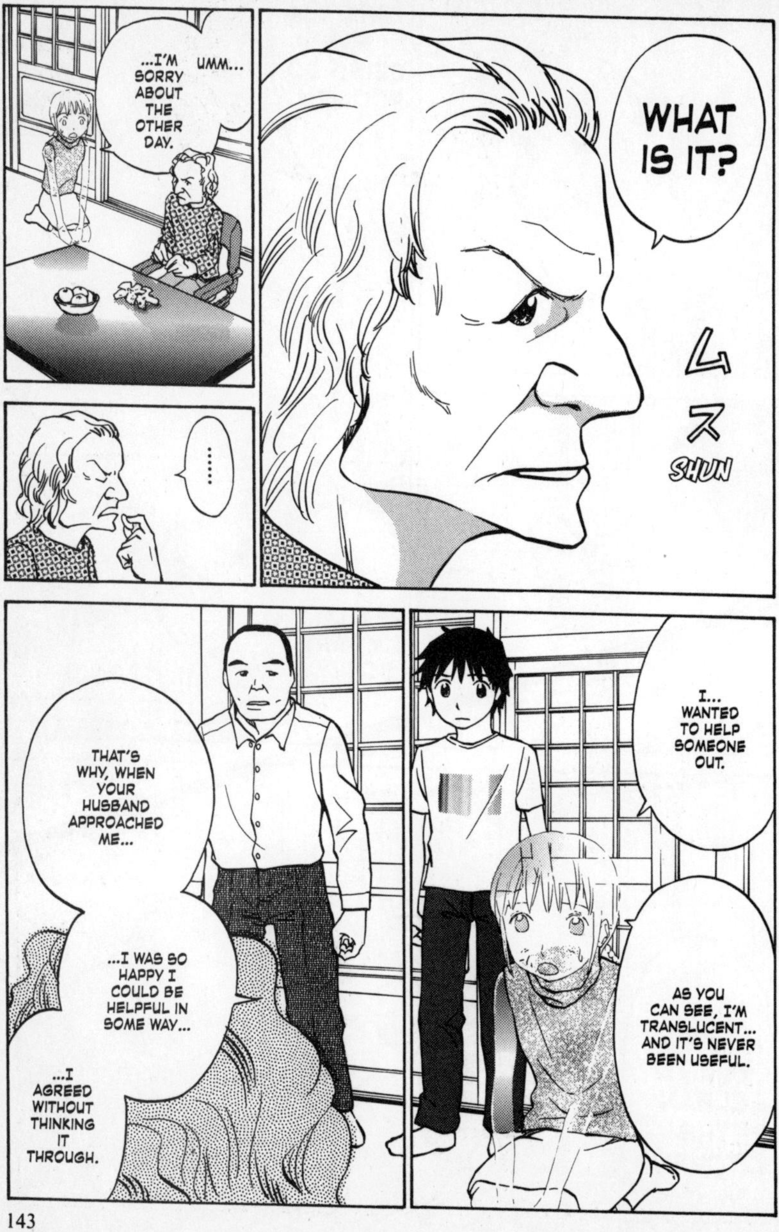
WHAT IS IT?
ムス
SHUN
UMM...
...I'M SORRY ABOUT THE OTHER DAY.
......
I... WANTED TO HELP SOMEONE OUT.
AS YOU CAN SEE, I'M TRANSLUCENT... AND IT'S NEVER BEEN USEFUL.
THAT'S WHY, WHEN YOUR HUSBAND APPROACHED ME...
...I WAS SO HAPPY I COULD BE HELPFUL IN SOME WAY...
...I AGREED WITHOUT THINKING IT THROUGH.

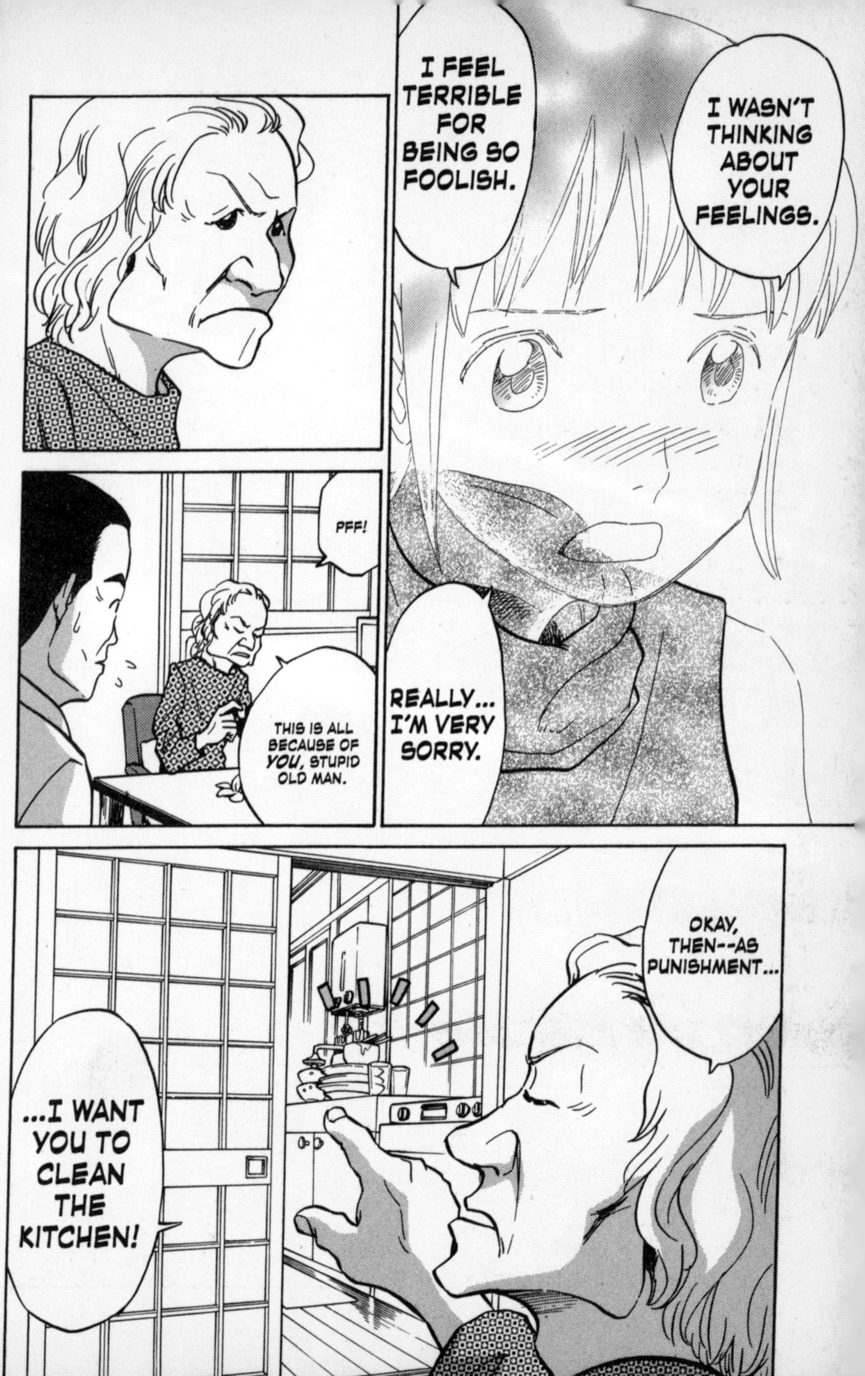
I WASN'T THINKING ABOUT YOUR FEELINGS.
I FEEL TERRIBLE FOR BEING SO FOOLISH.
REALLY... I'M VERY SORRY.
PFF!
THIS IS ALL BECAUSE OF *YOU*, STUPID OLD MAN.
OKAY, THEN--AS PUNISHMENT...
...I WANT YOU TO CLEAN THE KITCHEN!

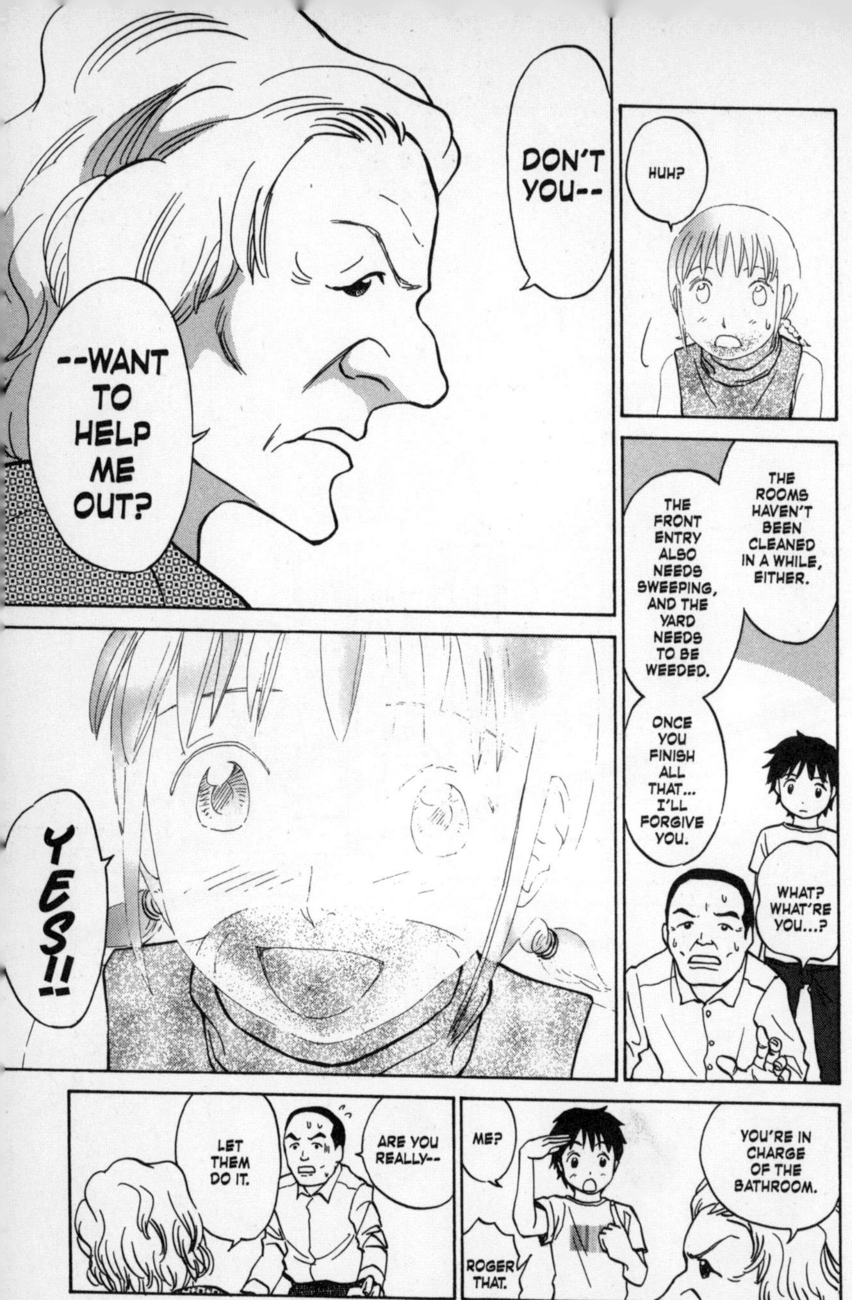
DON'T YOU--
--WANT TO HELP ME OUT?
HUH?
THE ROOMS HAVEN'T BEEN CLEANED IN A WHILE, EITHER.
THE FRONT ENTRY ALSO NEEDS SWEEPING, AND THE YARD NEEDS TO BE WEEDED.
ONCE YOU FINISH ALL THAT... I'LL FORGIVE YOU.
WHAT? WHAT'RE YOU...?
YES!!
YOU'RE IN CHARGE OF THE BATHROOM.
ME?
ROGER THAT.
ARE YOU REALLY--
LET THEM DO IT.

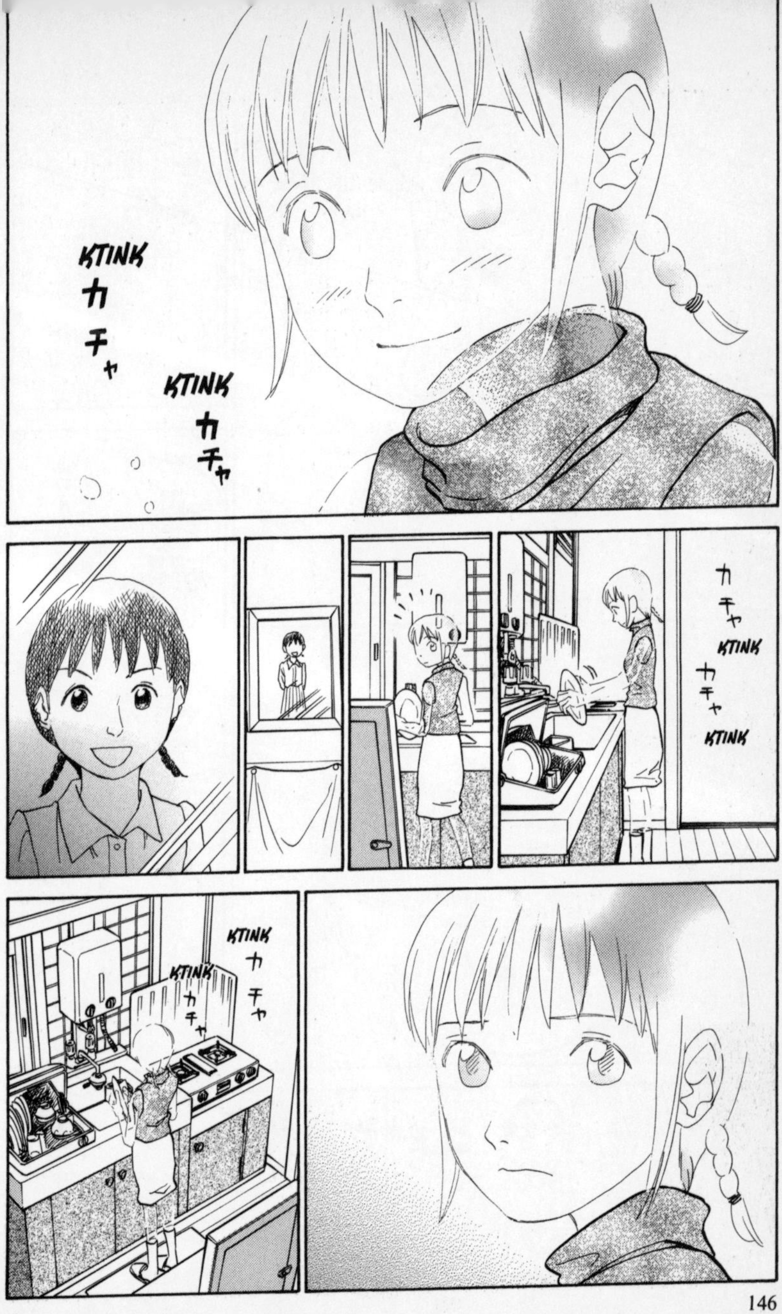
KTINK
カチャ
KTINK
カチャ
カチャ
KTINK
カチャ
KTINK
KTINK
カチャ
KTINK
カチャ

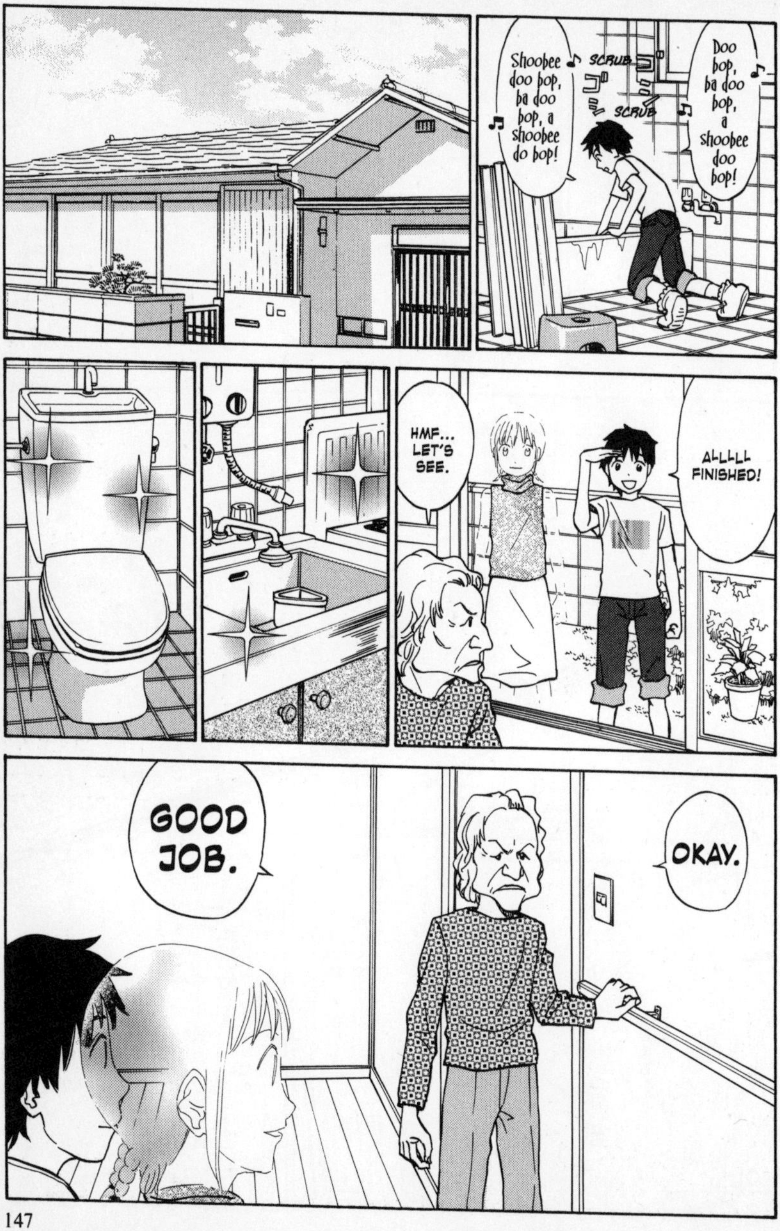
Doo bop, ba doo bop, a shoobee doo bop!
SCRUB
SCRUB
Shoobee doo bop, ba doo bop, a shoobee do bop!
ALLLLL FINISHED!
HMF... LET'S SEE.
OKAY.
GOOD JOB.

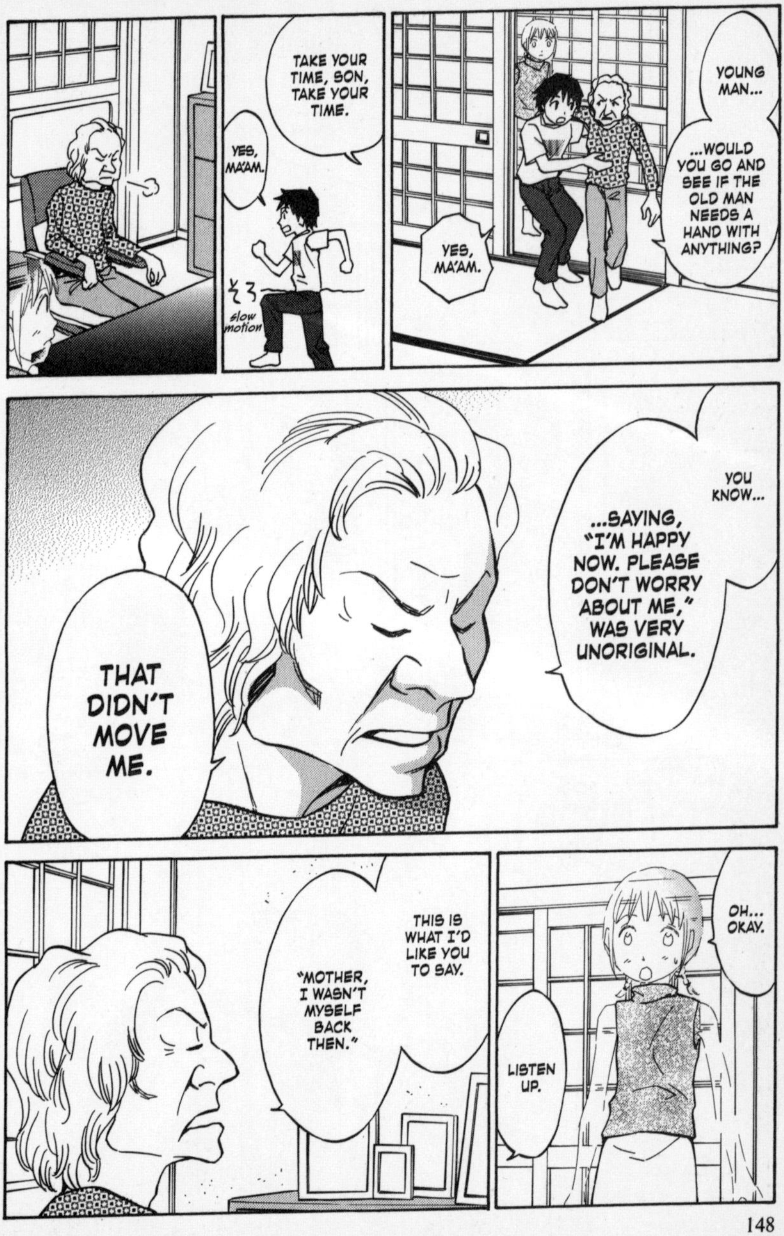
YOUNG MAN...
...WOULD YOU GO AND SEE IF THE OLD MAN NEEDS A HAND WITH ANYTHING?
YES, MA'AM.
TAKE YOUR TIME, SON, TAKE YOUR TIME.
YES, MA'AM.
そろ
slow motion
YOU KNOW...
...SAYING, "I'M HAPPY NOW. PLEASE DON'T WORRY ABOUT ME," WAS VERY UNORIGINAL.
THAT DIDN'T MOVE ME.
OH... OKAY.
LISTEN UP.
THIS IS WHAT I'D LIKE YOU TO SAY.
"MOTHER, I WASN'T MYSELF BACK THEN."

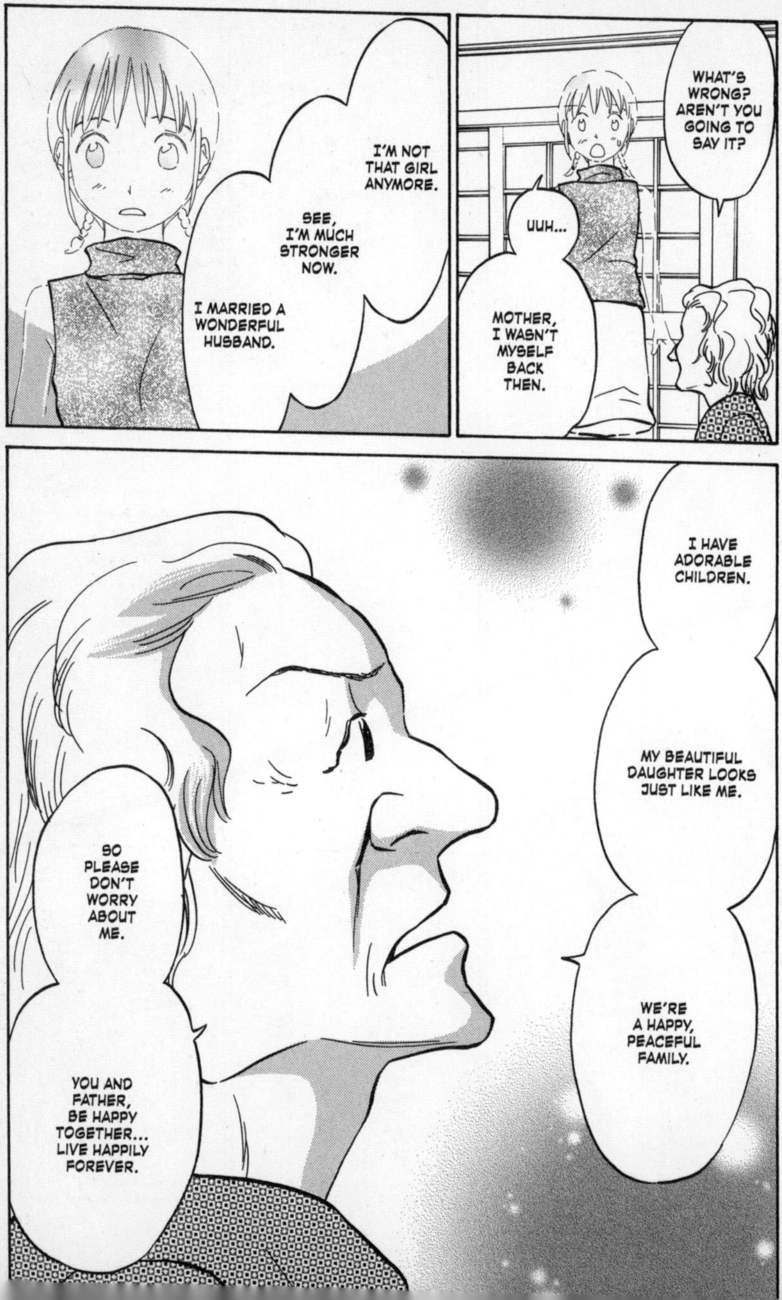
WHAT'S WRONG? AREN'T YOU GOING TO SAY IT?
UUH...
MOTHER, I WASN'T MYSELF BACK THEN.
I'M NOT THAT GIRL ANYMORE.
SEE, I'M MUCH STRONGER NOW.
I MARRIED A WONDERFUL HUSBAND.
I HAVE ADORABLE CHILDREN.
MY BEAUTIFUL DAUGHTER LOOKS JUST LIKE ME.
WE'RE A HAPPY, PEACEFUL FAMILY.
SO PLEASE DON'T WORRY ABOUT ME.
YOU AND FATHER, BE HAPPY TOGETHER... LIVE HAPPILY FOREVER.

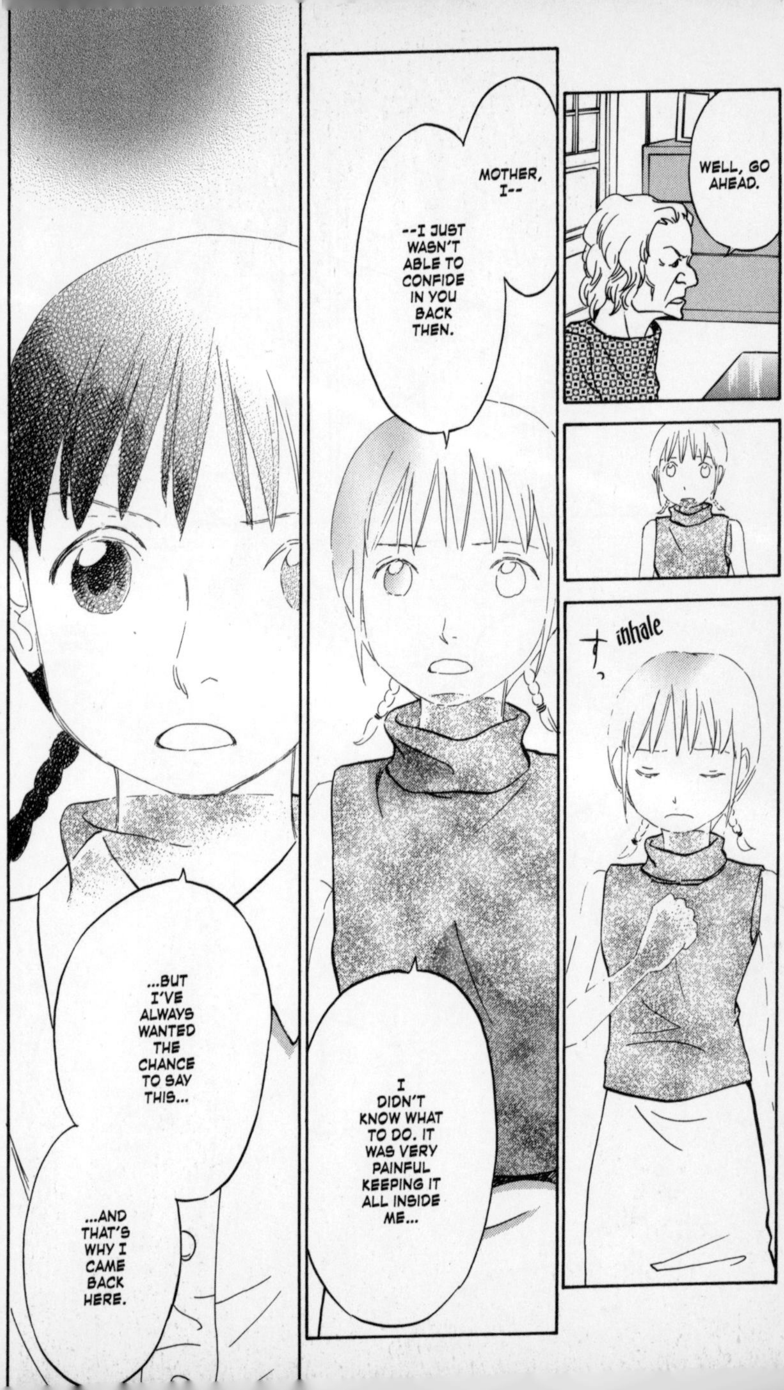
WELL, GO AHEAD.
inhale
MOTHER, I--
--I JUST WASN'T ABLE TO CONFIDE IN YOU BACK THEN.
I DIDN'T KNOW WHAT TO DO. IT WAS VERY PAINFUL KEEPING IT ALL INSIDE ME...
...BUT I'VE ALWAYS WANTED THE CHANCE TO SAY THIS...
...AND THAT'S WHY I CAME BACK HERE.

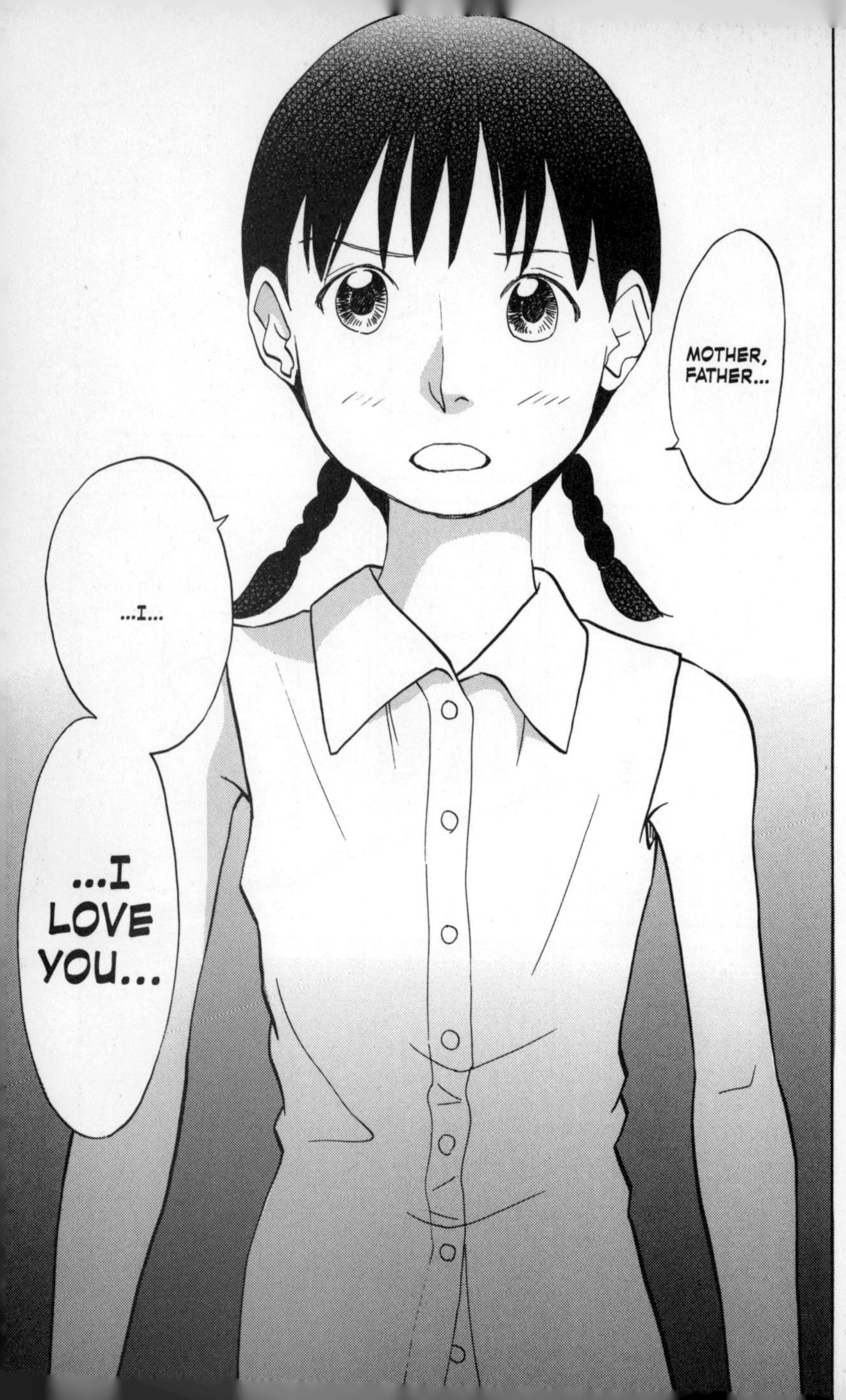
MOTHER, FATHER...
...I...
...I LOVE YOU...

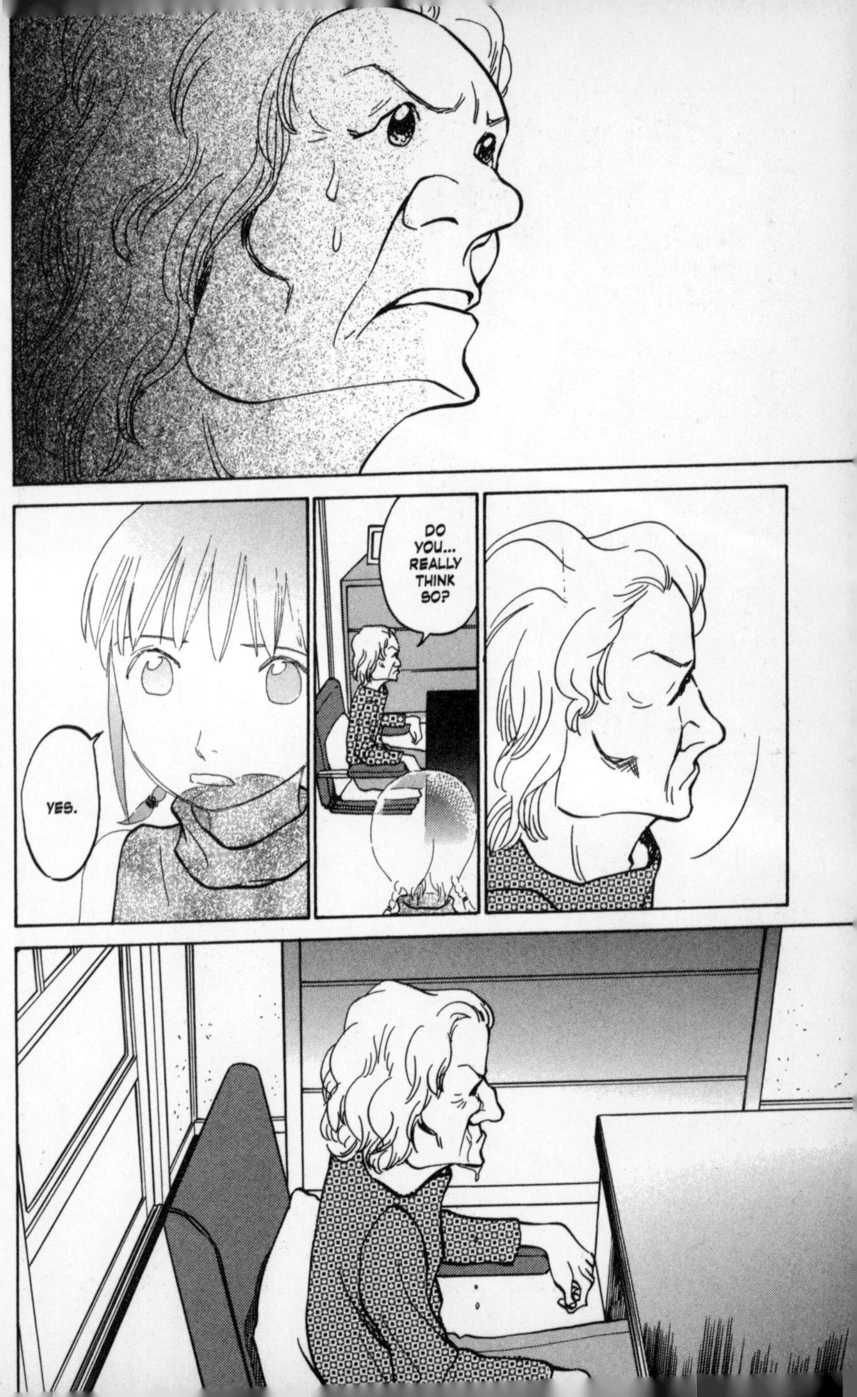
DO YOU... REALLY THINK SO?
YES.

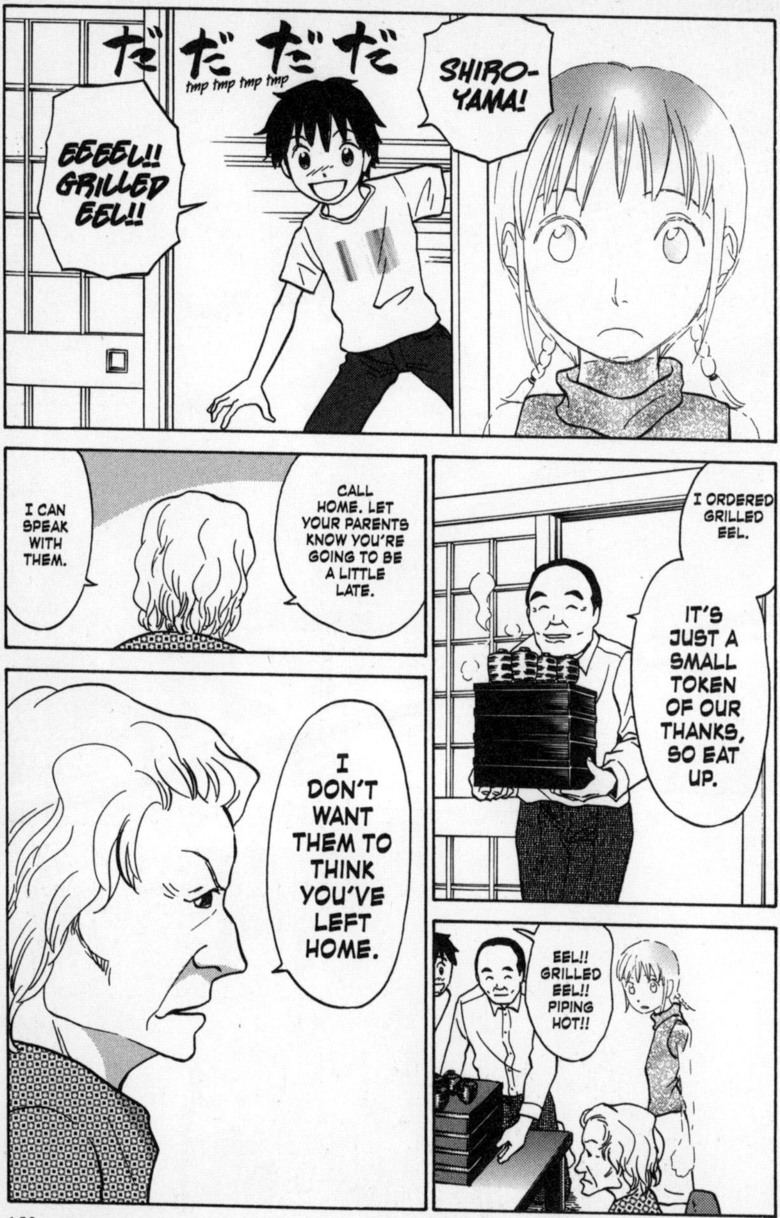
SHIRO-YAMA!
だだだだ
tmp tmp tmp tmp
EEEEL!! GRILLED EEL!!
I ORDERED GRILLED EEL.
IT'S JUST A SMALL TOKEN OF OUR THANKS, SO EAT UP.
CALL HOME. LET YOUR PARENTS KNOW YOU'RE GOING TO BE A LITTLE LATE.
I CAN SPEAK WITH THEM.
I DON'T WANT THEM TO THINK YOU'VE LEFT HOME.
EEL!! GRILLED EEL!! PIPING HOT!!

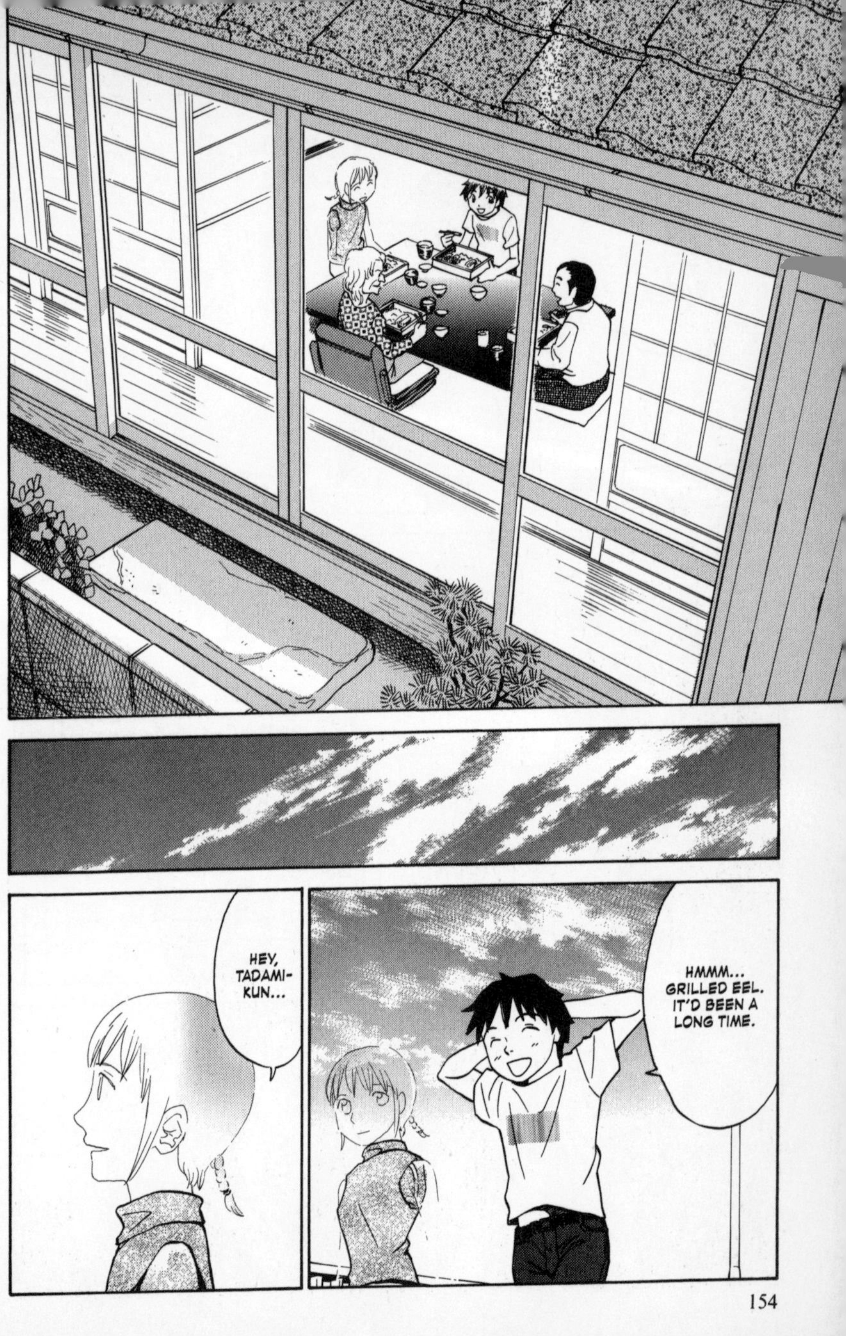
HMMM... GRILLED EEL. IT'D BEEN A LONG TIME.
HEY, TADAMI-KUN...

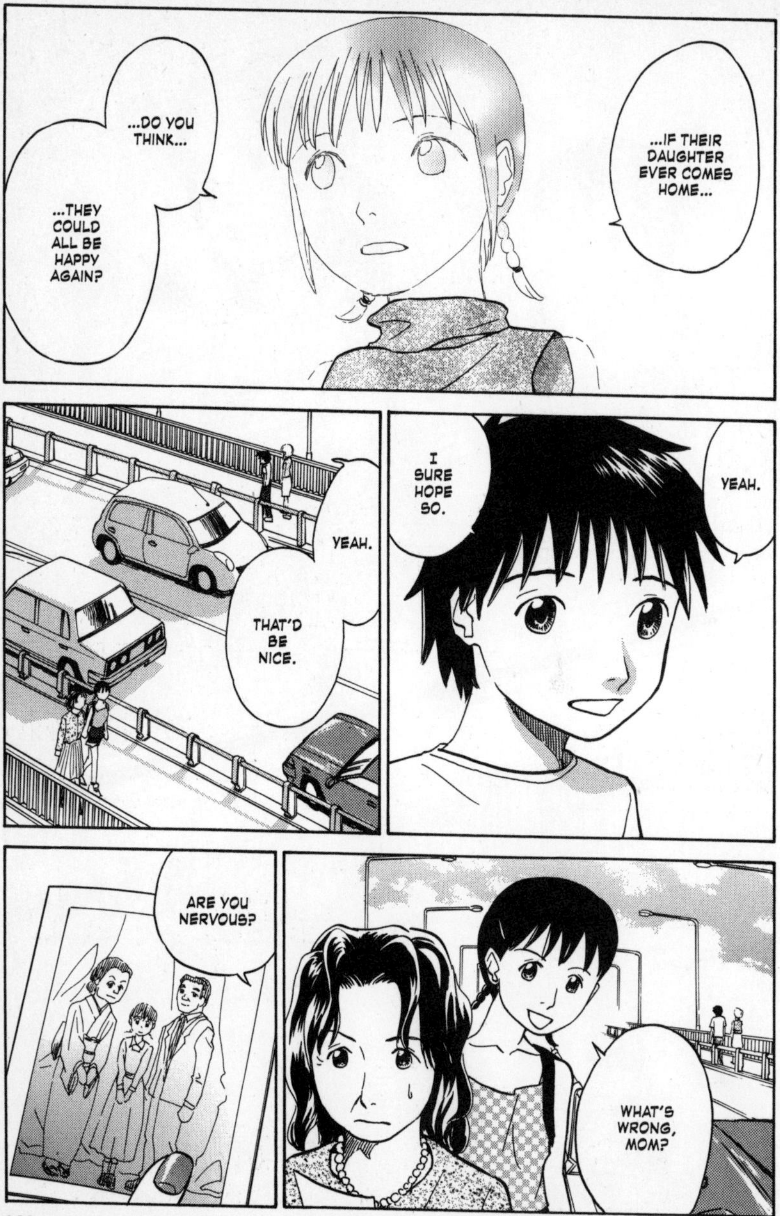
...IF THEIR DAUGHTER EVER COMES HOME...
...DO YOU THINK...
...THEY COULD ALL BE HAPPY AGAIN?
YEAH.
I SURE HOPE SO.
YEAH.
THAT'D BE NICE.
WHAT'S WRONG, MOM?
ARE YOU NERVOUS?

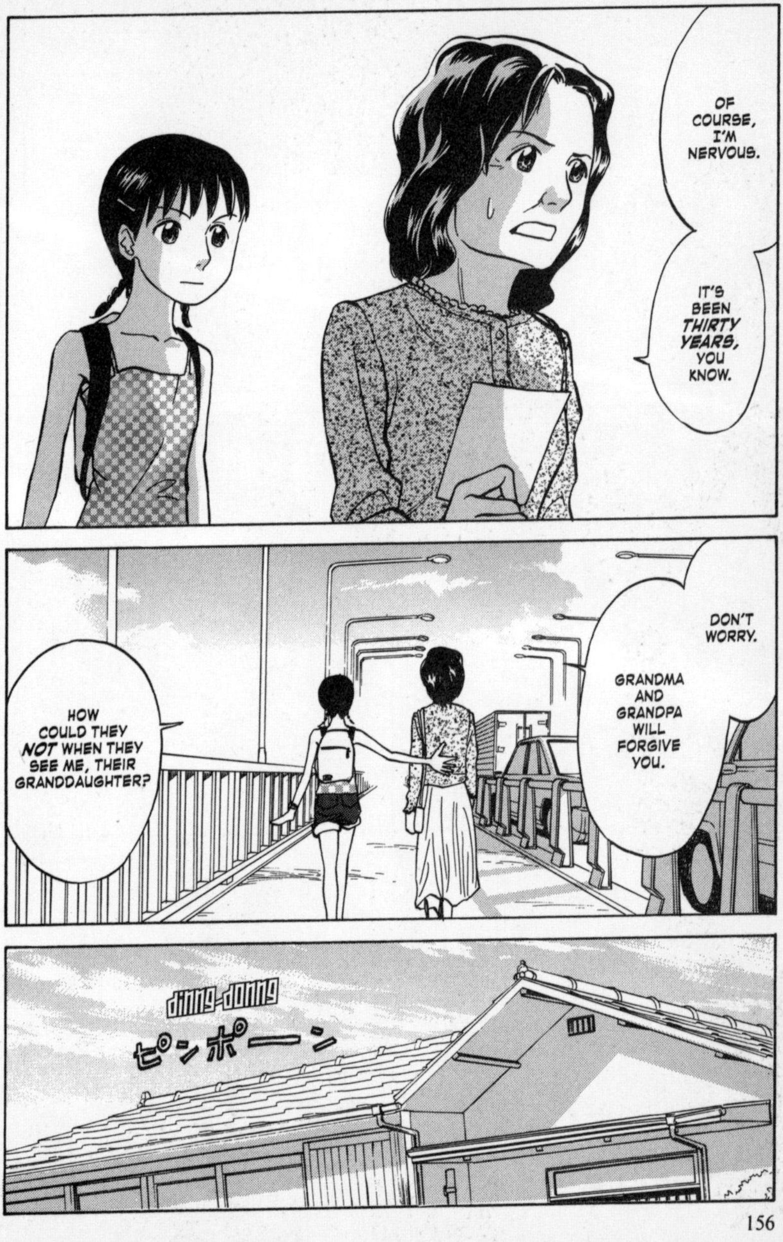
OF COURSE, I'M NERVOUS.
IT'S BEEN THIRTY YEARS, YOU KNOW.
DON'T WORRY.
GRANDMA AND GRANDPA WILL FORGIVE YOU.
HOW COULD THEY NOT WHEN THEY SEE ME, THEIR GRANDDAUGHTER?
dinng-donng
ピンポーン

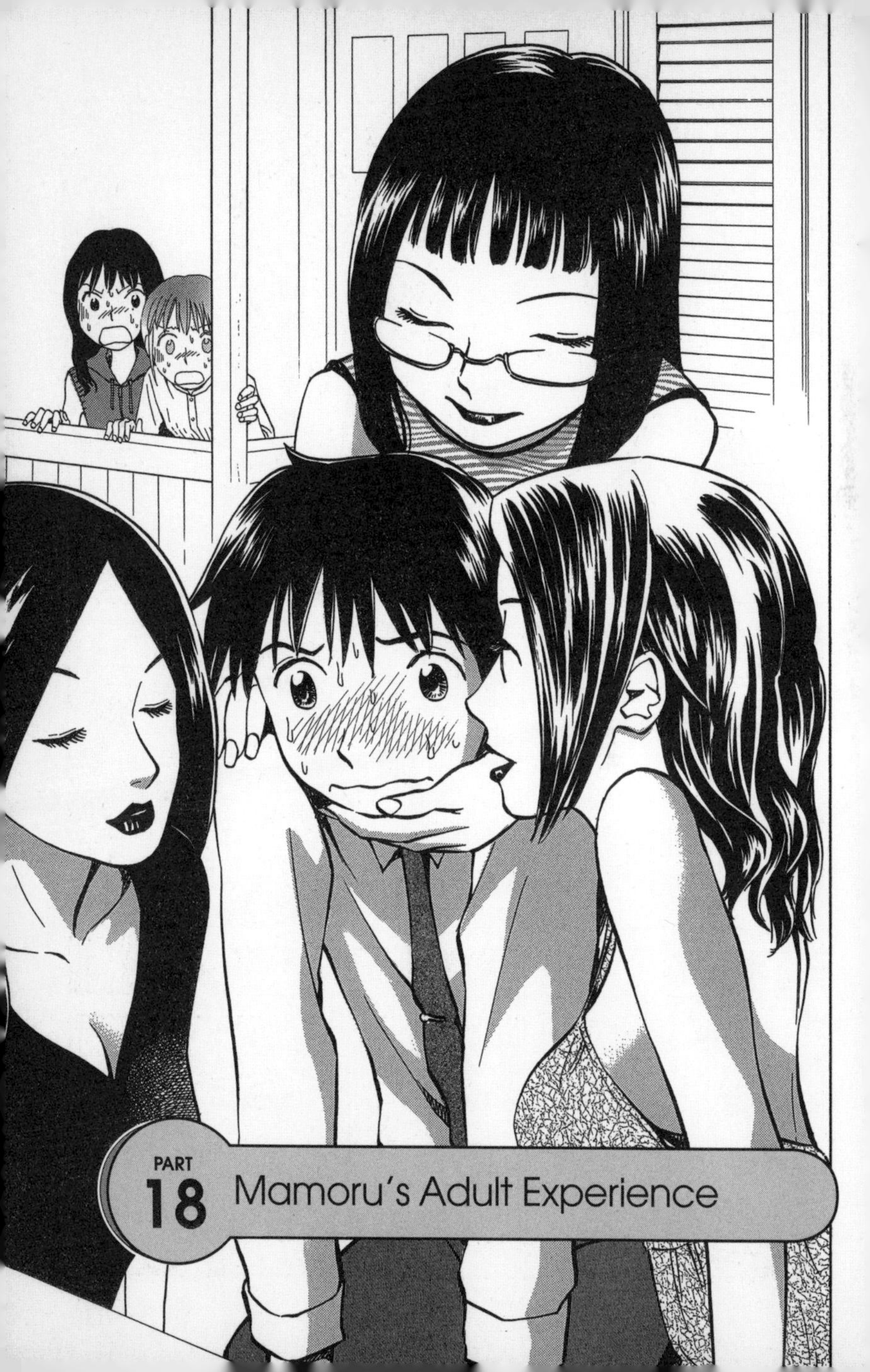
PART
18
Mamoru's Adult Experience

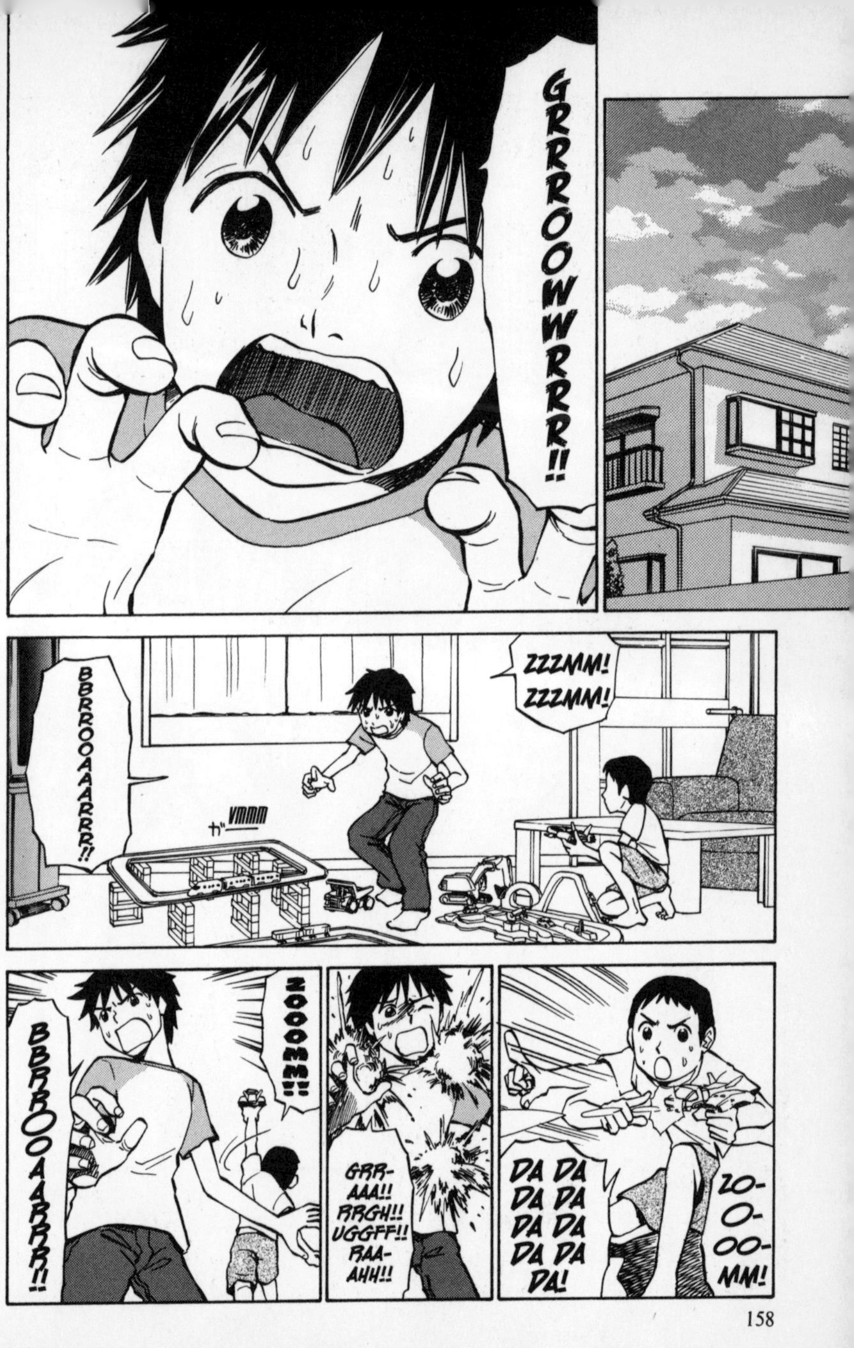
GRRROOWWRRR!!
ZZZMM!
ZZZMM!
ガ VMMM
BBRROOAAARRR!!
ZO-O-OO-MM!
DA DA
DA DA
DA DA
DA DA
DA!
GRR-AAA!! RRGH!! UGGFF!! RAA-AHH!!
ZOOOMM!!
BBRRROOAARRR!!

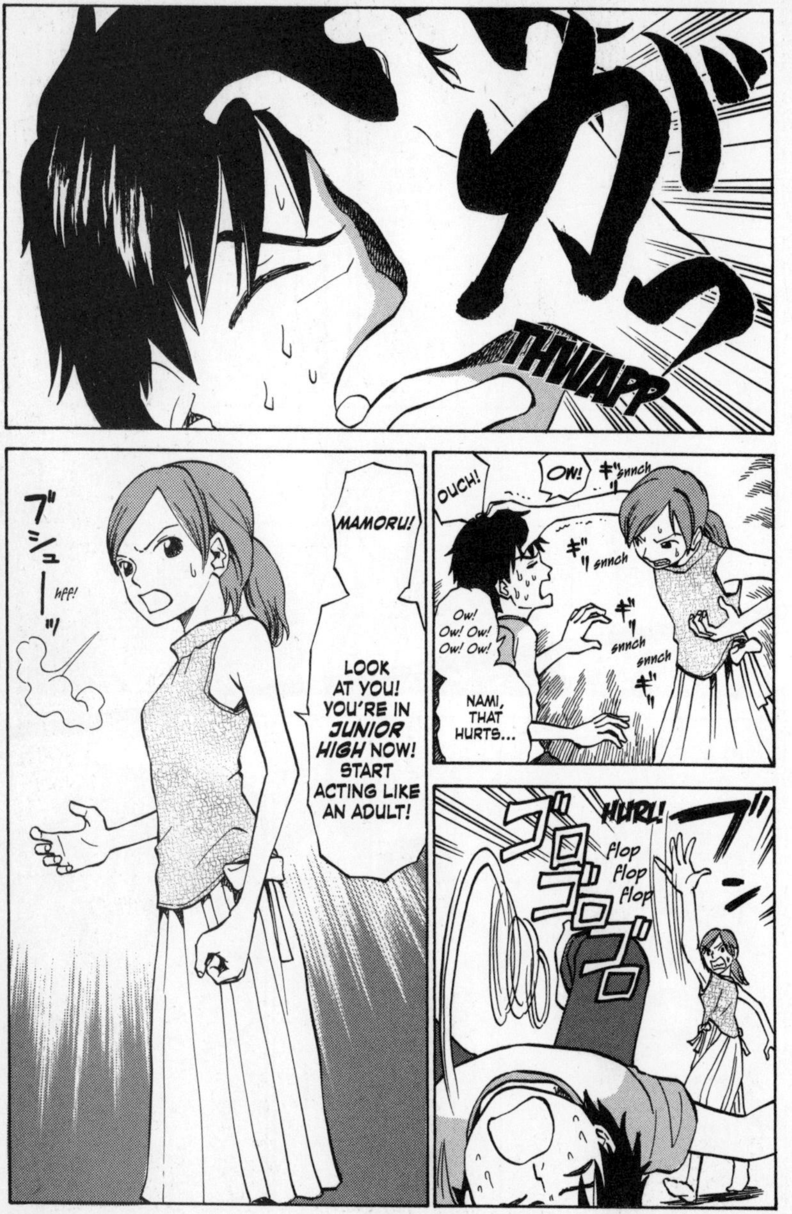

ガッ
THWAPP
OW!
OUCH!
ギ snnch
ギ snnch
ギ snnch
snnch
ギ
Ow! Ow! Ow! Ow! Ow!
NAMI, THAT HURTS...
ブン
HURL!
ゴロゴロゴロ
flop flop flop
MAMORU!
LOOK AT YOU! YOU'RE IN *JUNIOR HIGH* NOW! START ACTING LIKE AN ADULT!
ブシューッ
hff!

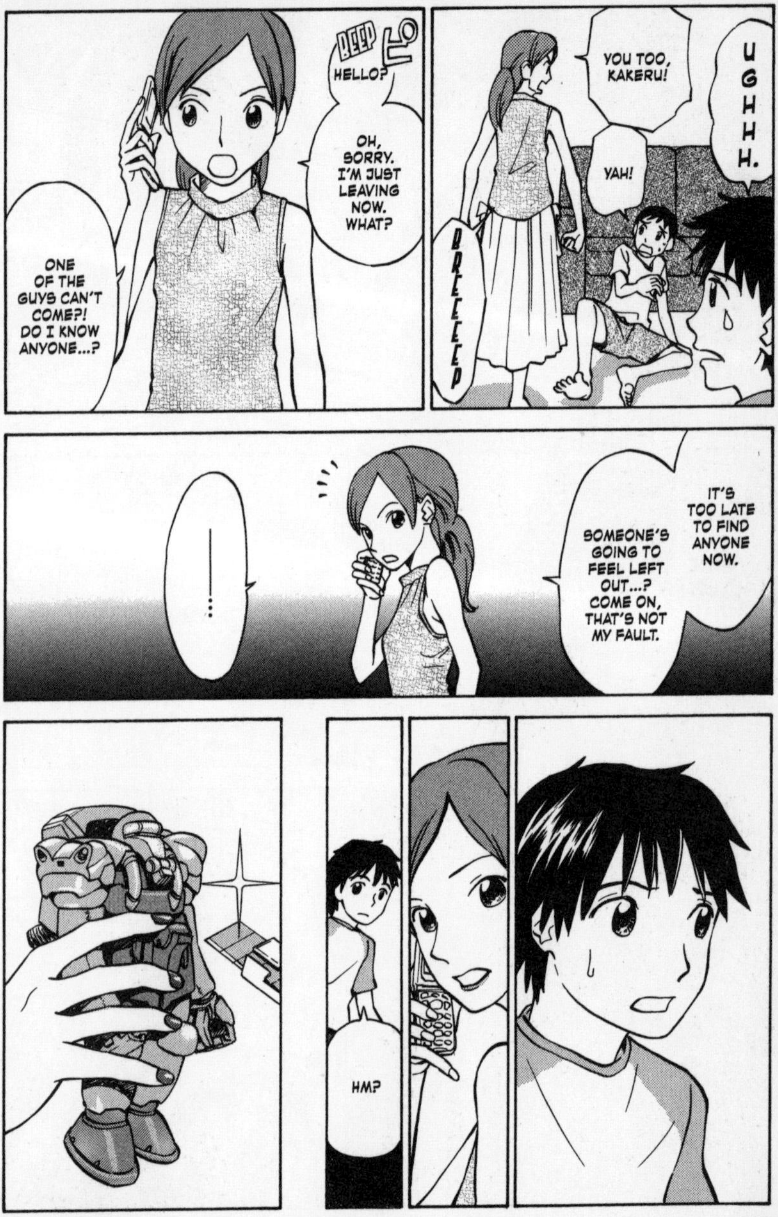
UGHHH.
YOU TOO, KAKERU!
YAH!
BREEEEEP
BEEP
HELLO?
OH, SORRY. I'M JUST LEAVING NOW. WHAT?
ONE OF THE GUYS CAN'T COME?! DO I KNOW ANYONE...?
IT'S TOO LATE TO FIND ANYONE NOW.
SOMEONE'S GOING TO FEEL LEFT OUT...? COME ON, THAT'S NOT MY FAULT.
HM?

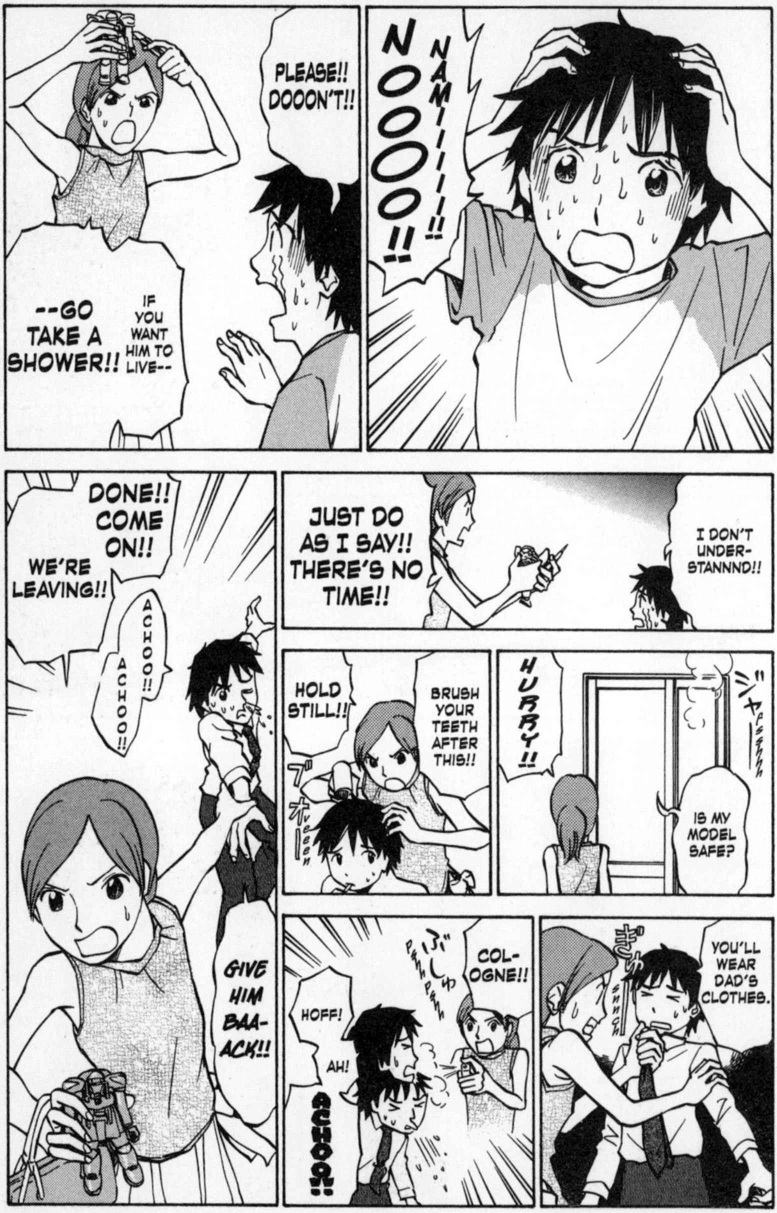
NAMI-!!!
NOOOO!!
PLEASE!! DOOON'T!!
IF YOU WANT HIM TO LIVE--
--GO TAKE A SHOWER!!
I DON'T UNDER-STANNND!!
JUST DO AS I SAY!! THERE'S NO TIME!!
ジャー
HURRY!!
IS MY MODEL SAFE?
BRUSH YOUR TEETH AFTER THIS!!
HOLD STILL!!
ブオー
YOU'LL WEAR DAD'S CLOTHES.
ぎゅ
COL-OGNE!!
ぷしゅ
HOFF!
AH!
ACHOO!!
DONE!! COME ON!!
WE'RE LEAVING!!
ACHOO!!
ACHOO!!
ACHOO!!
GIVE HIM BAA-ACK!!

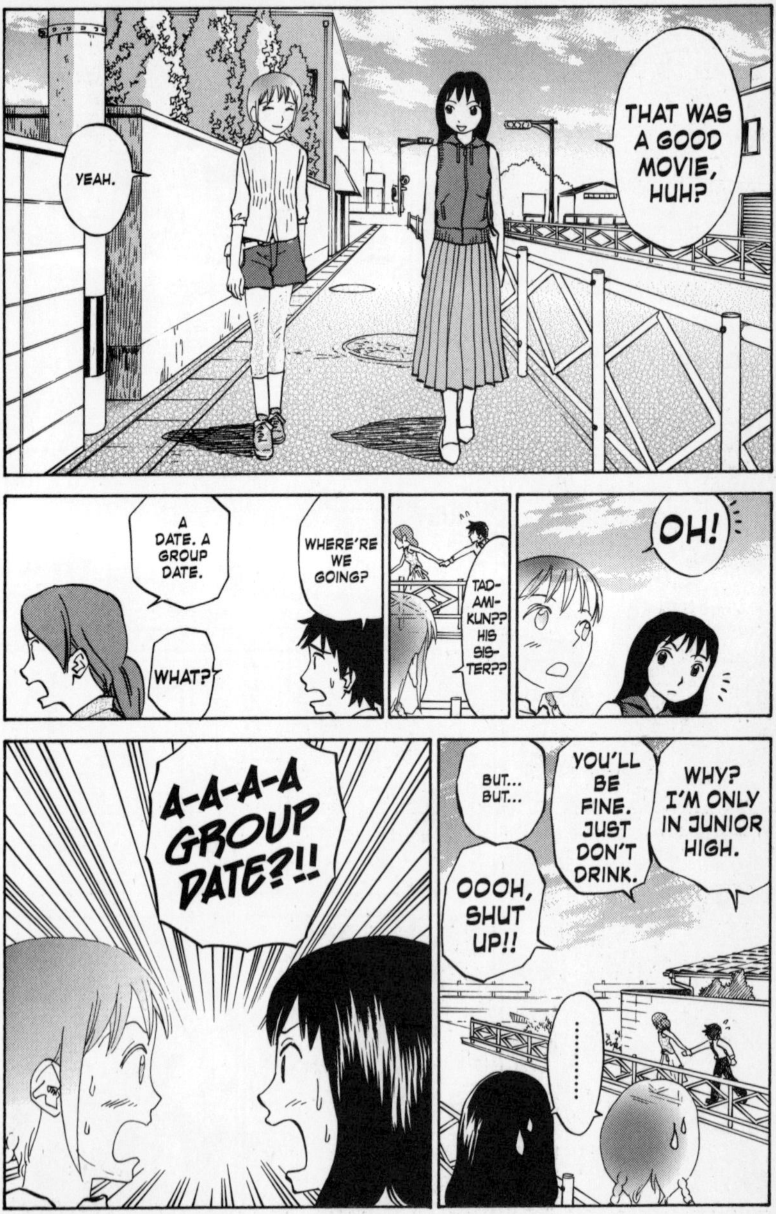
THAT WAS A GOOD MOVIE, HUH?
YEAH.
OH!
TADAMIKUN?? HIS SISTER??
WHERE'RE WE GOING?
A DATE. A GROUP DATE.
WHAT?
WHY? I'M ONLY IN JUNIOR HIGH.
YOU'LL BE FINE. JUST DON'T DRINK.
BUT... BUT...
OOOH, SHUT UP!!
......
A-A-A-A GROUP DATE?!!

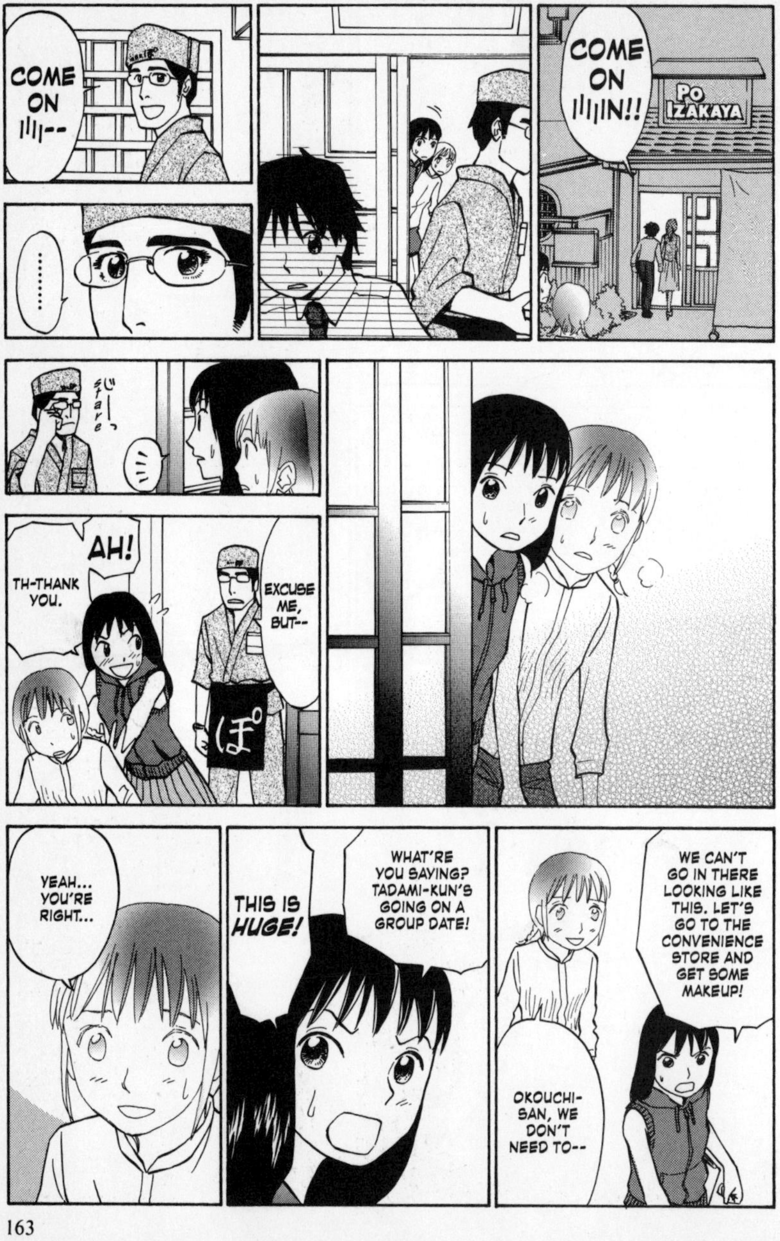
COME ON IN!!
PO IZAKAYA
COME ON I--
......
じーっ
stare
EXCUSE ME, BUT--
ぽ
AH!
TH-THANK YOU.
WE CAN'T GO IN THERE LOOKING LIKE THIS. LET'S GO TO THE CONVENIENCE STORE AND GET SOME MAKEUP!
OKOUCHI-SAN, WE DON'T NEED TO--
WHAT'RE YOU SAYING? TADAMI-KUN'S GOING ON A GROUP DATE!
THIS IS *HUGE!*
YEAH... YOU'RE RIGHT...

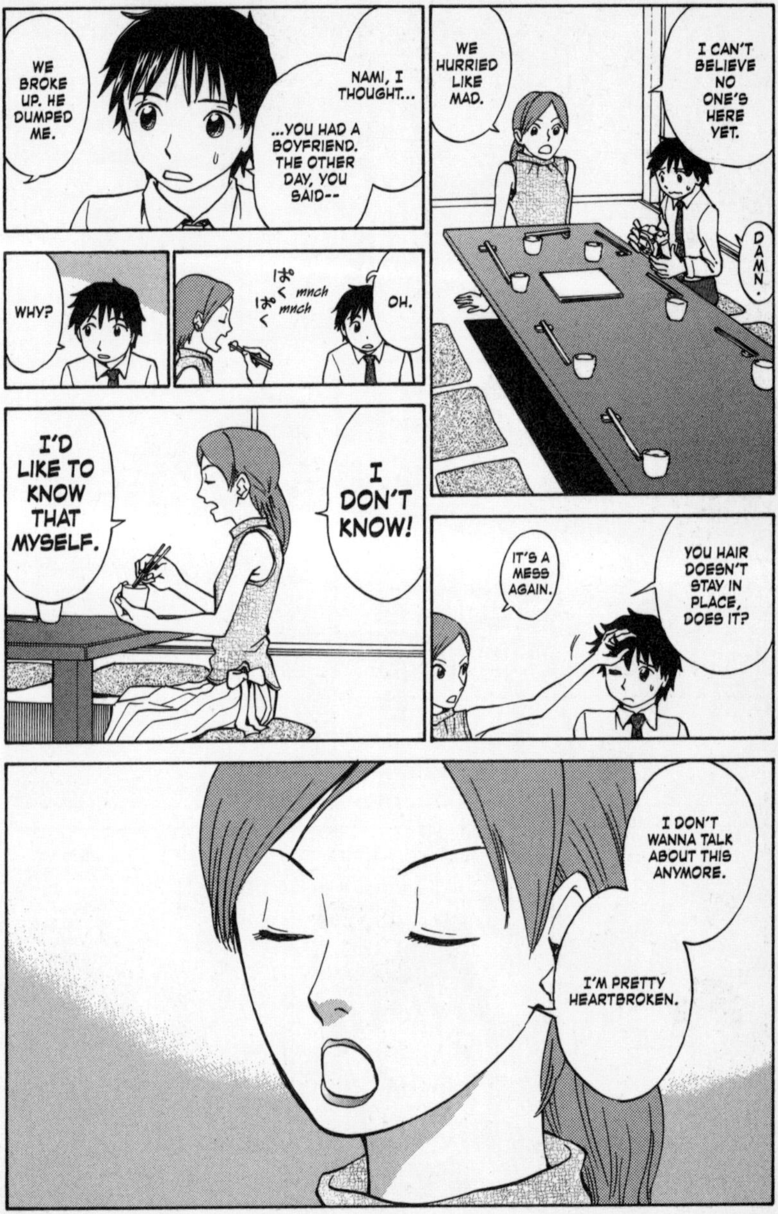
I CAN'T BELIEVE NO ONE'S HERE YET.
WE HURRIED LIKE MAD.
DAMN.
NAMI, I THOUGHT...
...YOU HAD A BOYFRIEND. THE OTHER DAY, YOU SAID--
WE BROKE UP. HE DUMPED ME.
OH.
ぱく mnch
ぱく mnch
WHY?
YOU HAIR DOESN'T STAY IN PLACE, DOES IT?
IT'S A MESS AGAIN.
I DON'T KNOW!
I'D LIKE TO KNOW THAT MYSELF.
I DON'T WANNA TALK ABOUT THIS ANYMORE.
I'M PRETTY HEARTBROKEN.

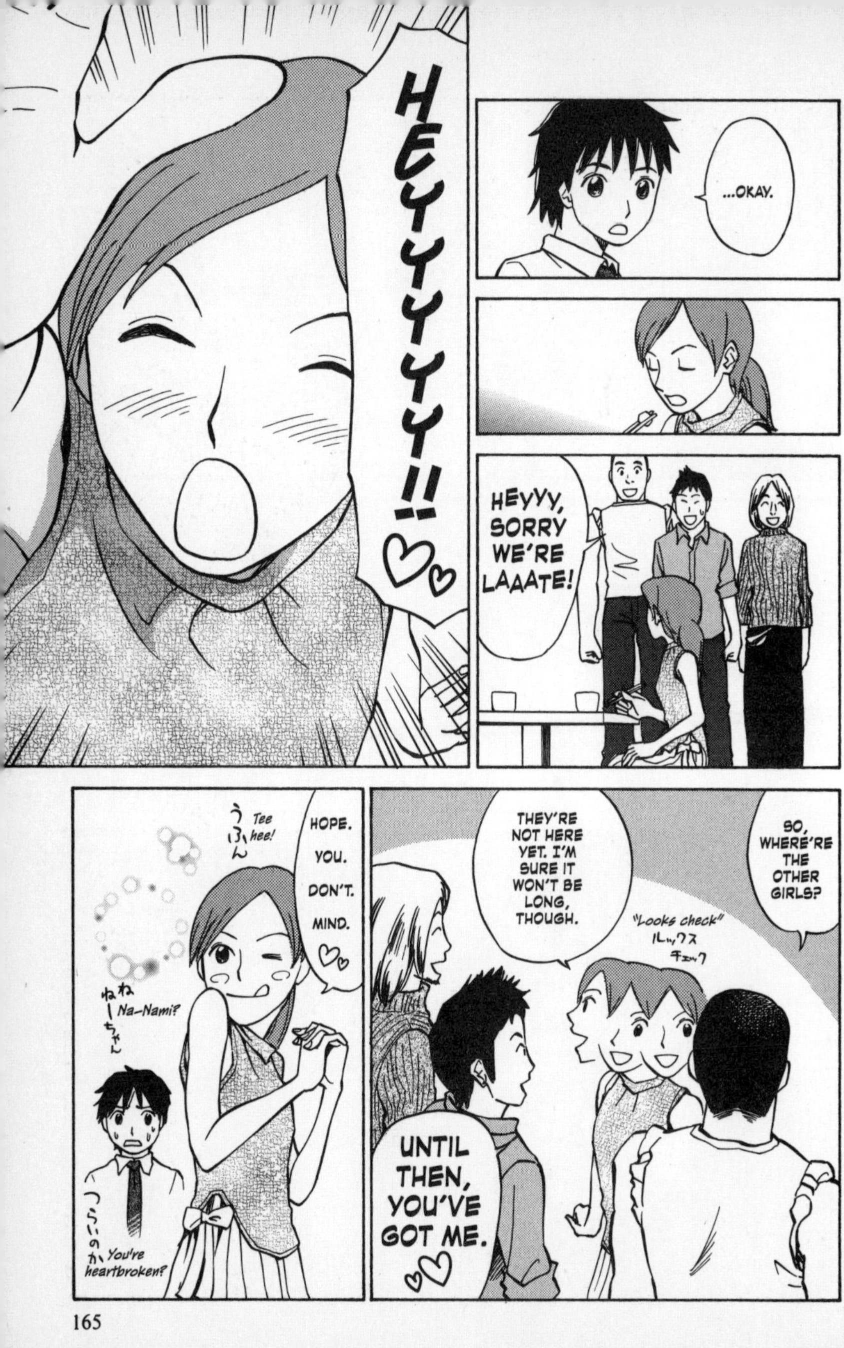
...OKAY.
HEYYY, SORRY WE'RE LAAATE!
HEYYYYYYY!!
SO, WHERE'RE THE OTHER GIRLS?
"Looks check" ルックスチェック
THEY'RE NOT HERE YET. I'M SURE IT WON'T BE LONG, THOUGH.
UNTIL THEN, YOU'VE GOT ME.
HOPE. YOU. DON'T. MIND.
うふん Tee hee!
ねねーちゃん Na-Nami?
つらいのか You're heartbroken?

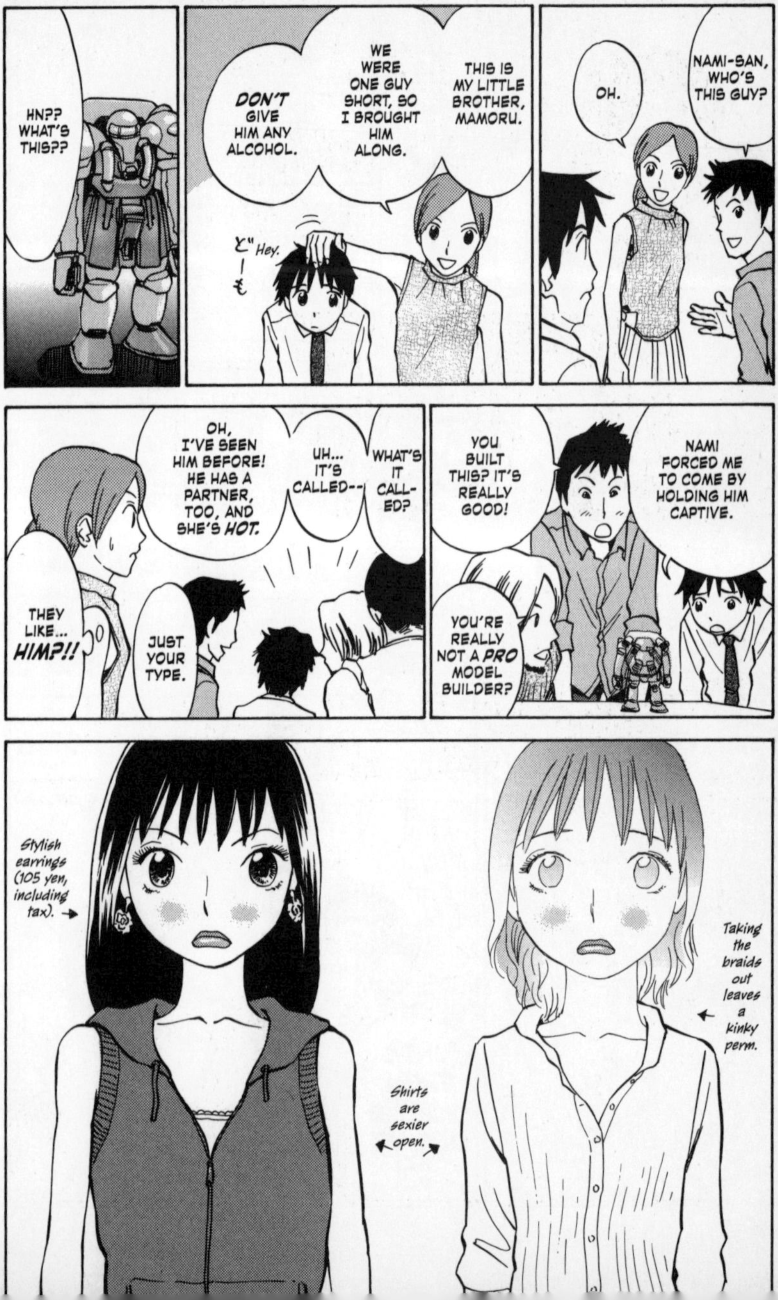
NAMI-SAN, WHO'S THIS GUY?
OH.
THIS IS MY LITTLE BROTHER, MAMORU.
WE WERE ONE GUY SHORT, SO I BROUGHT HIM ALONG.
DON'T GIVE HIM ANY ALCOHOL.
ど! も Hey.
HN?? WHAT'S THIS??
NAMI FORCED ME TO COME BY HOLDING HIM CAPTIVE.
YOU BUILT THIS? IT'S REALLY GOOD!
YOU'RE REALLY NOT A *PRO* MODEL BUILDER?
WHAT'S IT CALLED?
UH... IT'S CALLED--
OH, I'VE SEEN HIM BEFORE! HE HAS A PARTNER, TOO, AND SHE'S *HOT.*
JUST YOUR TYPE.
THEY LIKE... *HIM?!!*
Taking the braids out leaves a kinky perm.
Shirts are sexier open.
Stylish earrings (105 yen, including tax).

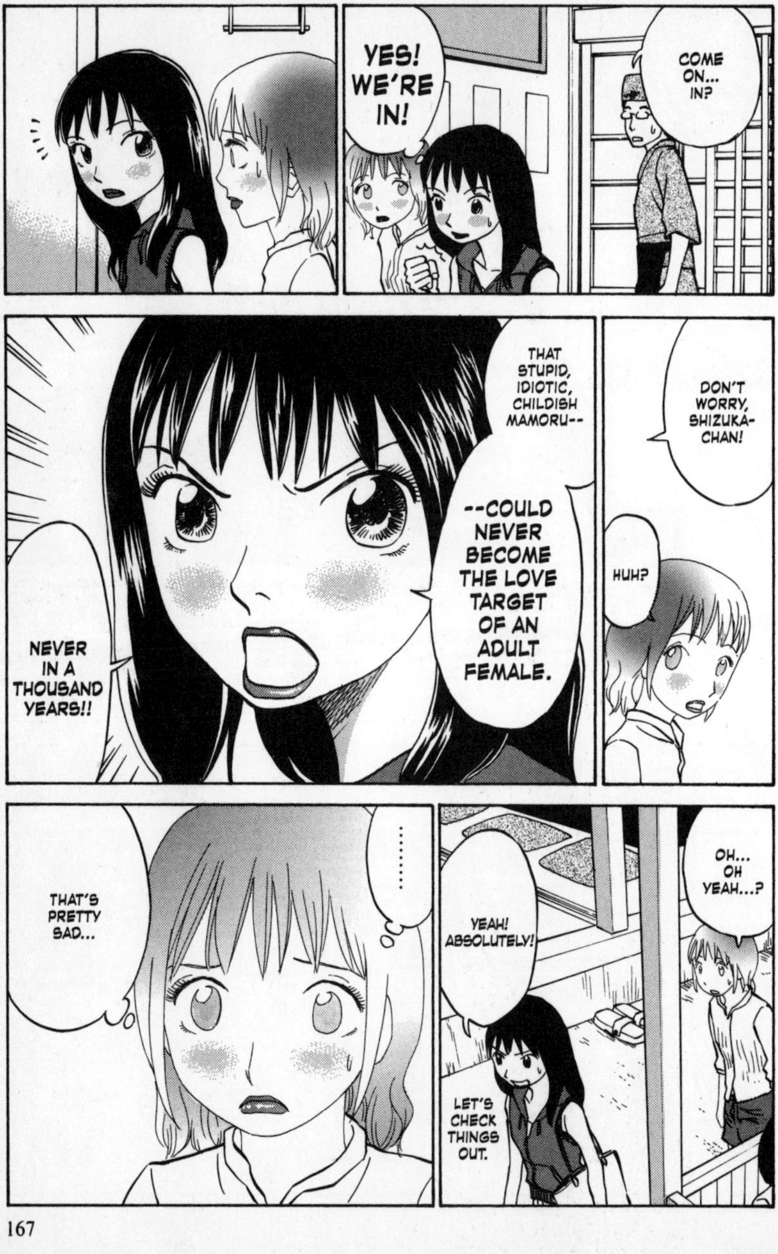
COME ON... IN?
YES! WE'RE IN!
DON'T WORRY, SHIZUKA-CHAN!
HUH?
THAT STUPID, IDIOTIC, CHILDISH MAMORU--
--COULD NEVER BECOME THE LOVE TARGET OF AN ADULT FEMALE.
NEVER IN A THOUSAND YEARS!!
OH... OH YEAH...?
YEAH! ABSOLUTELY!
LET'S CHECK THINGS OUT.
....
THAT'S PRETTY SAD...

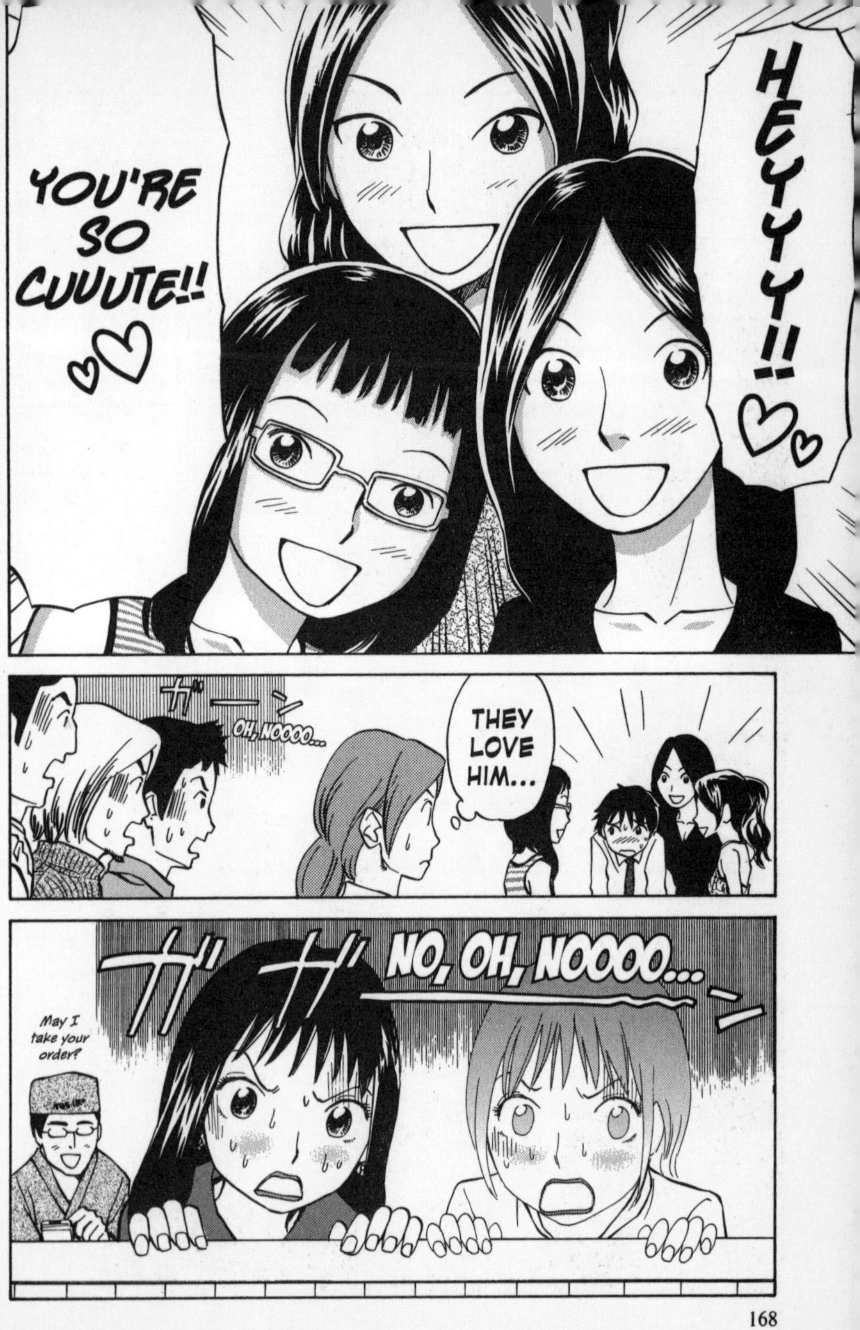
HEYYYY!!
YOU'RE SO CUUUTE!!
THEY LOVE HIM...
OH, NOOOO...
NO, OH, NOOOO...
May I take your order?

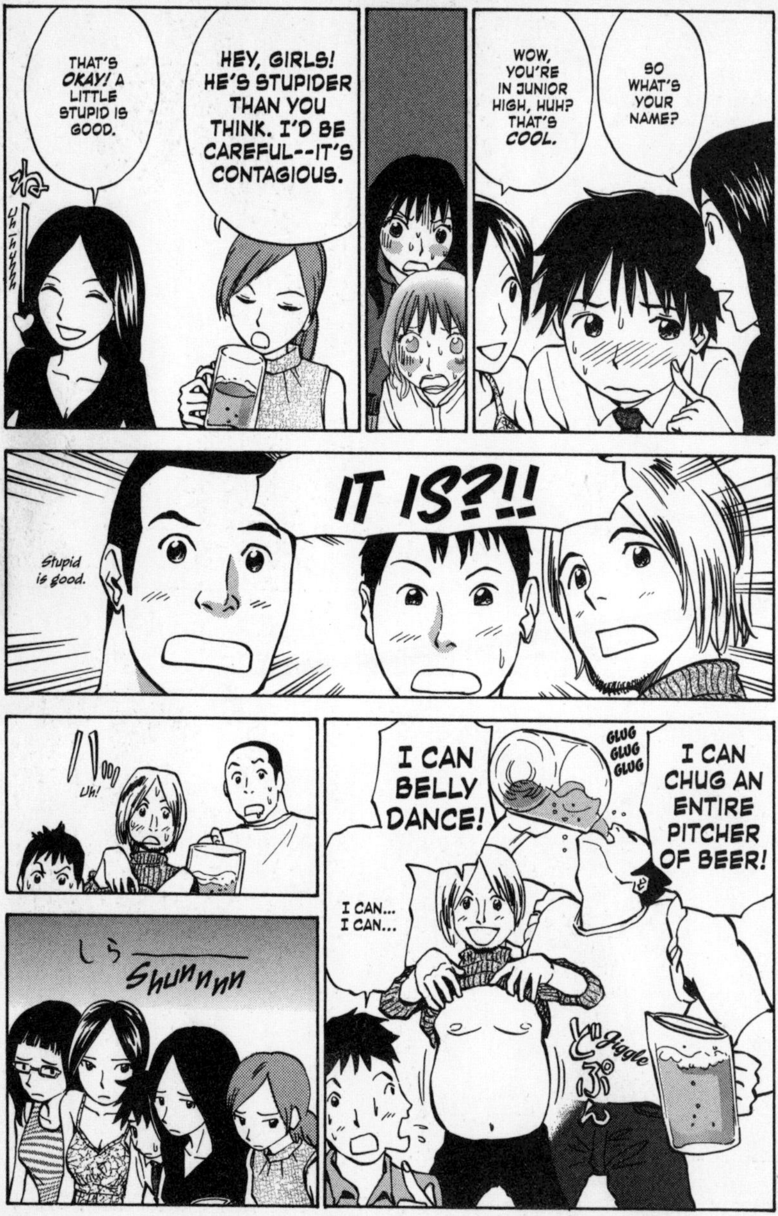
SO WHAT'S YOUR NAME?
WOW, YOU'RE IN JUNIOR HIGH, HUH? THAT'S *COOL.*
HEY, GIRLS! HE'S STUPIDER THAN YOU THINK. I'D BE CAREFUL--IT'S CONTAGIOUS.
THAT'S *OKAY!* A LITTLE STUPID IS GOOD.
IT IS?!!
Stupid is good.
I CAN CHUG AN ENTIRE PITCHER OF BEER!
GLUG GLUG GLUG
I CAN BELLY DANCE!
I CAN... I CAN...
Jiggle
どぷん
ハッ
Uh!
しら—
Shunnnn

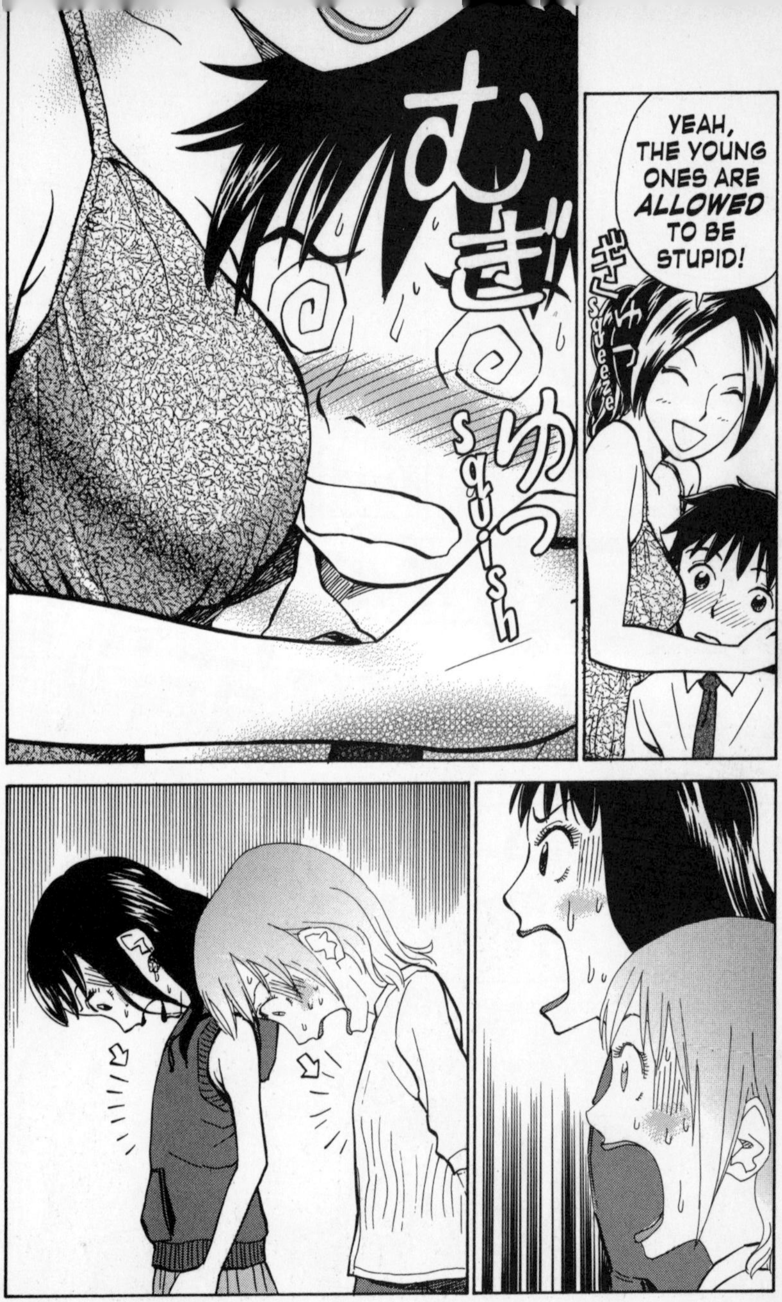
YEAH, THE YOUNG ONES ARE *ALLOWED* TO BE STUPID!
ぎゅっ
squeeze
むぎゅっ
squish

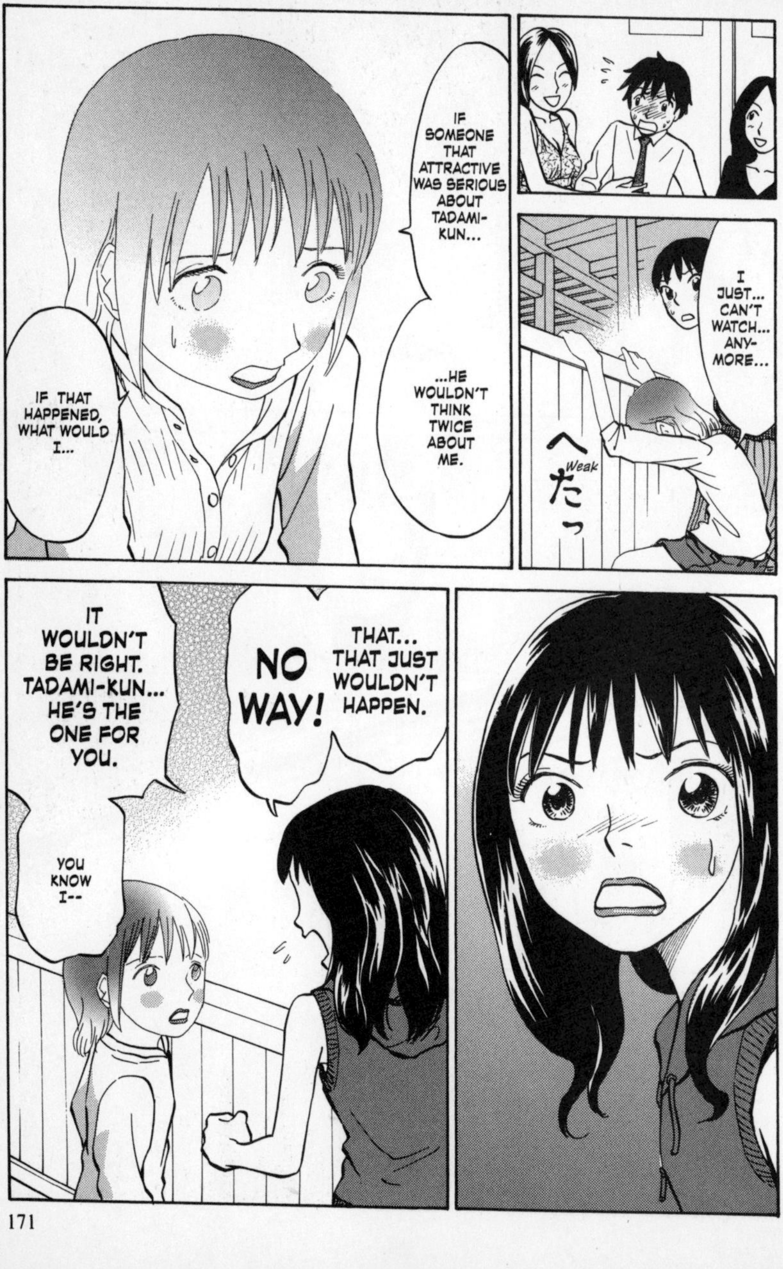
I JUST... CAN'T WATCH... ANYMORE...
へたっ
Weak
IF SOMEONE THAT ATTRACTIVE WAS SERIOUS ABOUT TADAMI-KUN...
...HE WOULDN'T THINK TWICE ABOUT ME.
IF THAT HAPPENED, WHAT WOULD I...
NO WAY!
THAT... THAT JUST WOULDN'T HAPPEN.
IT WOULDN'T BE RIGHT. TADAMI-KUN... HE'S THE ONE FOR YOU.
YOU KNOW I--

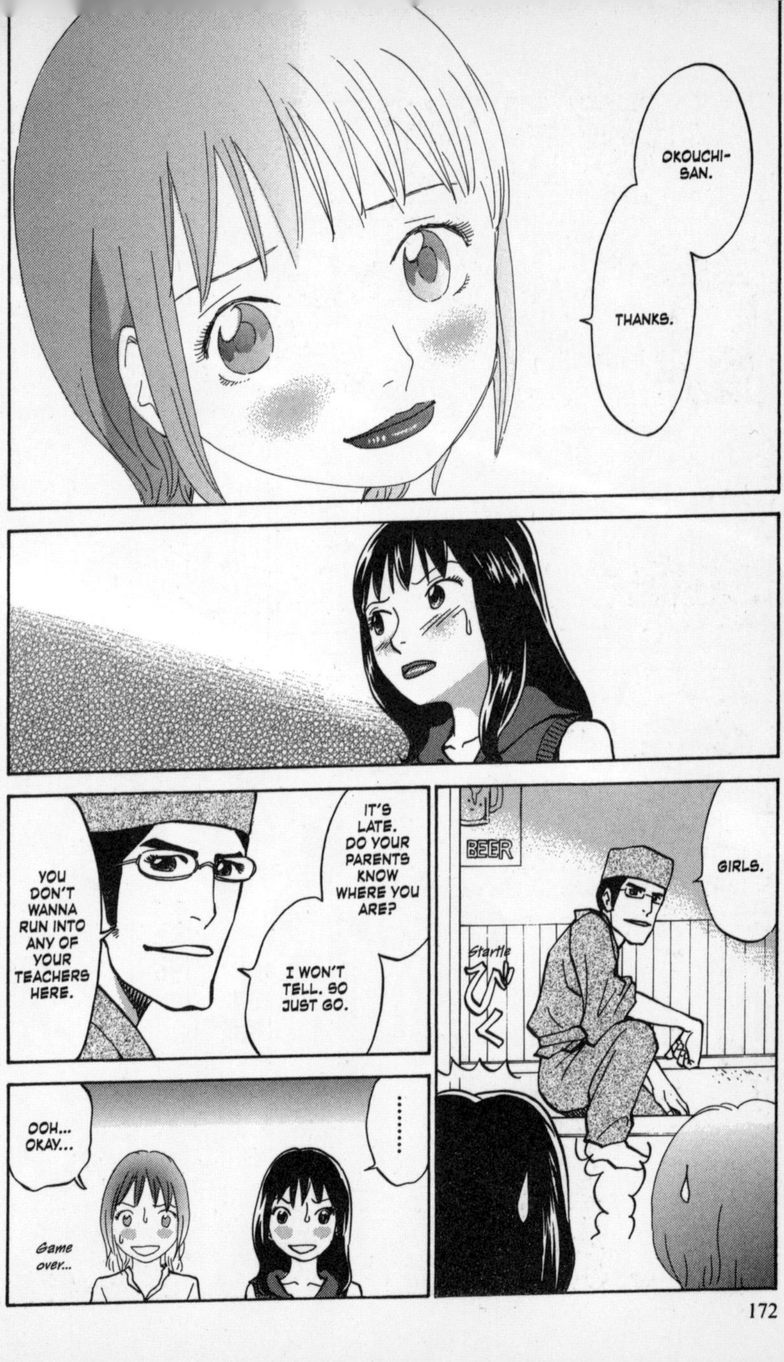
OKOUCHI-SAN.
THANKS.
GIRLS.
Startle
IT'S LATE. DO YOUR PARENTS KNOW WHERE YOU ARE?
I WON'T TELL. SO JUST GO.
YOU DON'T WANNA RUN INTO ANY OF YOUR TEACHERS HERE.
....
OOH... OKAY...
Game over...

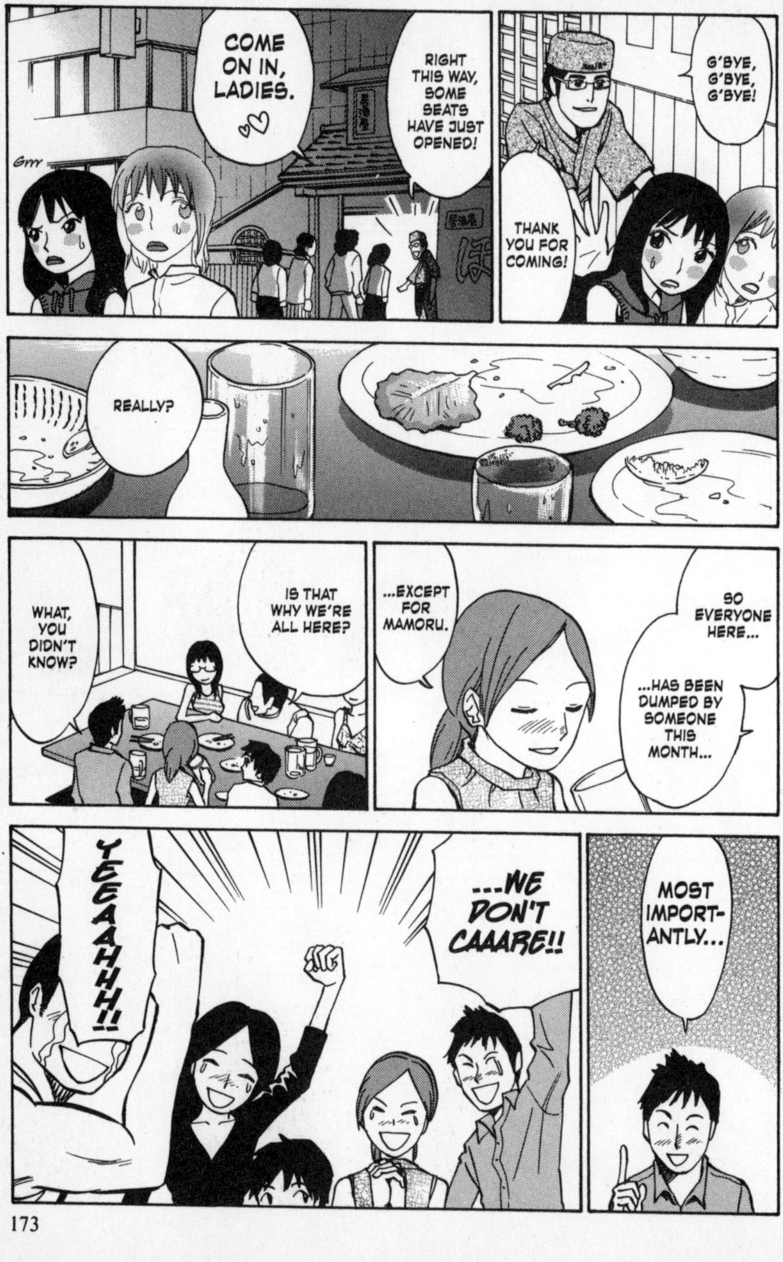
G'BYE, G'BYE, G'BYE!
THANK YOU FOR COMING!
RIGHT THIS WAY, SOME SEATS HAVE JUST OPENED!
COME ON IN, LADIES. ♡
Grrr
REALLY?
SO EVERYONE HERE...
...HAS BEEN DUMPED BY SOMEONE THIS MONTH...
...EXCEPT FOR MAMORU.
IS THAT WHY WE'RE ALL HERE?
WHAT, YOU DIDN'T KNOW?
MOST IMPORT-ANTLY...
...WE DON'T CAAARE!!
YEEAAHHH!!

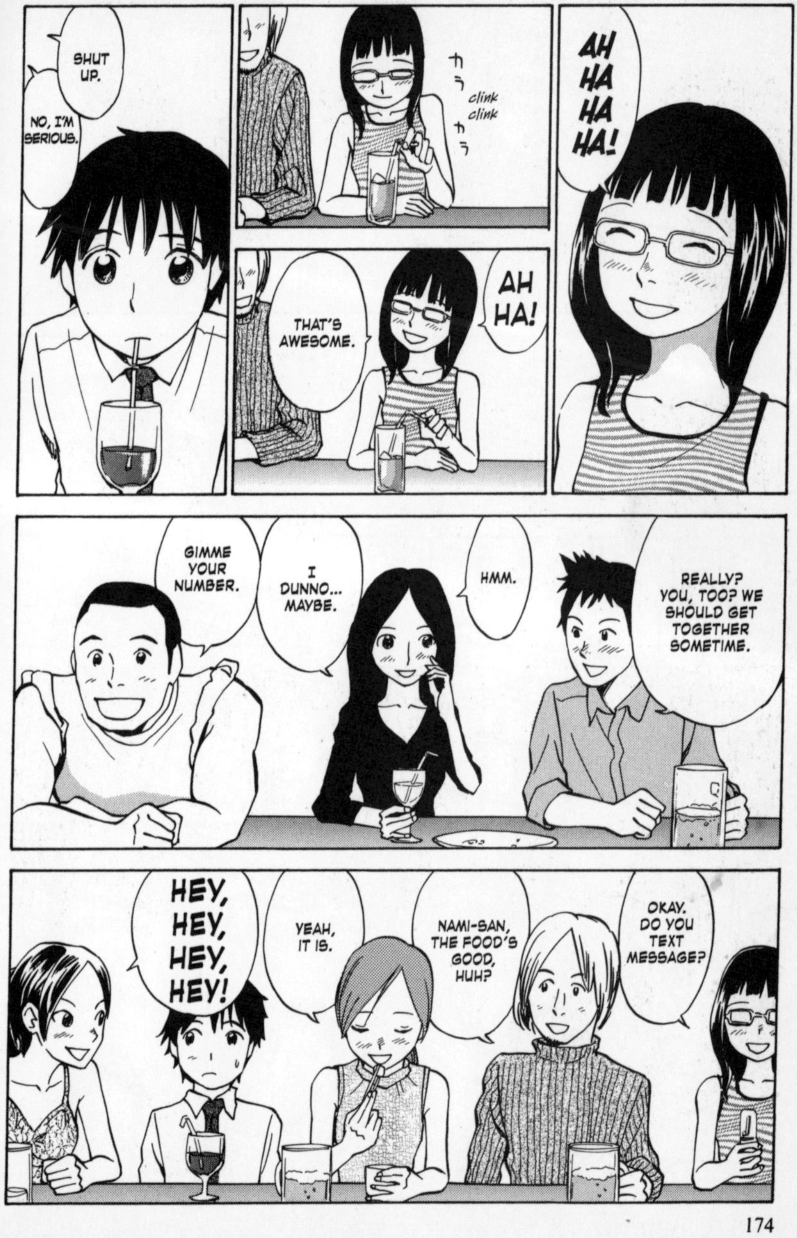
AH HA HA HA!
カラ カラ
clink clink
AH HA!
THAT'S AWESOME.
SHUT UP.
NO, I'M SERIOUS.
REALLY? YOU, TOO? WE SHOULD GET TOGETHER SOMETIME.
HMM.
I DUNNO... MAYBE.
GIMME YOUR NUMBER.
OKAY. DO YOU TEXT MESSAGE?
NAMI-SAN, THE FOOD'S GOOD, HUH?
YEAH, IT IS.
HEY, HEY, HEY, HEY!

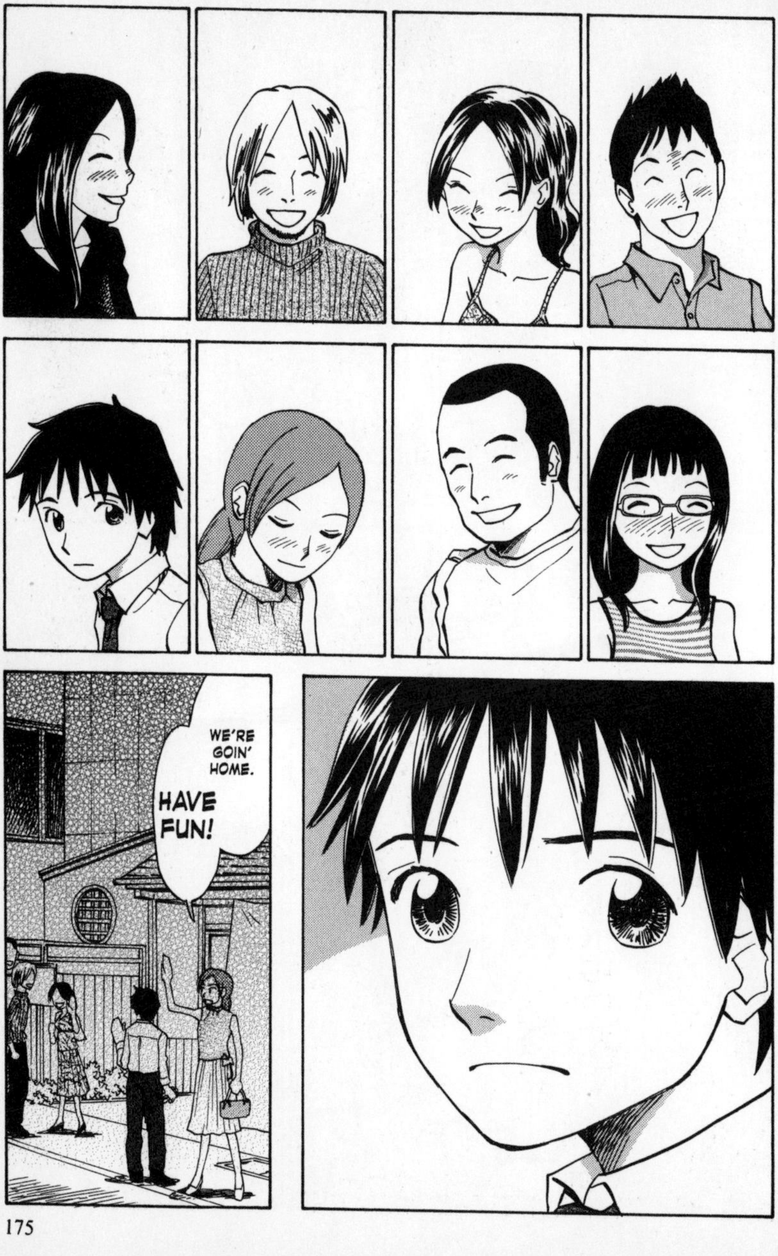
WE'RE GOIN' HOME.
HAVE FUN!

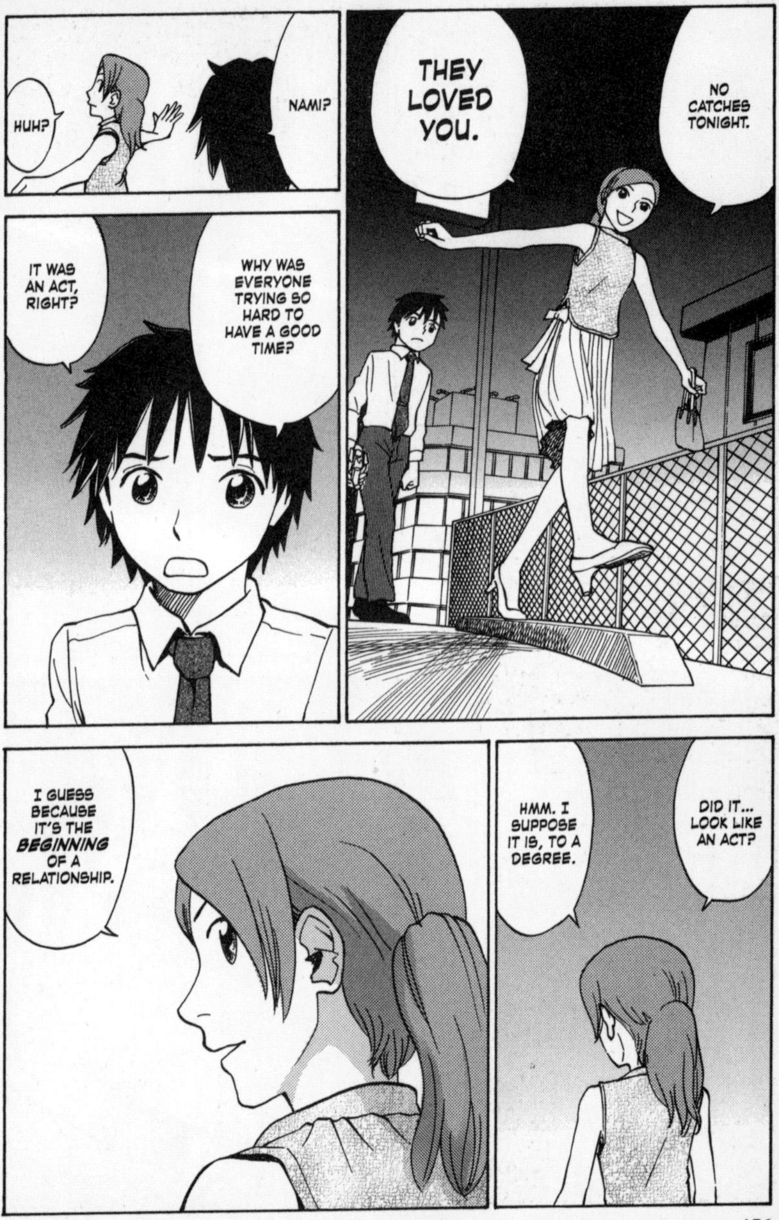
NO CATCHES TONIGHT.
THEY LOVED YOU.
NAMI?
HUH?
WHY WAS EVERYONE TRYING SO HARD TO HAVE A GOOD TIME?
IT WAS AN ACT, RIGHT?
DID IT... LOOK LIKE AN ACT?
HMM. I SUPPOSE IT IS, TO A DEGREE.
I GUESS BECAUSE IT'S THE *BEGINNING* OF A RELATIONSHIP.

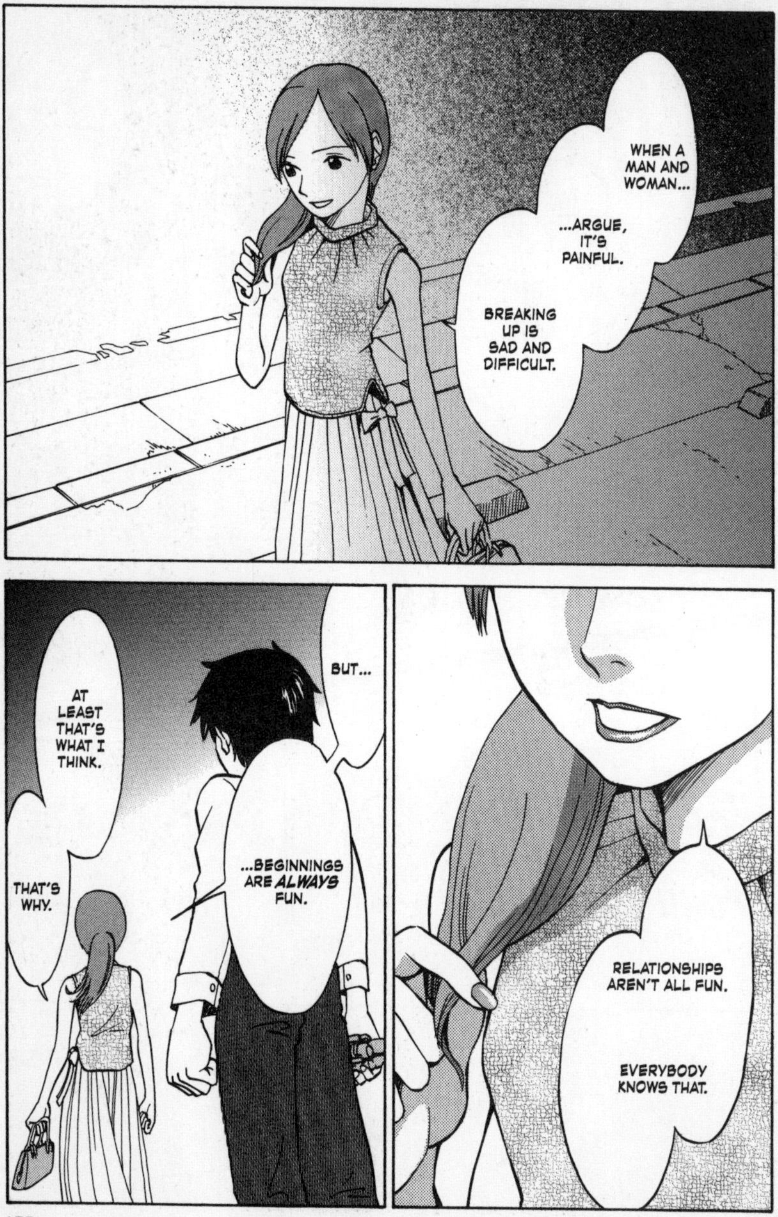
WHEN A MAN AND WOMAN...
...ARGUE, IT'S PAINFUL.
BREAKING UP IS SAD AND DIFFICULT.
RELATIONSHIPS AREN'T ALL FUN.
EVERYBODY KNOWS THAT.
BUT...
...BEGINNINGS ARE *ALWAYS* FUN.
AT LEAST THAT'S WHAT I THINK.
THAT'S WHY.

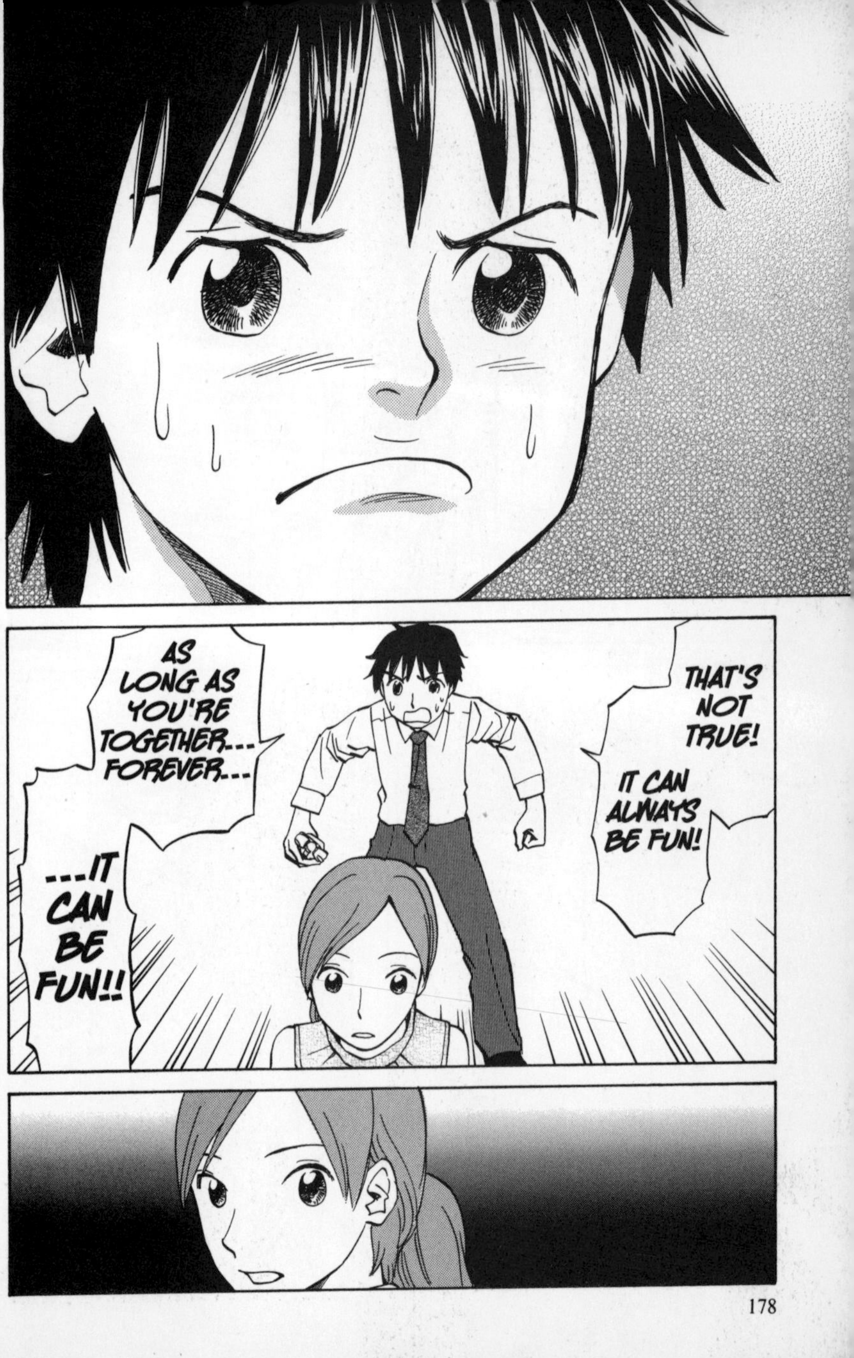
THAT'S NOT TRUE!
IT CAN ALWAYS BE FUN!
AS LONG AS YOU'RE TOGETHER... FOREVER...
...IT CAN BE FUN!!

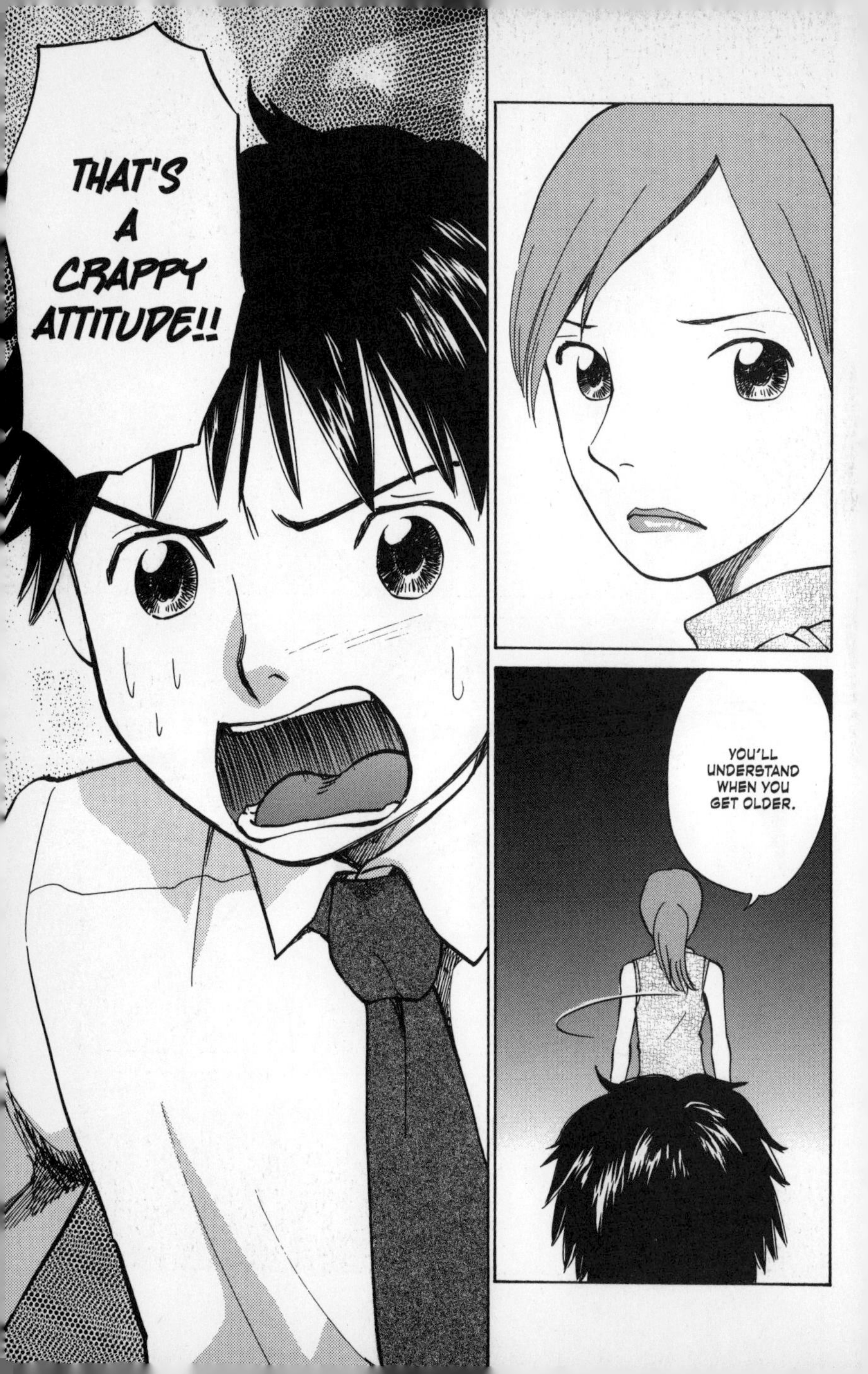
YOU'LL UNDERSTAND WHEN YOU GET OLDER.
THAT'S A CRAPPY ATTITUDE!!

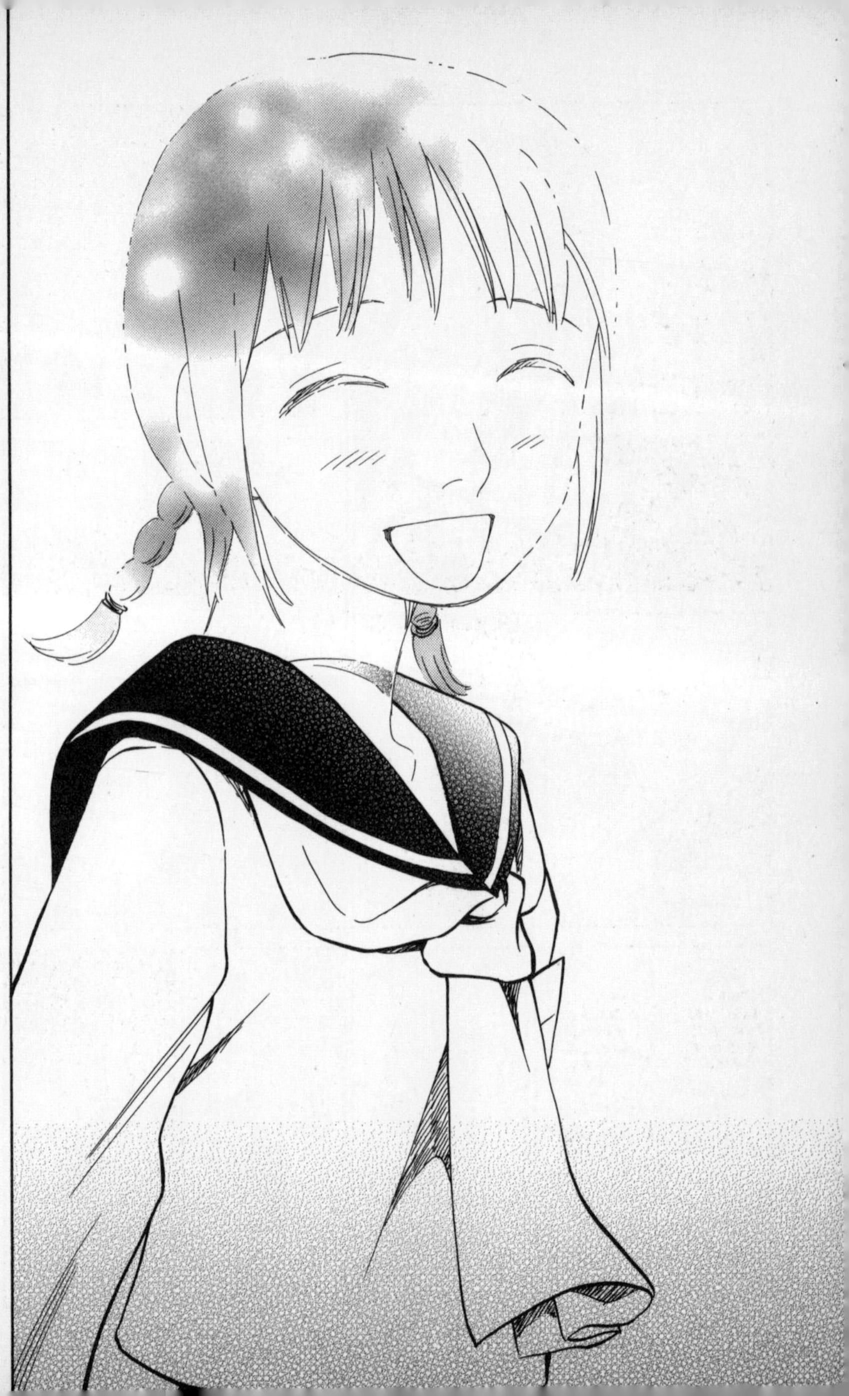

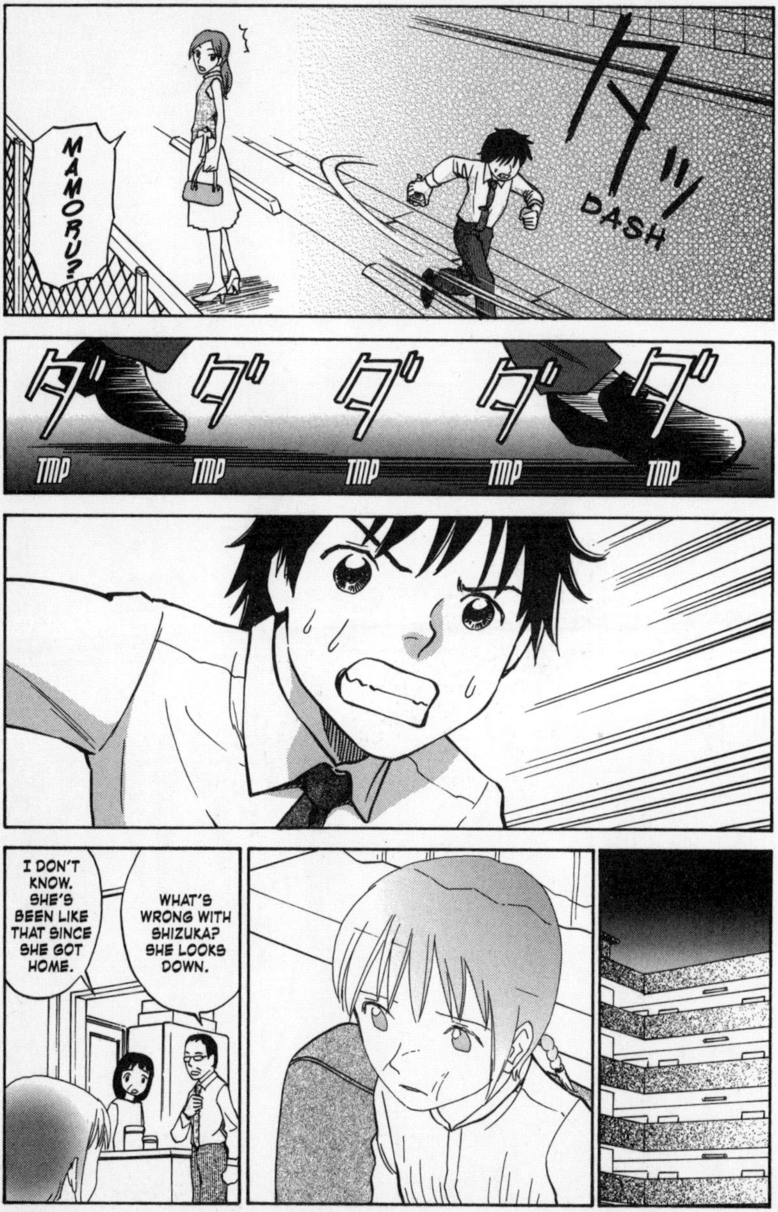
タッ
DASH
MAMORU?
ダダダダダ
TMP TMP TMP TMP TMP
WHAT'S WRONG WITH SHIZUKA? SHE LOOKS DOWN.
I DON'T KNOW. SHE'S BEEN LIKE THAT SINCE SHE GOT HOME.

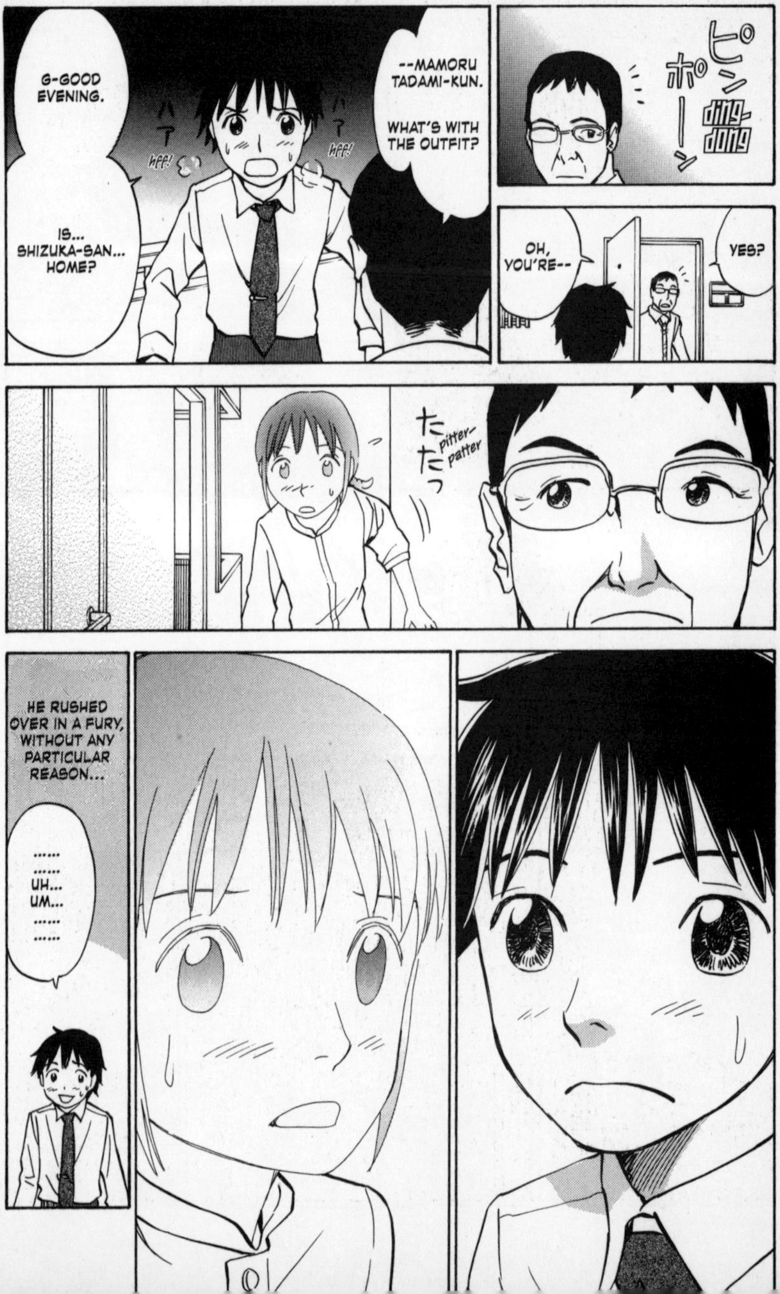
ピンポーン
ding-dong
YES?
OH, YOU'RE--
--MAMORU TADAMI-KUN.
WHAT'S WITH THE OUTFIT?
ハア huff!
ハア huff!
G-GOOD EVENING.
IS... SHIZUKA-SAN... HOME?
たたっ pitter-patter
HE RUSHED OVER IN A FURY, WITHOUT ANY PARTICULAR REASON...
.... UH... UM... ....

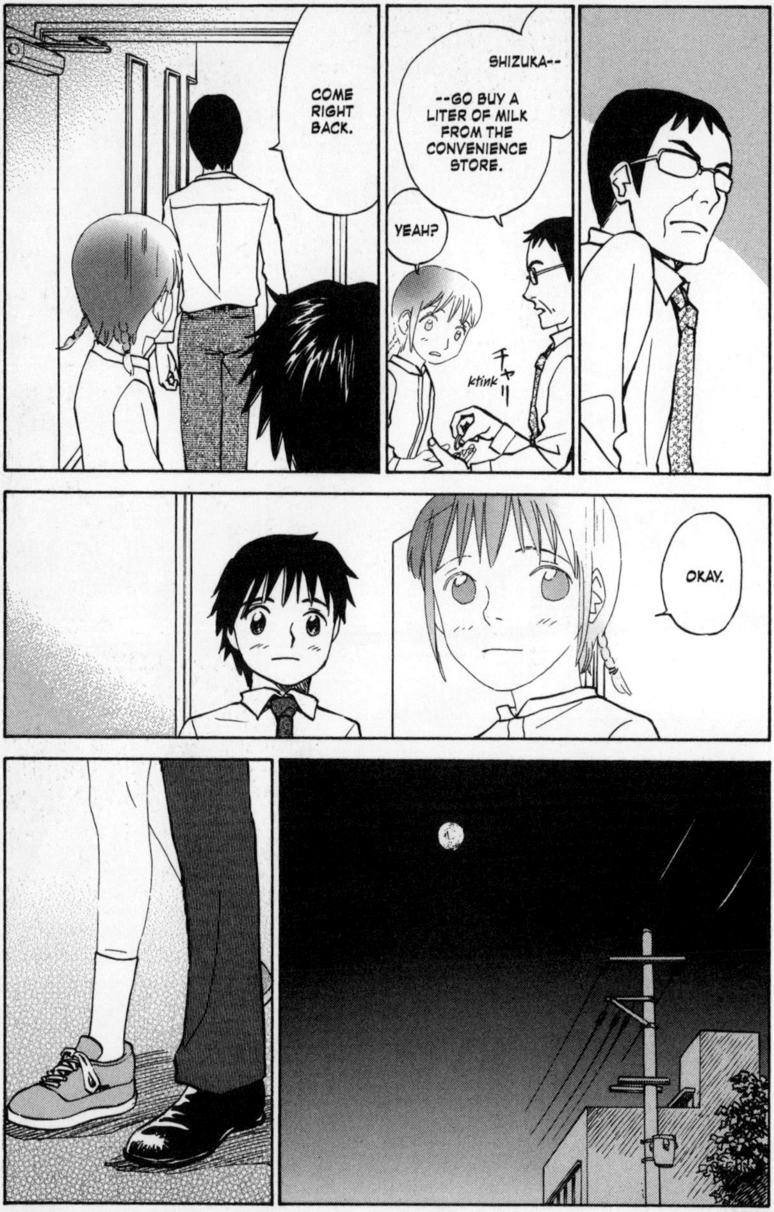
SHIZUKA--
--GO BUY A LITER OF MILK FROM THE CONVENIENCE STORE.
YEAH?
チャリ
ktink
COME RIGHT BACK.
OKAY.

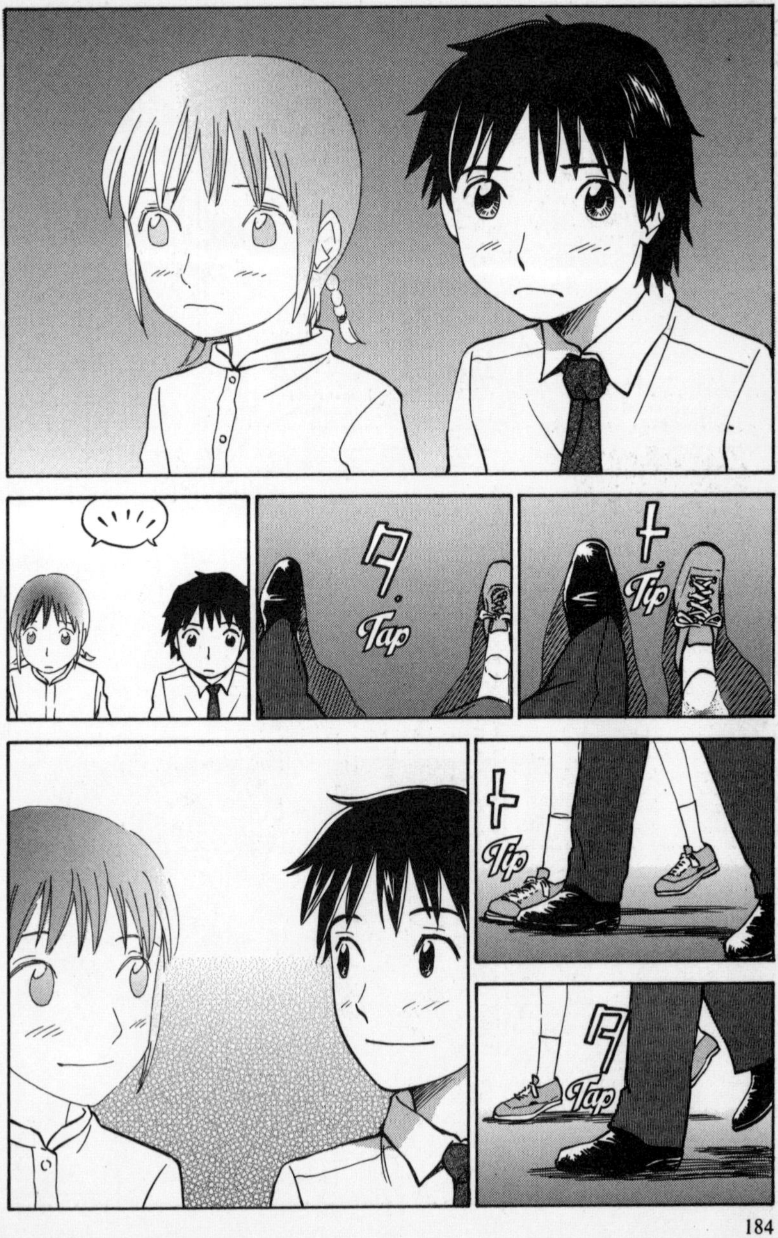
ト
Tip
タ
Tap
ト
Tip
タ
Tap

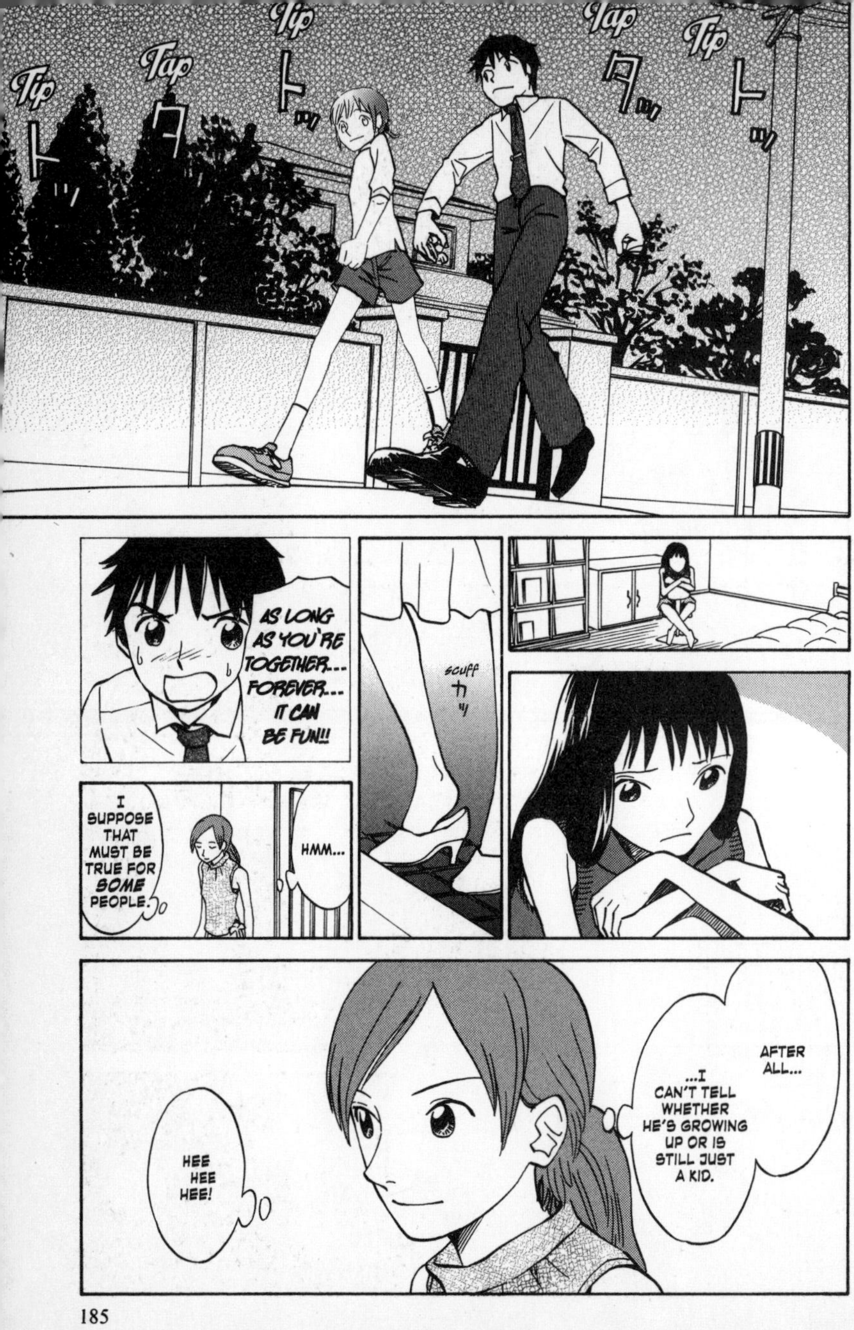
Tip
トッ
Tap
タッ
Tip
トッ
Tap
ク
Tip
ト
scuff
カッ
AS LONG AS YOU'RE TOGETHER... FOREVER... IT CAN BE FUN!!
HMM...
I SUPPOSE THAT MUST BE TRUE FOR SOME PEOPLE.
AFTER ALL...
...I CAN'T TELL WHETHER HE'S GROWING UP OR IS STILL JUST A KID.
HEE HEE HEE!

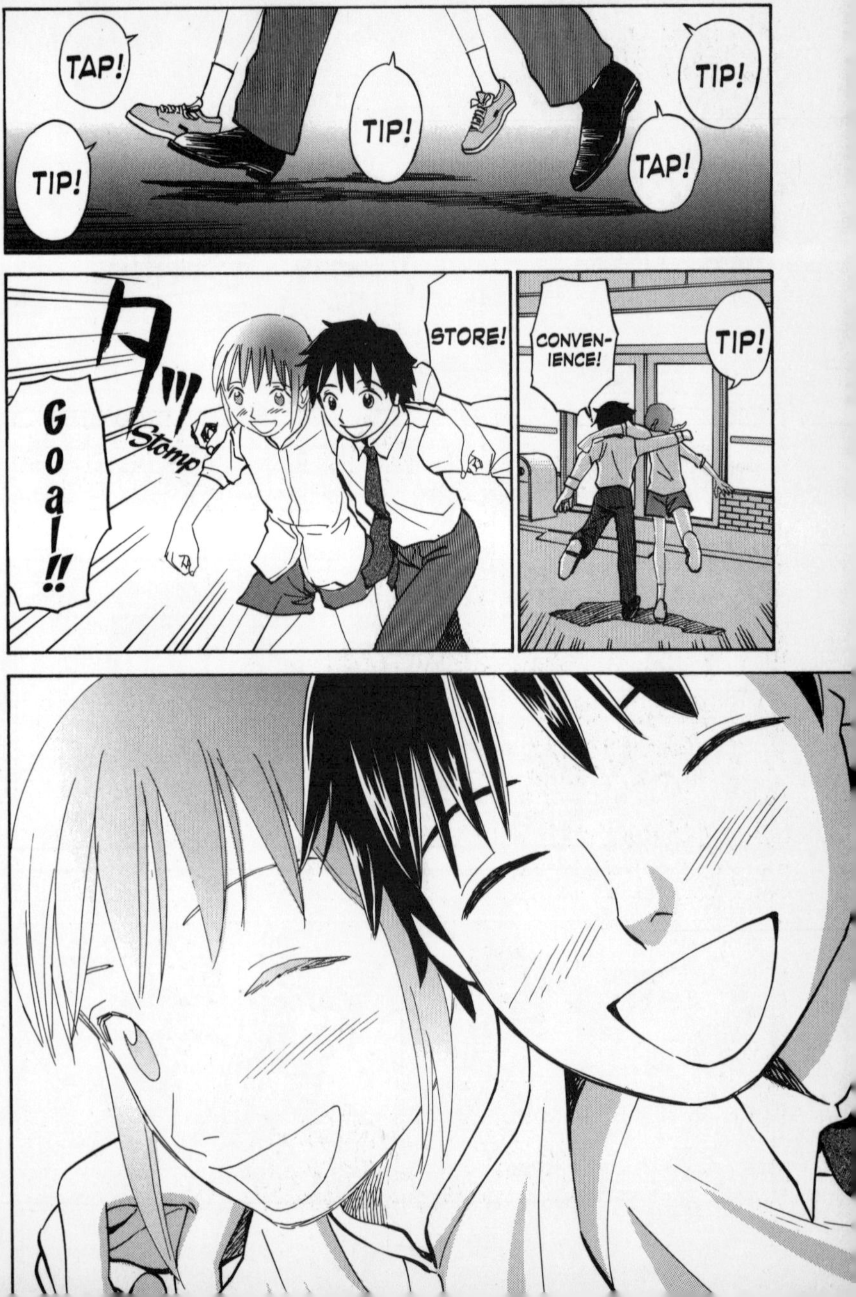
TIP!
TAP!
TIP!
TAP!
TIP!
TIP!
CONVEN-
IENCE!
STORE!
タッ
Stomp
Goal!!

OMAKE

ONE-PAGE BONUS MANGA #5

5

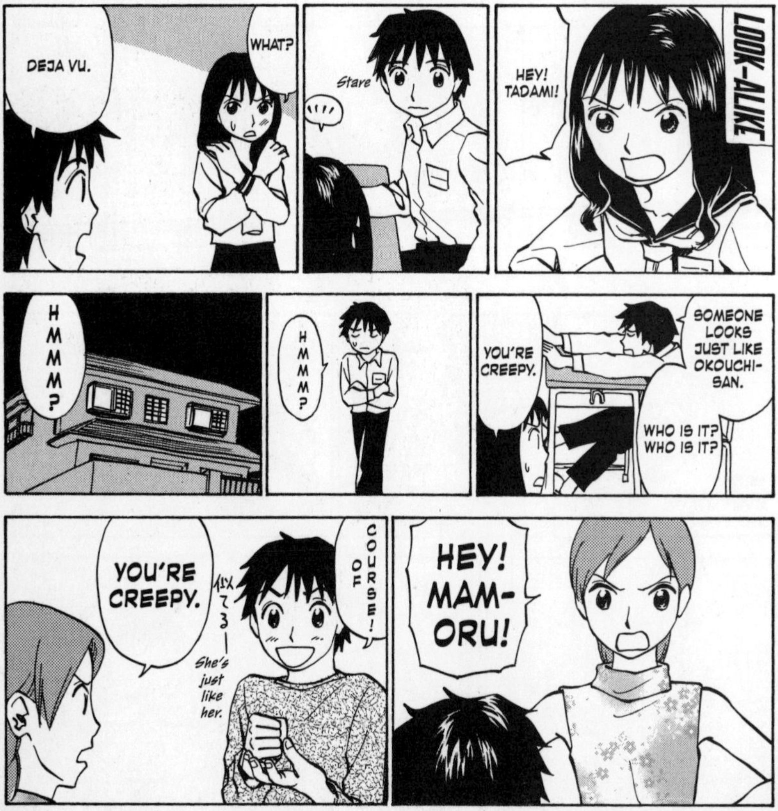
LOOK-ALIKE
HEY! TADAMI!
Stare
WHAT?
DEJA VU.
SOMEONE LOOKS JUST LIKE OKOUCHI-SAN.
WHO IS IT? WHO IS IT?
YOU'RE CREEPY.
HMMM?
HMMM?
HEY! MAM-ORU!
OF COURSE!
似てる
She's just like her.
YOU'RE CREEPY.

OMAKE

ONE-PAGE BONUS MANGA #6

6

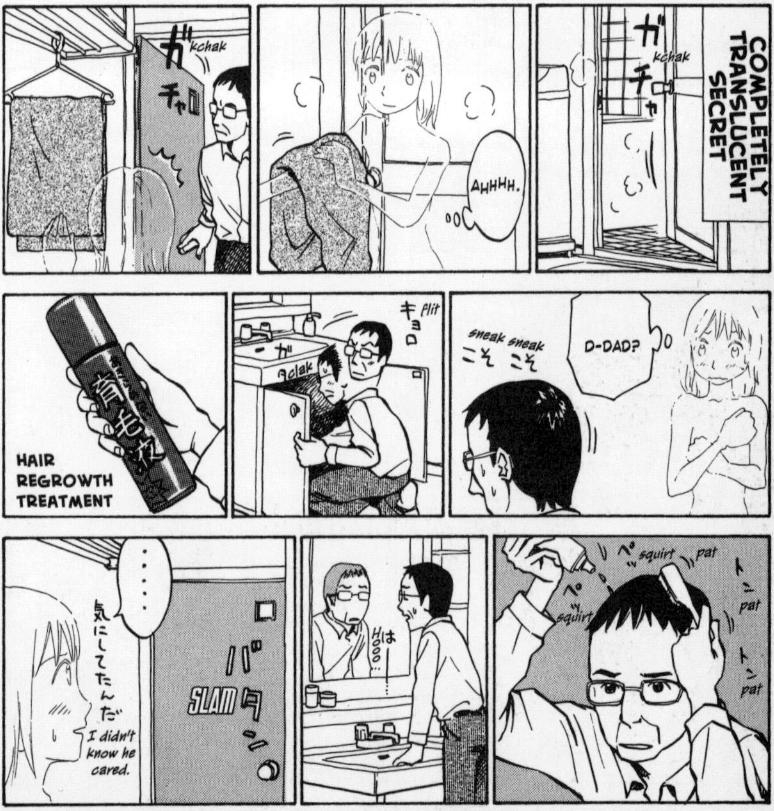
COMPLETELY TRANSLUCENT SECRET
ガチャ
kchak
AHHHH.
ガチャ
kchak
D-DAD?
こそこそ
sneak sneak
キョロ
flit
ガ
clak
育毛液
HAIR REGROWTH TREATMENT
ペッ
squirt
ペッ
squirt
pat
トン
pat
トン
pat
はぁ
Hooo...
....
気にしてたんだ
I didn't know he cared.
バタン
SLAM

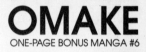

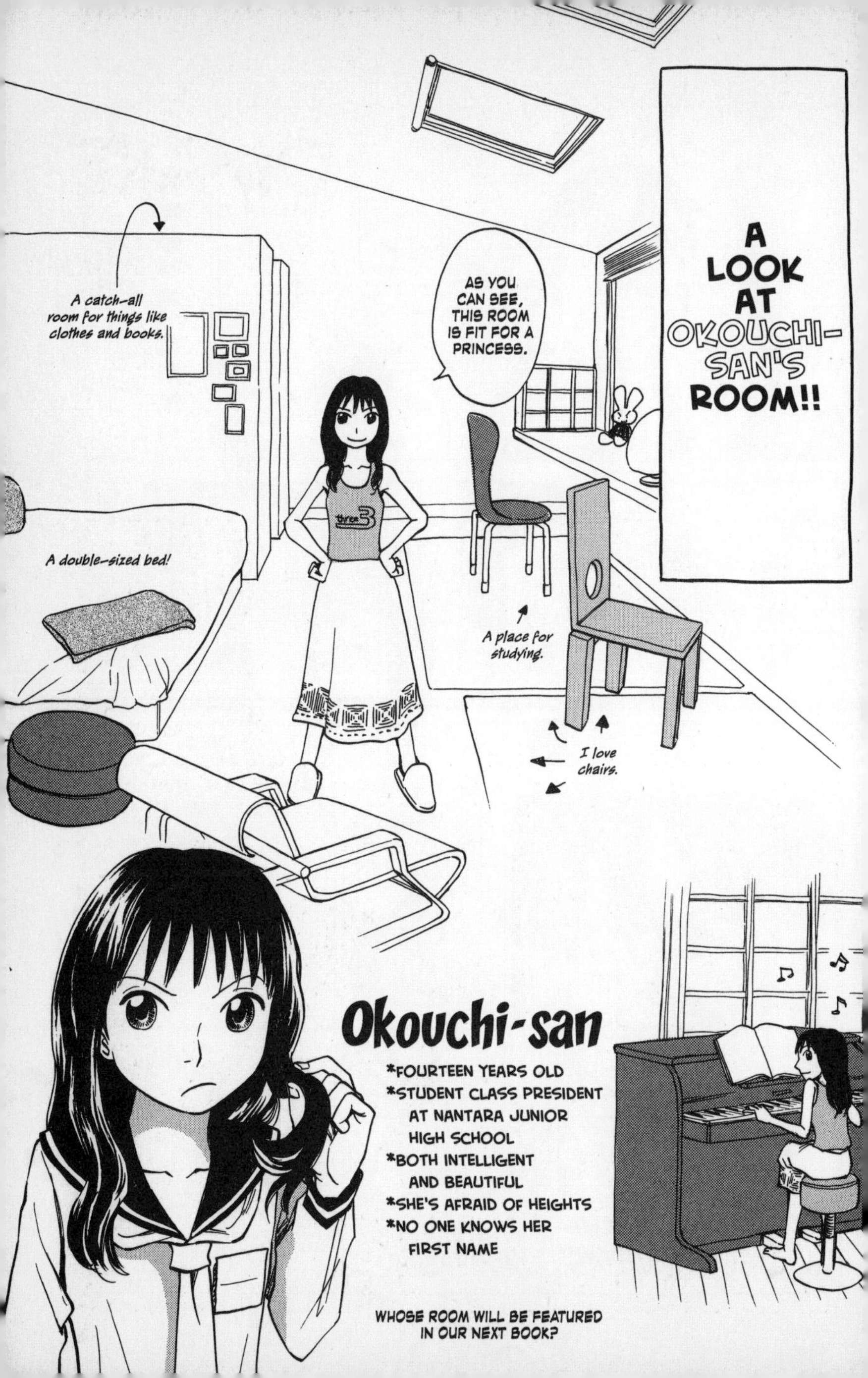
A LOOK AT OKOUCHI-SAN'S ROOM!!
AS YOU CAN SEE, THIS ROOM IS FIT FOR A PRINCESS.
A catch-all room for things like clothes and books.
A double-sized bed!
A place for studying.
I love chairs.
Okouchi-san
*FOURTEEN YEARS OLD
*STUDENT CLASS PRESIDENT AT NANTARA JUNIOR HIGH SCHOOL
*BOTH INTELLIGENT AND BEAUTIFUL
*SHE'S AFRAID OF HEIGHTS
*NO ONE KNOWS HER FIRST NAME
WHOSE ROOM WILL BE FEATURED IN OUR NEXT BOOK?

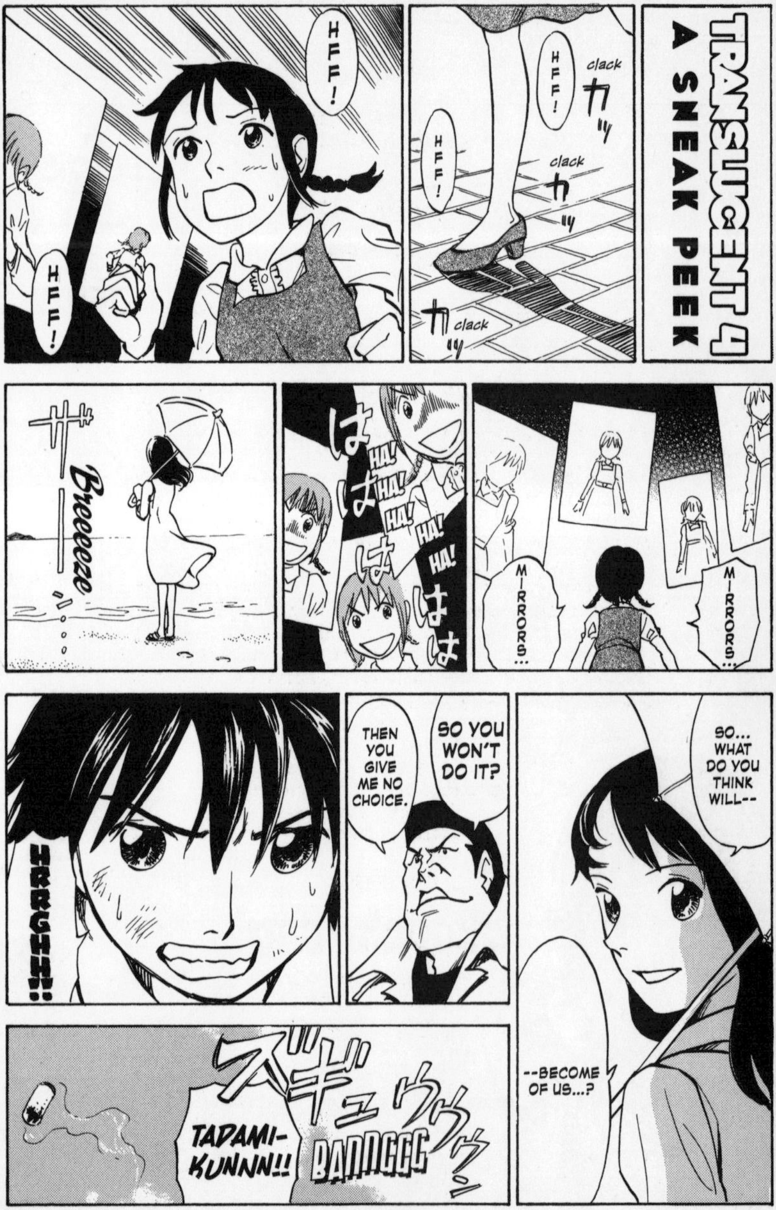
TRANSLUCENT 4
A SNEAK PEEK
HFF!
HFF!
clack
カッ
clack
カッ
カッ
clack
HFF!
HFF!
MIRRORS...
MIRRORS...
はは
HA! HA! HA! HA! HA!
はは
ザー
Breeeeeze
SO... WHAT DO YOU THINK WILL--
--BECOME OF US...?
SO YOU WON'T DO IT?
THEN YOU GIVE ME NO CHOICE.
HRRGHH!!
ズギュウウウ
BANNGGG
TADAMI-KUNNN!!

publisher
MIKE RICHARDSON

editor
PHILIP SIMON

editorial assistant
RYAN JORGENSEN

digital production
AREN KITTILSEN

collection designer
TONY ONG

art director
LIA RIBACCHI

Special thanks to Riko Frohnmayer and Michael Gombos.

English-language version produced by DARK HORSE COMICS.

Dark Horse Manga
A division of Dark Horse Comics, Inc.
10956 SE Main Street
Milwaukie, OR 97222

darkhorse.com

To find a comics shop in your area, call the Comic Shop Locator
Service toll-free at 1-888-266-4226

First edition: January 2008

ISBN 978-1-59307-679-5

1 3 5 7 9 10 8 6 4 2
Printed in the United States of America

STOP!

THIS IS THE BACK OF THE BOOK!

This manga collection is translated into English but oriented in a right-to-left reading format at the creator's request, maintaining the artwork's visual orientation as originally published in Japan. If you've never read manga in this way before, take a look at the diagram below to give yourself an idea of how to go about it. Basically, you'll be starting in the upper right corner and will read each balloon and panel moving right to left. It may take some getting used to, but you should get the hang of it very quickly. Enjoy—and thanks for reading!

1
C-COACH, I'M HERE!
2
OH, THERE YOU ARE.
3
I DIDN'T SEE YOU THERE, TRANSLUCENT GIRL.
4
HA HA HA HA
5
IT LOOKS LIKE YOU'RE BECOMING MORE TRANSPARENT AGAIN.
6
YEAH.
7
SUPPOSE IT WON'T BE LONG NOW...
8
...'CAUSE I USUALLY GO COMPLETELY TRANSPARENT EVERY FOUR WEEKS.
9
MY FACE AND RIGHT WRIST ARE THE LAST TO GO.

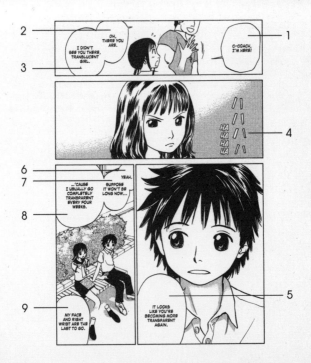